NATIONAL
ANTHEM

Richard Kluger

NATIONAL
ANTHEM

HARPER & ROW, PUBLISHERS 1817

NEW YORK, EVANSTON, AND LONDON

All the characters in this novel are fictitious. Any resemblance to people living or dead is purely coincidental.

FIRST EDITION

LIBRARY OF CONGRESS CATALOG CARD NUMBER: 69-15278

FOR MY MOTHER AND FATHER

NATIONAL ANTHEM

1

Oh, Say Can You See . . .

THE GROUND UNDER THE TENT IS ALREADY MUDDY FROM THE BEER and it is only Friday night. I squish through the foam-edged puddle that seeps from the base of the portable bar and bang my tankard on the counter for a refill. It will be my seventh since dinner, maybe eighth. Even tenth, conceivably. I would almost certainly be stupefied by now if the event was not being held out of doors and the night was not unusually crisp for mid-June. As it is, I have acquired a thoroughly satisfying buzz—a pleasant drifting sensation that propels me through the floodlit night full of good will and graceful phrases, all being quite sincerely if inexplicably dispensed toward these men, most of whom I have not seen since the day we graduated together ten years earlier. The source of my unexpectant mellowness, I suppose, is simply that they and I share this elemental frame of reference—we are aging together. No need to be glum about it, though, for this occasion, I tell myself, is nothing more than another routine rite of passage in the typical life cycle of the average college-educated, heterosexual, other-directed, upward-mobile, financially precarious, morally ambivalent, metaphysically unaffiliated American male.

Thus reflecting, I make my way to a can in the nearest dormitory, where I dimly sense that somebody next to me has begun to urinate

1

with noisy splashes into the large, low janitor's sink. It seems, as I think about it, a sensible thing for him to do, given the urgency the fellow evidently feels and the fact that I am using the only orthodox urinal there. I watch him obliquely—it is best not to gape under such circumstances—and only when the fellow is done and has replaced his large freckled member do I look up to see who its owner is. Shag Shaughnessy, a cigar inserted Mencken-like in the middle of his face, nods cordially. "They ought to run that beer through the horse again," he says.

I have not been in Shag's saloon on Third Avenue in almost a year, though it is only a few blocks from my office. As far as I know, he is the only saloonkeeper in our class. He had come out of the Marines and gone to work for a brokerage house and in no time at all was bored beyond endurance. To earn his keep, he started waiting on tables in East Side bars, mingling acquired efficiency with natural arrogance until he graduated to tending bar. In three years he had learned the business inside out, scraped together his savings, borrowed some capital, rented a run-down place on an unpromising stretch of the avenue, tossed checked cloths on the tables, installed a jukebox, hired a short-order cook who could concoct a decent bowl of chili, and turned the whole enterprise into a Place to Be Seen In— a chic pub attended by limber types and no unsightly lushes. But it was Shag himself who was the secret ingredient in the success of the place. He was always there, glad-handing and wisecracking and generally mouthing off with astonishing articulation to anyone who would listen about anything that moved him. A coterie of shifting composition surrounded him daily, offering token resistance to his tireless fulminating, which, in the last analysis, was the principal attraction of the place. For a while, I would drop by after work once a week just to listen to him. His thunder was sometimes diverting and occasionally even disarming. In time, though, new bars moved into the once-tattered neighborhood and Shag's place began to seem a bit seedy by comparison. More than that, Shag's performances had begun to turn tiresome, debilitating even, and so I started going straight home from work.

Partly out of guilt, then, I follow Shag Shaughnessy from the can and join his group at the end of the huge tent nearest the bar. We all have on our official class costume—open-neck sport shirts and matching Bermuda-length shorts, both splashed with an orange and black floral print, the orange clamorously dominant. A floppy straw planter's hat tops off the getup, which has been selected to represent the theme of a Tahitian tenth reunion. Why that, no one seems to know, or much care.

The moment he is back, Shag takes charge of the talk, which here and everywhere else under the tent is growing steadily louder and more indistinct. The topic has been America and the World, the course of the discussion inconclusive. When it reaches a particularly unproductive plateau, Shag rescues it by proposing the immediate annexation of Canada.

"Canada?" comes the hoped-for murmur of disbelief.

Shag rubs his belly with relish. "Yes," he says, "the vast, supine, and unsuspecting dominion to our, I believe, north. All three million six hundred and something thousand square miles of it. A lot of that, bear in mind, is one big frozen Popsicle, but still it is a pretty substantial package. Just think of it—overnight America will double in size. Overnight our flagging pride will be renewed. Overnight a vast new wilderness will open up and beckon our fabled ingenuity and matchless dynamism. The new frontier! A real one—not a lot of Kennedy blarney, may the dear men rest in peace."

How, someone asks, do we annex Canada?

"Strictly by protocol—to begin with. We write them a registered letter first. 'Dear Canada,' we say. 'You are hereby invited to join the United States of America in a more perfect union. We'll be glad to count each of your ten provinces as a state, which is more than most of them deserve, considering that you are mostly trackless wilderness. Together we will forge a mighty nation, which—it's time you faced it—you will never become on your own pitiful oar. We would appreciate your advising us at your earliest convenience. Trusting you will act affirmatively on this once-in-a-lifetime opportunity, we remain— Sincerely yours, The United States of America, Land of the Free and Home of the Brave.' "

And suppose, someone else asks, the Canadians decline the honor?

"Then," says Shag, disclosing a fist, "we kick the living crap out of her!"

"You mean *invade?*"

"We might give them twenty-four hours to surrender in first. That *would* be the decent thing."

"And suppose they think it's some sort of Orson Welles-Martian thing?"

"The President will go on television and explain that it is in our mutual interest. He's very sincere for the first ten minutes. They'll believe him. He'll invoke manifest destiny. Canada—the natural and divinely ordained extension of the Great Republic! Columbia the Gem of the Ocean is back in business! *E pluribus unum*—and the more *pluribuses* the better! Time for the great American powerhouse to start churning again! Time we stopped being pushed around by runty Asiatic fuckers! All right, you say—that's not our turf over there. But Canada! Canada is rightfully ours. Let's show the world we've still got balls!"

"And when the Canadians kick us in them?"

"In go the Marines. Two divisions can do it—and a lot of overflights. We move in at Sault Sainte Marie, march four hundred unopposed miles across Ontario to Hudson Bay, and bingo! the bastards are cut in half. Wham, bam, thank you, ma'am, and amber waves of grain."

Everyone is quiet for a moment. There is, undeniably, a certain mad attractiveness to the proposal.

"And where," someone finally asks, "will that leave Mexico?"

Shag finishes draining off a beer. "That," he says, wiping his mouth against the shoulder of his shirt, "brings me to Phase Two."

There is a short cheer in recognition of (a) his indefatigability and (b) his perversity.

"It is common knowledge," he goes on, acknowledging the outburst with a disparaging wave of the hand, "that the peons of Latin America are either in bondage to military dictators or at the mercy of Socialist bunglers. Ignorance, disease, unemployment, rampant inflation are their lot—and a choice between tyranny and anarchy. That is the picture for your typical ass-dragging Latino, am I right?"

You are right.

"So I ask you—you liberal and learned citizens of this blessed land that pledges unswerving allegiance to the Four Freedoms and the Rights of Man—I ask you, aren't all those ass-dragging, dung-grubbing, bug-bearing peons entitled to the dignity of a full belly, a roof over their heads, a little learning, and a decent job?"

Assenting murmurs.

"Not to mention head-to-toe fumigation on the house?"

Yes, yes, head to toe.

"Then I say to you that it is not imperialism but the fulfillment of America's destiny to deliver these helpless masses from bondage to venal rulers and medieval oligarchies. I see our glittering tanks rolling proudly down the sun-baked boulevards of Rio and Caracas to the thundering chant of approving millions. We will liberate, not subjugate. We will reach out our hands and gather all the sufferers gently to us and they will embrace us tearfully for their deliverance. I see a mighty nation of many peoples and many colors and many tongues in the tradition of the legendary American melting pot. I see an indomitable state stretching from Arctic waste to the storm-lashed tip of Tierra del Fuego—a true United States of America, of North *and* South America—a hemispheric monolith of boundless, luminous prospects."

New, heartfelt applause.

Shag downs the top half of a new beer an apostle has fetched him. "Gentlemen," he says, indicating by tone of voice that he has reached the peroration, "if the truth be told, the day of the nation-state as history has known it is at an end. Humanity demands it. The problems burdening us are too immense for each little piss-ant country to go it alone. Just as there will be a united North and South America, so, too, will there be a United States of Europe and a United States of Africa—oh, they will hurl the bloodied carcasses of the South Africans into the sea one day within our lifetime. India and Persia will unite with the Arabs. China with Japan and the rest of Asia. And Russia— Russia can have Turkey and a warm-water port. Down with petty despots! And once you have ended national sovereignty, there will be sustenance for every bedraggled bastard on earth. Every leviathan state will be so powerful that military solutions to any dispute will be unthinkable. The ultimate triumph of reason!" He reaches into his pocket for a fresh cigar. "Remember where you heard it first."

Shag Shaughnessy, visionary saloonkeeper, answerable to no known constituency. Shag Shaughnessy, between whose words and deeds there is a large and growing gap.

The music starts up again the instant Shag ceases, as if it has just been waiting for his mouth to close. The electronic go-go combo, plugged into the barely elevated bandstand at the edge of the tent, begins pulsing at a brain-damaging amplification. Two spangled go-go girls, hired to perform for five witless hours at twelve dollars a head, turn on at peak velocity at the inner edge of the platform. I detach myself from Shag's group and I turn and see the blurry light from the strung overhead bulbs swimming in Gibby Good's thick glasses.

"He is hugely hung," Gibby says admiringly of the stilled Shaughnessy. "Such a monument to polymorphous perversity."

2

The Silent Generation

HE HAD ROOMED WITH ME FOR OUR LAST TWO YEARS AS UNDER-graduates and we have remained moderately close, if not fast, friends ever since. Now he is Assistant Professor Gibby Good in the American Studies program at a large and not particularly stylish university in the city. On the ride down with our wives, we had tried to resurrect those bright college days which seem so much more antic in retrospect than they did at the time. It was, as a matter of fact, a singularly placid period, that undergraduate interlude of ours. It was before civil rights became a crisis, before sputniks and astronauts were to sunder earthbound visions, before John Kennedy had fired up the hormones with good words and good looks, before the New Left was accusing America of betraying the global revolution she had set in motion. We hoisted no picket signs, marched no marches, sat no sit-ins, rode no freedom rides, grew no beards, sampled no pot—in short directed no righteous rebuke at our elders for the world they were readying us to run. It was between wars, and everything was in neutral. It was hard, on any given day, to remember who was President of the United States. And harder still to fret over the starving children of India, who seemed scarcely more than a socioeconomic abstraction at the time. We dwelled amid a kind of mindless torpor, mostly studying and drinking and eating pizzas and cheering our teams and craving women and wholesomely having perhaps one or two of them down by the lake on weekend nights or illicitly in the dorm on Sunday morning. The Silent Generation, we were ungenerously dubbed by the reigning social commentators, who meant an

onus to be attached to the term, but so listless were we that no umbrage was taken. It had been a good, if feckless, time, and we were
glad of it, and have reassembled this weekend ten years later to com-
memorate it.

The accumulation of beer and talk and so many well-remembered
faces has left us too keyed up to turn off rapidly this first night.
Drunk but cautious, I drive Gibby and our wives back the dozen or
so miles to our baby-blue cinder-block motel on Route 1. Gibby in the
back seat rollickingly recounts the day's events as seen through the
roving eye of the trained social scientist. Eighteen per cent of the men,
he notes, have started to go gray or bald, and 11 per cent have
gone irretrievably to suet, but the startling thing is how little most of
the class seems to have changed physically. And yet Gibby is right in
detecting an almost palpable undertow of sadness to the occasion.
It is not merely that among us we have lived seven thousand irredeem-
able years since we have last assembled en masse. It is that, as Gibby
concludes after talking with them all day and studying the tenth-
reunion book published by the class, these years have set patterns
most of us will follow till our deaths are circumspectly reported in
agate type at the back of the alumni magazine. You can tell right
now, pretty much, which handful of us is likely to leave a mark in
the world while the rest play out all the fruitless rituals. "Except for
Shaughnessy," says Gibby, "who falls in neither category."

Back in the motel, we all kick our shoes off and Gibby recites the
statistical evidence from the reunion book. Ten years out of college,
the average man in the class has been married 5.8 years, has 2.6
children, weighs 176 pounds, earns $12,516.72 a year, reads 14½
books, sees 13 movies, goes to 6 plays-musicals-concerts and (though
this item is not in the tables, Gibby interpolates from a raft of un-
reliable sources) has intimate relations with his wife or someone
(almost certainly his wife) 68 times annually. Occupationally, 42%
are in one form or another of business (including sales, banking,
finance, real estate, and data processing), 18% are in law, 15% are

in medicine, 10% are in education, 6% are in engineering, 3% are in science, 2% are in architecture, 2% are in the ministry, one guy is an indigent poet, one is the jobless son of a deposed Latin-American tyrant, and one is a Negro from Newark now highly placed in the government of an emerging African mini-nation. Politically, 58% are Republicans, 24% are Democrats, 15% are independent, one guy is a Maoist, one is a Poujadist, and one is a Utopian working for Bertrand Russell's foundation in London. One-half live in the suburbs, one-third live in cities, 10% live in small towns, 5% live abroad, one guy lives on a houseboat in Sausalito, and one (presumably the indigent poet) lives in a cave. Eschatologically, 28% attend church once a week, 17% once a month, 17% once a quarter, 20% once a year, 18% never, and five are already dead. Joy-wise, 91% say they are happy in their home life, 9% say they are only moderately happy in their home life; 84% say they are happy in their work, 16% say they are only moderately happy in their work—leaving nobody who admits he is actively unhappy either place.

"And now," says Gibby, "a few case studies." He flips through the book. "Why, here's old Rollie Rutledge, whoever the hell he is, in the chips already out in Cleveland. Rollie reports he knocked around in the training programs of a few Eastern banks for a while before heading back home for manna. 'Two partners and I,' he writes, 'formed the real estate brokerage firm of Hinton, Parker & Rutledge. We also formed a land development company, Heartland, Incorporated, and a residential construction company, Heartland Homes Corporation. We now have eighteen sales representatives and a gross of four and a half million annually.'

"Oh, and Rollie adds that he belongs to the Cleveland Country Club and the Cleveland Power Squadron. His hobbies, he writes, are 'a forty-one-foot cruiser called *Peg o' My Heart* and a rack full of fishing rods.' His wife is named Maggie and they have three small Rutledges, two girls and a boy. All five of them, according to Rollie, are active in the affairs of their local Episcopal church, where their prayers, off the over-all evidence, are being generously answered."

"May God his gold refine," says Lynn Good. "Besides, I'll bet his boat's only thirty-nine feet."

"Next," says Gibby, "we have Calvin Coolidge Comorrant, who writes, 'Ever since I was a child I wanted to sell Yellow Pages advertising and thus joined the Reuben H. Donnelley organization as a management trainee. Having gotten used to receiving our Christmas bonus in the form of a frozen turkey, I've stayed with it for the seven years I've been out of the Navy and now find myself Sales Director-Metropolitan Accounts in the Greater Metropolitan Yellow Pages District. We live out in Manhasset, leading a typical vodka-Martini-drinking, James Bond-reading, videoing, puttering-around life. Linkswise I'm still in a fourteen-handicap rut and we're waiting impatiently to tailgate in the back of the Quadrangle at every home football game, as we do every year.' "

"Speaking of frozen turkeys," says Lynn.

Gibby is flipping the pages more rapidly now. "Tobey Taliaferro is trust investment officer of the First National Bank of Dallas, a member in good standing of the Dallas Society of Financial Analysts, an elder in the Presbyterian Church, a captain in the Texas Air National Guard, and the owner of a seventy-pound basset hound named Cedric. 'We lead a very pleasant life down here in the Great Southwest,' he says."

"Neglecting to add," says Lynn, "that for kicks on the weekend he buzzes the Mexican border and strafes stray wetbacks."

Gibby is about to fling the book aside when his eye is caught by one last entry. He lingers over it a moment. "And finally," he says, "I give you the quintessential member of the class, a bellwether of the Silent Generation, a living testament to the American way of life *in extremis*—Ronald Renfrew Redfield the Third, of Hollyhock, Virginia. Sandy-haired, straight-shouldered, keen-eyed Ron debarked from the hallowed halls and spent two memorable years in the Naval Reserve, where he served with distinction as a gunnery officer on a cruiser in the Mediterranean fleet. Following which he entered the University of Virginia Law School, where he was elected to the editorial board of the *Virginia Law Review*. He was the author of a Note published in the *Review* and, since graduating, has published an article in the *Review* on accident-compensation laws. He was also on the dean's list and was elected to the Order of the Coif—evidently a good thing to be elected to. And now I quote him directly: 'Since commencing to practice law, I have been very active in the Junior Bar Section of the Virginia State Bar Association and in the Young Lawyers Section of the American Bar Association. Since returning to Hollyhock to practice law, I have engaged in some political activity on behalf of the Virginia Democratic Party, which is the official arm of the National Democratic Party in Virginia except that its machinery moves next door every four years under the label of Democrats for Eisenhower, Democrats for Nixon, Democrats for Goldwater, et cetera. This is a very sensible political position as far as those of us who revere the memory of Harry Byrd are concerned. In the Democratic Party, I am presently a member of the Hollyhock Town Democratic Committee. I have also served an appointment on the subcommittee of the State Advisory Legislative Council which does legislative studies at the request of the Governor and the General Assembly. On the social side, I am a member of the Hollyhock Country Club (golf), the Deep Glen Hunt Club (fox hunting), the Prince Edward Cotillion (dancing), and the Hollyhock German (also dancing). My wife, Katie, is very active locally in the Prince Edward Junior League and on the State Women's Committee of the Richmond Symphony. For hobbies we both enjoy tennis, riding, and hunting. I also have a special love for sailing, and (I don't know whether this counts as a business or a hobby) I generally oversee the operations of my mother's plantation about five miles from Hollyhock. I am also the President of the Saint Bartholomew's Benevolent Corporation, a charitable group which finances the operations of a white private school in our county which has come into existence as a result of federally decreed racial integration in the public schools. It is not that I have anything against the Negro, but I do not believe the national government should have the power to force the mixture of the races, which defies all the laws of human nature.' " Gibby looks up. "He concludes: 'I trust that some sparks kindled at college shine through all this, though it may be difficult to so identify any single spark. I suppose this is the true effect and real meaning of a liberal education. At any rate, to all my friends in the class and to the great university of our meeting, I voice thanks for the company of ever-rich memories and the good Lord's blessings.' "

He snaps the book shut, and before Lynn can upstage him a final time, he says quietly, "It will not be difficult to identify Ronald Renfrew Redfield the Third in the alumni parade tomorrow. He will be costumed precisely like the rest of the class—except for his tapered satin hood. And if you lift that hood or look through the slits, you will see blood in those fierce little eyes."

Grim, grim as grim can be, all this. "Bring back the Lost Generation!" cries Lynn, despairing for the lot of us. Gibby declares the collective class personality to be hopelessly up-tight and discloses for the first time that he will propound potential therapeutic measures in his new book, for which he has been given a generous foundation grant to get him through the coming year's sabbatical. His first book, an expansion of his doctoral dissertation, was *The Mugwumps and How They Grew,* and it established him as one of the nation's reigning authorities on mugwumpery. But ever since, he has been moving more and more deeply into social history—in fact perilously close to the behavioral sciences. The new book will confirm his interdisciplinary appetite—and, he says, rescue the Silent Generation from oblivion. It is to be called *The New Dionysian Ego: A Study of the Liberated Libido in the American Puritan-Repressive Psyche.*

"What, precisely, is its point?"

"The point precisely," says Lynn, "is to get him tenure at the earliest possible moment."

For more than a year Gibby has been wallowing in all the Freudian, post-Freudian, neo-Freudian, and anti-Freudian literature he could lay his hands on, along with the canon of every even remotely related social thinker of any consequence: Norman O. Brown and Herbert Marcuse and Erich Fromm and Edgar Z. Friedenberg and Erik Erikson and Marshall McLuhan and Paul Goodman and Philip Rieff and Susan Sontag and Norman Mailer (the last particularly for his theory of liberation through tightrope-walking and balancing on precipices). Gibby has approached the subject with great caution, however. Not that he has doubted that, as his sources all argue in one way or another, the collision of intellect and libido is the crucial conflict within modern man. But he is by no means entirely sold on the therapeutic value of the whole Freudian legacy. In principle, of course, the prescriptions of these champions of the Unfettered Libido—or the Unzipped Fly, as he calls it in his less approving moments—seem unexceptionable enough. But in execution they have struck him as either impractical or unsavory. "I think," he explained to me some months before, "they're telling me to go out and fuck a dog—and I'm just not sure it'll do much for me."

To do his book right, though, he has decided he must put all the theorists to the test. He must practice what they, so far as he knows, merely preach. "Salvation through onanism!" he exclaims to us now. "As a basic part of my research, I will celebrate a month-long festival of the senses. Unfettered, I will experience an exquisitely protracted orgasm. Not specifically genital, though, you understand—that's important. Genital domination, as Norman O. Brown teaches us, is merely another form of repression. I am talking about extracting delight from the body in all its manifold variety. Constant, inventive, defiant gratification of all the senses—"

"Including dog-fucking?" I ask earnestly.

"See, you're still thinking genitally. You're just like all your classmates. There is so much else to the sensual life. I will explore every little orifice in me, every little promontory, every conceivable source of pleasure. There are countless little private ugly things to do with yourself that have nothing whatever to do with genital gratification. I like, for example, to remove patches of dead skin that accumulate between my perspiring toes. It's a very—fulfilling sensation. And it stops the itching. I like to drill a pinkie into my ear in quest of wax. And scout around my scalp for hidden scales of dandruff. I feel I'm purifying myself. I like to remove dirt jam from my fingernails with a paper clip—and then suck on the nails for a while before chewing them off. I like the feel of the nails yielding to my teeth. Things like that—all polymorphous perverse. Why, I'll bet there are erogenous zones that have never been tapped. They're hanging on somewhere, just waiting to be delighted in. Like the kneecap. I'll bet the kneecap, properly cultivated, has extraordinary libidinous potentiality. Patella Gratification, if will be called. You rub it clockwise five hundred times, then counterclockwise five hundred times, then stroke it and pet it and lave it with witch hazel till the calf starts to twitch and throb and tighten and tingle—exquisite! Instead of a climax, you experience a brief but very profound cramp."

"And you'll just ignore the genitals?"

"Who said that?"

"I thought you did."

"I said nothing of the kind. I said the genital part is by no means the whole story. To be *polymorphously* perverse means just what it says—undertaking perversions of every variety and intensity and shape. The taste buds, the toe buds, the ear buds, the eye buds, the fingernail buds—even, as I say, the kneecap buds. I will drive all my sensory apparatus to the limit—and perhaps beyond. Yes, almost certainly beyond, for how else will I know my limit? It will be the interior adventure of my life."

"But what about the goddam genitals?"

Gibby turns to Lynn. "Shall I tell them?"

"You might tell me first."

"I did—about the park."

"Oh, yes," she says to us, "we're going to do it in the park."

"But it'll be at night," says Gibby. "And we're going to use the particularly gymnastic technique Mailer cites in his next to latest novel."

"He prefers the ass," I say, "if I recall correctly."

"Then the ass it will be—though I'm dubious, frankly."

"*You're* dubious?" Lynn says. "It's *my* ass."

"I will attempt many varieties of coitus during the month with a variety of partners," he runs on.

"Just keep me in mind if you run across anything worthwhile," says Lynn.

"I will do it standing," Gibby says, "and I will do it sitting. I will do it upside down. I will do it on a seesaw. I will do it with floodlights on. I will do it in a coalbin."

"So far," Lynn says, "I'll pass."

"I will do it with a nymphomaniac to see how aroused one really gets. I will do it with a black to see how sinuous one can really be. I will do it with a Chinese to see how submissive one really is. I may even seek a homosexual experience that begins in the shower room at the Y."

"He gets restless during my period," Lynn says.

"Finally," says Gibby, "to externalize my experiences I will join one of those clubs for people who like to jump out of airplanes and fall through the air till they are a hundred feet from the ground. It is of course a thing that no normally repressed and reasonably prudent man would ever dream of doing. But by dint of sheer undiluted eros, I shall persevere. I shall become so good at it finally that I will amaze my fellow club members by masturbating during my free fall and achieving a climax at the symbolic moment my chute opens. And they will naturally make me a lifetime member. Now do you see how the genital thing can dovetail with everything else without necessarily dominating?"

"Beautiful," I say.

"Insane," Lynn says. "But it should do wonders for the sales of the book."

3

Kit

IT IS THE WEEK FOLLOWING THE REUNION AND I AM SUBMERGED in the daddy chair in our living room. I begin reading my copy of the tenth-reunion book that so depressed Gibby Good. I turn, of course, to my own entry first. Everyone was asked to provide two or three hundred words about his activities since college. My entry reads:

CHRISTOPHER PERRY KWAIT   "Kit"
   Home: 290 Central Park West, New York, N.Y. 10024.
   Occupation: Corporate Management, Continental Computron Corpo-
      ration (Assistant to Director of Market Research), 777 Lexington
      Avenue, New York, N.Y.
   Married: Anne Louise McNally ("Anne"), October 25, 1957.
   Children: Andrew, 6, and Elizabeth, 3.
   Military: None.
      I have spent the past ten years persevering. My wife is a good
   woman. My children are my hobby.

Most of the other entries are similarly devoid of drama, crisis, challenge, and triumph. But I rather prefer my own for its economy of statement. Is there no more to say about ten years of my life? In all candor, no, not really. But since the basic implausibility of all that follows stems precisely from this void, I will say a few somethings in self-defense of this Christopher Kwait, known as Kit, born of woman (half Episcopalian, half Unitarian), spawned of man (half Catholic, half Jewish), reared deep in the American heartland, tutored in all the tenets of free enterprise and self-aggrandizement, who came east to college where he studied fitfully, wrote two or three things for the campus magazine, wore a rumpled gray sweater all the time, had the rough edges buffed off him and graduated precisely in the middle of his class.

Declared unfit for military service because of an asthmatic wheeze (nicely cultivated by tens of thousands of cigarettes), he went dispassionately to work for the Continental Computron Corporation, a leviathan among guppies, whose products were in no measurable way superior to its competitors' but whose remarkable achievements stemmed precisely from ignoring that limitation. The company thrived because of its unswerving allegiance to a single operating principle, which, though never stated quite so baldly (indeed it was never stated at all), ran approximately: the more units you sell, the higher you raise your prices; the higher you raise your prices, the better the customers assume your product to be; the better the customers assume your product to be, the more units they will buy. Whatever misgivings Kit came in time to have about the sanctity of such a syllogism, there was no denying its efficacy. Every quarter now for twenty-four years running, Computron's corporate earnings have surpassed the corresponding figure for the year previous by no less than 12 per cent—a performance that had enshrined Computron stock in Wall Street's pantheon of blue chips and drove the price ever upward. A share of Computron bought at its opening price of $37.50 in 1924 and held ever since had a market price, the last time it was calculated, of $1,084. And since everyone who worked for the company had an option to buy its stock anytime at 20 per cent below the market price, the basic mendacity of its operations was hardly the object of continuing internal scrutiny.

They had started him as a salesman in one of the city's less promising territories. The youngest man in his office by five years, he nevertheless at once proved an excellent salesman—casual but persistent (as casual, that is, as one can be lugging a seventy-five-pound machine up and down stairs all day). And he obliged the petty regimen the company invoked. Every day he wore a white shirt and a dark suit and a dark tie with polite little doodads on it, and on his head he planted a gray fedora. He paid his token one dollar a year to join the Computron Country Club, because it was nice that they had a country club for all the fellows even if no city-dwelling employee ever bestirred himself to go to it. And each week he filed exemplary sales reports full of brisk prose and constructive ideas to improve the design and service of the product. By sweat and pluck and despite the unpromising territory, he made his sales quota and went to Florida each January with all the other sweat-and-pluckers around the country who had made their quotas, and they sat on the beach for two hours and went to the race track for two hours and spent the rest of the three days listening to talks on how they would make their (invariably higher) quotas next year. And they did make it. Except those who didn't, and they were told to go work someplace else.

He was, quite obviously, the stuff upper-management men are made of. And so in time the cast-iron machines were lifted from his slightly deformed back and Christopher Kwait, junior executive, was installed in a little office all his own. It had pale green walls and a glass door and it was at the farthest end of the Market Research Unit of the Sales and Marketing Department of the Products Division of the Industrial Group (as opposed to the Service Group and the Supply Group) of the Continental Computron Corporation.

Part of management now, he was less certain of himself at first. His new work, compared with the gut labor of his old field job, was abstract and isolating. What it was was thinking up better ways to sell the same old slightly remodeled, rejiggered, and basically overpriced machines. If he did that well, presumably they would move him to one of the task forces tirelessly contemplating (and invariably abandoning as too risky) a glittering array of new product lines. Mostly he wrote reports. His reports were based on other people's reports. And the other people's reports were based on still other peo-

ple's reports. They streamed into Market Research from the eighty-
seven field offices.

Kit read them all at first, every word, and within three weeks knew
the caliber of every man in the sales organization better than anyone else in the company did. Soon, though, Kit got tired of reading
every report and began instead to sample them. He would read a
dozen or so at the beginning of the morning and then he would think
about them. Then he would look at *Fortune* magazine, especially the
section in the front featuring the moguls of the month. Then he would
read three more reports. Then he would begin one of the articles in
Fortune, slow down about midway through, and finally push it away
before the end as fatigue set in. Then he would go to lunch. He liked
to eat lunch at a little-frequented Chinese restaurant on Second Avenue. The food was indifferent but they never bothered him when he
stayed an extra fifteen or twenty minutes to read the paperback he
always brought with him—usually a famous novel that he had not
been required to read in college, like *The Charterhouse of Parma.*
Then he went back to his office and lit a cigar and started in on
Business Week. Then he read a dozen more reports. Then he put in
some work on his weekly memo to Mooring—Malcolm McTavish
Mooring, Director of Market Research. Each week there was to be
a memo, just as there had been when he was in the field selling. Only
now his weekly memo was not just one of five thousand filed with
Sales Central but one of three that landed on Malcolm Mooring's
desk each Monday morning and presumably had something to do with
the company's over-all course of action.

His memos were effective in inverse proportion to the time and
effort he put into them. Bored with the task and lacking ultimate
passion for the company's primary purpose, he began to invent a
new kind of memo. He invented gingerly at first, dropping in a
literary allusion here and a strained but plausible analogy there. The
allusions and analogies began to reach out farther and farther until,
before he could check it, he had created the impression that he was

an intellectual. For a time there was real doubt whether it was a good thing for the company—a fellow like that, writing memos like that. But his conclusions and proposals generally made good sense, and it was refreshing to read memos that invoked Byron and Lord Acton and Arnold J. Toynbee. Someone was seriously suggesting—or so it seemed to management—that the selling of their machines was somehow related to the world at large, to the past and the future, to the great ideas that had been spurring men for thirty or forty centuries. It was inferentially flattering, and Kit's inventive reports, after the initial uncertainty about them, scored high. They began to come back to him with notes of commendation scrawled on the bottom, first from Mooring, who incorporated the best of them in *his* weekly reports, then from the higher-ups to whom Mooring occasionally sent them *in toto,* and then, one momentous day, from Sterling S. Steerage himself, corporate Vice-President in Charge of the Industrial Group and heir presumptive to the presidency. Which is to say the top man in his sector of the company apparently knew that Christopher Kwait was alive. Kit began, actually, to feel a twinge of fulfillment.

4

His Untimely Death at Thirty-two

THAT, IN AN OUTSIZED NUTSHELL AND IF ANYONE IS INTERESTED, is what there is to say about Christopher Kwait, called Kit, ten years out of college. In the way of hard substance, it does not amount to any more than the few lines his entry actually consumes in the reunion book. Indeed, he is the perfect embodiment, he decides, of the syndrome affecting most of these immediate peers of his: a sort of hemmed-in, cut-off, strapped-down feeling that the first half of their

lives has amounted to very little of any real value—and that prospects
for the second half are less than luminous. Nothing seems to warrant
their deepest fidelity—no cause, no hero, no enterprise or institution.
And so they speed ahead not without ambition but without passion,
without commitment, even to themselves. To break loose, to bust out,
to risk all, to pack the family in the wagon and head off into the sunrise—all that is inconceivable now. The time has passed for that, and
the place has changed. The forests have all been tracked now, rivers
all bridged, canyons all dammed, cities all built, fortunes all accumulated, wars all won (that had been worth fighting in the first
place). Those elemental arenas of fulfillment have dried up for them
and they sit, all the Kit Kwaits of the Silent Generation, in the dim
afterglow of a radiance once mythic, and they sift through the enormous jackpot at the end of that continental rainbow and worship the
totemic glitter of it. They see, in short, no purpose animating the great
republic that reared them. And that aimlessness, that zestlessness, that
disinclination to dare hugely for fear of losing what has been built
with such unflagging dynamism, shadows all their private pursuits.

Kit Kwait walks out on to his sooty terrace where his eye vaguely
registers the constellation of ten thousand incandescent windows on
every side. "Why have I surrendered?" he asks himself. "Am I living at all if I do not invest all my glands and sinews in the process?
If I hang back and let myself be wafted by the tide like straggling
flotsam?" He moves to the edge of the terrace and looks over the
side. Instant vertigo wheels over him. I am a moldering blob of
phobias, he thinks. A putrefying repository of repressions. A quivering quid of denied micro-urges. They dog my every waking moment:

I do not walk over gratings for fear they will cave in under me.

I do not pee in the shower even when I have a great yearning to,
even when the stench will be washed away and no one will know.

I do not go swimming because the water is so cold and wet and
wants badly to suck me under.

I do not go dancing because I do it lumpishly.

I do not ski for fear I will spill the marrow of my precious bones that have never been shattered. Or even fractured.

I do not fly because my plane is surely fated for obliteration and I for an ember that will settle for a moment on some treetop and then disappear forever.

I do not eat a meal without fretting whether it is still further bloating my soggy body.

I do not work in behalf of any civic cause because it all seems such fruitless bother.

I am thirty-two years old, a pillar of normality, a dedicated family man, without a trauma to my name, on agreeable (if distant) terms with my kin and most of the people I know on earth, working regular hours for good pay, materially deprived in no way—a paragon of decorum, a consummately civilized man. And dead.

He goes inside and tells his wife about it.

"Anne," I say to her as she knits in the dining alcove, "I am catastrophically hung up."

She knits on.

"I said something."

"Yes," she says, "I heard."

"Aren't you going to say anything?"

"I thought you were going to explain."

"What's there to explain? It's the basic fact of my existence."

"I didn't know that," she says, still tending her needles.

"I didn't either—till just now."

"What happened just now?"

"I've been thinking—about everything."

"Yes."

"I have not seen enough, done enough, suffered enough—in short, *lived* enough—to save the fiber in my soul."

"You want a divorce, is that it?"

"Look," I say, "I'm serious."

"Oh," she says, looking up. "Well, why do you want to suffer?"

"I don't—that's the problem."

"Why is it a problem?"

"Because without deprivation, there is no passion. Without adversity, there is no triumph. I am atrophying on the vine. So to speak."

She continues knitting. She is always knitting. She is a very good knitter. Once she knit a whole rug. Nine feet by twelve feet. It was cocoa color with little orange and red and deep brown squares sprinkled all over. By the time it was stretched and blocked and backed, it cost twice as much as any other nine-by-twelve rug in the world. But it fulfilled her. And when it was cleaned for the first time, it shrank unevenly and wrinkled all over. She told me the wrinkles would come out after it was put down on the floor again. Only they didn't. They got worse instead. I rolled it up and put it in the closet, hoping somehow the wrinkles would disappear in there. Only they didn't. I threw the rug out after three months. Meanwhile she had knitted three sweaters, a dress, a belted black coat and was well into a tapestry that would contain, when completed, 266,400 stitches. Old Flying Fingers, I call her.

"Would you like to have a crippling disease?" she asks me, fingers flying.

"No."

"Would you like to live in a steaming jungle and eat crunchy black bugs and teach salvation to natives with festers in their eyes?"

"No."

"Would you like to wear a green beret and stick bayonets into little Asian men in sneakers?"

"No."

"Would you like to puncture your veins with a needle twice a day and grovel on the floor in unbearable agony when they won't give you one?"

"No."

"Then what are you complaining about?"

"Because I want to know what it feels like to do all those things."

"Use your imagination. You don't have to stick your arm in a fire to know it hurts."

"I don't have an imagination any more."

"But you write those marvelous memos."

"Those memos are diddly-shit. So's the whole fucking company."

"Then why don't you become a ski bum or a whaling captain or—or—or a forest ranger and play checkers all day with Smokey the Bear?"

"Because I am a nice married fellow with a steady job and two adorable children who need their daddy or they will grow up queer."

"Besides which you're a coward."

"Besides which I'm a coward."

"Nonsense. You are a mature, responsible person. All those other things are escapism. They are indulged in by people who cannot bear to face life."

"You don't understand. *I'm* the one who's escaping, who isn't committed to anything. Everything I do is tentative. Defensive. I just go through the motions. The whole thing is totally dispassionate. There is not one gram of excitement."

She drops her knitting needles and sighs heavily. "I think maybe you need a vacation."

"You know," I say, "I'll tell you something. You're very conventional."

"I never claimed to be anything else."

I flop into a chair. "I suppose not."

She comes around behind me and runs her hands through my hair. "Aren't I nice, all the same?"

She cannot see my frown. "Very nice."

"And I don't make demands like a lot of grasping wives do."

"No, you don't."

"And you are unequivocally the boss and I am not out to de-ball you."

"No, you are not."

"And I cook nicely."

"When you cook."

"Cooking is a pain in the ass."

"It's your job."

"I feed the children well."

"Hamburgers five times a week."

"They *like* hamburgers. Besides, it's chopped round steak."

"And you never put my goddam shirts away. They sit around in laundry bundles for a week."

"You're right. I'm sorry."

"And lots of mornings there's no clean handkerchief in my drawer."

"I'm getting better about that, though."

"And you slurp when you drink your coffee."

"Just the tiniest bit—I love it so."

"And we don't screw often enough."

"Often enough for what?"

"For healthy, lusty adults."

"You're just sore because I don't like to do it upside down."

"You're *not* very adventurous that way, let's face it."

"Then maybe you ought to find a partner who is."

"Maybe I ought to."

"Just make sure she's clean."

Adultery! Yes—the very thing. Not a protracted messy affair—just a nice wholesome extramarital interlude. The perfect pick-me-up. The classic recreation. It is not the first time it has occurred to me, of course. But it has always seemed so unmanageable before this—so involving, so disruptive. And I have always lacked motivation. For the plain truth is that Kit Kwait loves Anne Kwait. Adores her, even. She is smart and she is gentle. She does not talk unless she has something to say. She derives large happiness from small joys. She never smokes on the street and never chews gum anywhere. She is as remarkably even-tempered as he is not. She is fond of the things he is fond of—people, food, movies, furniture (they are in their Art Nouveau period at the moment). All in all, and even though she does slurp her coffee occasionally (it is a tiny lapping noise, really, like a mouse might make, traceable to her habit of filling the cup to the absolute brim), she is a soul mate of singular congeniality.

All that, though, I tell myself now, is beside the point. The thing has nothing to do with my not loving her. It is just that, given the circumstances, adultery seems the one manageable adventure that may alleviate my long-latent and now suddenly exposed hang-up.

"It would have nothing to do with my not loving you," I say.

"I understand," she says.

"It's just that a little variety is good for everybody now and then."

"The spice of life."

"Exactly."

"It's all right with me," she says, "so long as equals are equals."

"Meaning—?"

"What's sauce for the goose is sauce for the gander." She glances up, brow furrowed slightly. "Or the other way around in this case."

"You wouldn't want to do a thing like that."

"Oh, I might."

"If you loved me all that much, you wouldn't even bring it up."

"I didn't bring it up—you did."

"I'm a man. Everyone knows men are allowed to philander."

"Oh, right. Fidelity is a drag."

"Absolute fidelity, anyway."

"That's redundant. You're either faithful or you're not—like being pregnant."

"My one real complaint with you is that you persist in seeing everything as black or white. I suppose it's a feminine prerogative."

She is knitting evenly now. "Anyway, whatever you do, make sure she's clean."

"Since when have you become such a bug on sanitation?"

"It's very important when doing it with strangers. I am all for liberation, especially if it cures your catastrophic hang-up, but I am definitely not interested in getting diseased."

5

Muffie

AND NOW I SEE THE SCARLET LETTER EVERYWHERE. EMBROIDERED with baroque serifs on my handkerchief each morning and my bath towel each night. Embossed along the edge of my attaché case. Flashing on and off subliminally in my dreams of thrashing liaisons. But instead of searing me with dread of venal sin, it beckons me like a signal in the dark toward a furtive rendezvous. Why, if the truth were known, Kit Kwait has never had any other woman since Anne McNally Kwait. The time, indisputably, has come.

I begin to look all around for the perfect collaborator. At fellow passengers in every bus I ride and on every elevator. At fellow pedestrians on every street I walk. At fellow eaters in every restaurant I patronize (having, with this quest in mind, at long last abandoned my Chinese lunch parlor). My head spins, my groin yearns. The lust is on me and I permit it to take hold in the name of Adventure.

In idle moments, which compose most of my time, I conjure up disembodied female parts that meet my requirements. The face I am to embrace can be any face, round or square or Picassoesque, so long as it is not blank or bristly. The breasts I will press can be modest mounds—I demand no gleaming warheads, thrust high and mounted for combat. Of the hips I ask only for flare without ungainliness. Of the ass I want heft, not quivering hemispheres that grossly overhang the toilet seats on which they hunker. Of the general pelvic region

I want mystery implied somehow in the drape of the skirt over the dark diadem that waits throbbing beneath it. When I reach the legs, though, my demands stiffen. No tubular ones of stately oak will ever cumbersomely entwine mine. Only kicky ones, diaphanously sheathed, can turn me on: the long lean ankle giving way to the supple musculature of the all-important calf, leading in turn to the not overly carbuncular knee at the threshold of sleekly tapered loins that promise numberless delights within ther springy clasp. Legs!

I survey the office secretarial corps. Svelte and single, all of them, and oh so pluckable. It is inconceivable that any of them is still chaste. Yet some even more perverse impulse steers my wanderlust toward married women—because the adultery would be doubled, I suppose, and therefore all the more thrilling. In a practical sense, moreover, a woman not unbearably matched to her husband would have as much to lose as I from any protracted involvement.

That decided, I find myself shepherding my children, one Sunday morning toward the end of June, to the playground in the park across the street from our apartment house. And there, having dispatched her own pair to the sandbox and surrounded now by the usual cluster of grown-up female admirers, is Muffie Miller, a friend of ours. Muffie Miller is easily the most demonstrative woman I have ever met. Her spherical face and soft features are outshone by saucer eyes that leap and spin as she rattles off one of her hyperbolic monologues that make her the commanding focus of any conversation she is part of. She is the only woman I have ever met who can tell a joke straight. She carries it all off with a put-on chic, compounded of good leather, cheap baubles, ungussy dresses, and unthinkable quantities of eye makeup. She comes on strong and goes off, if at all, unwillingly. Running a household bored her and rearing two kids bored her worse, so she began teaching college history to freshmen on the strength of her master's from Barnard and purposeful, if vague, promises that she is about to begin pursuing her doctorate. Muffie Miller: tough, tirelessly

self-centered, staggeringly self-possessed, and furiously competitive.
I think she badly wishes she had been born with a penis.

Marvin Miller, it is widely assumed, had. A slouching heavyweight,
he is further assumed to possess three virtues in his wife's eyes: (1)
he provides her with an appreciative audience, (2) the paper-bag
business he runs with his father produces the comparative posh to
which she has become accustomed, and (3) he ruts with the gusto of
a prize mustang. But, leaning back now against a seesaw and listening
to her patter on about her new maid, I begin to re-examine the Miller
situation.

"This is a *gem*," she spouts, "a three-hundred-and-fifty-two-pound
gem. The glitter *defies* belief! And she's still growing. All day she
eats. The doorbell's always ringing and it's another gross of doughnuts for Sadie. Only Sadie doesn't move fast enough to get the bell.
A large ant could spot Sadie ninety yards and win a hundred-yard
dash by *minutes*. So I'm always bringing in her doughnuts. But Sadie's
bright. That makes up for a lot. Her I.Q. could not possibly be
under—oh, twenty-three. Well, maybe twenty. She had a lot of
trouble with all those big words on the Pablum box the other day,
so she gave my little one a mess of Swans Down cake mix for supper.
The kid loved it. I may keep him on it. Honestly, though, it's a little
hard to communicate with Sadie because she speaks sort of Advanced
Aborigine. Margaret Mead's coming over next week to check it for
us. But Sadie's clean. I mean *immaculate*. Not the house—just Sadie.
She scrubs down from head to toe after every doughnut. Which leaves
about a six-inch layer of powdered sugar all over the floor. Sometimes
we get drifts. And she's devout. Every time I say 'Oh, shit,' she falls
on her knees and starts praying for me in Aborigine. Now we have
copies of the *Watchtower* on every table in the apartment—and a
dozen in the liquor cabinet. We're going to have a round-table discussion on blood transfusions tomorrow night—Sadie and me. She's
against blood transfusions. The Bible says it's wrong. We may open

the whole thing up, if the moderator lets us, and get into fluoridation, too. It's on Channel 13, eight o'clock. Sadie looks thinner on television than she really is. They can only get part of her on the screen at any one time. . . ."

What a scream you are, Muffie Miller, what a panic you are, Muffie Miller, what a cruel funny bitch.

She goes to scoop sand out of one of her kids' eyes and the rest of them begin talking about where they are headed the following week for the summer. Muffie elbows her way back into the middle of it and in another minute is explaining how her Marvin did not score at Amagansett the summer before.

"You have to *picture* it. Here are half the beautiful people in the Western Hemisphere sprawled on this one beach—the most *exquisite* people on earth, bar none. Acres and acres of *mar*velously toasted bodies draped all over the sand and literally *bursting* out of their loincloths. I mean I've seen bikinis and bikinis but these were cut to the *vulva*. Honestly. And the men—I mean you didn't even have to stare to see how well-hung they were. And, I swear, there was one guy—or whatever—wearing a paisley jockstrap. And everyone of course had on these enormous sunglasses—really huge goggles, like from Mount Palomar—and they're all lying around under these terribly campy umbrellas drinking ice-cold Marys and telling the rottenest jokes they know. Ethnic jokes were very big last year— especially Polish ones. Very snide. Very hip. The sexiest, hippest beach in the world. Like Saint-Tropez is Outsville compared with Amagansett. I mean I *died* for it. And here comes my Marvin out to join the swingers, my beautiful Marvin. Every eye on the beach is arrested by his striking figure as he strides manfully across the sand—in his floppy gray swim trunks that come down almost to his knees. And his big black clumpy city shoes—with wing tips! And a button-down shirt. And a tie. And the tie is knotted right up to his nose. A jacket he's got slung casually over his shoulder—with the Barney's label prominently on display. And he's squinting something awful trying to find me. He doesn't know from sunglasses. And he couldn't have stumbled on the sand more than—oh, eight or ten times. What a sensation! He was not to be believed. I let him wander around for an hour, squinting and stumbling like an epileptic. I mean it was just hor*rend*ous!"

Muffie Miller, you wicked vixen, you. No devoted wife uses her husband like that for gag material. You are telling the world something, and I am listening, Muffie Miller, I am listening.

The performance breaks up soon afterward and I find myself staring idly up at our apartment house, looming like a mammoth citadel over the park. Its twin towers of sandy brick dimly gave back the early-summer sunlight.

"Hey," a playful voice breaks my reverie, "what're you doing— casing the joint?"

I turned to face her narrowed eyes. "Me?"

"Oh, I won't say a word. I mean I approve. Entirely. You're the perfect robber for it. Who'd ever figure on an inside job in a nice ritzy building like that?"

"Yes," I say. "That's what I'm counting on."

"Actually," she says, "the city would be a helluva lot safer if a better class of people went in for robbing. Why should the profession be so left to a bunch of lowlifes?"

"Why indeed?"

"I mean a really first-class robbery requires imagination and finesse. And courage, of course. It's a very existential conception if you stop to think about it—the commitment in it, I mean."

"Why don't you come along?"

"Oh, I wouldn't dream of horning in. It has to be an utterly private thing, I'm sure of it. There's nothing heightening about it if you need help. It has to be the robber against the world."

"You're missing the point. It's like intercourse. It has to be a shared charge. A one-man robbery is like masturbating."

She is not used to having her whimsy batted back at her. "Well, maybe," she says. "Let me think about it." She runs a hand through her prettily disarranged hair. "You're coming out to Amagansett for a weekend, you know. I told Anne. I mean you've got to. It's an absolutely enormous place. With huge lawns and lots of trees. You'll *die* for it. Come—with the kids. And we'll plan our robbery." She puts a hand on my wrist. "Promise you'll come." The imperative gains force from the slight squeeze she adds.

"I wouldn't miss it for the world." Because I want your ass, Muffie Miller. You scintillating emasculating sensational snatch, you.

6

The Wallet

ANNE AND I TAKE THE SATURDAY MORNING TRAIN TO EAST HAMPTON the first weekend in August. At Muffie's urging, we have left the kids home with a sitter.

From the moment I lay eyes on her at the station, she is in motion, talking and drinking and cooking and playing games—desperate not to miss the slightest bit of the action. We throw our bags upstairs at the house and, Muffie at the wheel, speed out past Gurney's Inn to the seafood place at the shanty tip of Montauk. Wolfing down fried shrimp and not very cold beer, she chatters away about the unexcelled marvelousness of the whole Hampton scene. All the while, her eyes rove past us to see who really important is there. I am close to moving my chair out of the way so she can have an unobstructed view. Her back, of course, is to the sea; it she has seen already.

"How are you guys on poker?" she asks, almost rhetorically.

"Indifferent," I say.

"I *die* for it. We play every day." She turns to Marvin. "I could go some right now."

"I could go a nap," he says.

"Oh, Christ, I forgot—it's Saturday. The croquet crowd'll be over at three." She feigns a worried look. "Shit, I didn't ask Leo and Sally to the party."

"Why not?"

She turns, by way of answer, to Anne. "Would you believe a *Leo*? He's the only human Leo left on earth. And he's an un*bear*able drag. And *she* still has acne. Thirty years old and acne. She's a whiz at tennis, though. We play every morning. I actually beat her twice this week. I think she was easing up." She turns to Marvin. "Maybe she heard about the party and figured I'd ask her if she let me win a few times. Maybe I ought to. You think four hours' notice is too short?" She cranks out a hollow laugh.

Leo has a beard, it turns out, and someone named Alfred is almost utterly bald, and I miss the rest of the names except for a too-fat dark-haired girl named Vicki, whose chest is climbing out of her navy sweat shirt. Muffie is everywhere on the enormous lawn, urging drinks on the players, goading them to misplays, drilling rival balls to the edge of the enormous lawn with laughing gusto. Between shots, she darts into the house, a cigarette dangling from her mouth, to check with the girl in the kitchen who is helping her cook for the fifty people they are having in for a buffet at seven-thirty. At five, she orders Anne and me into swimsuits, and while Marvin naps and the croquet goes on unabated she drives us to the beach.

"It's sort of rough today," she says, leading us to a strategically located spot. "Everyone's just about gone now." She waves to a far-off blanket. Somebody waves back. "That's one of our neighbors. He's living with another woman. His wife's living with him, too, but so is this other one. I think he tells his kids she's his cousin or something."

"Doesn't his wife mind a little?" Anne asks.

"She's a dyke, I think. Sort of late-blooming. It all seems to be working out very well. They're coming to dinner."

"Which one does he bring?"

"Both of them, I guess. I just said, 'Come.' He's a shrink—a disciple of Sullivan. They're allowed to do *any*thing. So he does." She whips on a bathing cap. "He's very serious about it." She heads for the water. "Coming?"

"Too cold for me," Anne says.

She beckons me.

How I want to take her hand and plunge through the waves with her and afterward grovel with her at the water's edge, the way Burt Lancaster did with Deborah Kerr in *From Here to Eternity*. But I am an absurdly bad swimmer. I can swim perhaps a hundred yards— a hundred and ten if my life depended on it. "No," I say, "I've got pneumonia. The sun's good for it."

She is no toe-in-the-water wetsy-poo. I watch her square her shoulders and race into the foaming surf. She bobs on the waves, then begins arching over them like a helmeted porpoise. The water is there to serve her, and she uses it. Soon she is racing back toward us, a full-striding, big-bottomed, womanly woman, tossing her hair back and head up and casting a fine shower of droplets from her deeply toasted body with every step. "I *die* for it," she says and dives onto the blanket, spreading her cool, still-glinting limbs for the sun to bake in a jiffy.

We start on Bloody Marys as soon as we get back and before any- one has dressed. We drink on the little brick patio at the side of the house. Muffie keeps crossing and uncrossing her legs as she runs over the roster of guests with rising apprehension. The sight of those brown flanks in constant flux excites me more than her ceaseless patter puts me off. Suddenly she ducks off into the outdoor shower at the edge of the patio, a tiny stockade-like enclosure through the cracks of which my eyes flick hungrily but catch no more than shimmering slivers of her nakedness. Wrapped in a towel, she darts out barefoot and bounds upstairs to get dressed.

The accumulated liquor has begun to work on me by the time Anne and I come down for dinner. I start humming along with the hi-fi, which is pouring out a creamy bossa nova too loud, and snapping my fingers with unaccustomed fidelity to the beat.

Muffie, in a raucous Pucci jump suit, spins barefoot through the crowd like a dervish, dispensing contagious laughter to the women and brushing coquettish fingertips against the men. She thrusts an arm through mine for a moment and, smiling hugely but speaking in a muffle, asks, "Are you hating it? I can tell—you disapprove. You think they're all shallow nothings—galloping nonentities—great red-faced beasts without a drop of—"

I cut her short. "I am having a spectacular time. And I have never been more thoroughly disarming in my life. You go take a poll and see if they don't vote me the most thoroughly disarming fellow on my side of the room. And if they don't, I'll—"

"You *must* go in and eat," she says, not acknowledging my banter. "There are one million Swedish meatballs being utterly ignored."

"One million Swedish meatballs can't all be wrong."

But she is off, caressing another forearm and spraying another burst of canned laughter into the nearest corner.

I run out of cigars at about this point and go up to our bedroom on the sceond floor for some more. Cigars somehow seem to add to my buoyancy; besides, no one else is smoking them. I take three from the tin I have brought along and stored on the night table. Stripping the cellophane from one as I head out the door, I stop short and remember dimly that I left my wallet beside the cigars before going downstairs. And now the wallet is not there. I go back to the table. No, it is definitely not there. I look on the floor. I bend down and look behind the table. Nothing. I check my back pocket. Empty. My blazer pockets. No. My eyes race around the room. Not on the

dresser. Or the bed. Or anywhere. Stolen. The bedroom door had
been left open. And it had been right there. Anyone could have stuck
his head in, seen it, grabbed it, and gone back downstairs in a twinkling. Many of them are just casual friends of Muffie's—she has said
as much. All kinds of people in a crowd like this. Son of a bitch!
There was at least a hundred dollars in it. Plus our train tickets home.
Whoever took it is probably still here, still in the house or out on
the patio. But there are fifty or sixty people. And none of them looks
like a thief. On second thought, they all look like thieves. Who knows
what thieves look like any more? Should I tell Muffie? Maybe she
can solve it with a burst of laughter and some ready explanation like
"Oh, Salome Sims must have snatched it—she's a well-known kleptomaniac. Wait, I'll get it right back." Maybe, but probably not. Maybe
it would be better if I just go to the head of the landing, call for
attention, and come right out with it. "Someone in this house has
stolen my wallet," I will say, "and I mean to get it back." There will
be a charged murmur and much spinning of heads. Then I will say,
"Since we are all gentlemen and ladies, I do not of course intend to
embarrass the thief. If he or she will just have a discreet word with
me sometime during the next hour, the matter will end right there.
If nobody comes forward, I'm afraid I shall have to insist that everyone be searched and I will then have no choice but to press charges
against the culprit." Probably they will think it is a game. Surely it
will restore excitement to the evening, which is beginning to show
signs of running down. But no, I cannot do that. It will mortify
Muffie. She will never forgive me for ruining her otherwise dazzling
performance. I will simply have to circulate among the guests and
try to figure out who the criminal is and then let him or her know
by thinly veiled barbs that I *know*.

I go downstairs, my eyes suspicious slits, and back a fat man in a
turtleneck sweater against the wall. "What would you do if you were
me," I say menacingly, "and you just discovered that someone here
had stolen your wallet?"

The fat man has no fewer than three Swedish meatballs in his mouth at the moment. He chews them carefully while he ruminates. Then, licking his lips, he says slowly, "I'd probably cry." He lifts his plate and, indicating a dozen meatballs that form a little pyre on it, adds, "Say, have you tried these? They're out of this world."

Repulsed so offhandedly, I begin drinking again. It will be fruitless, this insinuating process, so I decide just to chalk it up as a very expensive night and confide in the Millers the next morning when, of course, it will be too late to do anything about the wallet. I drink and, feeling sorry for myself, drink some more. The laughter grows shrill, the room warmer. It is all turning into a bad dream.

In another hour, the house is empty except for Anne and me and the Millers and the girl in the kitchen. Muffie, instead of showing the signs of exhaustion any normal woman might have felt after a day like hers, is moving toward an emotional crest of some sort. "We're going over to Otto Oberdorfer's for poker," she announces from the sofa. There is nothing solicitous or tentative about it. She wills it; it is going to occur. As an afterthought, she asks me, "You liked Otto, didn't you?"

"The one with the two wives?"

"No, that's Mike Morgenstern—the beard in the pale blue slacks and the sandals. He has very expressive toes, did you notice? He likes men, too. Did he rub up against you? He's always rubbing up against likely prospects—of either sex. It's a basic animal thing, he says." She glances at me and flicks away her cigarette. "Of course your pants aren't really clutchy enough in the crotch for him."

"I would've soaked them in the sink all afternoon if you'd given me half a clue."

"No, dear," she says, "either you are or you aren't. You aren't." She climbs out of the sofa. "Anyway, Otto's the tall, marvelous one with the shoulders of Hercules and the brain of Goliath. I have to pee."

"She's in love with Otto," says Marvin, bestirring himself in the corner. "That's this week. Last week it was Morgenstern. Each week it's someone else. She says it makes the summer go faster."

The game is already in progress when we get there. There are only three places left at the table. Muffie grabs one, Marvin another, and Anne, at my urging, takes the last one. I have not played cards since college, and then it had been bridge, which I liked very little. It took too much thinking, and if I had to think, I preferred to think about something better. The game now is seven-card high-low, at which Muffie, apparently, has become adept. She instructs Anne for the first few hands.

I sit back and follow the game with decreasing interest. It is a curiously joyless ritual the way they go at it, Muffie especially, hard eyes flicking uncommunicatively about the table for a telltale look after stealing an expressionless glance at each card she draws. She bets with a short, decisive thrust of chips and wins or loses with a knowing little nod. She smokes throughout the game, a giveaway to her intensity. After a dozen or so hands, her cigarettes are gone. She reaches down into her purse for another pack. The purse is on the floor just in front of my chair. The way she opens it, I can see the contents clearly. My wallet is in there.

She fishes around in it without taking her eye off the table and finds the extra pack of cigarettes. The game, though, begins to go badly against her. She stays in to the end of five straight hands and loses them all. She quits the next two early, then goes all the way on three more and loses. It is her deal and she has barely a dollar left in chips. "Five-card draw," she says, and deals quickly. One of the cards flips over by accident. She has to reshuffle and deal over. This time she skips one of the players. Reshuffle, redeal, nostrils beginning to flare. On her third try, the cards just fall out of her hands as she shuffles. "I've had it," she says, rising dramatically. She signals to Marvin. "Here, you bail us out, baby—Mommy's going night-night before she throws an epileptic fit." And she is gone.

Anne, meanwhile, by combining luck and timidity, is actually a little bit ahead. Clearly she is not about to retire from the game. She is in fact so caught up in it that I slip out of the room without bothering to tell her. I cover the few hundred yards back to the Miller house slowly, thinking how I will handle the confrontation. Before settling on a graceful strategy, I am at the driveway. I can see the vast lawn harshly floodlit in the moonless night. And, in a few more steps, I can see Muffie at the far end, bashing a croquet ball up toward me. Her jump suit lies in a heap, inside out, next to the double wicket at my end. She has on only a white bra and a pantie girdle. In the incandescent glare they contrast severely with the tanned face and square shoulders, the solid, not yet thick, midriff, the long muscularly faceted legs. Her feet are bare.

The ball rolls dead a foot from my foot. "Hi, Stuff," she calls to me.

"Hi, yourself."

"Sort of a bad exit back there," she says, tossing her hair back but staying at her end of the lawn.

"You were tired."

"I was losing," she says, coming toward me now slowly and swinging her mallet like a golf club as she comes.

"And you don't like to lose."

"No," she says. "Do you?"

"Can't bear it."

She is beside me now. "Of course not," she says, and reaches into my shirt pocket for my last cigar. "You can't bear it so much you don't even like to play." She begins laughing. "And if you don't play, you don't lose—do you, Stuff?" She plants one of her bare feet painlessly on the toe of my loafer and presses. "I know all about you," she says huskily, and looks up at me. "You're a non-player from way back." She looks away. "How 'bout a light, Stuff?"

Now—now I will take her, must take her, right here, right now, floodlights and all. She is inviting it, blatantly, and I have thought of nothing else since arriving. Her moans will attract the whole poker crowd down the road, and they will line the edge of the lawn and cheer us madly to a simultaneous and protracted climax. And when it is done, Anne will show me the fifty dollars she has won at poker and tell me to button my fly.

But. I. Do. Not. Take. Her. I—I—what I do is clamp my eyes shut for a long instant to keep from fainting. And when I open them, she is still there, still sparsely clad, still waiting for a light. I poke into three pockets and finally find some matches in a fourth. "Thanks," she says.

"I notice you're not wearing very much."

"You noticed that."

"Yes."

"Very good for a non-playing Stuff."

"Yes," I say. "Well, it's very bright here with all these lights."

"Yes," she says. "Well, I was very warm."

"Yes," I say. "That would explain it."

"I hope I'm not embarrassing you."

"Not at all."

She takes her foot off my loafer, crosses her legs, and draws deeply on the cigar. "Very nice," she says.

"I'm glad."

"How'd you like everything?"

"Fine," I say, looking at her sternly now, "except somebody stole my wallet."

"Oh, I know," she says, unflinching. "I did."

"You?"

"It's right in my purse there—under the clothes." She kicks the jump suit away.

"You always steal your guests' wallets?"

"Always," she says, scooping up the jump suit and flinging it over her shoulder. "That's how I know so much about robbing. You remember our little talk in the park?"

"Oh, very well. I haven't stopped thinking about it."

She snares her purse between her big and second toe and lifts it to her hand. "Yours wasn't much of a challenge, I'm afraid."

"Sorry about that."

"Usually I grab it while my victim has it on him. It's much more of a charge. Or I get him pantsless and help myself while he's still recovering from the indescribable thrills of my exquisite body." She hands the wallet back to me. "I saw it lying there and took it before someone else did." She turns toward the house. "I meant to stick it in your pocket the instant I got downstairs." She is retreating toward the house now. "I guess I forgot in the excitement."

"Yes. There was a lot of excitement."

"Sorry if it upset you," she says over her shoulder.

"Sure."

She opens the screen door. "Promise you won't leave it around like that again?"

"I promise."

"Okay," she says, "then, g'night." The door bangs shut behind her.

"G'night." You indefatigable adventuress, you uncontainable whirlwind, you raging temptress, you barefaced liar, you fucking thief, you. You Muffie Miller.

7

Big and Little Mothers

EVERYONE KNOWS WHEN MUFFIE IS BACK IN TOWN FROM HER summer in the Hamptons. Her welcome-home bash, dubbed the Super-E-Go-Go, has been the talk of the playground for two solid weeks before the event itself at the end of September. Muffie, by now, has begun teaching again and does comparatively little to stir up excitement, other than telling everyone in the world she knows about the party and inviting them all to invite their best-looking friends.

In the Miller living room the sound detonates and turns quickly to a ceaseless throbbing. I unleash Anne, get a drink, and plant an elbow on the end of the mantel, smoking and drinking and watching the gyrations of the Five Little Mothers, the volume buttons on their electric guitars turned up all the way. One of the Little Mothers begins caterwauling, the words lovingly slurred and all but drowned out by the hairy Little Mother on the drums. *C'mon-a-hump-little lover-a-hump-an' show me-a-hump-that you care-a-whompa-whompa-whompa-whomp. Show me-ahump-again-ahump-again-ahump and again-ahumpa-whompa-whomp.* . . . After two or three numbers the room starts hotting up. The sound builds. The bleating turns falsetto. Five little castrados, their tousled teen-age heads bobbing grotesquely. My ears and crotch vie for aching worse. *Awhompa-whomp!* Tiny straight-haired molls who evidently belong to the Little Mothers thrash authentically with each other amid the grownups like so much saucy jailbait. I snap my fingers to their swiveling flanks. Go, you twitchy little she-rebels! Go, you cacophonous Little Mothers! Go, you big-assed sweaty-pitted grown-up fleshpots! *As they tugged him-whang-from the crackup-whang-they heard him say-whang-"Tell Laurie"-whang whang-"that I loved her"-whang whang- "all the way" -awhanga-whanga-whompa-whompa-whang.* . . . Anne's rump, in a gilded jump suit, flashes by me. Two years ago I would have whipped it for doing things like that in public.

In the middle of it all, shoes off, short-short hem flying high, ample trunk undulating in syncopation with flailing limbs, is Muffie Miller. Her long loose hair swishes from shoulder to shoulder as she punctuates every other beat with a jerk that burns up a month of hormones. Her sockets swivel with every granule of her energy. She is fighting, she is kicking, she is biting, she is lashing herself to a ritualistic climax, her substance crying out frantically for merciful release. And her pace never slackens. I watch her and feel myself being sucked ever nearer a deep dark vortex. Go, you untamable terror! Go, you frantic ball-busting bitch.

Suddenly she is bobbing and weaving toward me like an Indian rain dancer desperate for the heavens to open up. Something deep inside me begins to unravel. The collision of impulse and dignity. The unraveling whirls me right off the coil and I am free. Airborne. I grab one of her flying wrists and snap her to me and let her burning breasts drill into me. And I say to her, I say, "Hi, Toynbee," in a low growl.

"Hi, Stuff," she says, grinding away and not looking at me. "How's the haul so far?"

I thrust my pelvis three-quarters of the way to hers and with-draw it with a hernial wrench. "I don't go much," I say, "for this two-bit action." I drive my shoulders toward her in alternating wedge-like moves that would smack her to the floor were they to connect. "How much have *you* grabbed?"

"Up yours," she says, and Indian-backsteps from me. In a second she is thrashing away opposite someone else.

In the foyer I see the six-feet-three of Marvin Miller fretting over the police who are even now pounding heavily on the door and threatening him with his third summons of the night for disturbing the peace.

I elbow through the crowd to Marvin's side. "Here," I say, "try this," and push a fin into his hand. "Better add one of your own."

"You think so?"

"The most they can do is pinch you."

Marvin blinks a few times. "Yeah, but suppose they do? It's plain bribery."

"Right."

"I'll go to jail."

"We'll bail you right out. It'll be a gas."

"For who?"

"You'll be a martyr. We'll come picket."

Marvin takes out a five, adds it to mine, opens the door a crack, and pokes his arm out, flapping the bills in their faces.

They arrest him.

I wave goodbye gaily, give an extended wink, and make a reassuring circle with the thumb and index finger of my right hand, the one without the drink in it. When the door is safely closed, I drain the drink, go to get a refill, light a fresh cigar, and take up my regular station by the mantel. In a while I catch Muffie's eye and curl my index finger at her. She waves. I keep curling. Gradually she comes. "Why don't you snatch the choker from the old broad in the dining room?" she says, her feet never slowing. "She's my mother."

"I was saving it for dessert," I say. "Tell me something, baby."

"Anything, Stuff."

"You love your husband?"

She stops moving for the first time all evening and tosses her hair back, her characteristic gesture when she can think of nothing else to do. Her heavy flush is apparent even in the dim light. "More or less," she says. "Why?"

"The fuzz just took him away."

"Marvin?" Her voice rises.

"Big guy—about six-three—makes paper bags—"

"No!"

"Yes."

She looks toward the foyer where she last saw him perhaps two hours earlier. "Impossible!"

"He went quietly."

"Without even *telling* me?"

"He didn't want to break up your party."

"Oh," she says, "the dear. Isn't he a dear?"

I nod. "But dumb."

She puts on an indignant face, so I tell her how it happened. She shakes her head mournfully. "I'm surprised. I mean he's never bribed a cop in his life."

"His record's still intact."

"Actually," she says, "I think it's stupendous! It's the perfect climax for the party."

"Shall we all go down to the jail and have the Little Mothers serenade him from the street?"

"Oh, jail," she says. "I forgot."

"Does your old lady have bail money stashed away in that magnificently endowed bodice or will we have to hock her choker?"

"She's not really my old lady. She belongs to one of the Little Mothers."

"A Little Mother's mother?"

"Right."

"Better yet."

Muffie thinks for a moment. "We could take up a collection."

"He's already got my five bucks."

"Oh," she says. "Well, you've done enough."

"Yes."

"Of course we could leave him there—just overnight, I mean. That would make it really legitimate."

"He might be grateful, actually. Every man ought to spend at least one night of his life in jail. It gives him a chance to reflect on things."

"I've heard a lot of men come out of prison the better for it and begin all over."

"Yes, I've heard that," I say. "The only thing is—"

"I'll bet it would be the thrill of his life."

"I promised him we'd bail him out."

Her eyes narrow. "Bigmouth," she says.

"You're having lunch with me next Thursday—you read me?"

"Now you're talking, Stuff."

8

Mafioso

THE PLACE IS BETWEEN A CANDY STORE AND A LUMBERYARD. FROM the bar I watch her get out of the taxi, hoist her sunglasses to her forehead, and squint in disbelief at the street number. She glances up and down the block, gives a small shrug, as if she knows someone is watching, and hurries in.

"Welcome to the underworld," I say, brushing my lips over her gloved hand.

"Sorry to be so overdressed," she says, scanning the place, "but my good sweat shirt's still at the cleaner's."

"Don't be deceived by the gloom. It's all very calculated. Some of the most discriminating tax evaders in the world eat here with great regularity." I ask the bartender to send double vodka Martinis to our table.

"Actually," she says, peeling off her gloves as we sit, "I *adore* it. It's so—so—*Mafioso*-looking."

"Sh-h-h," I say. "It's the Syndicate's national headquarters."

"I don't doubt it."

"They even run extension courses at night. I'm taking Introductory Larceny. It's supposed to be the best in the world, this side of Palermo." I wave across the room at no one in particular. "Don't look now," I say, "but there's Machine Gun Mike Manicotti."

"I don't think I know the gentleman."

"He'd be unhappy if you did. His turf's Cleveland. He comes into town about once a month to settle accounts."

"What's his racket?"

"All of them. He's got the whole Lake Erie scene under absolute lock. Numbers, junk, protection—it's a model operation. Owns fifty thousand people body and soul. He's got twelve parish priests who come to *him* for confession."

Her eyes widen.

I nod toward the opposite corner. "Among our other guests today is Pistol Pete Pasquale—heir apparent to the Hudson County take. There'll probably be a plenary session of the Jersey branch right after lunch to divvy up the new judgeships."

She laughs out loud at my performance. It is the first time I have ever seen her give in to someone else's routine. It bodes well.

We eat and banter easily. She confesses fatigue from her teaching load. "What I need is a year abroad," she says, turning to the big travel poster of Florence on the wall next to our table. "Like there, for instance. Firenze—peerless jewel of Tuscany. In fact if you'll make it worth my while, I may just grab the next plane over."

The moment has come for me to steer sharply in the direction I have had in mind from the start. "I hear," I say slowly, "that the paper-bag business isn't what it used to be over there."

"Oh, shit on the bag business," she says with no great passion.

"Marvin will need a livelihood while you're over there—"

"Marvin can't come. Marvin thinks the Pitti Palace is part of Disneyland."

"And the children?"

"Sadie can handle the children. It's not as if I'd be gone forever."

"And you'd send back lots of pictures for them to remember what you look like."

"Hundreds," she says. "Thousands."

"Taking pains, of course, to crop out your Italian lovers."

"Of course," she says, unsmiling.

"I'm told they're something special."

"Who?"

"Italian lovers."

"I wouldn't know," she says, "never having had any."

"But you wouldn't be against it—in principle?"

Her face is lowered now, but she is eying me at an angle. "Or in practice, either," she says. "Why—are you going in for international procuring?"

"Nothing that ambitious." I run a finger lightly over her forearm. "I have a domestic client in mind, as a matter of fact."

"What's he like?"

"Oh—rather nice, I'd say. Bright—amusing—passably attractive, certainly."

"And in bed?"

"A raging tiger, from what I hear."

"Maybe you ought to try the zoo, then," she says, and drains her wine. "Is he married?"

"He is."

"Don't tell me he's unhappy?"

"Quite the contrary. But he thinks unrelieved bliss is a great big bore."

"How modern," she says.

The assignation is set over dessert for the following week.

9

A-Day

DAILY MY MISGIVINGS MOUNT. SHE IS BOUND TO BE A CRUELLY demanding collaborator. I am certain now she has been caressed by a hundred prior lovers, all of legendary potency. And what, really, have I known of the flesh of Woman beyond a handful of frantic premarital encounters and the customary locker-room reports that they are all pink inside? Nor can I, in the time-honored way among manly men, ask my best friend for the low-down, since Anne was designated my best friend on our fifth anniversary (and I hers).

I get down our old marriage manual—the one that recommends a quickie before breakfast every day it can be managed—and begin boning up. I smuggle it in and out of the bathroom inside a towel. But the things that I fear cannot be cured by books, with their exquisite techniques and exotic logistics. No, it has more to do with plain physiology. Suppose she demands more flesh than I have been provided with? Suppose my manhood fails to rise to the occasion? Or, having risen, to sustain itself? Suppose, in her bottomless lust, she calls on me to service her again and again when, for me, one satisfactory service is a full quota? Yes, I will call it off. My anticipation of the affair has generated enough emotional feedback to quench my appetite for it. The climax can only prove disastrously anticlimactic.

But it is too late for that. Too much ego has been committed. Once set in motion, the cycle cannot be halted at any cost less than total soul-shriveling humiliation. I have to see it through now if it takes a splint and a rubber band to make it.

I begin looking through the Sunday real-estate section for a cheap furnished two-room apartment, the cheaper the better—it adds to the depravity and the excitement. I note with interest a "1 rm kitchnte, $20 wk" on West Seventy-seventh Street and circle it. Anne notices.

"I admit it would be more economical," she says, "but there *are* four of us now and I'd do almost anything not to have to sleep on a Murphy bed again."

"I'm taking a mistress," I say.

"Oh," she says. "Well, you ought to find someplace nicer than that."

"I didn't want to take the bread from our children's mouths."

"They'll have bread," she says, "if I have to sell violets in the rain. I'd just hate to see you skimp on something as important as this. Suppose a rat crawls out of the woodwork and bites you in the privates?" She thinks that over a moment. "It would serve you right, of course, but that's not the point. If you're going in for adultery, you might as well go in style."

"You talked me into it," I say, and together we pick out a $32.50-a-week suite on West Sixty-eighth Street.

The next morning, though, on the way to work I stop in a phone booth and call a rather nice hotel in the Murray Hill area. "This is Peter Packer Parkinson from Pottsville, Pennsylvania," I say. "My wife and I would like a room next Thursday with a nice double bed."

"Of course," says the room clerk. "And how long will you and Mrs. Packer be staying with us?"

About an hour should do it, I suppose. Unless she has a double-header in mind or maybe even a three-game series, in which case I'll have to have a stunt man waiting in the closet. Or perhaps the room clerk will oblige.

I awake on A-Day with a terrible emptiness in the loins. Not a drop of seed in the pouch. I ache all over like an old man. All my joints are swollen. I watch Anne spring out of bed on little cat's paws and touch her toes ten quick times. My pajamas droop on the way to the breakfast table, nearly tripping me, and my belly bunches badly as I sit. There is one banana left for my cold cereal and it turns out, when peeled, to be consumed by rot. Whereupon my daughter spills a full tumbler of orange juice all over the table, for which I strike her more sharply than intended. Shaving, I cut myself in four places and bleed as if my fibrinogen has been entirely depleted. In the clothes closet, all my suits look rumpled as I stand among the knee-deep debris and snarl at Anne for the disorder. She, just then, is hummingly completing her twenty-fifth sit-up. Putting on my cordovans, finally, I snap a lace; there being no spare in any of the first twenty drawers I try, I am forced to laboriously transplant one from a pair of dusty black formals in a barely penetrable corner of the dishevelment.

By noon, though, I am beginning to revive. For lunch I have three drinks and a nearly raw steak, well-known restorative for flagging virility. I take a massage and a cool (decidedly not cold) shower at my college club, soaping my genitalia an extra time as if preparing them for some sacramental rite. However inadequate they may prove, they will, at least, be spotless. Then I stop by a leather-goods store and pick up a new cheap suitcase, passing up the invitation to have my initials embossed free. At a newsstand nearby I buy a dozen papers and shovel them quickly into the bag. Finally I call my office and tell my secretary I have some work to do at the public library. "I'll call in later," I say.

"Good luck," she says cryptically.

"Thanks," I say, feeling suddenly damp.

I check into the hotel fifteen minutes early and explain that Mrs. Parkinson will be along shortly. The clerk nods. "Oh," he says, checking the registration form, "would you please let us have your street address, Mr. Parkinson?"

I write, "28 Pineapple Place."

"All 'P's," says the clerk, studying the form.

"Yes, we think it's terribly amusing."

"Terribly," says the clerk, ringing for the bellboy.

The room has the requested double bed. The sight of it turns me instantly numb. Listlessly I inspect the rest of the room—the fake-gilded mirror over the dresser, the cheery little Dubuffets on the wall, the faded green carpet harboring the microscopic residue of a thousand earlier transients who have padded barefoot over it. The parts are reassuring in the collective homeliness. It is an utterly commonplace room—and what is about to happen in it, I remind myself, is equally commonplace. My incipient trauma begins to ebb. I look out the window. Other windows look back—there is no view. I lower the shade. And that clandestine gesture stirs the glandular root of my sex. I know then I will be all right.

I have another drink at the hotel bar and practice signing "Peter

Packer Parkinson" a dozen ways on a napkin. She comes fifteen minutes late.

"Hi, Toynbee," I say, not quite standing up for her, "what do you hear from Gibbon?"

"Not a helluva lot," she says. "Get me a drink."

She splashes it down as if dousing a fire. It eases her obvious tension. Then coolly she loops an arm through mine and we promenade through the lobby like any respectable couple from Pottsville, Pennsylvania.

"Watch your step," the elevator man says, looking me in the eye.

Her arm tightens around mine as we walk slowly down the hall. I am unexpectedly, almost guiltily, calm. I pull out the room key with a little jingling flourish. I plunge it cleanly into the lock. It sticks. I kick the door. It still sticks. I rattle the knob and give another kick, and the door springs open. She darts in. I follow slowly. With quiet ceremony I close the door and snap the lock. The knob at the end of the chain lock slides smoothly down its slot. Flushed with passion, I turn now to face my co-conspirator.

"How big is it?" she says, softly but unmistakably, her back toward me as she lifts the window shade a little.

"How big is what?"

"Your thing."

I feel my throat constrict. All my subdued misgivings of the past week suddenly awake. "Why," I say, trying to combat the spasm that has seized my vocal cords, "is there a minimum entrance requirement?"

She gives a cold little laugh. "I just like to know."

I see my face stiffen in the phony-gilt mirror. "Sorry," I say, "I haven't measured it in years."

"It stops growing by the time you're fifteen," she says, turning to me deadpan.

"I was a late bloomer."

"Come on," she says, sounding almost kittenish now. "Every guy knows how big his is."

Now I understand. A smile creeps over my face in the mirror. It is simply her opening gambit, a prurient put-on. She is just trying to hot me up with the perversity of the question, precisely the way that using dirty names for the sex organs is infinitely more provocative than the clean, clinical-sounding, Latinate ones. "I'll tell you what," I say, "you can bring a ruler next time."

"I will," she says. "And a tape measure, too—for circumference. Circumference is critical." She begins rubbing up against me. "Length without width," she says in her huskiest, "is like eggs without the bacon"—she slides a leg between mine—"or a flagpole without the flag." I clasp her in my arms. She yields fluidly. "Remember, though," she whispers, "no kissing."

"Why not?" I say, nuzzling the downy nape of her pulsing neck.

"Germs," she says.

"Come off it," I say, working around to the underside of her chin.

"No," she says, pulling back. "Really—it makes the whole thing so—so *personal*." She turns around. "Here, help me out of this."

Puzzled but not gravely perturbed, I zip down her dress. She has nothing on underneath. I nearly ejaculate.

"I'll take a smoke in the bathroom if you want."

"For what?"

"If you want to fix yourself up."

"I'm fixed," she says.

"Oh," I say, "of course."

She thrusts the covers back on the bed and coils herself onto the sheets. Her body slides back and forth and up and down as if trying to find just the right groove. Settling in, she stretches one leg as far as it will go, points it, and gives its toes a little wiggle. She bends the other leg up at the knee and folds her hands together behind her head. "Come on, tiger," she says, "let's see what you've got."

She is going all the way with the gambit and it works, fiercely. I claw off my clothes. She gives a soft low admiring whistle. I move to the edge of the bed, my million ganglia taut with anticipation of hot flesh pressing hard against them in another instant.

"Hold it," she says.

"Wha'?"

"Pay me."

"Huh?"

"Pay me."

"Hardy-har."

She slaps the bed next to her. "Fifty bucks—right there."

"Big joke."

"Get it up."

"C'mon, will ya?"

"Get it up," she says, "or the deal's off." She crosses her legs.

"You're kidding."

"Like hell I am." She tosses her hair back defiantly.

My thing begins to droop. "I don't believe it."

She reaches out for her bag beside the bed and draws out a cigarette. "Start trying, buster."

"I—refuse."

"Forget it, then."

"You mean you're a—*whore?*" It comes out like a croak.

"No," she says, "I'm a country girl from a little mining town out West. Only I don't happen to turn on, baby, unless I get paid first."

I throw back my head, put my hands on my eyes, and draw them down over my face and neck and chest. "But that's terrible."

"Oh, fuck off," she says, shaking the match out angrily. "You think you're so fantastically sexy I'm going to go down for you for nothing?"

I open my eyes slowly and see the fierceness in her face. "I—thought we were friends."

"Sure, sure, we're friends—you don't think I let just anyone get in me?"

My throat goes taut again. "I—didn't know you were for hire."

"Now you know. And don't expect one on the house—not with that tiny tool of yours. I've seen cocker spaniels better hung than that!" She blows a mouthful of smoke at me. "You couldn't turn on a muskrat in heat with *that*."

"I'll tell you something—"

"Tell me something, baby."

"You're a sick bitch."

"Cut the sermon, sweetie. Just pay or get out."

"What do I need you for if I want to buy it?"

"Because I'm a hot piece of ass."

"There's a dozen on every block in town."

"And you couldn't knock one of 'em off if you were stuck with it on a desert island."

I am in my underwear by now. "You ought to do something about it, you know—see a shrink or somebody."

"On second thought," she says, looking at the ceiling, "you'll pay anyway—for my inconvenience—and for being such a sanctimonious bastard."

"Make me." I button my shirt.

"You'll pay," she says, "or I'll tell Anne."

My fury rises. "I'll tell Marvin baby."

"Ha!"

"What does that mean?"

"What do *you* think?"

"He—*knows?*"

"He hasn't raised one in ten years."

I stop dressing for a moment and just stare at her shameless nakedness. "Your children—they're not his?

Her head pivots toward me. "What kind of slut do you think I am?"

"I give up."

"They're his friggin' kids, all right—but it took some doing. If you want a real laugh sometime, try getting laid by a syringe."

I feel nausea coming on. "And because he's—that way, you do this?"

The top half of her body knifes upright and she glares at me. "Is that so hateful? I'm a healthy sexy woman. I need action. What am I supposed to do—have my bottom cut out?"

"Better that than selling it." I move toward the door, knotting my tie en route.

"Just leave the money on the dresser."

"No money, baby."

"I'll tell—I swear to Christ I will."

The room dizzies in on me. "No, you won't."

"Why not?"

Hand tense on the doorknob, temples pounding, black waves of hatred foaming through my brain, I turn and say very slowly, with a quiver that means I mean it, "Because I'll kill you if you do."

She is still for a long second—long enough to show she thinks I just might.

"You!" she says, trying to salvage something from the encounter. "Some killer you'd make!" She snorts smoke. "You don't have the balls to grab a cupcake from the corner baker!"

"See you in my dreams, baby."

"Go play with yourself, you asshole fairy!"

I'll kill you, you sick smart sad funny bitch, I'll kill you if you tell.

10

Jolly Roger

HAVING THUS SEVERED THE FETTERS OF PROPRIETY, HAVING leaped free, having reached out to touch another life and charge the droning tempo of my own, I, Christopher Kwait, known as Kit, should by all rights tuck my tail between my hairy legs and scuttle back home in shame.

And yet it does not happen that way. The abortive affair works on me as a bellows on a flagging fire. It has done something irreparable to my glandular thermostats. It has supercharged my nervous system and galvanized my psychic metabolism. It has made me, at every waking moment for its duration, immeasurably more aware of being alive. Of being.

And so I seek a great new unsanctionable adventure—a quest so remarkably irresponsible and utterly uncharacteristic that I am astonished at the ambition. I will not, this time, I *cannot,* fail.

Actually, the banter with Muffie Miller was not entirely idle: I have always wanted to be a robber. Not your habitual, dirty-necked thug, of course, but an occasional and very daring one—and then only on the proviso that the victim be some monolithic enterprise that can go for years without missing the loot. Everyone in America has it, I tell myself now—this impulse to larceny—without meaning anything much by it. There's just so much here to rob. If, after all, we have done so well for ourselves conspicuously consuming, isn't *in*conspicuous consumption equally in the national interest? Most of us, of course, repress these outlaw urges, and my own toward robbery has been particularly well muted. Or perhaps I have just lacked the fiber to try my hand at it. Either way, I never have stolen, not even as a child, in whom such waywardness would presumably have been forgiven. As I got older, my needs naturally grew, and so therefore did my motive to steal. But so, necessarily, did my repression, a complementary process which in turn produced some truly spectacular feats of fantasized banditry.

In time, all my feckless schemes were surpassed daily by desperadoes in the headlines, like the self-exiled Portuguese sea captain who commandeered a Brazilian freighter to protest tyranny in his homeland, like those Cuban zealots who put a gun to the back of an American pilot's scalp and order him to fly his jet to Havana. So I turned back to more conventionally perverse skylarking, like how to snatch priceless artifacts from indifferently guarded museums. And then those fellows came along and, with the supreme artistry displayed only in old Alec Guinness films, made off with storied jewels from the Museum of Natural History. What did all that ceaseless derring-do leave for an armchair robber to dream up?

Robbery as an abstract concept had nevertheless continued to prey upon my fantasy life. And now, as that life begins to annex portions of my real one and render its restraining mechanisms inoperative, I seek a specific arena for converting that lingering, freshly dredged impulse to overt action. Thus it is with new and narrowed eyes that I find myself inspecting the twin-towered apartment house in which I live and the six or seven hundred other tenants with whom I share the address.

I start assembling mischievous equipment at a novelty shop near the office. I buy a joy buzzer for shaking hands with in a distractingly amusing manner, a box of simulated dog turds to leave on my neighbors' hall mat, and a great hairy soup-strainer mustache to confound the authorities in general. Then I go to F. A. O. Schwarz.

There is a very large panda in the window. Not quite so large as a real one, but large. About as large as a person—me, for example. I will buy it and scoop out its insides and climb in and perform my perversions thus camouflaged. It would have a certain flair to it: PANDA THIEF IN 200G HEIST! Oh, but the getaway would prove formidable. I could install a zipper, of course, and slip right out. But they'd trace me easily. How many man-sized pandas could Schwarz sell in a week?

I dawdle downstairs looking at the cases of antique toys and thinking that all the cherubs who played with them when they were painted and shiny are dead now, or close to it. I cannot imagine why I should think *that* on seeing those tarnished artifacts of childhood—the uninnocent nature of my mission, undoubtedly. I climb the wide marble stairway at the back of the store up to the second floor and ask forthrightly to see their gun collection. The saleswoman just points me to it and lets me play by myself. It is a disappointing selection. Mostly machine guns and rifles with telescopic lenses. And not a laser ray in the batch. I am after a pistol, and what is offered is manifestly unsatisfactory. They all look like nothing so much as toy guns. Very silvery, very plastic-handled, very unmenacing. I signal the saleswoman. "Have you," I ask, "any models of guns? Real-looking models?"

"They don't make them any more," she says. "People would pull holdups with them if they did."

"Oh," I say. "I hadn't thought about that."

"No," she says, "you don't look like the type who would."

"No, I really don't, do I?"

"But you never know."

"No, you never do," I say. "Tell me, where are your masks?"

"Masks are across the aisle," she says. "Someone else will help you."

There is no one in the mask department. I go into a corner and, my back to the aisle, put on my false mustache. It itches. But it is essential. For everything has to be done right from the start or it will all end in disaster. Hundreds of stores in town sell toy guns but rather fewer sell masks, and probably very few sell ones as distinctive as Schwarz's. Thus I could be readily traced if I were not somehow disguised. True, the mustache may attract greater attention than my regular face. But the latter, so far as I had discovered, is not detachable. Weighing the odds—and there are odds to weigh at every point—I conclude that the mustache will be remembered vividly and the rest of me not at all.

There is an outstanding assortment of masks. It is important to pick the right one. The mask, after all, will become my trademark. The rubber ones are by far the most fetching. Besides, they come with holes in the nostrils. I put on a gorilla mask, look in the mirror, and barely stifle a gasp. Marvelously hideous. I try flaring the nostrils. They work beautifully. It is everything you would ever want in a gorilla mask. Yet the symbolism of it doesn't sit quite right. I try some others. I am in the midst of modeling a pig mask when the saleswoman comes up behind me. I turn, too swiftly, and she gives a little start.

"We'd prefer," she says, gathering herself together, "that you didn't try them on."

"How will I know if it fits?" My voice is nicely muffled.

"They're all the same size."

"Oh," I say, reluctantly unpigging.

She gives another, smaller start at the sight of my soup-strainer mustache, as if I have on a mask under my mask, which of course is very nearly the case.

I settle finally on a perfectly dreadful pirate mask. It is the fiercest face I have ever seen. The eyebrows are Stalinesque, hideously black and thick and slanted severely upward. The nose is rumpled and red and huge, and the skin is almost prune-like in the number and depth of its wrinkles. Its teeth are furiously clenched, and its tangled jet mustache overflows onto the great scraggly beard. I put it on and it snarls at me in the mirror. Perfect: a face of unyoked rapaciousness—cold and cruel and altogether redoubtable. It is made by the Keystone

Rubber Company in Bethel, Connecticut, it says on the back. I take it.

To cover my tracks, I buy two others, one of a woman with a perfectly gold face, save for her fireman-red lips and brunette pageboy, the other a little mauve oval mask like you wear to a costume ball, just covering the eyes and nose. That night I present the gold and mauve masks to my children with the promise they can wear them on Halloween, now two weeks away. The pirate mask I tuck in the back of the filing cabinet in my clothes closet, safely secreted while I turn to assembling the rest of my rig.

II

Forearmed

THE SUPREME TEST, ADMITTEDLY, WOULD BE TO CARRY NO WEAPON whatever—to pull it off on sheer bluff and gall. A weapon is a crudity, a barbarism. Why, anyone can inflict terror by waving a weapon at a defenseless victim. But am I an actor? Unarmed, could I ever inject enough conviction into my voice and behavior? No, there has to be a weapon.

There is never any question, of course, of my killing anyone if it comes to that. If a victim resists my commands, then he resists; that's all there is to it. He will win and I will lose. But it must never come to that. I must appear to be willing and able to kill. Or at least wound. Or at the very least disable, one way or another. Hypnotism would be ideal except that it requires the cooperation of the victim. Some sort of tear-gas bomb, I suppose, would be next best. In fact I see an advertisement for a certain kind in a mail-order catalogue—Ward-Off, it is called ("so irritates face and eyes it's bound to stop any would-be assailant, human or animal—*without corneal damage, permanent injury!* Sprays 15'; can be used 25 times. Pocket-sized, 4" x ¾". $1"). The very thing! Of all conceivable weapons, it sounds most humane. I consider ordering one and trying it on my children. Just one tiny little squirt. On reflection, though, the soft crumple of their little bodies gasping with pain would prove nothing really beyond a certain dispassion on my part: any even marginally courageous victim, suspecting the worst damage his assailant can inflict is a dose of temporary pain in the eye, is as likely as not to shield his face with one hand and use the other to bring his tormentor down with a flying tackle. And if more than one victim at a time is to be held at bay, something more potent will obviously be necessary. But what?

Well, there is something to be said for a knife. For one thing, the very sight of one immediately conjures debilitating images of severed flesh and spurting blood. And suggests a more purposeful—i.e., maniacal—assailant. And its quietness is not to be denied. If I were going to assail someone in a library, there could be no other choice. But my intention is to assail no one, and so its quietness is of no practical importance. Its limitations, though, obviously are. Knives are notoriously less effective discouragements to valor when flashed across a room than when held against a hostile bellybutton. They are, moreover, not readily retractable, a characteristic that would require me, upon confronting several victims at once, to display a fistful of daggers—an unwieldy strategy at best.

I toy a bit with the concept of a lasso. It, too, is quiet. And, unlike the knife, can be used to disable at a distance without drawing blood. Of course I might end up strangling someone quite by accident in the unlikely event that I developed the marksmanship to rope a moving target (or even a stationary one). But lassos have the same shortcoming as knives—they take a bit of managing and are not really meant to render harmless a roomful of adversaries.

I consider, too, the bow and arrow, vials of acid, and a vicious German shepherd trained to spring at the first false move by anyone in the room. Each has certain merits but is flawed by one or another critical weakness. The dog, as a matter of fact, has more going for it than any of the other ideas I have had till now. But I hate dogs. And they know it; some sort of hate waves radiate from my nostrils to theirs. Which convinces me that at our first opportunity to strike, my Schotzie would take a big bound, pivot picturesquely, and, with a single slash of his outsized fangs, remove the greater portion of my neck.

My arsenal of prospects is reduced to a single, banal possibility —a gun. A real gun. Which leads me, as it would any tasteful fellow about to launch his criminal career, to Abercrombie & Fitch.

They have quite a big gun room at Abercrombie & Fitch, with many guns in it. All kinds of guns. And I, except for a few rounds at the penny arcades of my youth, have never fired a gun in my life. And not without reason. My reason is that I think it is bad to shoot guns at living things, because you may kill them. Not that there aren't some living things that, under certain trying circumstances, shouldn't be killed—a snake about to strike, say. But experience, however circumscribed, and instinct, however encumbered, have left me believing that those who derive a charge in the scrotum from firing guns are not likely to restrict their targets to venomous beasts at the instant of striking. Their cramped libidos must get an airing or else they will go berserk—and so, I guess, it is better that they puncture a dozen deer or ducks or foxes to exorcise their clamoring demons than wing a plaza full of people from a handy perch on a bell tower. Still, I am uneasy about all the unseen and unscented blood implicit in the air of the Abercrombie & Fitch gun room; what is seen and scented is the oiled wood and steel of several hundred death-dealing machines of various sizes, none of which I know anything about.

The gun man is remarkably cordial, especially considering a certain mandatory lack of candor on my part. I start with the pistols. There are any number of them—some, I notice with surprise, that look

almost exactly like the toy ones at F. A. O. Schwarz—antique Western
ones with steer heads and stars carved into the ivory handles. Those,
though, seem a bit festive, even show-offish, for the occasion. I want
something handy, discreet, and very businesslike. My eye falls on two
used Colt .38s, a sort of nondescript house revolver for $90, and a
big black ugly Commando for $50. I am inclined toward the more
conservative, more expensive one.

"I'll try that one," I say, stabbing my trigger finger against the
glass case.

The gun man, who has on a shirt with a big suède patch below the
shoulder (for resting a rifle butt against, I gather), takes it out carefully, spins the cartridge case expertly, and presents it for my inspection. It is heavy. I don't know what to do with it except squint
down the business end of the barrel, and something tells me that that
is probably very poor form indeed. So I give it a few little jiggles to
test its heft. It has heft. "Nice," I say, handing it back gingerly and
nodding to indicate it is a deal.

"You'll have to let me see your permit, you know," he says.

"Oh," I say.

"It's the law, you know," he says.

"Oh," I say. "I think that's a very good law. Where do I get a
permit?"

"Where do you live?"

"In the city."

"Then you apply to the police captain of your local precinct."

"Oh," I say, sorry that I have never cultivated the captain properly.
"Is he likely to be sticky about it?"

"Not if you have a good reason."

"What's a good reason?"

"I wouldn't know offhand."

"I mean does it have to be something like there's someone in the
building trying to kill me?"

"I think the police would probably prefer to handle something like that themselves."

"Not that there *is* anyone in the building trying to kill me—"

"I understand."

"It's the black panther loose in the basement that worries me a little."

He puts the gun away.

"Do I need a permit to buy any gun in the store?"

"Oh, no," he says. "You can get a rifle without one."

"Why is that?"

"I don't know."

"I guess it's a little harder to pull a robbery with a rifle."

"I suppose that's one reason."

He looks around to see if there is any more promising sales prospect in the vicinity. But I, clearly, am not about to go away. "Would you like to see the rifles?" he asks, resigned to servicing me to the fruitless end.

"I think I would, as a matter of fact."

I study the rifle rack for what seems an appropriate few minutes, then point to what turns out to be a Remington Deluxe pump-action .22, with a Du Pont-developed wood finish, custom checkering, big-game-type sights, tapered barrel, crowned muzzle, fluted comb cuts on the stock, attractive grip cap, big cartridge capacity, positive cross-bolt safety, a special design to prevent jamming, and a receiver for tip-off scope mounts. It is beautiful. And rather a lot of money. And, as I have observed, a bit unwieldy for pulling a stickup. But it is available without a permit.

"Of course," the gun man says, "we take your name and address."

I look at his fingernails for traces of congealed bear blood. "Of course," I say, and give the .22 a hoist to my shoulder. Bang bang bang, you are dead, gun man of Abercrombie & Fitch, slain by one of your own machines of destruction. He walks away to help someone else for a moment while I play by myself.

I loiter a bit longer and am about to leave in despair when my eye falls on a case proudly exhibiting air-powered weaponry by the Crosman Arms Company. "Authentic in looks, heft and handle," the accompanying literature proclaims, and indeed they do look authentic. "Shooting's fun all year round . . . with Crosman guns," the brochure adds, and displays a handsome assortment of seven pistols and revolvers, the most expensive selling for $29.95. I go to find my gun man, who is plainly depressed at the renewed sight of me.

"I don't need a permit for those BB guns, I take it?" My delight in the discovery borders on smugness. It is the ideal solution: a real-looking gun that can, if called upon, disable without necessarily doing severe damage. "The firing of a Crosman gun," the pamphlet goes on, "is practically silent compared to the noise level of other types of guns." And it is capable, I read with growing excitement, of firing as many as ten shots in three seconds. Who can ask for anything more?

"I'm afraid they're illegal within the city limits," the gun man says.

With the doggedness of a monomaniac, which I am in the conscious and quite rapid process of becoming, I immediately consider renting a post-office box in the first suburb across the city line.

"Thank you very much for your time and trouble," I say, promising myself to spare him if our paths should cross one day while I am on a rampage.

The rest of the day and into the evening I mull the merits and shortcomings of pneumatic air guns. The merits are apparent enough, and since my new perverse covenant with myself, while granting me considerable liberty, requires that I stop short of maiming anyone, the limited capacity of BBs to immobilize onrushing bodies seems more a virtue than a drawback. I am about to settle on a Crosman ten-shot semiautomatic CO_2 Pellgun (weight 44 oz., length $9\frac{1}{2}''$, swing-feed boltless loading, all steel Tru-Flyte button-rifled barrel, micro-click rear sight fully adjustable for windage and elevation) when Gordimer, the neighbors' cur, begins yapping next door. Yes, dammit, I forgot about dogs. What happens if I barge into an apartment with a slobbering Cerberus just waiting by the door to mangle my shins and bay for the cops? Will a BB be enough? Suppose the foaming beast just keeps coming at me? It is one thing to forbear from wounding someone who does not yield gracefully to my threats; it is quite another not to be equipped to check any man, woman, child, or animal that may try to interrupt my tactical retreat. And a BB gun seems, on reflection, not quite up to the task, particularly of felling a large, mad, and unreasonable animal. No, there has to be something else.

The next day I find it. The people at the A.S.P.C.A. are delighted with my guarded inquiry, made in the name of a new wildlife magazine I say I am writing for.

"You could dope a plate of chopped meat," says one of them, a little Scotty of a fellow, "and coax the dog to eat it."

"Of course a well-trained dog probably wouldn't accept food from a stranger," says another, Dalmatian-lean with pricked ears.

"You might try chloroforming the dog," says the Scotty.

"Of course you might lose an arm in the process," says the Dalmatian.

"How about a swift kick in the rib cage?" I ask.

"That would probably hurt the dog," says Scotty, "and we're really *not* supposed to encourage that sort of thing. Actually, though, it might be quite effective."

"Of course you might lose a leg in the process," says Dalmatian.

Scotty suddenly snaps his fingers. "I know what you want! Get one of those Cap-Chur guns. It's an air gun that fires a syringe with some kind of nicotine solution in it. Knocks the dog right on its ass."

I ask where I can get one and naturally they have no idea. But the people at the Bronx Zoo will probably know. I thank them.

"Oh, what did you say the name of your magazine was again?"

"I didn't say."

"What is it?"

"It's going to be called *Stalk and Fetch*—it's for hunters."

"Oh," they say together.

"It will have marvelous features no other magazine has. Like how to disembowel your catch with the least possible mess."

"Oh, oh," they say.

"And there'll be a regular section with all the bullfighting results—"

"Oh my," they say.

"And a schedule of all the upcoming cockfights—"

"Oh my, oh my," they say.

"And the first issue has a special color spread on how Alsatian farmers force-feed grain down the gullets of geese to improve the pâté-de-foie-gras yield."

They begin to cry.

"I could put you down for a subscription if you'd like."

The head honcho at the zoo refers me to the Palmer Chemical & Equipment Company, Douglasville, Georgia. A telephone call there from the managing editor of *Stalk and Fetch* establishes (1) that Cap-Chur guns are used mainly by big-game hunters, wardens in animal preserves, ranchers, and police; (2) that the gun is capable of knocking a dog on its ass in thirty seconds; (3) that it comes in both pistol and rifle versions; (4) that it is silent and fires without any kick; and (5) that no permit is necessary to purchase one.

"And does it work on people?"

"Hasn't been tried yet."

"Any reason?"

"Nope. It'd probably work fine—'cept o' course it might prove fatal. Shock an' all. Only if ya kept the dose low enough, likely wouldn't do no lastin' damage."

That afternoon *Stalk and Fetch* obtains a P.O. box in the name of its editor, Byron Blood. Cap-Chur gun literature is solicited by mail within minutes thereafter. The material arrives three days later, and in the next mail an order blank is dispatched to Douglasville, Georgia, for:

1 Short-Range Projector w/ Practice Syringes, Push Rod, and Instructions @ $104.25

1 Box of 5 CO_2 Powerlets @ $1.50
1 2-cc. Syringe with Nose Plug (Needle) No. NE2 @ $4.80
1 Silicone Lubricant @ $1.50
1 Box of 50 Cap-Chur Charges, 1 through 3 cc. @ $6
1 30-cc. Bottle 90 mg./cc. of Cap-Chur-Sol @ $1.50
accompanied by $119.55 in cash.

The Cap-Chur order is executed air express and proves, on arrival, to be a thing of rare beauty. I smuggle it home in my briefcase and lock myself in the bathroom with it before anyone else has arrived in the house. I examine each of its dreadful parts with care, lingering particularly over the construction of the barbed needle and familiarizing myself with all the instructions. ("The muscular area of the hindquarters generally makes the most satisfactory target for effective placement of the syringes in large animals; the effect of the drug will be more rapid on dogs and cats behind the thoracic cage.") Carefully I assemble it, making sure each part fits firmly. I hold it up to the light. There are tiny bubbles floating in the terrible potent liquid. I put on my pirate mask, heft the needle-nosed weapon into place, and face the mirror. Perfect! No man or beast alive will resist this fierce visage.

I hear our front door open with a crash and my children thundering down the hall.

12

The Mentor

PROFESSOR GIBBY GOOD, ON SABBATICAL FOR THE TERM AND
cultivating a grotesque beard that is growing every way but down,
has stayed in the city to finish his book *The New Dionysian Ego*,
parts of which have begun to appear in Establishment avant-garde
quarterlies like *Partisan Review* and more orthodox periodicals like
trans-ACTION and even several of the underground magazines like
underground and *Up Yours*. As a result, he has been acquiring a bit
of a reputation as a savant among the psychedelic set, albeit one with
impeccable scholarly credentials.

He is working in his office on the sixth floor of Krafft-Ebing Hall
on the sullen campus of Knickerbocker College when I walk in on
him, tell all, and then, unsnapping my attaché case, show him the
Cap-Chur gun.

Gibby pushes his books and notes to the side of his desk and
examines the gun with great care. Then he looks up and says, "It's
marvelous!"

"What is?"

"The whole concept—absolutely bloody marvelous!"

I move past the desk in silence and go to the window. A minute-
long look down into the soot-blown courtyard, then: "Yes, that's what
I thought you'd say."

Gibby runs a hand through his unruly beard. "What do you want
me to say—that you're a depraved maniac?"

"If that's what you really think, yes."

"But you *know* that's not what I think."

"Who can be sure with you? You trade in your -isms every year for a new set."

Gibby tugs at the beard. "Because I'm growing. Because I'm deepening."

A surly grunt from me.

He clamps his hands together and tilts back in his frayed leather swivel chair that needs oiling, or new springs, or both. "Shall I tell you what's so marvelous about what you're proposing—or do you just want to stand there and brood?"

"I'm not brooding. I'm thinking. I'm thinking about the risk. I'm thinking that I'm going out of my mind."

"But the risk is precisely the point of it! It's inherent in every adventure worth undertaking. How can you liberate yourself without incurring peril? It's a contradiction in terms. Nothing ventured, nothing gained. The uncertainty of the outcome is what makes the whole thing existentially valid, don't you see?"

"I don't think I do—no."

"Because *you're* doing the choosing, not someone else. Because you're opting for peril. It's your *will* that's driving you. You remember will, don't you? It used to be that fuzzy thing up there in the lobes somewhere that directed our acts when we acted—and *non*-acted. Ah, but the poor fuzzy little shat-upon will has fallen on hard times. All those external forces out there imploding on it—all those torques and valences and rheostats, all those semiconductors and antibodies and ionized particles, all the EDP and DNA and LSD, all those polyunsaturated psychoneurohydrodellaphobias bombarding it and atomizing it—Christ, there *is* no will any more! The Freudians administered last rites, like, fifty years ago. And now, to finish the whole bit off, the last metaphysicians have reported the death of God—may He rest in peace." He swivels around and looks gauntly at me. "So what's left, sweetheart? Just the ever-lovin' pleasure principle, that's what. And it's running around loose with its pants down, bumping into the leftovers of propriety or morality or whatever the hell you want to call it and getting its dangle all mashed in the collision."

"So?"

"So if there's no will left, baby, there's no such thing as a good man or a bad man. Or at least that's what our hot-rock social scientists are telling us all now. There's no such thing as malevolence, they're saying—no such animal as a man who makes a conscious choice to commit evil. No, he's *driven* to it, they say—driven by circumstances beyond his control. His fucking id hasn't been properly yoked, they say. His libido is running rampant, they say. And the fault? The fault, of course, lies with society. The perpetrator of evil today is, *ipso facto,* sick—victimized by his psychic maladjustment. He is to be pitied, not punished, for he is no longer morally responsible for his acts, because society, somehow or other, has deprived him of his right to develop acceptable social responses."

"So? *So?*"

"So what is implicit in all this garbage besides the rotting of our moral fiber is the dissolution of man's power to direct his acts. It is the utter abandonment of free will. But what you are proposing, don't you see, is an act that will strike a body blow at this whole lamentable erosion. For you are manifestly not depraved or deranged, and you were badly mistaken if you thought for even a minute I would tell you that you are. Quite the contrary. You are the most nearly normal product of your environment that I know—a nice respectable family man who probably showers every morning before breakfast and makes a lovely BM promptly after. You have been the beneficiary of nearly every blessing your society can bestow. And your conduct to this moment, so far as I know, has been entirely exemplary—which is to say a raging bore. And that, my most highly ethical friend, is what makes the course of action you are planning so terribly important—so absolutely marvelous. Those little demons that have been consuming you so long are symptomatic of what ails us all. And you, unbeknownst to yourself, are making a heroic gesture by freeing them. You are endorsing the power of men to act as they choose—even if the act they choose happens to be perverse. Because in the process of acting, they regain sovereignty over themselves; they become human again, alive and vital and growing and reaching, and stop being just an assemblage of deprived impulses. But if they do not make that critical liberating gesture you are about to make—if they do not end their psychic deprivations—they wind up trooping to the grave in routinized despair. Or else they explode one day and blow out the brains of the first ten people they find—and then their own."

I am looking out the window hard. "And you believe that? All of it?"

He swivels frontward and thinks for a long moment. "Yes," he says. "I think I do."

"Not very long ago you were more skeptical, if I recall."

"Sure—because I was as bourgeois and tight-assed and hung up as everyone else."

"And now? Are you homosexual and loving it?"

"No," he says, glancing at me sideways, "but at least I tried."

"No!"

"But yes! I said I was going to—remember?"

"You said you were going to try a lot of things."

"I was drunk."

"Maybe you should have stayed drunk."

"Maybe. Only that defeats the whole purpose. It's not *willed* if you're not sober."

"What happened?"

"When I got buggered?"

"Yes."

"I didn't find it especially rewarding."

"Maybe you weren't doing it right."

"I didn't do—I was done."

"What, and skipped your turn?"

"Yes, frankly."

"Isn't that the best part?"

"It—looked very sordid."

"But how do you know if you didn't try?"

"Well, I did, actually."

"And you didn't make it."

"I didn't make it. It was—very sordid."

I throw up my hands. "Why the Christ are you handing me the whole pitch if you finked out yourself?"

"Wait a minute! At least I tried it. At least I dared. I dared to do something unspeakable. It doesn't matter that it wasn't bliss. I didn't say all perversities were equally wonderful. Buggery just doesn't happen to be my bag. So I'll try something else. The point is that I dared."

"And now you feel wonderful and fulfilled."

"I didn't say that."

"Then what?"

He is stroking his beard again, slowly. "I feel—real. Alive. Bigger than a breadbox."

"Then come with me and help me do it."

Gibby shoots back in his chair. "Oh," he says, "so that's your little scheme."

"I wouldn't make it sound as calculated as all that."

Gibby shakes his head. "And here I thought you were turning to me to help translate your inarticulated yearnings into good, plain, psychotherapeutic jargon. And all you want to do is use me."

"Oh, fuck off! I just thought you'd get a kick out of coming along if you're such an emancipated hot rock."

Gibby sits scratching the forward edge of his scalp for a moment. "No," he says, "you've got to do it by yourself."

"Why?"

"Because it's not a heroic gesture otherwise."

"Why not?"

"Because it must be a private act or it's nothing. It's got to be all you or the force of the thing is vitiated. It's like asking another man to help you get laid—to put it in for you."

Translation: he is chicken. But then he has his pending tenure to think of. "If you don't come, I'll just have to tell the authorities I owe my entire criminal career to my mentor in perversity, Professor Gilbert Good, whose new book and renowned teachings will be the inspiration to a whole generation of hung-up zombies just like me."

"Uh-oh."

"You will be ruined."

"Ohhhh."

"Of course that would be blackmail."

"Uh-huh."

"And I wouldn't blackmail my mentor and long-time friend."

"No."

"Even when he turns out to be a spineless prophet."

"Now, wait—"

"And utter fraud."

"I resent that!"

"The evidence is overwhelming."

"I—"

"Yes?"

"I'm—thinking."

"What's there to think about? It's all visceral, not cranial."

"I know, I know."

"Rational motivation is anathema to psychic liberation."

Gibby falls deeper into the ruptured leather chair. "All right already."

"You'll do it?"

"You do it first, then check me in."

"In the interests of the behavioral sciences—"

"Precisely."

13

Alibi

TWO EVENTS NOW OCCUR AT COMPUTRON THAT SHARPLY REDUCE
the likelihood of my ever scaling the heights of big-time corpora-
tiondom—and confirm me in the wayward path I have veered onto.

One of the sacred rites of the Market Research team is to project
sales figures for the coming year. It is, at best, an inexact science.
You start with the sales figures of the past five years, consider the
prevailing money rates, check in with the Dow-Jones industrial average (which has already discounted next year's over-all economic performance), multiply by the market price of your weight in gold, divide
by the ebb tide off Cape May on the first Thursday of the coming
June—and then put down the number that top management expects,
regardless of all the foregoing.

For the first time, I am charged with spearheading the task force to
project next year's sales. Newly intrepid in all matters and frankly
indifferent toward company ritual, I try to project fearlessly and
realistically. I suggest that (1) in light of management's decision to
raise the price of the basic model #300 by another 15 per cent without (2) any compensating improvement in the productivity of the
machine itself or (3) any other substantive change in the marketing
plan, and in further light of (4) the price-cutting and (5) quality-
improvement programs embarked upon by our massed competition
whose machines are (6) in no measurable way functionally inferior
to the Computron #300, it is not inconceivable that (7) sales of
the #300 may fail to forge ahead at the pace achieved in recent
years. "Thus," the Kwait Projection concludes, "the company may

find its most basic, best-selling machine lodged on or close to a sales plateau. To prevent such a development, it is respectfully submitted that the decision to increase the #300 price by a full 15 per cent at this time be carefully re-evaluated."

My logic, of course, is unexceptionable. I am merely invoking the classic laws of supply and demand. The Kwait Projection is handed to Malcolm Mooring, Director of the Market Research Unit, who hands it to the Supervisor of the Sales and Marketing Department, who hands it to the General Manager of the Products Division, who hands it to the Vice-President in Charge of the Industrial Group, who hands it to the Executive Vice-President, who hands it to the Assistant to the President, who hands it gingerly to the President, who hands it still more gingerly to the Chairman of the Board, who, at that moment, is about to exercise his option to buy five thousand additional shares of Computron stock (at 20 per cent below the market).

"Sales plateau, my ass!" says the Chairman of the Board, and in fifteen minutes the Kwait Projection is back on the Kwait desk with a note attached from Director Mooring suggesting that Kwait prepare a new projection. Right away.

"Why?" I ask him.

"Because it is wrong," he says.

"How can a sales projection be wrong when the sales haven't happened yet?"

"Because you are projecting a sales plateau."

"Yes."

"But there can't be a sales plateau."

"Why not?"

"Because we won't permit it."

"But if we raise our prices while our competitors are lowering theirs?"

"The higher we raise our prices, the better our customers think our products are."

"Yes, but—"

"We are *número uno.*"

"And therefore charge all the traffic can bear."

"Naturally. We are in business, after all, to make profits."

"Yes, but the law of diminishing returns holds that—"

"Our sales force must be given new goals to achieve."

"Regardless of competitive circumstances?"

"Regardless."

"Oh."

"Good luck."

The second Kwait Projection anticipates a short-run downturn and a long-run upturn for the year ahead, culminating in record sales of no less than 18 per cent ahead of the current year. The projection is favorably received all the way up the line.

"Well done," says Malcolm Mooring.

"It was nothing."

But they have punched a little punch on my punch card. I can tell.

Having thus implicitly questioned the unslackening velocity with which the company pursues inordinate gain, I am a trifle surprised when, the following week, they offer me a promotion—to Chicago, where the marketing apparatus is badly in need of overhaul. Long-established company policy dictates, of course, that any serious contender for the ranks of upper management must first make his mark in sales (as I have done), then work out of the home office in a lower management position (as I have been doing), then put in three or four years in the hinterland in the middle management ranks—it gives you perspective—before returning to headquarters to assume grave new responsibilities at or near the top. Few can stay the course, but fewer still are chosen to try who have not acquiesced to the salutary ordeal of temporary exile. This is not merely Computron policy; it is universal policy within the American corporate infrastructure. It said so in *The Organization Man* (causing companies who had not already done so to adopt it as inflexible policy).

"Chicago?" says Anne.

"Chicago."

"Why Chicago?"

"My lucky day, I guess. Why—where would you rather go?"

"Go? I don't want to go anywhere. This is the most exciting place on earth."

"I know."

"Then tell them no."

"No," I tell them.

"No?" says Mooring.

"No."

"What do you mean no?"

"I mean I am very grateful to have been offered the opportunity but I would rather not move to Chicago."

"Oh."

"I like it here. My wife likes it here. What's happening is here."

"Oh. Oh my."

And so they punch another punch in my punch card. Two punches make you a marked man, moving sideways into your corporate future. And men who are moving sideways at Computron are, by definition, moving down. And eventually out.

I spend the rest of the morning at my desk reading Audax Minor in *The New Yorker* on a two-year-old bay gelding that starred at Hialeah the week before and Susan Sontag in *Partisan Review* on "The Illimitability of the Palpable in Recent French Cinema."

But I am not ready yet to burn my last bridge to the mainland. I want, as they say at the RAND Corporation, to keep my options open. There is no telling how my beckoning career in perversity will unfold. Meanwhile I continue to be dimly aware of mouths to feed and bills to pay. And so I make a token gesture of genuflection to the corporate ideal: I volunteer for a project no one else around the place wants to undertake. Computron is making elaborate preparations to market a remarkably versatile new gadget—a photocopier, dictating machine, and electric pencil sharpener combined in one glossy housing. The field obstacles will prove formidable since we are starting late in our effort to penetrate these markets (and our price will naturally be higher than the highest-priced photocopier, dictating machine, and electric pencil sharpener combined). And since Computron prefers to lacerate, not merely penetrate, any market it enters, a major research effort is being mounted to determine how best to package, promote, and sell Little Wonder #301 (as the new product is known affectionately around the shop).

Mooring is about to send an expeditionary force into the field for six weeks to gather data, interview potential customers, and otherwise sniff out the prevailing aroma of the marketplace so that a data-gorged presentation, strikingly mounted on multicolored graphs and charts, can be offered to management in support of policies and strategies already formulated and certain to be affected in no way by what Market Research has to say. Six unsupervised weeks out of the office! Six weeks on the company to ply my unwholesome wares! At the end of which, if I choose, I can fabricate a totally fascinating field report that will restore my flagging fortunes, management-wise, like a rocket booster.

I tell Mooring I am his man for this thankless but essential task.

"You?" He snorts. "I thought you were concentrating your glittering talents on the *Times* crossword puzzle."

"You have badly miscalculated your man."

"Is that so?"

"If you don't mind my saying so—yes. I am an uncut gem."

He hawks up a bit of guttural flotsam, strokes his cheek a few reflective times, studies the ceiling a bit, and then springs me.

14

The Bottom of the Barrel

I PUSH OUT OF THE ELEVATOR THE INSTANT THE DOOR OPENS, sideswiping young women and old men, and fall into the first bar I see. Alone and purposefully, I begin sopping up beer at a great rate, noting at each swallow how little I really like the taste and aroma and consistency of the golden bilge. But I cannot just sit somewhere —on a park bench, say—hands folded, and think thoughts. Pure thinking is pure agony. The beer, at least, acts as a sort of ballast, for my thoughts are on the verge of a vertical lift-off. All the trailing, scrambled tie lines to convention have been cut now. I am free to pursue my fate.

After an hour I leave and go two blocks north to Shag Shaughnessy's bar, which, I notice, has been rechristened again. Every year Shag likes to change its name. First it was called P. J. Shaughnessy's. Then it was Grandma's Bun. Then Orphan Annie's Thumb. Then some other things no one can remember. And now it is just The Bottom of the Barrel. Changing the name, Shag once said, is like opening an all-new bar. Everybody likes newness. And a lot of the old customers who had drifted away to someplace flashier come back every time, thinking there might have been a change of management and décor and ambience, only to find the same old musty cave with the same old wire-back chairs and the same old lethargically laundered tablecloths and the same old very good but unvaried food (of which chili is still the mainstay) served by the same old young, sleepy-eyed, tousle-haired waiters all looking as if they hope the Big Break in Show Biz will pluck them momentarily from this unspeakable tedium.

I wander tentatively through the door, half hoping Shag has not shown up yet. I am not really up to an extended session with the feisty tormentor, whom I have not seen since the class reunion five months earlier and whose saloon I have not visited for almost a year and a half now. But it is Shag I have very specifically come to see, and there is no putting off the interview any longer.

I head for the nearest vacant table and tumble into one of the wobbly chairs, which tilts as I land. Carrie Nation is still up there over the bar in tintype, twice as big as life, wielding a mighty battle-axe and wearing a mean righteous tight-twatted little snarl behind her fragile specs. And still marshaled all around are W.C.T.U. stalwarts, shown trudging unswervably to Jerusalem and looking as if they need nothing so much as a good swift lay. But there are some changes in the place, my ears tell me before my eyes, which have not quite ac-climated themselves to the gloaming. A steady chorus of little bells and buzzers comes from the other side of the partition that divides the room. I jack myself up and see a whole battery of pinball ma-chines being ardently tended by late-afternoon gamesmen on high stools. There is great animation among them as their scoreboards jangle raucously.

I slip slowly back into my chair. More than anything, I want to clunk my head down on the table and take a nap for five minutes, but the pinball racket is ceaseless. I settle instead for closing my eyes and counting to sixty. When I open them, the first thing I see is a white lifeguard's chair in the opposite corner of the room—a regular one from a regular beach, eight or nine feet high—and Shag Shaughnessy perched on top in a pith helmet, a sweat shirt reading "GOD IS CAMP," and khaki Bermuda shorts artfully frayed along the bottoms. I close my eyes again and count another ten. It is all still there when they reopen, only now Shag is standing up, his helmet practically touching the ceiling, and beating his chest rhythmically. No one pays any attention; it is evidently a frequent rite of his. And then he is clambering down barefoot from his lookout post, with a small wooden box held up by a thin shoulder strap bobbing at his side. The box, as he moves within range, looks more and more like a shoeshine kit. He gooses the waiters as he passes and then, suddenly, terribly, with unspeakable degradation, is spread-eagled on the floor, the box between his legs, seizing my left foot and propping it up on the shoe stand.

"What in Christ's name are you doing?" I ask, tugging my foot away.

Shag hangs on to it and yanks it back into position on the box. "I'm being depressive," he says, bending closer to the shoe to see what color it is.

"You're *what?*"

"Being depressive." He gestures with his head arcross the room. "When I sit up there too long, I get manic. So I come down and shine everybody's shoes."

I try to yank my foot away again. "But I don't *want* you to shine my shoes."

He reaches into the box for the polishing equipment. "Why not?" he asks. "I happen to do a goddam good job." He looks up. "Besides, it's free."

"I don't give a crap if *you* pay *me* five dollars," I say, trying to lift him up, "I don't want you groveling around down there like that."

"Everybody else lets me do it."

"Why?"

"Because they like their shoes shined free."

"And they think it's a riot for the boss to do it?"

"That's right," he says, clamping the shoe back in place and giving it a few exploratory strokes of the brush.

"Well, I don't."

"Yes, well, every once in a while someone like you comes along and finds the whole idea sickening."

"Then what do you do?"

"I throw them out on their ass," he says, whipping the polish can out from the box and, with one hand, removing the tight lid.

The pressure of his other hand holding the shoe firmly in place makes it clear he is entirely serious, so I yield to his newest idiosyncrasy. "Cordovan polish," I tell him, "if you have any."

"Cordovans are hopelessly square." And he begins applying black polish with precise little swirls of his fingertips.

I sit transfixed as he works expertly over the shoe, massaging the polish well into the grain. I hesitate to speak for fear of unsettling a craftsman at his trade. Finally, though, I ask softly, "Why are you doing this terrible thing?"

He pops the polishing rag a couple of times to make sure it is satisfactorily limber, and then begins furiously buffing away. "I told you," he says. "To stay sane."

"And when you're properly depressed from shining shoes, you climb back up on the chair and start beating your chest?"

"Only if I'm *very* depressed."

"And if you're only mildly depressed?"

"I play the pinball machines—three at a time."

"And what does that do for you?"

"It makes a lot of noise."

"And that's good, is it?"

"Yes, because it makes me think I'm actually doing something."

"But secretly you know that's not so?"

He pulls a flat tin of miniature cigars out of the shoe box and helps himself to one. Then he remembers to offer me one. I take it gratefully. "Well," he says, lighting us both, "it's all relative." He takes a big swig and balances the cigar carefully on the edge of the shoe box. "I would agree that playing pinball is not what would generally be called a socially useful activity. But then how many people you and I know are doing anything of demonstrably higher value?" And he resumes buffing away until the shoe gives off a rich gloss, even in that dim light. When he is done, he gives the sole a tap. I remove the shoe and, without arguing any more, proffer the other one. Now I begin to sense the stares of the couple at the next table, newcomers to the place evidently, judging by the way they rivet their looks on Shag and me and barely restrain themselves from laughing out loud at the ardor with which the shine is being executed. If Shag is aware of them, he gives no sign.

Just then a little old lady comes in, peddling wilted gardenias from a big box. She stands behind Shag for a moment until he fishes into his pocket for a coin. She whispers something in gratitude to him and pins a flower on his shoulder. She is about to offer one to me when she sees I have no one with me to give it to, and moves past me unsmilingly to the couple at the next table—the starers.

"Would you like to buy a lovely flower for the lovely lady?" she asks.

The fellow shakes his head and looks away.

"They're only fifty cents."

"No, thanks, really."

"They smell very beautiful."

"I said no!"

It comes out too sharply to suit Shag, who stands up. The fellow looks at him, then at the old lady, then back to his date.

"She's a poor old lady," says Shag.

The fellow looks up again, not understanding.

"She wants you to buy a flower from her."

"I know," the fellow says, "but I don't want to buy a flower just now."

"That really doesn't matter."

"Look, what is this?"

"It's called charity. Don't you believe in charity?"

"Not when someone twists my arm."

"She's not strong enough to twist a lemon."

"She shouldn't ask three times."

"You said no the first two."

"And the third time, too, Look, let her check into an old-age home instead of bothering people with her rotten old flowers."

"They're not rotten—I wouldn't let her in here if they were rotten."

"You shouldn't let her in regardless."

"Why not? Because it reminds rich, pudgy people that not every-one has it so good?"

"Do you always insult your customers?" the girl with the fellow asks.

Shag throws her a sizing-up look. "Just the bad apples," he says.

"Let's split," she says.

"No," the fellow says. "I'm not going to be intimidated."

Shag leans closer to him. "You get much off her?"

"Shut up," he snaps, "or I'll call the cops."

"It's *my* bar."

"That's doesn't give you the right to be abusive."

Shag leans close again but says loud enough for the girl to hear, "Frankly, she's got fat ankles."

"Will you please punch the bastard in the nose?" the girl says, standing now.

"That's just what he wants—he's got at least fifty pounds on me."

"Look," she says, "I'm not going to stay here and be insulted by this—this drunken pug."

"Sit down, bimbo," Shag says to her. "Or take me on yourself."

"I just might," she says.

"My table's in the back," Shag says. "Under the lifeguard's chair."

"Okay," she says, pushing out past her date.

"Brenda—where are you going?"

"With him," she says, "you chickenshit!"

"Brenda—you're making a scene."

"I'll be back in a minute," Shag says.

"Swell," she says.

"And your ankles aren't all that fat."

"Thanks," she says. "And you're not a pug—just a beast."

"Brenda!" the fellow says desperately.

Shag looks down at him. "Okay, now, Big Balls—either you buy one of the lady's gardenias or you're out on your ear."

The fellow heaves a great sigh, then surrenders a dollar bill. "Save the flower," he says to the old lady, tossing the dollar into her box.

"That's an insult to her," Shag says. "Take the flower."

He takes it and sticks it in a glass of water on the table.

"God bless you," the old lady says, and moves on unsinkably.

"Yeah, you, too," the fellow says after her.

"Okay," Shag says, hooking a finger under the fellow's lapel, "now hit the road."

"What for? I bought the flower."

"But you weren't sincere. Now start moving, buster, before you start flying."

He is up and back-pedaling.

"But what about Brenda?"

"She's in safe, if playful, hands."

"But you can't just take her like that."

"You're a douche bag."

"You'll hear from my lawyer in the morning."

"Besides which I didn't *take* her—she came by herself. I have thirty-seven witnesses, all of them my friends or employees." He takes a menacing step toward the slack-kneed loser. "She'll send you a post-card, sweetheart. And your bill's on the house—now blow!"

And he does, untouched by human hand.

Shag signals the bartender for two beers and drops into the chair next to me. "Thus," he says in his best Westbrook Van Voorhis, "I have become a legend in my own time."

"Right," I say. "Meanwhile your shoeshine box is on fire."

Shag glances down at the smoldering box. "Oh, shit, the cigar!" He bellows something to the bartender, who hurls the beers on the tray of the nearest waiter, who speeds them across the room to Shag, who, never moving from his chair, douses the smoking mess. "Two more," he tells the waiter.

"But you didn't finish my other shoe," I say.

"Say, that's right," he says. "Sorry, I'm all shined out at the moment. You come by tomorrow and I'll finish."

"That's all right."

"No, I mean it."

A newsboy comes in peddling the afternoon paper. He brings Shag the first copy. Then he offers one to me. I shake my head no. Shag looks up sharply. I fork up a quarter and say, "Keep the change."

Shag nods, then scans the racing results. "Two winners," he says.

The beers come and Shag toasts me without looking up from the paper.

"Look," I say, "I don't want to keep you from the lady."

"She's no lady." He puts the paper down. "Let her wait."

"How often do you pull a stunt like that?"

"Every chance I get."

"And to what do you attribute your legendary prowess?"

"To the fact that everyone else is dead—like Brenda's late beau. He should've punched me in the mouth very hard about twelve times. But, like she said, he was chickenshit. Everyone is. Nobody punches anyone in the mouth any more, no matter how great the provocation. They just sit there and get shat on. Including you."

"Precisely why I'm here." And, after chugging my beer and practically choking over the dregs, I proceed to tell him everything there is to tell about my plan.

When I am finished, Shag takes off his helmet, tosses it in the air, and fields it on one klopping bounce off the tabletop. "You are the hero of our time," he announces, and toasts me with the last of his beer.

"Also I am insane."

"They go together."

"Will you help?"

Shag slams the helmet back on his head. "You have come to precisely the right place." He gets up, walks across the room, and comes back a moment later with a small dapper man in tow. "Kit," he says, "this is Action. Action is the resident fence. The best in the business, I've been told. Action, of course, is not his real name. We don't use real names in the underworld."

Action offers his hand.

"And this is Kit," Shag adds, "also an alias. Kit is a robber—or about to be. How good a one we don't know yet, but he's got all the natural equipment. He's anxious to get off to a good start, so any counsel you have to offer he'd greatly appreciate."

I take the extended hand. It is slightly damp and distinctly scaly.

15

Over the Rainbow

I WILL BE DEAD, WHEN I DIE, FOR A VERY LONG TIME IS WHAT I am thinking. I then wonder briefly how many people who ever lived have had that same bleak thought. Quite a few, I decide, which suggests it is not worth dwelling on. And when I die, I decide further, there will be not a single paragraph about it on the *Times* obit page, and all the people who have never heard of me will have to read the paid death notices to learn that I am no longer here for them to ignore. The thought of my being dead fills me with momentary grief. And then, resentful, I decide I am against having a paid death notice. If I have done anything worth noting, they should register it free of charge for posterity to look up on microfilm; if I have not, I must vanish unlamented the way of most flesh.

"What will any of it matter in a hundred years?" Anne is fond of saying, by way of dismissing any little murmur I have ever let escape about the inconsequential drift of my diminishing life. Oh, she is sweet and means well, but that does not get us anywhere. For she has long since, like most people who are no longer children, surrendered to the concept of mortality. I, for my part, have not, though I am no longer a child. I am afraid to die, of course. For however short of ecstasy it keeps falling, however wearying and saddening it keeps being, I do not mind life at all. What I have minded is how it keeps intimidating me, how mastery of any part of it keeps eluding me. I secretly insist on my share of power and wealth and fame and some sort of ultimate wisdom. That these things are all transient, just like anyone who possesses them, and therefore unworthy of the effort that must be made and the price that must be paid to win them—well, that is what Anne, in her soft and sensible way, has always argued. But to me that is precisely the surrender I have decided I will no longer accept. I have, I say, an obligation to go down fighting. I look across the living room at Anne.

"I have a wonderful idea."

"What is your wonderful idea, dear?"

"Soon it will be Christmas vacation for our older child, what's-his-name—"

"Surely you remember what's-his-name's name—"

"I am being playful, my dear."

"What fun."

"I was saying—his vacation."

"Yes."

"My wonderful idea is for you to take the children to some winter wonderland for a week, at the end of which I shall join you, and then we shall frolic, the four of us together, skating and sledding and taking marvelous sleigh rides together at twilight, all cozy and warm under great furry blankets and watching our breath turn to frost as our little horse trots evenly across the silver landscape, twinkling merrily all the way."

"Where are you while we are there?"

"And then we shall drink creamy hot chocolate from thick china mugs as we sit before the huge fire blazing in the main house and softly sing songs like 'Side by Side' and 'Over the Rainbow.' "

"The first week—where are you?"

"I am here, in the foul, noisy city, working on my massive research project for the Little Wonder #301."

"Why do you want us to go away without you?"

"That is not the way to look at it."

"What is the way?"

"The way is to see that I want you and the children to have an extra week where the air is clean and crisp and their little bodies can gain strength. I cannot spare two weeks, but I do not want to deprive them—and you."

"Oh."

"Isn't that nice?"

"I don't think you are being entirely candid."

"Not entirely, no. The fact is I will get much more work done if their little bodies are not screaming their bloody heads off in my ear every third minute."

"Oh."

"You will love Lake Placid."

"But you've never been there."

"In my mind's eye."

"I don't like to be where you aren't."

"Nor I where you aren't."

"Good, then let's forget about it."

"No, it's settled. I am going to call the travel agent tomorrow and make the arrangements."

I do not like to see her cry, and she is crying. And I am full of deceit. But I am strong now, too, and cold, for I am propelled by forces she will never understand, so I do what must be done.

16

Dry Run

A LIMOUSINE COMES TO CARRY THEM OFF TO LAKE PLACID, SINCE of course there is no suitable train. It will take six hours. The children will grow terribly irritable. I proposed tranquilizers, but Anne insists it would be some sort of sin. And so, martyrlike, she disappears into the limousine, her eyes faintly rimmed with tears, the kids chirping mindlessly. Guilt wells within me for one barely containable instant, then gets hustled back into exile. I throw kisses. The driver, patent-leather peak of his cap glossy in the midmorning sun, salutes me reassuringly. I salute back. The big car moves off quietly. Little faces framed in the back window wave frantically. Then they are gone. And I—I finally, I irreversibly—am free.

I go back to the apartment, which seems to echo still with the howls and giggles of the children. Drifting through the rooms, I feel cool and detached and powerfully laden with vital liquids. Anne's menstrual cycle has prevented ejaculation for a week and I am aswarm with hormones. I theorize that all man's noble acts, all his daring acts —indeed every one of man's achievements of recognized magnitude— have stemmed from an undeposited surplus in the scrotum. I do not have the clinical evidence and would not care if it contradicted the theory. But I am certain that regular and frequent seminal discharge reduces a man to perpetual obeisance, renders him sluggish at best and defenseless at worst before the usurping forces ranged against him. The way of man is to crave the steady release of semen—a habit that leaves him in a condition of maximum vulnerability. He who can abstain the longest—he who bears a cocked phallus on his shield—that zealot has the rest of the race at a disadvantage for the duration of his celibacy.

I begin to assemble my equipment from the dust-choked depths of our main clothes closet. It is all together, in a worn-out suitcase. The pirate mask, which seems to have grown still woollier whiskers since I stashed it away. The BB pistol and the Cap-Chur gun, the latter easily the world's most Byzantine-looking weapon and twice as frightening as I remembered it. And the purchase of the past week from the hardware store on Twenty-third Street: three pairs of handcuffs, two pairs of white cotton gloves, and one pair of heavy shears. I spread it all out on the bed: the tools of my trade. My loins churn with anticipation. I put on the mask. It is hot and clammy inside. I keep it on to get used to it. Then I check the Cap-Chur gun for cleanliness. Then I assemble the firing mechanism. Then I move across the room and begin practice-firing it. My target is a pillow on the bed. The first time I overshoot and the needle ends up in a lamp-shade. The next time I undershoot and bag a soiled sock. The third time I connect. But what are the odds on my winging a moving target on the first real try? Long. Very long. I keep practicing. Then I try manipulating the handcuffs. It is harder than it looks in the movies. And impossible to manage with one hand, which is all I will have available unless I am going to ask my victims to hold the gun while I snap the bracelets on them. Perhaps I will not use the handcuffs at all. It will depend on the situation. Then I try on the white gloves. They look like Mickey Mouse's. I try firing both guns with them on. It is harder yet. I try working the handcuffs with them on. Clumsiness beyond belief. They will laugh me out of the crime business. Sweat has collected in a small pond inside the mask. I decide I must practice everything for another day or two. Particularly the voice I will be using. I have not decided which of my many terrible accents would be best. I could use my "Amos 'n' Andy" accent, of course— that would be easiest. But why exacerbate the race struggle? My Scandinavian one is good, too, but everyone knows there are no

Scandinavian robbers, and so they will think I am harmless. My German one is left over from old B movies about the Nazis, and I like to think of myself as a sympathetic criminal. My new Gaelic accent has been coming along nicely since I saw *Hogan's Goat* at the American Place Theatre. But it is too stagey to work effectively under the circumstances. No, it will have to be a plain old thug accent: the nasal sound, as if the passages are permanently congested with tar, and the pronunciation lumpishly slurred, with every sixth word being "like" as in: "Like, shut de daw, man, aw like I'll kick yaw goddam face in, like." The dumber I sound, the more violent they will take me for. Now, do I need a black leather jacket with twelve zipper pockets and death's-head epaulets? And where will I dispose of my getup when the deed is done? To say nothing of the loot. Oh, the details are endless.

In between practicing with the gun, the handcuffs, and the accent, I carefully consider who my first victim shall be. It is no casual matter. All kinds of factors enter into the decision. He (or they) must be (1) manageable, (2) loaded, (3) bad, and (4) at home. *Manageable* because I will be a beginner and at least as frightened as he (or they) and more likely to shoot myself in the toe than to bring down some sturdy fool trying a flying tackle on me. *Loaded* because this is no mere thrill robbery, no mere therapeutic happening; I am after money and jewels and other valuables (which lets out my immediate neighbor, who, I have discovered from the doorman, an invaluable source to me these days, is a chiropodist). *Bad* so that I will do good by taking from them, by bringing this affliction down upon their fatted insolence. *At home* because I am no crummy second-story sneak thief; it is the confrontation, that moment of supremely heightened emotion, that is critical.

And so, after endless guarded inquiries and due deliberation, I settle at last on Mr. and Mrs. Leonard Lifeline in 15J. Lifeline is a builder of buildings all of which look precisely alike, all of which have self-service elevators and long corridors continuously filled with

Muzak by Mantovani, and all of which will fall apart exactly twenty years from the day they were topped out. Lifeline, of course, does not own any of the buildings he builds. He sells them to syndicates of wily investors who hold on to them just long enough to extract maximum tax advantage from the properties before selling them to another set of wily investors, who in turn sell them to someone else and then lease them back for still more sophisticated tax benefits. Lifeline has built at least thirty of his identical buildings, each one presumably more profitable than the last, since he is renowned for having brought the art of corner-cutting to levels never before achieved in the construction industry, of which he is a lofty and revered pillar—or beam, if you will. Also an art collector of some standing, Lifeline lives two floors above me in a nine-room apartment presumably protected by a delicate burglar alarm that is about to face its sternest test: a robber who has no idea of how it's done. Lifeline also probably has at least one resident servant, who, rather than springing to the master's rescue, will more than likely be secretly pleased at his getting taken to the cleaners.

Leonard Lifeline, prepare to meet your avenger.

17

Breakfast Epiphanies

THE DAY OF DAYS. I WAKE WITH A SMALL HEADACHE CORKSCREWING around somewhere deep in a rear lobe. I will master it; it will not deflect me from my purpose. My hands, as always first thing in the morning, are swollen, the knuckles puffy. Aches prosper at every joint. I am naked. I rarely sleep naked, even in summer—especially in summer, because the air conditioner invariably drops the room temperature to the frost level by morning. Now, though, I rather prefer my nakedness. It is a small but easily staged show of rebellion, a tiny triumph of id over superego, and at the moment I am counting all victories, however miniature.

I reach behind me on the headboard for my pirate mask. I must become thoroughly accustomed to it. I put it on. It is soon clammy inside, but less so than it seemed yesterday. I creak slowly out of bed and go nakedly to the front door, bending painfully and thrusting an arm out through the crack for the newspaper. I take it into the living room and throw open the shutters. Fine, the sky is gray. A bright crisp day would have been much too intrusive.

I plant my bare behind on the blue silk sofa and stretch out with the newspaper. I love to read the newspaper; it is how I know I am alive. Especially reading the obituaries. Two interesting casualties in the death department this morning. A blue-eyed, dark-haired, 45-year-old daredevil drowned yesterday when his 30-foot-long jet-powered speedboat, roaring across the surface of a 5½-mile lake in northwest England at better than 300 miles per hour, suddenly climbed out of the water like an airplane, turned a complete backward loop, smacked down right side up, turned end over end several times in a great plume of spray—and sank quickly. Terrific. He couldn't have wanted to go any other way. Not so very many miles away—in Aberdeen, Scotland, as a matter of fact—a famous soprano who was once the stellar attraction of the Chicago Civic Opera Company, was going, as all stellar attractions one day must, to her final reward, at the age of ninety-two. She was, the obituary said, quoting her biographer, "a condor, an eagle, a panther, a society dame, a gallery of moving pictures, a siren, an indomitable fighter, a human woman with a heart as big as a house, a lover of sport, a canny Scotch lassie, a superwoman." There was no immediate cause of death given (though she was not, apparently, driving a jet speedboat at anything approaching three hundred miles an hour at the time of her demise). Rest ye well, dear panther, on yon bonnie banks.

I turn next to the sports pages, which I relish above all other parts
of the paper. I relish them because of the unambiguity of what is
recorded there. The scores separate the winners from the losers, the
gifted from the hapless, as they are rarely separated elsewhere in life.
It does not matter at all that these athletic performances are morally
neuter. It matters only that an arena remains where a man alone, by
name and measurable performance, may demonstrate his prowess,
and his prowess will be readily apprehended by multitudes because of
its very physicality. On the sidelines, nobody has a body any more.
So I note, with compulsive interest, that Willis Reed, a local professional basketball player, is averaging 19.8 points and just over 14
rebounds per game at the moment—not, on the face of it, an astonishing performance for a man six feet ten but in fact a remarkably
creditable one, given his displacement from the fruitful center slot
several seasons back by an even taller but noticeably sluggish player.
I have not, of course, ever seen Willis Reed play in person. Nor have
I been to a basketball game in eleven years. Nor am I likely ever to
see another.

Finally, I check the stock tables to learn the closing price of
Computron, of which I currently own twenty-five shares. It ended
trading yesterday at 325½, up 2. Bringing my portfolio up to a paper
value of $8,137.50. Which, added to the $1,788.57 in my hard-
pressed checking account, the $2,500 in my listless savings account,
the $25,000 face value of my remorseless term insurance policy, and
the $10,000 group policy my benevolent employer pushes in my
face to prove it has a heart, brings the gross disposable worth of my
estate to $47,426.07 (not counting the hockable value of Anne's
engagement ring, our canned goods, our sagging beds, our soiled
carpets, and one exquisitely wickered baby carriage, vintage 1890,
purchased on a whim two years ago as late high camp and this very
moment grandly standing in the corner opposite me—the most magnificent, and useless, piece in the living room). Not, as net worths
go these days, anything to get excited about—paltry enough, in fact,

to place just plain money at the head of the list of exotic motives propelling me toward this evening's moment of truth.

By now, I am sweltering under the hairy pirate mask. I pull it off and go scramble eggs. I am one of the world's better egg scramblers, principally because my wife is not. She never gives the eggs a chance to settle, preferring to rake her fork back and forth across the pan, a technique producing a cluster of unattractively coagulated, badly connected, hard, tasteless yellow particles that, on transfer to the plate, break up like a hammered blob of quicksilver. I, on the other hand, work only around the edges of the pan, folding the cooked area in toward the center with a graceful pivot of the wrist while the runny parts hurry out to the edges for their brief moment of intense heat. This mini-skill of mine pleases me and someday soon I shall move on to omelettes. At the moment, though, what is most remarkable is not my virtuosity at the stove but that my headache, somehow, has vanished and been replaced by galloping pangs of hunger I must quell at once.

The butter hisses in the pan and spits impatiently at my moderately haired chest as I beat half a dozen large eggs to a golden froth. I lower the flame and send the mix cascading into the pan till there is nothing left but a trickle of beaded dregs. A bright warm soft edible disc smiles up at me, wetly shimmering. While it begins to cook, I slash three oranges in half and extract their sweetness on the electric juicer that whirs too loud by half. Bathed in a riot of gay colors, I suddenly conceive of breakfast as a kind of rite—a celebration of self-renewal. The finished eggs, fluffy and inventively patterned, fill the better part of a gleaming white plate. The squeezed juice, cool and fresh and thick but seedless, fills a twelve-ounce rose-colored plastic goblet just shy of the brim. I disengage four small spongy toast-brown rolls from a family of them in a crackling plastic bag and, not bothering to pry them open, apply fat wads of whipped butter to their irregular tops and spread them unevenly. About a spoonful of salt on the eggs, and then I am ready: The Last Breakfast. I shovel it all down at an unbelievable speed, never removing my eye from the new number of the *Bulletin of the Atomic Scientists,* the most exotic entry on my periodical shelf but one that I am incapable of confronting for more than two consecutive minutes— and then only at the breakfast table or on the toilet. Astonishingly, I am still hungry. And thirsty. I chop two ample slices from a half-gone salami and squeeze three more oranges. Then two cups of coffee and countless small chocolate cookies and a handful of dry-roasted peanuts. Finally, a cigar, to help focus on coming events.

I begin thinking of promising hiding places for my impending haul: a hollowed-out loaf of bread, the heel pieces kept intact; a disemboweled chicken, a zipper installed in its crotch; the insides of cereal boxes, a layer of tiny taste treats retained on top for camouflage. Inspired, I start roaming the apartment in quest of other unfindable hollows. In the dining room: the bookshelves, of course, though it will be costly. There are no less than a thousand books in nine high-tiered cases. With a razor blade, I will chop out a cover-to-cover hole inside six of them (three thick ones, three thin), retaining a thin margin on the top, bottom, and sides, and replace them on shelves, waiting repositories for fabulous heirlooms. In the bedroom: the high round wicker hamper where Anne stores her leftover knitting yarn in snarled skeins, dozens and dozens of them, in the impenetrable middles of which whole handfuls of gems may readily be embedded. In the foyer: the false-bottom drawer in the roll-top desk. No—absolutely not! All roll-top desks, it is well known, contain false-bottom drawers. No, nothing very promising in the foyer. On to the living room: how about the window seats? Too obvious. The fireplace? Up the unused flue? No, terrible. They are all automatic up-the-flue lookers. Behind the painted white bricks? No, they will speedily detect telltale fissures in the mortar. I am seized by a moment of panic. If they come to search, they will search indefatigably and leave no replaced brick, hollowed book, tangled yarn, or zippered chicken unturned; industry is their substitute for inspiration.

But why should they come here to search? There are two hundred apartments in the building. Will they ransack every closet, rip up every rug, eviscerate every mattress? That's crazy. Cool it, baby. A little prudence, a little practice, and a whole lot of cool and it's all going to work like a charm. Just don't leave the loot in a pile on the living-room rug is all. Shove the ice inside that throw pillow over there, or an old shoe or the clothes hamper. Stash the thousand-dollar bills behind the cardboard in every laundered shirt. Assuming there will be some to stash.

I am feeling better. Excellent, in fact. I go take target practice in the bedroom, re-donning my pirate mask and talking to myself like the glue-tongued Brando counseling the pigeons in *On the Water-front*. I am becoming first-class at all these skills. I start to tingle vaguely all over. Things I have put off till now spring to mind—things I should have worked out long before. Like how, precisely, I am going to get inside the door that separates Leonard Lifeline and his gathered spoils from all of us who would unburden him of them. And how, precisely, once I am inside, I am going to conduct the un-burdening. Not that I have not thought about all this many times in the past few months. Quite the contrary. Indeed I have been thinking of little else but. I have read widely on the entry problem in par-ticular. There is, of course, the time-honored wax-impression method, whereby I make a mold of Leonard Lifeline's lock and have a key fashioned to fit it. How awkward, though, to be caught in the im-pression-making act by Mrs. Lifeline, who may open the door by chance and cause me to fly across the threshold and land on my bare face. It would be easier, in theory, to steal the passkey. But how does one steal a passkey? And which passkey is it? Answer: one hits the superintendent on the head with a lead pipe and takes *all* the pass-keys. Yes, but *how* does one manage to hit the superintendent with a lead pipe without his recalling, upon reviving, who hit him? And what if the superintendent's head is as thick as the pipe and more un-yielding? Even assuming it is not, how does one discover which of

the fifty passkeys opens the desired door? Trial and error, of course—
an unsatisfactory solution under the circumstances. No, something more
artful is necessary. Like "loiding" open the lock. I have read about
that in *The New Yorker*. They ran a series on robbers once, and
"loiding," I learned, is S.O.P. You slide a strip from a celluloid playing card or wallet calendar through the crack in the door and slip it
gently up and down until you work the catch out of its groove. Only
it takes practice. And I cannot stand in the corridor beside even my
apartment door and keep poking at the lock indefinitely with a celluloid strip; someone will notice, and sooner rather than later. No,
I must gain entry quickly, and without any cumbersome or unper-
fected techniques. Just how, though, I have left unresolved. And now
I must resolve it. Without further hesitation I decide I will walk up
the fire stairs and go to the service entrance at 10 P.M. and ring the
bell. If there is a peephole, I will put my thumb over it. They will
ask who is there. I will say it is the plumber and that there is an
emergency—a leak downstairs—and that I have to check their back
bathroom. They will say why can't we see you through the peephole,
and I will say because the hall light is out. And they will let me in.
Just like that. And if not? If not, I will beat the door down in a
frenzy. Or sit down and cry.

But I am not really worrying about any of that. One way or another I will get inside the door—precisely because I am not worrying
about it. Precisely because the whole undertaking must, in large
part, be spontaneous and therefore capable of being performed with
all the more conviction. I shall confront my victims with masked
countenance and exotic weaponry and brutish voice, and they will
shrink at once, with trembling nausea, before the dark power my
entire bearing will bespeak.

The tingling has reached my genitals. It is 10 A.M. Half a day to
go.

18

Brinkmanship

I DRINK THE AFTERNOON AWAY AT THE BOTTOM OF THE BARREL, where Shag Shaughnessy has imported a rinky-dink spinet and is even now assailing us with his very own, very blasphemous Christmas carols. Only the melodies remain. As in (to "God Rest Ye, Merry Gentlemen"): "Why curb my loins' propensities/Or wenches' fears allay/When I am so superbly hung/That I can come all day?" Newcomers, drawn by the gaiety, crowd in to listen. Half of them, sickened by the lyrics, depart at once. The other half piles on top of the earlier mob that urges Shag on to still greater outrages.

I am drinking vodka gimlets and inching, sip by sip, up some spangled spiral to euphoria. Drinking and not thinking, I scarcely notice Action as he plunks down at the table and hands me a claw. It is waving insistently in my face, so I grasp it, wondering who that is on the other end. He looks familiar but not very, mainly because he has not removed his fur cap. "Who are you, again?"

"Very funny," he says, and takes the hat off.

"You didn't say the password."

He looks more dour than I remember. "You sure you know what you're doing?" he asks, almost avuncularly.

"All signals go." I toast him.

"Okay," he says. "It's no skin off my ass."

"That's not a very festive thing to say."

He notes my lack of sobriety and squints at me. "You don't work when you're loaded, do you?"

"Why—isn't that how everyone does it?"

He reaches for his hat. "You don't need a fence. You need a lawyer."

I put my hand on his arm. "I'm kidding."

"Sure." He's getting up now.

"I take two twenty-minute freezing showers with a quart of steaming coffee in between before I go on. Does wonders for my trigger finger."

"Sure, sure." He begins turning.

"Sit down, punk!"

He spins around.

"You don't want to handle the job, I'll get someone bigger."

He sits.

"The job's tonight."

"Yeah?"

"Yeah. I'll be in at four tomorrow to give you the rundown."

"No," he says, "wait a day."

"Yeah?"

"Yeah."

"All right, then—four the day after."

"Okay."

"One little thing—"

"What?"

"The word around is that you do pretty good for yourself."

"I get by."

"Like, uh, I hear you end up with nine-tenths of the action and, uh, like I wind up with hind titty. Which means, uh, like I'm working for you, dad, and not the other way around."

"Who says that?"

"Everybody I talk with."

"You talk too much." He begins to get up again.

"I got to know who I'm dealing with, don't I?"

"Look, don't do me no favors, chum. I do a nice business. I got a nice reputation. I don't need you dumpin' on it. You wanna work with me, fine. I take your merchandise, you get the going rate. You don't like the setup, go look in the Yellow Pages, dig?"

I throw down the rest of my drink. We are each maneuvering for some slight advantage, but in fact I have nothing going for me but vodka-fueled nerve. I look at him. He will not come into focus. It is not my fault entirely; it has something to do with his face. It looks as if it is made of plastic dough that he kneads every fifteen minutes or so to keep from getting identified in police line-ups. It is sort of lumpy and bloated and asymmetrical. He is easily the ugliest man in the room. All the others have square jaws and close shaves, and even though it is in mid-December some have detectable tans. But not one of them, probably, is a fence. And a fence is what I will happen to need very badly in, uh, like forty-eight hours. So I stand up and stick my face in front of his, which is changing shape before my very eyes, and I say, "Okay, sweetheart, I'll go to the well once with anybody—only my pail's gonna have more than three drops in it when I check in at the bottom of the hill or your ass ends up in a sling."

He starts to laugh at me, and his nose slides over under one eye. "You been seein' too many movies, pal. I'll see you in two days if you don't shit in your pants first." And off he goes, switching his nose to under the other eye.

I am pleased with my performance, all the more because it was unplanned. I have not begun to exploit my charismatic power. I am feeling unstoppably potent. But since I have quenched the old yearning to spill my seed on schedule every third day or so, I take in the assorted ginch around the place with disdainful eyes as if I am hermaphroditically self-sustaining. It is evidently irresistible, this Robert Mitchum look of mine: uninvited, a long-lashed thing with smoky blonde hair to her shoulders falls in beside me.

"I'm gay," I say to discourage her.

"We're not talking about you," she says. "This is about me. Me me me."

"Go have your identity crisis somewhere else."

She tilts her chin up, revealing a lithe, unlined throat. "There's no other seat in the place, so I'm staying, dad."

"Okay. You have lovely hair."

"I buy my own drinks, thanks."

"And very classy elocution."

She puts her elbow on the table and cups her chin in her hand. "My problem is," she says, bending toward me a little, "that *Playboy* wants me to be its Playmate of the Month."

I frown. "Gee, that's terrible."

"For four thousand dollars."

I smile. "Gee, that's terrific."

"Only where I come from you don't do that sort of thing for any kind of money. It makes you a whore."

"What does—peeling to the buff and showing the world your swell gifts?"

She nods.

"Maybe your gifts aren't all that swell."

She squints hard at me, then quickly unbottons her jacket and unfurls a sweatered chest of legendary roundness and fullness and protrusion. She makes sure I have had a good look and then locks them up again. "They're all mine, too."

"They're beauties. I apologize." My fingers expand and contract involuntarily. "In fact a steal at two thou apiece."

"Thanks."

"You owe it to the world to share your blessings."

"You're not being serious."

"But I am. Think how many male members of all ages, races and religions will be aroused by the sight. Placed end to end, they will reach the moon."

"Now you're being dirty."

"What dirty? It's a perfectly normal, healthy glandular response.

And if you were honest with yourself, you'd admit what a terrific thrill in the crotch the prospect gives you."

Her eyes are big and busy and pale-something—it's too dark to tell the color—and not overly made up as is the fashion. They look at me for a moment and then slowly narrow. "You know," she says, "you are right. I don't know how you knew, but the thought of it excites me terribly." She reaches over and takes a sip of my drink. "You know what I want to do sometimes? I want to run down the street naked, with everything jiggling wildly and the sidewalks all crowded with men in loincloths, and at the end of the street there is one of those cute little Aztec-type pyramids with steps running up it, and at the top is the high priest in a long white linen gown and a mask—he's a eunuch, see—and he blesses me and anoints me all over with some kind of glittery gunk and from the altar he picks up a foot-long tapered knife that gleams in the sun and he hands it to me and I lift it way above my head, tip up, and give a really fierce scream—at which point all the men lining the street tear off their loincloths and rush up the steps of the pyramid, eyes fixed on my perfect, glistening body. And as they file by one by one, I give a short but still very fierce scream and then slice their stiffs off with a single stroke that sends them away howling and clutching their terrible wounds."

She does seem to have a problem. "And what do you do," I ask after a seemly pause for reflection, "with all their severed things?"

"*Do* with them?"

"I mean do you save them for dildos or give them to the priest to play with—or what?"

"Christ, I don't know. I'm not *that* sick."

"I'm glad," I say, and shove the rest of my drink at her and signal the waiter for another. "Well, we can't have you running around the countryside unmanning the entire *Playboy* subscription list. I suggest you have a long, frank talk with your family clergyman."

"My father is my family clergyman and he is a not-to-be-believed drag."

"Because your mother unmanned him—"

"Yes."

"And you have never forgiven your father for letting her do it to him."

"Yes, yes."

"So you want to take your revenge on the entire male population."

"Bull's-eye."

I lean back in my chair and clasp my hands behind my head. Then I look at her commiseratingly. "You have a lot stored up inside you—"

"Yes—oh, yes."

"And you can contain it no longer."

"You are a brilliant man, whoever you are."

"Yes, well, I would say the *Playboy* gig will do wonders for chasing out those demons. And if you feel uneasy about the money, give me half of it as a token of gratitude for my excellent counsel."

"Take me." Her voice has a fierce imperative timbre to it that summons my corked groin to activity.

"Take you where?"

"Take me anywhere"—her hand is on my knee—"and give it to me good."

Not entirely spiritual, that hand, that voice, that Playmate chest. It is all so unlikely that I do not doubt her for a moment. Lust rages in my glands, boils in my enzymes, ignites in my blood. But how do I know she won't, at the crucial moment, produce that great glittery knife and slice off my member? Or, like Muffie Miller, hit me for a payoff just before delivering the goods?

"*I'll* pay *you*," she says, as if reading my mind. "Not much, but something."

It is a supreme temptation. My bed is empty and beckoning. My evening's plans can be postponed twenty-four hours. My throat con-

stricts as is its habit at palpitant moments. There is a rightness in
the casual form of our encounter: two total strangers who can fill
each other's momentary psychic and chemical needs, no questions
asked. I must just take her home—now, without a moment's delay.

"No. I cannot be your stud tonight."

She frowns. "But why? Aren't I attractive? Or is it my aggressive-
ness?"

"No, you're just fine."

"Then what is it? You're married? I'll die if you're married!"

"I told you at the beginning—I'm gay."

"The hell you are."

"I know I don't sound it or look it, but I am—in a very masculine
sort of way."

"Oh, come off it."

I take some of my drink. It strangely strengthens my fading resolve. "All right—I'll tell you the truth." I look at her eyes. They are
already beginning to rove past me. "I'm a robber and I've got a job
to pull tonight."

"Oh, for chrissakes!"

"And I need all my fifty million spermatozoa to pull a job."

She gives a little groan of despair and turns away from me toward
the sudden commotion around the door. A wedge of bodies enters
and moves toward the bar. In the middle is a stocky fellow with a
smiling head, short-cropped and graying a little, turning this way
and that as it bellows warm greetings to admiring hands that wave
at it from every corner. His entourage stops for a quick drink and
then burrows its way to a booth next to the piano that Shag has
stopped playing. Shag clears the booth for them—actually throws
out the people who were in it—and gives the ringleader a solid
thump on the back.

"Who's that?" I ask my girl friend, who had joined in the general
arm-waving at the newcomer.

"Daryl Divot," she said. "Isn't he adorable?"

"Daryl Divot, the columnist?"

"The column isn't the half of it. It's *him* that's so special. He knows every actor, playwright, novelist, editor, athlete, saloonkeeper, politician, gangster, and prostitute in town. He makes every exciting party every night of the week and doesn't quit till four. He drinks enough for five men and never loses his mind. He's writing three books, doing four TV spots, being syndicated in twelve newspapers, lecturing twice a week at Columbia Journalism School, and getting in the pants of three women a night."

"How do you know all that?"

"He got in mine once."

"I thought you didn't go in for that sort of thing."

"I was lying—I'm an actress. And I haven't been a virgin since I was fourteen."

I nod. I am slightly numb from the liquor and therefore not very startled by anything she has said since she sat down, including this last revelation. Still, I am vaguely disappointed: there was a certain engaging element in her implausible story that, like my own, made it seem plausible, especially in a place like this, on an afternoon like this, in a town like this, in a year like this, in a world like this, where everything is calculable and nothing adds up.

"And your father," I say, "he's not really a minister?"

"Oh, he is. And he deflowers virgins." She grabs my drink, the second one she has appropriated, and begins guzzling. "He even did me."

"I don't believe it."

"I didn't either—till I missed my period." She looks sad for a second. "I haven't been home since."

A roar erupts from Divot's sector. They are all laughing and talking and drinking and smoking, and it looks as if no one is listening to anyone else. The din they raise is infectious, and soon the whole place is uproariously buoyant and wanting to know what they're saying at Divot's table. My exquisitely chested girl friend has peeled her jacket off entirely and is heading over that way. I watch her grind her way through the crowd till she is hovering on the edge of the action and, after a moment of maneuvering, is engulfed by it. All the *glamorosi* and would-be *glamorosi* in the place are drawn toward Divot like filings to a magnet. He has it all—ceaseless excitement, far-flung fame, entrée to chambers that wealth cannot buy, friends beyond count, allies in high councils, the power to say who shall flourish and who shall flounder, and a front-row seat on the whole frantic cavalcade. Naturally, I hate him. I hate him because he has talent and looks and extra testosterone glands, and I do not. Because he is propelled at an all-day, all-night, death-defying pace that divides the quick from the zombies, and I am a zombie. And then I remember that all that is about to be changed in only hours now, and I am less angry at Daryl Divot, for he embodies my heart's every desire. And when Shag pokes through the crowd and points directly at me, I am surprised and pleased because I did not think he knew I was there. He waves insistently for me to join them, and I go.

He tells me who is there. There is Sheila, the lady wrestler turned writer who recently got raves on her first novel. There is Wilkie, whose smash-hit Broadway comedy has just been bought by Hollywood for well up in six figures. There is George, the season's hottest society pianist and the Newport sailing crowd's favorite to star on the next America's Cup crew. There is Roland, the Mayor's new executive assistant and top speech writer. There is Jo-Jo, the star pro quarterback with the trick elbow and incurable habit of passing twice a game to an enemy safety man. And hanging on the fringes are assorted talentless straight men and long-lashed, heavy-boobed candidates for the show-business meat chopper like my minister's daughter, who turns out to be called Oriole Odell.

Sheila is playing Jazz Trivia with Roland, who is trying to remember who blew alto on Duke's original "A Train." "I can hear it,"

Roland says, "I can *hear* it." And he raps his fist against his temple in mock anguish.

Wilkie is telling George how Peter Pomerance, thirty-one-year-old critic, poet, and editor of the determinedly highbrow *New Angst Review*, which runs more Scotch ads than any other ethnocentric monthly in the world, has just written his autobiography. "You're *nobody* if you haven't published your autobiography before you're thirty-five."

Daryl Divot is telling Jo-Jo that he goddam well should get better pass protection or demand to be traded. "You are not a scrambling quarterback," he says, "and if they make you rush the bomb ten times a game, you are going to have two or three picked off on you every time out." Jo-Jo, eyeing Oriole Odell's heaving forward wall, agrees.

Shag, ignoring the tumult, asks me how everything is going, and I tell him tonight is the night. He is delighted and at once orders a good-luck magnum of champagne for the table. I suggest that perhaps such showiness is a trifle indiscreet, but he waves me aside and oversees the placement of the champagne glasses. Somebody asks what the occasion is and Shag tinkles for attention.

"This is my old friend Fritz Fetlock," he says, poking a finger in my sternum, "and we are celebrating his début tonight as a big-time criminal."

I feel my eyes close and my neck heat up. I do not understand what he is up to. Shag is well known to be eccentric and unpredictable but I would not have thought he would violate a serious confidence in quite so public a way.

"What sort of criminal is he?" Sheila asks Shag.

"None yet," Shag says. "He's just beginning."

"Beginning at what?"

"Don't tell us," Wilkie says. "Let's guess."

"He's an apprentice arsonist," Sheila says, "and he's going to burn down Lincoln Center—and I will help him."

"That's wrong," says Shag. "One down, nine to go."

"He's a counterfeiter," says Roland, "and he's passing out a million dollars' worth of plastic quarters which are slightly heavier than the new government ones."

"That's wrong," says Shag. "Two down, eight to go."

"He's an Albanian spy," says Sheila, "and he's stealing the *Spirit of St. Louis* from the Smithsonian Institution at 4 A.M. with the help of Francis Gary Powers."

"Wrong," says Shag. "Seven to go."

"He's a rapist," says Jo-Jo, "and he's giving it to a blind lady newsdealer in Washington Heights."

"He is not a rapist," Oriole Odell puts in from the sidelines, and all heads turn to her quizzically for a moment.

"We give up," says George. "What are you about to become?"

I turn to Shag. My face must be scarlet. What the hell are you doing to me, my eyes radio him.

"Fritz," he says, oblivious to my signal, "is launching his life of crime as a robber."

"Ohhhh," says Sheila, her tone tripping down the scale, *"très ordinaire."*

"Not at all," Shag runs on. "He's giving up a perfectly good, conventional life as a master glass blower to make the plunge."

"What's he robbing?" Roland asks. "Chase Manhattan or a gumball machine?"

"I don't know," Shag says, and looks at me. "Do you want to tell everybody, Fritzie?"

The craziness of the thing begins to hit me. He is blurting out my darkest secret—disclosing an event that, within hours, will utterly alter the structure of my life—and he is doing it as matter-of-factly as if he were introducing the day's line-up of attendant curiosities at his cabaret, as if my act will be followed by a one-armed juggler who keeps a dozen bowling balls in the air and a one-eyed archer who, for openers, will bag a fly on an apple on top of the bartender's head.

I say, "Why doesn't the whole crowd just come along with me and be surprised?"

"Terrific," says Wilkie. "I'll call Andy and the crowd and tell them to bring buckets of silver paint to douse the victim."

"I'll call the Mayor," says Roland. "He loves to take an active role in the teeming life of our dynamic city."

"I'll call the city desk," says Daryl Divot, coming to life now. "Suicides, abortions, and electrocutions I've covered, but never a live robbery." He zeros in on me as if I were suddenly a somebody. "Or would that be cramping your style, tiger?"

"How can he have a style?" Sheila asks. "He hasn't ever done it before."

"It's a joke," George says. "He's no more a robber than I am."

"Joke," Roland says.

"Joke," Wilkie echoes.

They all look at Shag, who has just invented me for their instant amusement. Shag looks at me. The alarm my eyes had flashed him is gone. I am all inscrutable. He pauses a second to gauge me. Then he pops the cork and says, "Hell, no. It's no joke. Fritzie's pulling his first caper tonight." And he begins pouring the champagne, as much on the table as in the glasses.

" 'Sthat right?" Divot asks me.

"It's his champagne," I say cryptically.

Divot takes out a pressed handkerchief and wraps it around my glass. "Roland's not to be trusted. He'll go running with your finger-prints to the Police Commissioner."

I thank him. Then I say quietly, "You can come along if you like, but actually I think it might be dangerous."

"You're right. I'll just interview you here—and then maybe we'll do a follow-up tomorrow in jail."

"Oh, I'm not going to jail."

"How can you tell?"

"Because I will be an excellent robber."

"But you're untested."

"So was Columbus."

He smiles. It's his kind of material. He takes out a ball-point pen and starts taking notes on a cloth napkin. "Why are you turning to a life of crime?"

"Because I feel it will be very rewarding. It's exciting work—and the pay is good for the technically proficient—and there is a great deal of room for individual initiative if the government does not intrude in yet another field historically reserved for the private sector of the economy."

He nods. It is good copy, what I'm giving him. His wheels are spinning. "But what makes a family man give up security—"

"Who said I'm a family man?"

"Well, I assume—from what Shag said—"

"Good reporters don't assume. They ask. That's what Jimmy Stewart said in *Call Northside 777*. Or didn't you see that?"

Divot smiles. "I quit after *Citizen Kane*."

"What did it say on the sled?"

"What sled?"

"The sled they find in the junk heap at the end of *Citizen Kane*."

"I don't remember."

"It was the key to the movie."

"So sue me." He has stopped smiling.

"You should know that."

"Why?"

"It's part of the folklore of our times."

"You're full of shit."

"You're overcompensating."

"You want to be interviewed or not?"

"Interviews are pseudo-events."

"What does that mean?"

"It means they are contrived to fill all those endless blank columns in the daily newspapers."

"You are rapidly developing into a pain in the ass."

"You are losing your cool, oh famous columnist."

He tosses the napkin aside in pique. "Let's skip it."

"Actually, I *am* a family man."

"No," he says, turning aside, "we're all done. You've had the schnitzel, Fritzie."

"Speaking of family men, Divot, I hear you cop a lot of ass."

His head swings back. "Where'd you hear that?"

"From an unimpeachable source."

"I'm a happily married man."

"Then you shouldn't cheat on your wife."

He is angry now, but he is trying manfully to control himself. "Look, buster, what's eating you?"

"Nothing." I cannot resist. "Who's eating you?"

I see his teeth clench. "In ten seconds," he says very slowly, "I am going to push your face down your throat."

"No, you're not."

"I'm counting."

"Don't you even want to know what it says on the sled?"

His fist rams my jaw and knocks me out of the booth. There are no other blows. I am lying on the floor. I see their feet. I think they are about to kick me, fast and hard and all together. But nothing happens. They are just drinking my champagne and talking. I hear their voices.

"Offhand, I'd say he should stick to glass blowing," says one of the girls.

I stay down there for a while. Nobody helps me.

"His recuperative powers seem a little on the sluggish side," says one of the men.

I struggle to my feet and brush myself off with great dignity. They are all watching. I straighten my tie. Then I look at Divot. "My best to Mrs. Divot."

He jumps up. "I'm gonna have you killed," he says in a low, even voice. "Dead." He levels a finger at me. "You ever bug me again, boy, I'll open your belly with a blade."

"Rosebud," I say.

"What?"

"That's what it says on the sled in *Citizen Kane*—Rosebud."

He lunges across the table at me. I step back. He loses balance, crashes onto the tabletop, sends the glasses flying, and sustains a nasty cut on the chin.

Shag sees me to the door. "Good show," he says.

My jaw is hurting now. "What was with the champagne action?" I ask him painfully.

"I thought you'd like a big send-off."

"But now they all know."

"What do they know? They didn't believe a word of it. You heard them. It was a gag. But what's the point of doing it if the world isn't told? You don't want to go skulking around dark alleys like any old robber—you want to be notorious, right?"

"I also don't want to get caught."

"Now don't start going up-tight, dad." He pats my backside. "Stay loose."

It is beginning to snow. Dimly I hear Shag's piano start up again and then fade behind me.

19

The Deep End

HEAD CLEARING, I MAKE MY WAY UP MADISON AVENUE THROUGH a light, cheering snow.

What I see in the windows of the endless small swank shops adds to the gaiety rising in me now even as the liquor's grip is loosening. I adore everything I see and want terribly to have it, to stack it all up in room after room of a town house I will buy and use solely to store the collected artifacts of my age. The silver sequined dress in the window of the latest far-out boutique seems to shimmy as the rotating colored floodlight plays over it; it is sinuous and pagan and blatant, and I love it fiercely. It ends about four or five inches above the knee. All the skirts are like that now, showing all those sinuous and pagan and blatant legs on all the marvelous girls who are loving showing what they have, and I, even celibate, am loving seeing it. I turn and watch every set of passing legs. How I yearn to run my hand down the backs of all those exposed thighs and seize their calves firmly and squeeze them hard and long. But I dare permit myself no lusty fantasies and so sail on uptown.

Rich people in evening clothes are being picked up by a charcoal-brown limousine in front of the Carlyle as I pass. For one impulsive moment I want to push in there beside them, to squeeze the women's calves and snitch the men's plump billfolds while we all laugh and pass around a flask and sing dirty college songs on the ride to Darien or Cold Spring Harbor or wherever we are going. But I am bent on another mission.

I cross to the other side of the street at Seventy-ninth and pause before the Carlebach Gallery, transfixed by the chess set on display. It has six-inch-high, intricately carved pieces of what I take to be jade and lapis lazuli in starting position on a board of inlaid ivory and onyx, and cannot, I am sure, cost less than twenty-five thousand dollars. It is a feat of superb and unconscionably conspicuous craftsmanship, rendered long ago for some prince of Tuscany or Levantine despot and available now to any passerby of infinite means and no hesitation about squandering them. It will be among the very first purchases I will make with the ill-gotten proceeds of my impending crime. It will be, purely and simply, a gesture of outrageous indulgence, and I mean to make it, for if I do not, I will be confessing that there can be no such thing for civilized man as a step taken without reference to its moral implications and that therefore no man can be both truly liberated and truly moral at the same time.

I swing west toward Central Park. Nearing Fifth Avenue, I see the twin towers of my apartment house thrusting way above the adjacent skyline on the far side of the park. The orange lights on the tips of its towers glow invitingly. I cross Fifth Avenue and make my way into the park heading toward the reservoir. There are few other people in the park this late. I would not normally ever walk across it except in full daylight. Yet now I feel immune to danger because I am changing, this very minute, from defender to offender, from potential victim to imminent perpetrator—in short, from being fearful to fearsome. It is exhilarating, this dark throb of menace I now bear within me.

I am ready—in the name of liberation, in the name of retribution, in the name of catharsis, in the name of Dionysus and a thousand other gods long since banished from the pantheon of men's permitted idols—in all those names, I am ready now to stop absorbing and to start inflicting.

I could try, a final time, as I move more briskly, through the deepening dark here at the dead center of the park, to *explain* to you what is inexplicable. I could try to *justify* what is unjustifiable, and that would be even more tedious, for it is a basic miscalculation of our age, a basic narcotic that humanism has been avidly dispensing for some centuries now, to think that the rest of mankind gives a good flying fuck about our justifications, yours and mine, for how we pee our lives away. Just do it, whatever you are doing, however you are doing it, for whatever reasons you may have, and shut up about it. No one else cares—no one *really* cares—unless you are perhaps a saint or a genius or an exquisitely gifted charlatan. Do it and do not worry what the world thinks of you, because almost certainly it does not think of you at all. And so, being neither saint nor genius nor charlatan of the first rank, I am doing it. I am going ahead without further tedious justifications that you would not, in any event, accept. I spend a large part of my final hour of preparation in the shower. It is a fine, old-fashioned sort of shower. It has six nozzles set in the side walls, two each at shoulder, navel, and crotch levels, which are stimulating me horizontally while the overhead valve, its openings tightened to pinheads, is tingling my scalp to ecstasy. The bottom of the stall is filling up faster than the drain can carry it all away, and soon I am ankle-deep in it. I am being impinged upon top and bottom, front and back, left side and right. I pretend that it is fetal liquid I am floating in. My eyes are shut tight and I am suspended in a state of shapelessness and placelessness and timelessness—a spell, an equilibrium I dare not jar by moving. Dimly I am aware that I shall drown if I do not retain a sense of where I am. But don't I want to drown, to let go, to abandon this madness that has seized me and is propelling me toward perversions so unthinkable just a little while ago? Don't I want to relapse to that flexless life I have with such bravado resolved to quit—and in relapsing, drown? I am bored by the questions. I can no longer cope with questions. I cannot bear the prospect of constructing labored and coherent answers. I am riding the crest of a wave I cannot, I will not, fathom. I have entered a state neither natural nor unnatural but supranatural—beyond all conventional categories of deportment, beyond all redeeming rites of passage or prostration.

I turn off the shower. A jet of cold blows up my tail. But it does not dispel the heady looping aerial sensation that wafts me, as if I have been steadily inhaling pure oxygen for an hour. My mind is radiantly clear and deliciously uncluttered. I am in total command of all my extremities. I towel down, and up, and sing loud.

The phone rings, and I plummet. I will wrench the cord out of the wall. But I must answer, must to prove that I remain very much corporeal while sustaining this erection of the soul, this parabolic thrust even now approaching its apex.

It is Anne.

"Where were you? I've called three times."

"I—I—"

"Where have you been? Didn't you remember I was going to call?"

"You're hysterical."

"Who wouldn't be? Where on earth have you been?"

"I've been laying my secretary on a park bench."

"Very funny. Very damn funny."

"How's the winter wonderland?"

"Terrible, if you want to know. When are you coming up?"

"Monday, I guess. What's wrong with it?"

"Monday! I thought Saturday."

"I have to finish some things."

"What things?"

"What's wrong with the place?"

"Oh, nothing—I'm just dying, that's all."

"From what?"

"From playing Wonder Woman. What do you think I do all day—drink toddies by the fireplace? I'm out with the kids from dawn till I drop. And even that's not enough for them."

"It's good for you."

"Oh, absolutely marvelous—especially when I took Beth skating and fell directly on my pelvis. And when I took Andy in a skimobile and practically turned the thing over. And when I took them both in a toboggan and crashed into a tree."

"Why don't you stick to toddies by the fireplace and let them build a snowman outside the window?"

"Very funny. When are you coming? Why aren't you coming Saturday? What are you doing down there? Don't you love me?" She is still for a second. "Save me!"

There is poignancy in her voice. It is pitiable enough in its un-varnished appeal—deep enough in its guileless pull—to wrench me from my soaring course and bring me back to earth, to her, to what

we share, to decorum, to my senses, to a life of sighs and unfulfill-
able gestures, to an existence bereft of drama, of exhilarating pin-
nacles, of sustained—sustained anything. But I cannot, I will not, allow
it. I tell her to pull herself together. I tell her not to fall on her pelvis
any more. I tell her to keep the hell away from the skimobiles and
toboggans. I tell her I am coming in just a few days and not to panic
in the interim.

"I love you," she whispers at the end.

And that is the most maddening, most intimidating, most excruciating thing of all. She loves me. I love her. Beauty is truth, truth
beauty. Yes, love. Yes, truth. Yes, beauty. But it is not enough, and
never has been. Tranquility is the deadliest of sins, stasis the most
pernicious sickness. My life is so blessedly, blissfully tolerable that
I cannot bear it. Anne McNally Kwait, you have given me no more
reason to go off the deep end now than you ever gave me to be un-
faithful. It has nothing to do with you, Anne—don't you see that
finally? Won't you try to see? It has to do with life, *my* life, the briefness of it, the unbearable briefness, the intolerable knowing that it
will be over before there has been any living, any growing, any peril,
any triumph. It is careering by, and I reach out after the whirlwind
and catch hold of nothing, because I am afraid to catch hold for
fear of not knowing where it will take me and what I will find. But
now you are away from me, there on the other end of the phone,
upstate and away, and I am breathing freely and openly and deeply.
It is all unfurling for me, all unfolding, all unraveled, and I am beginning to sense joy in this impending overflow of life.

"I love you always, Anne." Kiss kiss.

I love you, Anne Kwait, I love you. I *adore* you. I *cherish* you.
Wherever you are and wherever I am. But that, my adorable cher-
ished pelvis-bruised ceaselessly loved and loving wife of my life—
that is not the end of it. Not for me. No longer.

I climb into khaki pants, tennis sneakers, an old gray sweat shirt, and
a blue wool-lined canvas jacket with snap buttons. I load my guns (I

had picked up a second, toy one at the five-and-ten to supplement my arsenal). I stuff the three pairs of handcuffs, a pillowcase, and the heavy shears into my coat pockets. I put on my pirate mask. The clock strikes ten. I go to our back door, the service entrance, and unlatch it. I peek out. No one is there. I go out into the poorly lit gray-painted hall. My tread is light. I dart up the back stairway. Two flights. My heart should be pounding, but I am not aware of it because all of me is pounding. Fiercely pounding. I pause at the landing door. There is no prayer to make, and no one to make it to. There is only—NOW.

20

The Robber

LEONARD LIFELINE, AGED FIFTY-SIX, IS SITTING IN A LARGE UP-holstered chair drawn up to the teak trestle-based dining-room table in his $475-a-month (utilities included) apartment. He can afford to pay ten or, say, twenty times that much rent. He can afford to maintain a large mildewed château in, say, Gascony. Or a very long yacht called the *Briny Spume* with a year-round crew of, say, six. Or a racing stable in Kentucky with, say, fifty thoroughbreds and a silk pennant in colors of his choice (gold and aquamarine would have been his choice, since the lobbies of all his buildings are in those) snapping smartly from a pole on the stable roof. Or, conceivably, all these things. But he has chosen to lavish his fortune on none of these emblems of self-indulged wealth. Instead, he has spent freely, often excessively, in accumulating—and promptly dispersing—a superb, if notably eclectic, collection of paintings.

Almost all the paintings that Leonard Lifeline has bought hang in museums and other institutions throughout the world. Each one of them bears a small copper plate on the bottom that says, in black scroll lettering that their donor insists on, "A Gift of Mr. and Mrs. Leonard Lifeline, New York." Which, by Leonard Lifeline's lights, is class. Authentic class. For the paintings, if he himself is any judge, will outlast all the buildings he has erected over the years—structures meant to be serviceable, not commemorative; lucrative, not philanthropic. He does not, he has readily confessed to friends, know a great deal about art. "All I know," he is fond of saying, "is what I like." To other, closer friends, he has added that any painter whose paintings cost a lot of money—say, twenty thousand dollars or so a throw—must be good or why would anyone pay that much for them? And Leonard Lifeline almost never buys a painting—certainly not these days—that costs less than twenty thousand.

At this very moment, sitting at his dining-room table, which has been cleared for some time now of the dinner dishes, Leonard Lifeline is sifting through the loose-leaf book in which he lists all the paintings he has ever bought, the prices paid for them, and the museums, universities, hospitals, libraries, churches, synagogues, and YMCAs in which they are currently hanging. Counting the big Chagall and the little Klee watercolor he bought the weekend previous, the Lifeline Collection, if it were ever collected, would number two hundred and fifty-four. The total price of the purchases has now mounted to $3,868,700. All but a dozen of these superb paintings have either been given away for good or lent as promised gifts (the latter procedure allowing the donor to benefit, in calculating his income tax, from the inevitable rise in the appraisal value between the date the painting is placed on loan and the date it is finally and formally handed over to the recipient institution). Of the dozen paintings remaining in his personal possession, three hang on the bottle-green walls of his office—an early Géricault (huge), a 1934 Picasso (medium size), and a vintage Degas (little). He makes a point of looking at them each day for at least a minute (that is, twenty seconds each—but twenty truly contemplative seconds). Any visitor who fails to take fawning note of them on his first visit is likely to be written off as a lowlife and handled with even more contempt than Leonard Lifeline normally dispenses to all comers.

The other nine undonated paintings hang here, in the Lifeline apartment. The new Chagall has the place of honor over the fireplace. It is flanked by a Caravaggio and a Stuart Davis. On the other long living-room wall hang an enormous, slashing Hans Hofmann and a smallish candy cane of a Renoir. In the dining room, a medium-sized weblike Jackson Pollock on the long wall vies with a Frans Hals portrait of a merchant king from Ostend on the short wall. The foyer is graced by a single spotlighted Poussin. And the new little Klee watercolor, for which Lifeline knows he has paid more dearly than he should have, hangs gaily in the guest bathroom. They cost him, these paintings in his home, a total of $665,900, and he is very proud of them—and of himself for having accumulated the money to own them. They have made his home into a veritable museum, and that is nice. That is class. Genuine class, class that châteaux and yachts and throughbreds do not bring. Important people in the art world come to see his paintings. And he receives requests to donate one or another of them no fewer than a dozen times a week. Just now, in fact, he is seriously entertaining a request from the Phoenix Museum for the Hals portrait. He bought it twelve years ago for $37,500. Surely it would go for four or five times that today. But Leonard Lifeline is inordinately fond of the Hals portrait; indeed he has identified closely with it these dozen years. Were he to donate it, he thinks, he would commission someone of the first rank—Wyeth, say, or (since he is becoming more daring in his taste) even Warhol—to paint *his* portrait. Neither, probably, is undertaking commissions these days, but Leonard Lifeline is prepared to pay them handsomely.

While Leonard Lifeline is surveying his riches at the dining-room table, his wife, Cynthia, is spread across the entire length of one of the matched purple sofas that face each other before the living-room fire-place. Cynthia Lifeline is wearing a pair of orange and green lounging pajamas and reading a book. Actually, she is reading two books. She always reads two books at a time. She feels she is accomplishing more that way. Certainly it is more of a challenge to keep track of two plots and sets of characters at the same time.

At the moment she is reading *The Source* by James Michener and *The Charterhouse of Parma* by Stendhal. For a while she thought that *The Charterhouse of Parma* was the superior book but then she noticed a brief introductory comment advising that Stendhal wrote it in only seven weeks; *The Source,* she reflected, must have taken at least two years—probably more. But what, she decided, was the point of comparing two such different books? Each was very good in its way, and that was what mattered. Wasn't that exactly what Leonard said of the paintings he bought? And Leonard was a man of some cultivation. True, some people, they had heard, said he was a phi-listine who scurried around buying indiscriminately. They said that because, first, he bought such different kinds of paintings from so many different periods ("I am very wide-ranging in my taste," Leonard had told more than one interviewer from the art magazines, "and I don't see a blessed thing wrong with that"), and because, second, they were jealous. Well, they could all go shit in a hat, Leonard and she had decided, and they went right on buying and giving away absolutely marvelous paintings, keeping an occasional one for their private delight.

This, then, is the putative scene of domestic tranquility in the apartment of the Leonard Lifelines: Leonard savoring his riches in the dining room, Cynthia alternating between two famous novels on a living-room sofa. And Mirabel, their large and toothless black Ven-ezuelan housekeeper, is locked away in the maid's room in front of a television tube twenty-one inches wide which produces images of low fidelity and sounds of alarming amplification. The time, accord-ing to the clock on the kitchen stove, is 10:03 P.M.

Suddenly, jarringly, the back doorbell rings.

Cynthia Lifeline, in the living room, does not hear the ring at all. Mirabel, in the maid's room, a scant dozen feet from the back door, is so absorbed with the yammering television set that she does not hear the ring, either. Leonard Lifeline hears it through the closed kitchen door, but only dimly—so dimly that at first he thinks he is mistaken. At any rate, Mirabel is closer and will attend to it if she is awake. He returns to his reverie.

It rings again, unmistakably and unwelcomely insistent.

Odd, thinks Lifeline, someone at the back door this time of night. He listens to hear if Mirabel is stirring. There is no detectable movement—only the dull, far-off murmur of the television set. He gets up, more curious than annoyed. He pushes through the swinging door to the pantry and supposes it is a neighbor in distress. Briefly he considers the likelihood of there being a robber on the other side of the door. But the service elevator shuts down at five every afternoon. And the back stairway ends in the lobby, not the basement, and there are never less than half a dozen doormen and elevator men on duty in the lobby. This, moreover, is the fifteenth floor and what robber would climb fourteen flights—especially without a promising means of escape at his disposal? No, it is too remote a possibility to merit serious consideration. Still, he vaguely wishes he had heeded the advice of the insurance company, which has been pointing out for several years now the folly of his having installed the intricate and costly alarm system sprung to go off the instant any of the paintings is lifted so much as a fraction off its moorings without his having then taken the additional precaution of putting a peephole and a chain lock on the rear door like those on the front door. He has been meaning to do it all along. Indeed he had asked Cynthia to attend to it as soon as it was first suggested, and she had said she would. But at that moment she had been deeply involved with *Don Quixote* by Miguel de Cervantes and *The Prize* by Irving Wallace, both of which she was enjoying inordinately, and so she promptly forgot about it. On his occasional trips to the kitchen, he would notice that she had not taken care of the door yet, and he would say, "Will you have the chain lock and peephole installed on the back door, please, darling, or am I going to have to close down all your charge accounts and kick you in the head?" And she would laugh lustily and promise to do it the next morning. But by then, of course, she would be immersed in the new Herman Wouk novel or John O'Hara's latest collection of short stories, along with one or another volumes of *Remembrance of Things Past* by Marcel Proust, or *The Golden Bowl* by Henry James —she did so love to combine reading old books and new books like that—and so she would always forget. And so would Leonard until the next time he threatened to do her violence for failing to attend to the matter.

He is standing right beside that door now when its bell rings a third time. Heard that close, it sounds undeniably imperative. "Who is it, please?"

A terrible rasping sound comes from the other side of the door, as of a thoroughly clogged throat being cleared.

"Who is it?"

Murkily a voice answers, "The night handyman."

"The who?"

"Night handyman—leak downstairs—have to check—sorry to bother—"

Vague, gravelly, unconvincing voice. If there were a peephole on the door, Leonard Lifeline would surely be peeping through it now. And if there were a chain lock, he would almost certainly not have undone it before opening the door a fraction to confirm his late caller's claim. It would have been normal prudence. But there is no peephole, and there is no chain. And Leonard Lifeline has already made the judgment that no one up to mischief would intrude at this time of night, at this altitude, in this building. Besides, robbers do not rob homes when people are likely to be in them—that is well known. And so Leonard Lifeline twists the lock and throws open the door.

It is hard to say who of the two is more stricken by the confrontation—Leonard Lifeline, gaping at the hideously demonic pirate face and the needle-nosed gun, or the intruder, presented point-blank with the round, corrupt, and vulnerable countenance of his very first victim. Both quell an exploding impulse to pivot and, shrieking at the top of their lungs, fly from each other at full throttle. The intruder, the panic on his face hidden from the victim, stifles it first by a decisive moment and drives a leg across the threshold before the other recoils enough to slam the door on him. He shoves his terrible-looking weapon in the puffy and still-thunderstruck face of Leonard Lifeline and growls, with no effort to mimic the denizens of the underworld, "Open your mouth and you're a dead man."

Lifeline backs two small steps. The vandal flashes through the door and brushes it closed behind him with his gunless hand.

"You're—crazy—mister," Lifeline whispers, eyes like fried eggs.

"All the worse for you, then."

"You'll—never—get away with this!"

"They've never caught me yet."

"There's—no way—out of the building. They'll see you."

"They didn't see me come in and they won't see me go out."

"But how?"

"I'm a human fly. I walked up the side of the building." He takes half a step forward and pokes the horrid needle of his gun into Leonard Lifeline's sagging chest. "Now shut your face, mister, and listen to me."

Leonard Lifeline's jaw hangs slack. The starkness of the moment has penetrated. There, inches from him, masked and armed and threatening death, is a robber. He has never seen a robber before— not an official robber. But instead of terror, he feels something strangely close to relief at his sense of helplessness. The robber, bristling at him behind his dreadful hairy mask, is in command—and it has been many years since Leonard Lifeline has found himself in a situation he did not command. He has almost forgotten the sensation.

"You play ball with me," says the robber, "and nobody gets hurt, see? But you just try any cute stuff"—he wags the gun so that its needle nearly brushes the extra flap of flesh below Lifeline's quivering chin—"and zap! you get it in the neck. You read me?"

Lifeline nods.

"I am wanted for murder in twelve states, mister, so don't press me."

Lifeline nods.

"I slit the last guy's belly open and hung his guts out the window like a string of sausages." And he gives a little snort. "Okay, now who else is home?"

"My—wife is in the living room, and"—he gestures toward the heavy murmur of the television set behind the door at the far end of the kitchen—"the maid's in there."

"Okay, get over there against the stove."

Lifeline gets.

The robber pulls a pair of sheers from his pocket and lays his needle-nosed gun on the kitchen counter, its business end aimed at the abject victim. A second is visible tucked inside his belt. "One move, mister, and you're a goner." With one cotton-gloved hand, he picks up the wire to the telephone sitting on the edge of the kitchen counter and, with his other hand, shears it in two. "Now let's visit the missus."

Lifeline is frozen in place.

"March, mister!"

Lifeline marches—gallops almost. Through the swinging door to the dining room, past it to the foyer, and under the open archway to the living room.

Cynthia Lifeline, reclining voluptuously on cushions of purple silk, looks up and gives a little cry of terror. Her books slide off her lap.

"Don't panic, dear!" Leonard Lifeline tells her.

She jerks herself upright. "But—who is it?"

"He didn't give me his card."

"Is he a—a—?"

"He seems to be."

She peers nearsightedly across the room. "It can't be."

"That's what I thought."

She gives a hard, uncertain laugh. "Oh, come on—both of you!"
And she points a finger at the masked man. "Now, who is it? Oh, I
know—it's Steve Stutz!" She stands up and takes a step toward him.
"Oh, you're adorable in that, Steve—"

"Don't take another step, lady!"

She looks over at her husband and gives a second little snorting
nervous laugh. "He's not for real."

"I'm afraid he is, dear."

"Oh, stop! I see that silly gun. I can tell from here it's a fake."

"I don't think so, dear."

"It's a toy or something."

"I don't think so, dear."

Cynthia stares at the gun again for a long moment, then glances
back at her husband. "Oh, stop it already! Enough's enough! Say it's
a joke. Steve, it is you, isn't it? Or is it Paul Pelikan? Yes, that's who
it is—it's Paul. I can tell Paul's voice anywhere."

"Paul is in Bermuda, dear."

She crosses her arms over her chest. "All right, let's get this
silliness over with."

"This is an air gun," the robber says evenly. "It is mounted with
a syringe. The syringe contains a deadly acid. If you scream or take
one step I don't tell you to, I will shoot you through the heart and
you will die in three seconds."

"Bullshit!" says Cynthia, and bursts into laughter.

"Cynthia!" Her husband takes a step toward her, then remembers
what he is doing and checks himself. "Cynthia, he'll kill you!"

"Leonard, will you please stop it? And you, too," she tells the
robber, "whoever you are."

Leonard Lifeline's head pops back as if delivered a sharp jab on
the chin. "Sweetheart, are you dreaming? Wake up! This is real! This

is our living room and this man is not Steve Stutz or Paul Pelikan. He is a robber with a gun."

"Will you please tell me what kind of robber talks like that?"

Leonard looks over at him for help.

"I'm a Harvard dropout, lady. I tried blackmailing the dean and he didn't like it—okay?"

Cynthia is still for a second, sizing up the intruder. "You're a fake!"

At that the robber reaches out with his free hand and grabs a porcelain plate off of a small end table just inside the open archway. He holds it up like a fragile full moon and says, "Lady, is this worth much?"

She is startled by the gesture but recovers quickly. "Well, no," she says. "Not all that much—it's just delft."

"That's good," says the robber. "Then you won't miss it." And he sends the dish spinning across the room with a sharp backhand flip. It shatters against the fireplace with a musical resonance befitting its hallmark.

Cynthia Lifeline bursts into tears at the small spectacle. "Oh, you didn't have to do that!" She blubbers and collapses onto the sofa.

"All right," the robber says, "the game's over." And he sends a bronze lamp and a crystal ashtray crashing off the end table that a moment ago also held the delft plate. "We'll collect everything right here," he says, dusting off the tabletop, "starting with your wallet." And he aims a finger at Leonard Lifeline. "Okay, cough it up, Charlie."

"Don't you give it to him!" Cynthia suddenly shrills.

Her husband is visibly moved by the unreasonableness of her valor. "Cynthia! Stop being an idiot!"

"Besides," she says, ignoring him, "your wallet's in the bedroom."

Leonard looks at her hard and then at the robber.

"Turn around," the robber orders.

He turns around.

"What's that bump on your ass?"

"My wallet."

"Ohhh!" Cynthia moans. "I thought you had some guts," she yells at him. "He'll turn and run the second you stand up to him!"

"Cynthia, you've been reading too much rotten fiction—"

"Leonard, now you just tell that creature to go fuck himself and see what happens."

Leonard puts his hands on his temples and brings them down in despair along the sides of his face till they meet in a prayerful clasp just below his chin.

"Go ahead, Leonard—tell him!"

Leonard nods several times.

"Now!"

"Okay—go fuck yourself, buddy."

"Not like that! Say it like you mean it, for crissakes!"

"Go fuck yourself, buddy—and I mean it!"

"Good!" his wife says and turns to watch the result.

"Okay, Charlie, you get two points for heroism—now just toss the wallet over."

Lifeline digs into his back pocket.

"Leonard!"

His dilemma—a choice between bravura and survival—is written on his soft spherical face in a bright flush.

"Now, mister!"

"Tell him to come and get it!"

Leonard nods hopelessly. "Come and get it." It is said with the defiance of a tired mouse.

"Oh, Leonard!" his wife groans and buries her face in her hands.

"Come and get it!" he suddenly blurts, startling everyone, including himself.

The robber advances a stride into the room. "If I have to come and get it," he says calmly, "I'm going to pick up that big pewter ashtray on the coffee table and smash you unconscious with it. And then I'm going to ravage your wife, who looks to me as if she's just begging for it. And then I'll take what I came for anyway. So why don't you make it easier for both of us, mister, and just flip the wallet over here?"

Lifeline flips it.

There are seven hundred-dollar bills and a wad of small ones in it. The robber dumps them out onto the table and tosses the wallet back. "And now, mister, you will kindly open the wall safe."

The Lifelines eye each other in silence.

"Now, mister."

Lifeline says nothing.

"There isn't any," Cynthia says.

Lifeline, after a moment's hesitation, chimes in. "Yes, there isn't."

The robber takes another step toward Cynthia Lifeline. "Lady, I think you are making a bad mistake. You are letting yourself be misled by my good manners and extensive vocabulary. The fact is I'm a hardened criminal who turns into a vicious maniac when aroused" —his voice grows noticeably sterner at this point—"and you are beginning to arouse me." He looks over at Lifeline. "You better tell her to button that big fat red gash of a mouth, mister, or you're going to be a widower when I walk out of here."

"Cynthia, shut your face—I'll handle him from now on."

And Lifeline's fiber does seem to stiffen a bit, for when the robber again asks him to open the wall safe, he says, with some conviction this time, "You heard us, mister—we don't have one."

"Then where do you keep your big money and the lady's jewels— in a cookie jar?"

"All my cash is in the wallet."

"And the jewels?"

"She doesn't like jewelry. She's just got her ring and a few smaller things."

"Okay—then we'll start with the ring."

"Give him the ring, Cynthia. It's insured."

"No!"

"Cynthia—this is exactly what the insurance is for!"

"I don't care about the insurance!"

"Cynthia—you're being stupid again."

"He's bluffing, I know it!"

"Take it from her, mister," says the robber.

She recoils as her husband nears. "Cynthia—stop it!"

"It's mine, goddammit! You keep away, you—you—gutless—fairy!"

"Take it from her, mister!"

"She won't give it."

"Make her."

"How?"

"Crack her in the face."

"I—can't do that."

"Try."

He looks at her.

"Leonard!"

He looks harder.

"Leonard—don't you dare!"

"Then give it over!"

"No!"

"Give it, you silly bitch!"

"Never!"

He wallops her in the face.

With instant recoil, she knees him in the groin. He falls moaning on top of her, pinning her in place, and they wrestle over the sofa until they fall off it and onto the rug, her claws flailing at his eyes and crotch, his knees searching for her neck. Finally, by sheer weight, he wins.

"Pull it off her," the robber says.

Lifeline wrenches it off her now flaccid finger.

"Give it here."

From his still-prone position he flips it glittering across the room—an oval of no less than seven spectacular carats—and then rolls off the vanquished Cynthia, who screams, "You ball-less bastard," and begins blubbering out her fury anew.

"Okay, champ," says the robber, "now the safe."

Though secretly grateful to the intruder for having provided him the opportunity to sock that venomous bloodsucking maw of hers, Leonard Lifeline now faces the prospect of his wife's scorn till death do them part. And so to mitigate his complicity, he decides to make some modest show of manliness. When the robber renews his demand to open the wall safe, Leonard Lifeline says, "Look, you bum, I told you—there is none!"

"You're pressing your luck, Charlie."

Lifeline glares at him—or at least it is the semblance of a glare. "Look, I can't open what's not there!"

"Okay, Charlie, we'll play it your way. I'm going to count out loud to three. And when I'm done counting, I'm going to walk over to the fireplace and pick up one of those big jagged slivers from the plate I busted. And if you still tell me there's no safe, I'm going to jab that sliver right into the middle of that big ugly painting over the fireplace. And if you *still* tell me there's no safe, I'm going to start ripping the picture—first one way, then the other—until it's in so many shreds that a brain surgeon couldn't put it back together."

Lifeline looks stunned.

"Good!" comes a caw from the floor. "Good good good good good!"

"ONE," says the robber.

Lifeline's eyes are glazed.

"Rip rip rip," comes a jeer from the floor.

"TWO," says the robber.

Lifeline is paralyzed by indecision.

"Slish slash," mocks the voice on the floor, "down with trash."

"THREE!"

"NO!" Lifeline shrieks.

"YES!" the floor witch counters.

The robber begins walking toward the fireplace.

Lifeline falls on his knees. "I swear it—there is none!"

The robber reaches the fireplace.

"Why don't you believe me—in the name of God?"

The robber bends, keeping an eye fixed on his victims, and picks up the sharpest shard he can find.

"You can't do such a terrible thing!" Lifeline gasps, rolling the whites of his eyes up at the robber.

"Why can't I?"

"Only a barbarian would do such a terrible senseless thing!"

"What makes you think I'm not a barbarian?"

"I—because you don't seem like one."

"I'm a desperate man."

"You don't seem desperate. You seem very calm and—and—professional."

"Thank you. Now would you like to open the wall safe for me?"

Lifeline closes his eyes and throws out his hands, palms up.

The robber lifts the jagged piece of china in the air and half turns slowly toward the painting over the mantel.

"Leonard!" Cynthia screams, scrambling to her knees. "For God's sakes, tell him!"

Lifeline's face, rigid with tension, suddenly sags. "Oh, you big-mouthed bitch!"

"But he was going to do it!"

"He was bluffing, you moron!"

"The hell he was!"

"I told you to butt out, didn't I? I told you I'd handle him, didn't I?"

"But he was going to do it—I swear to you, darling!"

"He was bluffing."

She looks up at the robber. "Tell him you were going to do it."

"Say please, lady."

"Please tell him."

"I was going to do it."

"There, you see?"

Lifeline just shakes his head.

"Okay, Charlie," the robber says, gesturing with his gun, "let's get the show on the road."

Slowly Lifeline climbs to his feet. Disgust is drawn in large gray swatches across his wet face. He materializes limb by limb before the Stuart Davis painting to the left of the fireplace.

"In back of it?" the robber asks.

Lifeline, the corners of his mouth pinched, nods.

"You were lying to me."

Lifeline frowns uncomprehendingly.

"You were lying—you said there was no safe."

"But—you're a robber."

"Two wrongs don't make a right."

Lifeline, having found him till now more reasonable and more agreeable than his wife, is beginning to have second thoughts about the reliability of his tormentor. "What do you want me to do—give you a certificate of commendation?"

"But I said no tricks."

"Look, I didn't exactly invite you in here."

"I said I'd kill you if you played tricks."

"I don't *want* you to rob me—I don't *like* to be robbed."

"Do you want me to kill you? I will if you want me to."

"I don't want you to kill me. I want you to go away and leave me alone."

"I'll go as soon as I get what I came for. Now, you were doing very nicely till you started lying."

Lifeline emits a mighty sigh and says to the wall, "So sue me— I lied to a robber."

"But we had an agreement—no tricks. Didn't we have an agreement? Yes, and you broke it. Do you know what I do to people who break agreements with me?"

"You slit their bellies open and hang their guts out the window like a string of sausages"

"Very good. Now open the safe."

Lifeline hesitates.

"I said open it."

Lifeline still hesitates.

"What's the matter?"

"I'm thinking."

"Stop thinking and start opening—or your thinking days'll be over for good."

Lifeline grips the side of the painting firmly, preparatory to lifting it. But he does not lift it. And he keeps on not lifting it.

"What's the matter—you got a hernia?"

"Not yet."

The robber is still for a moment, puzzling over the noncompliant turn in his victim. Then he understands. "Okay, Charlie—hands off it."

Lifeline is visibly relieved.

"Turn off the switch."

"Ohhh," moans the re-emergent Cynthia. "Why did you wait, you *putz?*" she snaps at her husband. "Why didn't you just lift it?"

"Because he would have shot us both."

"He would've turned and run with his fucking tail between his legs."

"He doesn't have a tail. He just has a gun."

"Guns," the robber corrects him.

She turns to the robber. "Wouldn't you have run like hell? I mean if the alarm was really jangling loud?"

"Cynthia, for crissakes! He is a very unstable person. Unstable people do very erratic things."

"Actually," says the robber, "I'm not at all unstable. I'm *very* stable. That's why I became a robber."

"See?" she says to her husband.

"Shall we have him to our next dinner party?" he asks her.

She laughs grimly. "Ha."

"We'll tell all our guests to wear their best jewels."

"Yes, yes," she says, warming to the idea, "and we can split the take with him." She turns to the robber. "Or don't you ever work that way?"

"It's never come up before."

"We'd make everybody come in a mask so you wouldn't feel out of place."

"I'm not against the idea in principle."

"See?" she says again to her husband. "He's a perfectly reasonable person. And so he would've taken off like a bat out of hell if you'd set off the alarm."

"Frankly, ma'am," says the robber, "you're right—"

"See?"

"And so's your husband."

"What do you mean?"

"I mean I would've shot you both and *then* I'd have run like hell." And he motions to her husband to fix the alarm.

Almost smiling, Leonard Lifeline goes over to the fireplace, reaches a hand under its lip, and throws the switch. Then he goes back to the Stuart Davis, lifts it carefully off its hooks, and leans it against the base of the wall. Then he sets to work on the combination. He dials and dials and dials. Nothing happens. He glances over at the robber sheepishly. "Sorry," he says.

The robber motions him back to work. Then he asks Cynthia, "When is the party?"

"What party?"

"The dinner party you're having me to."

"Oh—that."

"Yes, when will it be? I wouldn't want to schedule another job the same night."

"I—haven't really decided."

"It doesn't make much difference, really. If I do have a job planned that night, I'd just excuse myself early—would that be all right?"

"Well—yes, I suppose." She looks over at her husband uncertainly. Lifeline, though, is focused on the safe, which still refuses to open. He turns back to the robber. "Look, I know what you're thinking, but honestly—I'm not getting it."

"Try harder."

Lifeline mops his brow and returns to the task.

"Actually," the robber says to Cynthia, "I think you're kidding about the whole thing."

"No," she says quickly. "Oh, no. I think it's a wonderful idea. My friends would all love to be robbed by the best robber in New York."

"That's all right, ma'am—you don't have to lie to me. I know robbers are socially undesirable. That's why I'm trying to set an example."

"Well, then, you shouldn't have broken my plate."

"I'm sorry about the plate, ma'am, but you were being very uncooperative."

"But I didn't know how much fun this was going to be."

"Oh, I see," says the robber. "Would you like your ring back?"

"Well," she says cautiously, "yes—I think I would."

"Son of a bitch!" Leonard Lifeline screams at the safe. He turns, panicking, to the robber. "I think it's broken—really!"

"You try one more time, then—nice and slowly."

Relieved, Lifeline complies.

"The ring," Cynthia says.

"Yes," the robber says.

"May I have it back?"

"Only if you have me to the party."

"I promise."

"I'll keep it till then."

"Oh." Then she brightens. "But where shall I send the invitation?"

"I could just call you on the telephone in a few days and you could tell me."

"Yes, of course. Do."

"Finally!" cries Lifeline, and the little round door swings open.

"Okay, Charlie, now get away from it."

Lifeline retreats half a dozen steps.

"*All* the way away."

Lifeline joins his wife by the sofa.

The robber walks swiftly to the safe and begins scooping out its contents. Everything is in envelopes—cash, stock certificates, jewelry. Lots and lots of envelopes. He scoops and scoops till it is empty. Then he carts the armful of envelopes across the room to the end table where the wallet and the diamond ring are.

"And now," he says, "we're going to get the maid."

"The maid?" Cynthia Lifeline's voice is suddenly shrill. "Oh, leave her out of it—she doesn't know she's alive. In fact she's not."

"So much the better. March, both of you."

She is large and very black and wearing a lace-ruffled nightie and cap and her eyeballs are spiraling something wild as Cynthia Lifeline leads her out of her cell. "This," says Cynthia, "is Mirabel."

"How do you do, Mirabel?"

Mirabel is not doing very well at all. But she is definitely alive.

"I'm not going to hurt you, Mirabel, so long as you do what I say. Understand?"

"She's from Venezuela."

"Doesn't she understand English?"

"Sometimes." Cynthia turns to her. "*Comprende al—ladrón?*"

"*Sí sí sí sí sí sí.*"

Single file, they march back to the living room, the robber in the rear. He stations the Lifelines at the far end of the room and Mirabel at his end. She sees it all at once—the shattered plate, the knocked-over lamp, the picture off the wall, the safe door open, the pile of valuables on the end table—and begins to shake all over. Her tooth-less mouth flies open and she gives a loud groan, just one, and then is still.

"Mirabel, I want you to go into the lady's room and bring me the rest of her jewelry. *Comprende?*"

Now there seems to be some real question of Mirabel's being alive. The eyes are half closed. The mouth is hanging open. The face is expressionless.

"Jewels—I want them. You get them—now! *Comprende? Pronto!*"

Nothing.

"Or I'll kill you!"

She groans a terrible new groan and looks across the room at her master and mistress.

"He's a bad man," Lifeline says to her. "You'd better do as he says."

"Don't you dare, Mirabel! I forbid it!"

"Oh, now, for crissakes, Cynthia!"

"They're *my* jewels and I forbid it!"

"You're toying with *her* life."

"I'm standing up to this—this fraud—that's what I'm doing. Be-sides, Mirabel doesn't know where my things are."

"They're in Mrs. Lifeline's bottom drawer, over on the right. Now, go get them."

Mirabel gapes, nods, then goes.

Cynthia puts both hands to her mouth to contain the shriek that is about to break from it.

In a moment Mirabel is back, gems spilling out of her great cupped hands as if they are molten. She adds them to the pile on the table beside the robber. He stakes out half the pile of valuables and pushes it to the edge of the table nearest to Mirabel, who is hypnotized by the shimmering cluster. "Take them," he says to her.

She looks at him, not understanding.

"Take them, take them all—and as much of the money as you want. Go pack your bag and put the jewels in it and go—and don't ever come back."

She understands but does not want to.

"Go back to where you came from and sell them and live well and help your family and your friends."

Mirabel does not stir. Until at last the big head begins to move sideways, and the liquid eyes open wide and say they understand the kindness intended but that it cannot be, that they would stalk her black ass to the ends of the earth and when they found it they would whip it to shreds and throw it in jail to rot forever. "No," she whispers. "No no no."

The robber nods, then pulls out two sets of handcuffs from his pockets and shows Mirabel how they work. "Put this one on the *señora*," he says, "and this one on the *señor*."

Numbly she moves to obey. Cynthia, as if grateful for Mirabel's decision, offers no resistance. Leonard Lifeline, though, is beginning to bristle noticeably at the magnitude of the crime being perpetrated against him in his own living room, and waves Mirabel and her cold metal clamp away from him. The robber eyes him warily now lest in a flash of irrationality he should spring across the gap between them and smite the intruder a furious clop in the eye. But Mirabel is stalking Lifeline openly now, as if she were the robber's unabashed accomplice. Again he steps aside.

"I suggest you cooperate with Miss Mirabel," the robber says, "because if I have to do it, I may just catch a vein or two."

Lifeline looks up broodingly. "Why do you have to handcuff us?"

"To humble you, of course."

"Haven't you done enough of that?"

"Enough? Why, Mr. Lifeline—don't you want to go to heaven?"

Leonard Lifeline's face turns tomato. "How do you know my name?"

"How? Why, everyone knows *your* name, Mr. Lifeline. You're a pillar of the *community*, Mr. Lifeline. All those *wonderful* buildings you've built. All those *magnificent* paintings you've donated. What an *exemplary* life you've led, Mr. Lifeline. Why, if I weren't my kind of robber, Mr. Lifeline, I'd give my eyeteeth to be your kind."

"Why, you dirty son of a bitch! What is this—a *personal* robbery?"

"Oh, definitely."

"Who put you up to this?"

"Oh, no one, Mr. Lifeline—I'm naturally depraved. It's just that I have a passionate preference for deserving victims."

"And I'm one?"

"Oh, you're in the highest category."

"Why? Why? Just because I'm fabulously successful? Just because I'm rich beyond most men's wildest dreams?"

"Oh, I'm not a Communist robber, Mr. Lifeline. I'm not begrudging you your success and money."

"Then what are you bitching about?"

"It's how you got them."

" 'How'? What do you mean 'how'?" The circuit of capillaries just beneath the surface of Leonard Lifeline's face is spastic now with rage. "I pulled myself up by my own bootstraps, mister. Nothing was handed to me on a silver platter, mister. I've worked my ass off, mister. Nothing I got wasn't deserved, mister. Why, it's people like me, goddammit, who made this country great—tough, gutsy, far-sighted people like me, who aren't afraid to boot a few behinds if they have to to get the job done, and don't you forget it, you dirty thieving lying smart-assed bum!"

He is panting when he is done.

The robber waits a moment for the rage to subside. Then he says, aiming his gun directly between the other's eyes, "Leonard Lifeline, you are a monument to corruption in our time. You are the very model of the single-minded predator who takes everything from life and gives nothing in return. Your paintings? You think your paintings will exonerate you. You think you can buy forgiveness with a dose or two of charity. But it doesn't work. And that is why I am here —an avenger for that fatted cow out there that you've been milking so long and so hard that its great bursting udder is raw from your grasping hands. And that is why you must think of me as a friend— as an angel of retribution. Because if you add up all the acts of villainy you have committed, all the acts of deceit and duplicity that have gone hand in hand with your mountainous greed, you will see that you have a great deal of soul-scrubbing to do before you may qualify to walk humbly with your God."

"Amen," whispers the co-avenging Mirabel as she snaps the remaining handcuff on Leonard Lifeline's limp wrist.

So there they are, like three linked frankfurters, stubby Mirabel in the middle, a Lifeline dangling on either wrist—the entire unit reduced, for all practical purposes, to immobility.

The robber, total triumph within grasp, directs the trio toward the grand piano in the far corner of the room. Mirabel leads the way like a plucky tugboat. Leonard Lifeline is propelled in her wake. Cynthia lets herself be dragged across the rug.

"For crissakes, Cynthia, get up!" her husband snarls.

"Up yours!" Cynthia snarls back with her last drop of passive resistance.

The robber goes swiftly to them, snaps one handcuff of his remaining pair on Cynthia's free wrist and the other around the nearest piano leg. Then he tests the links that Mirabel has applied. They are on quite firmly, as if she had been expressing her gratitude toward him in the process.

Now the robber pokes a gloved hand in Leonard Lifeline's bloated, beaten face. "From this day on, you will pay Miss Mirabel two hundred and fifty dollars a month, plus room and board. And she will be off all day Thursday in addition to Sunday after breakfast. Is that clear?"

The corners of Lifeline's mouth turn down sourly.

"I said, 'Is that clear?' "

Lifeline nods vaguely.

"And tomorrow morning you are going to sit down and write out a check for ten thousand dollars. And you are going to make it payable to Mirabel's nearest of kin. And you will not declare it as a deductible gift on your tax return, for that would not be an act of pure charity. No, you will simply reduce your net worth by that amount, and I will know if you have done it, because I have colleagues in high places just as you have, Mr. Lifeline, and mine will keep me advised as to how faithfully you stick to our little bargain. Is that clear?"

No answer.

"I can't hear you."

An almost imperceptibly murmured "Yes."

"That's fine," the robber says. Then he strolls to the fireplace. "And now tell me which of your priceless paintings I'm going to steal."

Having complied so readily from the start except for a few token sorties of resistance, Leonard Lifeline is incapable now of summoning the adrenalin necessary to vent his outrage with any conviction. Instead, he loosens a few ineffectual sputters that quickly ebb, then throws his unshackled hand in the air as if to convey the abject quality of his surrender. The next moment, there is further evidence he is persuaded that mankind's judgment of his works and days is in fact being visited upon him in the person of this strangely articulate masked man: Leonard Lifeline, on the brink of losing the merest fraction of the plunder he has so assiduously gathered, is weeping at the prospect.

"Let me put it to you another way," the robber says matter-of-factly. "Which one is worth the most?"

The weeper's tears do not abate. But his wife rallies in the face of his extreme prostration. "That one," she says. "The one he took down for you."

She indicates the Stuart Davis leaning against the wall, its bright and vibrant jigsawed shapes and lapidary hieroglyphics bouncing around the canvas. But this, as has been established in the minds of all present, is no ordinary robber, and so his cultivated eye wanders instead to the large painting with the brilliant lights and somber shadows on the far side of the mantel. He goes to it and reads the small gold tab affixed to the bottom of the frame. "Saint John with a Ram," it says. "Michelangelo Merisi da Caravaggio." A sad-eyed young shepherd leans back against what must have been a chair in the artist's studio, but the chair cannot be seen for the exquisitely rendered drapery of a large russet cloth spread over it. The ram, buttocks to the viewer, nestles close to the boy, who never wavers in his fidelity to the pose. The figures are highlighted in melodramatic contrast with the undefined chocolate-brown background. It looks the way a famous old painting should: expensive. Irreplaceable. Priceless, in fact, is the word that springs to the robber's mind.

"That's a copy," Cynthia blurts.

The robber inspects the delicate web of veinlike cracks that have long since infiltrated the glossy surface.

"All right," she says, "a contemporary forgery."

The robber puts the superb brushwork under even fiercer scrutiny. Then he puts down his gun and takes a handhold on both sides of the heavy rococo frame.

"All right," she says, as if relenting, "I'll tell the truth. It's an almost finished study for a much larger version that's in the Borghese Gallery." She pauses, then adds, "In Rome."

The robber gives it a trial heft. It is heavy but manageable.

"The experts are divided about the one in Rome," Cynthia hurries on, almost desperately. "Some think it's authentic—some think it's by a student of his."

The robber lifts it. Grunt. Off. There. Beautiful. Priceless! He tries hoisting it by the hanging wire on the back. Yes, he can manage it with one arm—and the rest of the booty in his pillowcase with the other. O magnificent haul! O new star in the firmament of the underworld!

"No!" Cynthia screams.

"Nice try, lady."

"You'll ruin it!"

"I'll be careful, lady."

"You idiot! You'll never be able to sell it—the whole art world will know it's stolen."

"I'll put it in mothballs for ten years, lady." He drops his Cap-Chur gun into the pillowcase and throws the pillowcase over his shoulder. He hoists the painting and then turns toward his captives a final time. "In five minutes I will have escaped. In ten minutes I will call the police and tell them what has happened. In twenty minutes you will be rescued. So there is no point, really, in screaming your lungs out the moment I leave. I suggest that, instead, you each reflect soberly on what has happened to you and what steps you will take to purify your lives starting the moment you're set free. See, all the really good robberies benefit the victims at least as much as the robber." He moves off a few steps, then stops at the archway to the living room. "My regards to the insurance company," he says, and gives his head a little farewell bob.

"Hey, you!" Cynthia barks.

The robber glances back. "Yes, duchess?"

More softly, she says, "I'm sorry for you, whoever you are."

"Then we're even."

"No," she says, "you're still way behind."

"Fine," says the robber and turns away again.

"Why do you do it?" Cynthia persists even as he fades into the foyer.

"I'm poor and dumb."

"No—tell me."

"I'm a cop who never took a bribe and got bored from it."

"Stop it! Tell me! What are you disturbed about?"

"People like you."

"We make the world go round."

"Exactly."

"I'll bet it's your sex life—you don't have one, do you?"

"You see right through me, duchess."

"Love—you need love and never had any—isn't that it? I'll bet you're impotent—and you channel it all into—into this sort of thing. Isn't that it?"

"Actually, I'm quite a skilled rapist when I'm not busy robbing."

"No one who's loved would ever be driven to this sort of thing."

The robber halts and turns sharply. "And who loves *you,* duchess? And how's *your* sex life, duchess? When's the last time you were getting it steady, duchess? Ole Lenny, there—up straight now, Lenny, paunch in—old Lenny's probably been giving it to his secretary with the big knockers for the past five years."

"That's a lie! You see—you're a terribly sick man. You can't conceive of a normal love relationship—like Leonard's and mine."

"Yes—I noticed the loving way he walloped you."

"This thing tonight is a totally abnormal situation. It's enough to make anyone say and do things they don't mean. Actually we're very devoted."

"That's swell, lady," says the robber over his shoulder as he hustles out through the dining room. "See you in the funny papers."

"Aren't we, Leonard?"

Leonard is still.

"Aren't we?"

Nothing.

"Leonard!"

Leonard lifts his head slowly.

"Tell him, Leonard!"

"He's right," Leonard says softly.

"Who's right?"

"The robber."

"Right about what?"

"I've been giving it to my secretary for the past five years."

"Just what I thought!" she screams. "You dirty lousy stinking cheating filthy lousy bastard!" And she starts climbing over Mirabel, her claws flying after him. Mirabel deflects her handily and cradles Leonard's tear-streaked face against her vast mothering bosom.

21

Half of Xanadu City

AT TWO IN THE AFTERNOON THE FOLLOWING DAY, I RETURN TO The Bottom of the Barrel, where I am warmly hailed by Shag's retainers for the exemplary aptitude I displayed the night before for taking a punch and falling down. Shag himself is popeyed with joy at the sight of me and, pumping my hand with lavish zeal, says through teeth clenching a cigar, "You got lots more in the *cojones* department than I ever figured."

I take neither inventory nor umbrage but thank him for the esteem implicit in this manliest encomium and follow him to his booth at the rear, where all the newspapers are spread open to the stories of the robbery. The *Daily News* account, headlined "CPW PIRATE HEFTS $400G TREASURE CHEST," is the most extensive, reporting that neighbors summoned police to the Lifeline apartment just after midnight by which time the masked thief, "remarkably well-spoken, according to the victims," had long since vanished, bearing gems valued at $275,000, a seventeenth-century masterpiece by "Carravagio" (*sic*) said to be worth an estimated $100,000, and about $25,000 in cash.

"That's big-time, baby," says Shag, and promptly offers to sell me half of The Bottom of the Barrel. "There's no rush—take about two minutes to decide. If it takes longer, you're not the guy I want in with me."

I do not bat an eyelash. "But why," I ask, "should a big-time robber become a tavern keeper?"

"That's what all big-time robbers become. It's like an annuity when they stop robbing. No self-respecting robber wants to wind up running a toy store or a delicatessen, right?"

There is something very persuasive about Shag Shaughnessy's spontaneity. "Yes," I say, "but how do I know you are not trying to bilk me? If your tavern is doing well, why do you want to sell me half? If it is not doing well, why should I want to buy in?"

Shag signals for two beers. Then he says, "Good, I like your candor—you come right out with it. Those are perfectly fair questions—very astute, very pertinent. Clearly you are a man I will be able to work with in absolute harmony. And that's the only arrangement that makes any sense. Who needs a partner he's going to argue with all day? Who needs a guy who pussyfoots around for an hour before he comes out with what's eating him? Not me, I'll tell you that. Now, what about the name—do you think we should change it? I like to change it every once in a while. It keeps us out of a rut. Besides which it's great fun. We make long lists of new names and poll all the customers. Then we call it what I want to call it. Right now I'm thinking we ought to call it something vaguely psychedelic— nothing blatant, of course, because that would suggest we're just following a fad, which I am against. It just ought to suggest a very bright, sort of shimmering image, you know? Something like, uh, Xanadu City." He pauses to swallow beer. "How's that grab you?"

"My questions," I say.

"What questions?"

"The astute, pertinent ones."

"Right—what about them?"

"You haven't answered them. And my two minutes are nearly up."

"Oh—I thought they were rhetorical."

"Well, not entirely."

"What? You mean you actually think I'd try to get you to buy half of a lemon?"

"I didn't say that. I was just after some particulars."

"But that's petty. It's character that counts in a partnership."

"Granted—but I thought it might be nice to know exactly what I'm being asked to buy."

"Hold it, Smiley. You're not being *asked* to buy. You're being *invited*."

"Sorry."

"As to this 'exactly' business, I can't really help you. What you're buying is a franchise—and most of that is good will. I've never offered to let anyone buy half of that before."

"Why am I the lucky first?"

"Partly because you've got some loose money."

"That's what I figured."

"But that's only part if it. The main thing is it's more laughs when you're in with someone else. I get tired of talking to myself all day."

"I can understand that."

"Then it's all settled."

"But you haven't answered my questions yet."

"They don't matter."

"Why?"

"Because I'm going to blackmail you if you say no."

"You wouldn't do that."

"Try me."

"But that's not a nice thing to do."

"I know. But I'm desperate."

"The place is that much in the hole?"

"Oh, no, the place is fine. It's boredom I'm desperate from."

"Then why don't you sell the place and buy a yacht or something?"

"I have a yacht—or at least a very substantial cabin cruiser."

"So go sail it to Singapore."

"That's a drag. Besides, I crave air pollution."

"How much do you want me to pay?"

"Whatever you think's fair."

"What do you gross?"

"About half what we will when we fix the place up with your dough."

"That's is not responsive to the question."

"Okay, the bar pulls about a hundred and ten thou a year, the kitchen between fifteen and twenty, the juke between six and seven. What's that come to? Say about a hundred twenty-five, a hundred thirty. I take away about twenty a year. If we can jack the gross up to two hundred, the take should be between forty or fifty—plus all the booze you can handle."

I nod. "Okay, I'll pay ten thousand for a half interest."

"I was thinking of about fifty."

"Okay, twenty—provided you keep running the place."

"But you've got to show up every day for at least an hour."

"Sold. And Xanadu City is fine with me."

Delighted, he tosses the rest of his beer in my face and says rollickingly, "That's to baptize the deal." So I throw mine in his and we perform a wet and manly hug. Still dripping, we agree there will be no papers, no lawyers, no anything—just our sacred words.

"And when will I get the money?" he asks.

"When Action comes through."

"Has he got the stuff?"

"No, I'm supposed to see him here tomorrow. He wants it to cool for a day."

"So where is it?"

"I'm not going to tell any blackmailing bastard a thing like that."

"I was bluffing, schmuck."

"Okay, it's in a locker at the Port Authority Bus Terminal."

"Including the painting?"

"Yeah, I took the frame off and rolled the canvas up in linen."

"You *rolled* it? Didn't the paint crack?"

"Remember Bobby Butterfield from college?"

"The faggot—"

"The very one. Well, it turns out he's an associate curator at the Met—we worked the whole thing out this morning."

"What whole thing?"

"He came over to look at it. He says everyone knows the Lifeline Collection and there's no question that it's quite genuine. And he showed me how to roll it up so I wouldn't ruin it."

"Why did he do that?"

"I promised to let him play with my body when the deal goes through."

"What deal?"

"Oh, well, I'm going to let the museum buy the painting from me at half price. Of course museums don't generally buy stolen paintings, so we had to work out something ingenious. What we're doing is that I'm going to send Bobby an anonymous note asking the museum to get Lifeline's permission to keep the painting as a donation from him, and if he says yes I will mail it to the museum, and Bobby, in strictest confidence, will get me the fifty thousand. If Lifeline or the museum says no, the note says the painting will be destroyed in forty-eight hours."

"Suppose they don't go for it?"

"Why shouldn't they go for it? Lifeline'll get a big fat tax deduction, the museum'll have a major new acquisition for half what they'd have to pay at an auction, Bobby'll be a hero—and I'll have my fifty thou under the table."

"Suppose Bobby doesn't come through with the money?"

"Then I won't let him play with me."

"Suppose he pays, plays, and rats on you later?"

"I'll say he took a cut."

Shag nods admiringly and then proceeds, with withering tedium, to initiate me into the innermost mysteries of our new saloon business. He tells me the house brand of Scotch costs $4.15 a quart, yields about thirty drinks, and grosses roughly $25. I pretend to be interested, so he goes on. Supplies, like candles, glasses, and cleaning materials, cost $15 a week, machine repairs $20 a week, the accountant $25 a week, the porter $35 a week, and the insurance $40 a week. I am stupefied by the news. And when he begins explaining the kitchen situation—"the chef gets three bills an hour but only puts out at about half capacity"—I am faint with boredom and practically ready to cancel the deal. But then he says, "Of course I won't bother you with all this crap. In fact I don't bother with it myself. Jimbo Jeheavensocker—he's the waiter with the handlebar mustache —runs the place for me. He's very reliable, discounting what he steals from the register. But I know what the take should be any given night, going by the size of the crowd, and figure what he steals is what he'd be earning if he had some kind of bonus arrangement, which I of course steadfastly refuse to give him, believing, as I always have, that labor is a commodity. So it all works out very nicely, and Jimbo gets the added charge of thinking he's putting something over on me, which is very good for his morale."

I am on the verge of suggesting that perhaps some slightly more orderly arrangement, like a percentage of the gross, might be worked out for Jimbo, but I refrain, deciding that would be to contest Shag's ideology when all I really care about is that I should earn no less than one hundred per cent annually on my investment and be able to tank up free anytime I have a hankering.

And a hankering, a large hankering, is precisely what I have at the moment. A celebration over the way things have been happening is in order, and very soon I am feeling no pain whatever. I begin feeding quarters to the jukebox and reconnoitering with a proprietary air among the late-afternoon customers, whom I amuse with a variety of stage dialects, Buffoon Irish and Gesticulatory Yiddish the most affecting of them, and whose shoes I occasionally shine with Shag's shoeshine kit, a service for which I charge a mere dollar or insist on being stood to a beer.

At a corner table, I come upon a girl sitting alone and reading a book. She looks at me over the top of it without moving her head a jot. Her hair is sandy and short, in the French pixie manner. Her eyes are green-blue and combative and not a little playful. It is a thinnish face, the cheeks severely planed, and altogether it is neither lovely nor ghastly; what it is is animated and intelligent-looking. It speaks before I do. Still hiding behind its book, it says, "I've been watching you. You are behaving like a perfect ass. Do you know that?"

"The saints preserve us if it isn't lit-tle Sally Straightlace herself, readin' her ti-ny limpid eyes out over in the dankest caw-ner of the bloomin' establishment."

"You are very unfunny," she says. "You are the unfunniest person I have seen all day."

"And where whoult it be hur-thin' you, child, that you should berate a penniless wayfarer like meself who means no harm t' no one and brings a smile'r two t' the lips of—"

"You are not only unfunny, you are also boring. Go away—you're blocking my light."

"And I thought I was being rather amusing."

She pretends to be reading.

"Besides, I don't see why I ought to take your word for it. Who says you're any judge of what's funny?"

She keeps reading.

"People at the other tables think I'm funny."

Reading.

"Don't *they* have any taste?"

"No. Now go away."

"You're very hostile."

No bite.

"*Why* are you hostile?"

Still none.

"Do you hate men?"

"Just crude, tasteless men," she says, still not looking up.

"Are you waiting for someone?"

Nothing.

"Is there someone who you cherish?"

"Whom I cherish."

"Yes, whom."

"There is—and I am marrying him three months from today—and if you keep being a pest, I will call him on the telephone and he will come beat you up with his large fists."

I sit down at her table.

She puts the book face down on the table. "Don't you believe me?"

"Oh, sure. But I like you. You're funny."

"Funnier than you, anyway."

"Yes."

"Are you trying to pick me up?"

"I'm just being a friendly person."

"Oh. Well, I want to read my book. You're interrupting me."

"Why are you sitting in a bustling saloon if you want to read your book?"

"Because I like it here. It's very—tacky. I like tacky places."

"Don't you have a tacky home to read in?"

"It's squalid, not tacky—they're different things."

"Why don't you desqualidify it?"

"Because I'm getting married in four months and I'll be moving to new squalor."

"I thought it was three months."

"Three or four—it doesn't matter."

"Oh." I put the shoeshine kit on the table. "What are you reading?"

"Something hard."

"Does it have a name?"

"It's in French."

"Oh. Sorry, I don't know French."

"I can tell."

"Why are you reading something French?"

"Everything I read is French."

"Oh."

"It is an extremely beautiful and expressive language, and anyone who doesn't know it is not very—couth."

"Oh."

"It just so happens, though, that what I am reading at the moment is neither very beautiful nor very expressive. In fact I hate it."

"Then why don't you read something else?"

"Because I'm a graduate student, and this is for a seminar. And since I am a brilliant student, I am of course reading it with fanatic attention, which means very slowly because it is terribly dense stuff. Also somewhat idiotic. Do you know about the genetic structuralists?"

"I—"

"Half the time I call them the structural geneticists. And frankly I'm not sure it makes any great difference if you get it backward."

In short order and with a minimum of further prompting, I am also advised that she: (1) never reads the newspapers, except the help-wanted pages lately because she is thinking of quitting school and getting an exotic job if she can discover one; (2) has studied classical guitar for six years and subscribes to the *Guitar Review,* the only periodical she follows faithfully; (3) prefers, *really* prefers, classical Greek literature, which she devours at the rate of forty-five lines an hour, to all contemporary literature, but her principal cultural involvement is with Assyrian and ancient Near Eastern art and archaeology, about which she knows a great deal; (4) cannot—literally *cannot*—multiply or do percentages or keep a checkbook; (5) worked at Japanese brush-painting for about a year—and nothing else in life, nothing—until she noticed in one non-levitating, blindingly scrutable flash of insight that she had absolutely no gift for it; (6) always thought the Golden Rule was "ladies first"; (7) owns fifty skirts, a hundred blouses, and two hundred pairs of shoes, none of which does anything for her, because she eats too much because she likes to cook for her auto-racing Venezuelan fiancé, who is much loathed by her untiringly acquisitive upper-middle-class family, which is in the leather business and does not understand a thing about her except that she is obviously quite brilliant and headstrong; (8) is twenty-two years old; (9) is named Olivia Ottway; and (10) thinks she looks like a rat.

"A rat?"

"Yes. I look like a rat."

"I never saw a rat with—sort of blue eyes."

"Well—if a rat had blue eyes, I'm what it would look like."

"Well—maybe just a little."

"No, a lot."

"Do you hate yourself?"

"Because I look like a rat?"

"Yes."

"No, I love myself. I'm just very objective about my weaknesses."

I once knew a girl who looked precisely like a kinkajou, no ifs, ands, or buts, but I volunteer nothing about her—or myself—and she asks nothing and so we go on about her, and the more I hear, the more I like, but she will not let me buy her a drink, drinks only wine, as a matter of fact, taking decorous little sips every ten or so minutes, and after an hour with her I am relishing her and her rattiness and before long am sneaking prurient looks at her breasts, which have a hint of real heft to them under the demurely loose but clearly inviolable silk blouse. However intimate her disclosures, she nevertheless retains a definite air of detachment, as if to say we are only toying, and I (Olivia Ottway) am rather special merchandise and not for purchase or winning but am just here, now, talking with you for however long it amuses me to do so. She is very young and very smart and very knowing and, withal, very vulnerable.

And then I see Action come in. He sees me the same instant and his look reveals at once that he is displeased with me for having violated our arrangement. He brushes by our table and says, sideways and abrasively, "I thought we said tomorrow."

"Right. I just came to celebrate."

He shakes his head and keeps going.

"Who," Olivia asks, "is that?"

"That's Action. He's a fence."

"What's *that?*"

"A purveyor of stolen merchandise."

"Oh," she says, and purses her thin lips. "Do you do business with him?"

"I'm about to."

"And do you steal things?"

"Not habitually. I've just begun, to tell the truth."

"But isn't that quite dangerous?"

"Yes, quite. That's why I do it."

She senses at once that she is not being put on and so responds with immediate and serious interest, engorging me, in turn, with excitement and drawing from me perhaps imprudent candor.

"But suppose they catch you?" she asks.

"I'll probably plead temporary insanity."

She sips more wine and meditates. Then she says, "Look, don't tell me your name, all right?"

"All right."

"I wouldn't want to get you in trouble."

"Nor I you. Shall I go away now?"

"Oh, no! I'm fascinated now. Tell me what you've stolen."

I drain my beer. Then I say, "Come home with me and I'll show you."

Her dark smart eyes open wide and void their whimsy but stay fixed on mine and say, without her saying anything, that it is not impossible but that I must give reassurances. "Yes, come and cook me dinner and I'll show you. And then you can go away and never know who the mysterious robber was."

She keeps looking at me and mulling it. "I have a class tonight."

"Go after dinner."

"I've already made up my mind I'm cutting."

"Then cut with me."

"How do I know you're not a fiend?"

"Oh, I *am* a fiend. I'm a werewolf with a close shave."

"No, I mean it."

"Okay. I swear I'm not a fiend. I swear I don't want to violate your young and tender body."

"Or kill me."

"Or kill you."

She gives a series of little nods and smiles for the first time—a little smile—and says, "What would you like for dinner?"

22

Stew

STEW IS WHAT WE DECIDE ON. STEW IS WHAT SHE MAKES BEST, because she can invent as she goes along. Never uses a cookbook. Puts in whatever the spirit moves her to. We buy beef, greens, cabbage, onions, chickpeas, walnuts (not for the stew, she explains), tomatoes, several kinds of cheeses, and several kinds of crackers. It costs fifteen dollars, which, since I do not own half the store, I must pay. Grudgingly.

In the cab home we chatter merrily, then take the elevator past the somber and habitually disapproving countenance of Fitzroy, the elevator operator, who reports that a total of ten inches of snow is due by morning.

It occurs to me only as we sail through the door that I have brought Miss Olivia Ottway here under false pretenses, for the swag is all safely stashed at the Port Authority Bus Terminal, and I tell Olivia that the moment I remember it, which is not till we are across the threshold. I see her flash a look of disappointment, followed by the reflection that I am a phony and a mad rapist. And so I trot out my robber's gear—masks, guns, handcuffs—and volunteer to run her down to the bus terminal at once to prove I am an honest-to-goodness thief. But she points out that might be risky and settles for my telling her what the haul was exactly. I pick up the evening paper from the hall mat where it is delivered nightly and thumb through it for the story, which I proudly poke under her nose. She takes the paper, throws off her coat, and, falling onto the living-room sofa, gives a low long whistle of admiration as she reads.

"Oh my," she says, "that's really outstanding. And you've never done it before?"

"No, never."

"And will you do more?"

"Well, I don't know. I haven't decided yet."

"Oh, but you must. You sound perfectly brilliant at it." She tucks her legs under her. "Now I'll confess—I'm a robber, too, which is why your whole thing fascinates me."

"No—you can't be a robber."

"Neither can you. But we are. Of course I'm strictly small-time. I mean I just snitch things from department stores and bookstores and sewing stores. But it comes to quite a bit when you add it all up."

"It sounds as if you're just a flourishing kleptomaniac."

"Oh, no, not at all. I mean I know just what I'm doing. I'm not compelled or anything. I just see something I want and don't have enough money to buy—or don't want *enough* to pay for—and zing! I snatch it. Or get people I'm with to snatch it. I'm more the brains of the outfit than a regular thief. Here, I'll make up a list of every-thing I've taken." And she takes a pen and a little notebook out of her bag and starts scribbling. "You go put the food away."

I go put the food away. And hummingly fix two drinks.

"No," she says to the drink with unequivocal finality. Then, "What is it?"

"It's half Pouilly-Fuissé, half club soda."

"Well, okay—as long as we understand each other."

"You are sacred and inviolable—and quite young."

"But very sophisticated."

"Yes, quite."

"And engaged."

"Yes, you are promised to another and we have nothing in common but our avocation."

"Right. Now read my list."

I read:

Partial List of Articles Stolen by Olivia Olgivy Ottway

FROM BONWIT TELLER:
One real ivory bangle bracelet,
one fake gold bangle bracelet,
seventeen assorted silk (chiffon) scarves,
one pair of imported Italian sunglasses,
one very long fake gold chain necklace (not stolen, really; I took the new one and put my old one back in stock),
several rather expensive men's ties (Pauline Trigère and one Pucci, but Pucci ties tie badly),
one pair of small fake gold earrings,
one pair of navy nylon gloves (but they tore and I got my money back).

FROM THE COLUMBIA BOOKSTORE:
Innumerable quantities of Pentels, Bics, pencils, erasers, tubes of oil paints, nibs for Rapidographs, small notebooks (this one), loose-leaf fillers, one record (by a Brazilian guitarist of whom you have never heard), funny greeting cards, a Columbia T shirt (for Paul), a few

hardback textbooks (an Italian reader comes to mind), and a great many paperbacks.

NOTE: The Columbia articles were acquired with the combined efforts of Olivia and Paul.

FROM THE ROCHESTER MUSEUM OF ART (my B.A. is from Skidmore):
One dodecahedron, brass, Mexican paperweight,
one very small reproduction of a Cretan (Minoan) bull statuette,
several small art books,
some earth from the potted plants for *my* rubber plant,
two champagne glasses (from the members' opening of the Wyeth show),
one tin Mexican bird,
one tin Mexican pineapple.
(Attempted but failed to get: one small Matisse statue, which was nailed to its base, which was nailed to the floor.)

FROM ALBANY DEPARTMENT STORES:
Minor cosmetics.

"It's not really complete," she says. "There are lots of sewing things I could add. I particularly remember a scarlet lining for a skirt I made. And some big snaps for a navy coat—"

"Don't be apologetic. It's a perfectly decent showing for a young woman."

She smiles. Her whole thinnish face goes into the smile. "You really think so?"

"I do. Who's Paul?"

"My fiancé."

"Oh."

"What's the matter?"

"I was just wondering if it was good for both of you to be thieves."

"He's not really one. I just make him do it once in a while. It's not that he doesn't know right from wrong."

"And do you?"

"Of course! That's why I do it. I can't *bear* doing right things all the time. Like coming home with you—it's dangerous, right?"

"Right."

"That's why I'm here."

"Are you really going to marry Paul?"

"Yes—of course." She sips at her drink. "If he wants to. I mean *I* want to and he *says* he wants to. But we're a little uncertain of the date, that's all."

"Do you mind that?"

"Just a little. Actually, I'm quite fond of him, even if he is rather stupid at times—and very inefficient. But he's the first one I really want to marry. I mean lots of people have wanted to marry *me*—or said they do. About eight by now, including one professor who tried to seduce me first. He was quite nice about it, actually—"

She spins on and on and I hang on every word. It is happening by itself, without any premeditation on my end, except, of course, for a frame of mind newly receptive to some form or other of extramarital congress. Suddenly I know I am not going to join Anne and the children in winter wonderland. No, I am going to spend every waking moment I can, and perhaps some sleeping ones, these next few days with this zany, disarming, irresistibly, inexhaustibly exuberant young thing—if she'll have me.

She whirls into the kitchen and takes total command, scraping, slicing, washing, chopping, spicing, basting, mixing, tasting, and never ceasing her flow of marvelous chatter. As eating time nears, she is rattling on about kites. She flies kites. All the time she flies kites. She loves to fly kites.

"It's like holding down a piece of the sky," she says. "And if you let yourself go a little, you think you're up there on it, or that it's you, and you're dipping and swooping in the wind. It's an absolutely wonderful feeling. I do it all the time. I run around the Sheep Meadow like a lunatic—the meadow, in the park—I have special kite friends there. They have clubs. I don't belong to any of them. I'm not a club person. But I know a lot about kites. Did you know that during the First World War they used kites as a weapon—to drop bombs, I think. I mean they put a man in the kite and then they gave him a bomb—he held it on his lap or something—and then up he went and flipped out the bomb where it would do most damage. Only I don't think his aim was very good, usually. It took a very big kite to do all that, like thirty-five feet high or so."

"*Very* big kite."

There is really not much to say back to her. It is just a matter of letting her charm me with her endless string of wonderful irrelevancies. Not that she expects me to burst out laughing. She settles nicely for that look of mild but steady amusement her chatter shapes on my attentive, grown-up face.

The stew is splendid, the meat flaky, the potatoes crumbly, the vegetables flavory, and everything else is of an excellence exaggerated by the unlikelihood of the entire encounter. Buoyed by either the wine or her own uncorkable effervescence or, more likely, both, O. O. O., as I am now calling her, is soaring off every moment on new flights of fancy, and I am her more-than-willing passenger. All at once, though, she stops and looks me in the eye.

"I have a terrible confession to make," she says.

"I know—you're a brownie."

"What's a brownie?"

"A pixie. An elf. An imaginary creature, born supernaturally and full of whimsy."

"Yes, well, of course I'm that. But that's not my confession."

"I know—you're a sixty-six-year-old nymphomaniac when you take your mask off."

"Wrong. My confession is that I am not really Olivia Olgivy Ottway. That's a pseudonym. But it's my real pseudonym—"

"What's a real pseudonym, as opposed to a pseudo-pseudonym?"

"It's one I've been using for a long time. Lots of people call me it. Some of them think it's my real name. But most of them just know it's my other name."

"Why do you have two names?"

"Oh, lots of reasons. It's fun, for one thing. It's my invention, for another, and most people don't have much choice about what they're called. And then it's quite convenient sometimes to have an extra name—when you don't want someone to know your real one."

"Like me, for instance."

"Yes. Well, up to now, anyway. But I'm confessing to you."

"And who are you really?"

"I am really Connie Capehart Colton. But all the magazines I subscribe to are addressed to Olivia Olgivy Ottway. I even have a telephone in that name. It's sort of mysterious. I like being mysterious. Paul, of course, thinks I'm a little crazy. But it's all perfectly harmless."

"You're sure? I mean there aren't certain times when you're Olivia and certain other times when you're Connie?"

"You mean am I schizoid? No, nothing like that. I can be either one anytime I like. It's a very nice feeling. I'm much more maneuverable than most people. Also, I have a third name."

"A third name?"

"Just when I sculpt or paint. I sign everything Cricket."

"Cricket?"

"See how much fun it is to say?"

It is decided I am to call her any of the three names I care to— or any other mutually agreeable one. I suggest she has offered me a wide enough selection as it is, and my preference, if she doesn't mind, is Connie. Connie says she is not *against* being called Connie, never has been, and I should understand that.

23

The Nances of Isis

FILLED WITH GOOD FOOD AND WELL-BEING BORDERING ON GIDDI-
ness, we consider what should happen to us next.

There are three possibilities. First, Connie should go away immediately and we should never lay eyes on each other again. I am
against that. Second, we should go directly to bed and bring that
shared giddiness to a rapturous consummation. Connie is against that.
Third, we should commit a robbery together. A little robbery.

"But I just committed one last night."

"No," Connie says, "that was a big one. I mean a teeny one."

"It's sort of hard to control. You have to take whatever's there to
take."

"I don't see why. Why can't you just take one or two things, and
not be a pig about it?"

Logically there is no denying her. It just goes against my nature.
But my nature now is swollen with affection for this weird and em-
braceable creature, and I will do anything to keep her from going out
the door and disappearing from my life. We plan a teeny robbery.

We pick a pair of nances on the seventeenth floor: Jerry and Terry,
fashion photographers, according to my informant, the doorman.
They are in their jockey shorts when we arrive, I am in my standard
pirate getup, Connie is in the gold woman's mask and a sweater and
pair of Anne's slacks that I lent her. The lads are perfectly bare, save
for their shorts, the pouches of which are stuffed with washcloths or
bean-bags or some sort of padding to heighten their allure. On their

arms, each is wearing a hammered-gold bracelet in the shape of a coiled serpent.

"Why do you want to rob *us,* of all people, for goodness' sakes?" asks Jerry. "I mean we don't have a *thing* worth robbing—not a blessed thing."

"Besides which," says Terry, "we love you. Yes, we do. You are outcasts of society and we identify with you. We moral rebels share something worth sharing, you and we—don't we and they, Jerry sweetie, when you think of it *that* way?"

"Within limits, Terry honey. But I don't think we should *assume* they see it quite that way. All they can see, as a matter of fact, is a pair of queens running around in loincloths and caught practically *in flagrante delicto.* No matter how fascinated they are, they are almost certainly *recoiling* at the sight—"

"And assuming this is our habitual costume and posture."

"Exactly."

"Well, I don't care if they *do.* I am what I am, and I'm not going to get on my knees to apologize to a couple of pitiful thieves who barge right in on our privacy."

"You're *entirely* right."

"There they are standing ramrod straight, pointing their big potent guns at us and pretending they're here to rob us when what they really want is for us to put on a little exhibition for them."

"Oh, I'll bet you're *entirely* right—entirely."

"As if we're their surrogate lovers and they want us to do things they want desperately to do themselves but don't have the courage and the honesty to do—"

"Oh, I *know* you're right."

"As if they feel so uncertain of their own sexuality, so inadequate about the frequency and intensity of their own erotic performance, that they are *bristling* with latent hostility toward all candidly practicing homosexuals—"

"Yes, yes, right."

"As if their own endowments are so meager that they can scarcely wait to see how big and juicy ours are—"

"Yes, right, right."

"And what we do with them to derive the kind of satisfaction they crave and don't know how to get—"

"Oh, God, you are *so* right I could scream."

"I certainly don't think we ought to oblige a pair of frustrated perverts like these just because they're armed."

"Oh, I couldn't agree more."

"Unless, of course, they promise not to rob us of the few paltry possessions they may mistakenly think are worth robbing."

"What good would their promise be?"

"Well, I for one have never entirely *believed* this business about there being no honor among thieves. I think they're probably as honorable as everyone else."

"Well, you're *certainly* more of a gambler than I, is all I can say."

And together they look at us for some sign of assent. I glance down at Connie, who shrugs. It is clear they passionately want spectators for their rites of perversity, and any covenant between us pertaining to not robbing them is purely incidental. To deny them an audience would be the worse offense, and so I dip my gun slightly in a gesture of complicity.

What follows is a scene left over from Fellini's cutting-room floor. They move—and we follow—into a living room ablaze with Art Nouveau objects: cut-glass vases and bronze candlesticks and silver samovars and opal-encrusted dishes and a ten-bulb lily-pond lamp and a bottle-green tureen with a dozen turquoises set in the flaring metal base and a pair of Van de Velde chairs and pewter picture frames of intertwined flowers and horses' heads and a big clock set between arched back-to-back Circes and a huge glassed-in bookcase with panels of unbelievably convoluted filigree. Before the fireplace is a screen of such swirling exquisiteness that Connie gives a gasp, producing a brief lecture by Terry honey, who explains that it is made of carved ash with applied oak, zebrawood, and sabicu; the marquetry is of amboyna and walnut; it is by the Frenchman Emile Gallé, and it is dated at the very *fin de siècle*. On the walls are large unframed black-and-white photographs of rooms and buildings that demonstrate the highest state ever reached by the exotic movement: the Metro entrance at the Place de l'Etoile for the Paris Exhibition of 1900, the Atelier Elvira in the Treppenhaus in Munich, and, most astonishing of all, the interior of the Owatonna Farmers National Bank (Louis Sullivan, 1907). The net effect is of a beauty so unbearably overwrought that its decomposition is almost palpable in the cellular structure of the assembled *objets d'art*. And about this spectacularly unwholesome setting flounce our two grotesques. They proceed through some sort of ritualistic minuet, draping limbs in arabesques of pliant gesture as if to mirror the supreme curvilinear suppleness of all the artifacts in the room. With grace defying the human eye, they are suddenly seen totally bare, except for the golden serpents wriggling up their thrashing arms. They are whirling through their *ballet bouffe* now at a genitalia-blurring speed, and all that is clear is that they have shaved their pubic regions to the nub. Faster and faster they fly till all at once they are on each other, meshed like the classically complementary Yin and Yang, rolling over and over and emitting regular *castrado* squeals of ecstasy over the perfectly performed rite of *fellatio*.

I am transfixed by the spectacle. Fascination mingles with revulsion as their coupled bodies roll on in unison, noisily feeding on each other. It is not the sort of intimacy I have been privy to before, and however unattractive I find the notion of changing places with either of them, I am not about to disrupt their proceeding with the perversion to its unspeakable climax—indeed I am consumed with curiosity to see just how they will manage it. But then I hear a low moaning from Connie, who can bear it no longer and makes me make them stop. They must be pried apart, members still rigid with anticipation.

"You scrummy son of a bitch!" one of them shrills, and for a moment I fear they will turn their tumescent fury on me and grab the
gun. But I back off rapidly. They sprawl on the floor as if spent,
members swiftly dwindling. Connie and I scan the room now, figuring
what is worth taking and what, in fact, is capable of being moved. We
take the lily-pond lamp, the Circe clock, and one of the opal-studded
dishes. The nances are surly and silent as we go about our business.
Then Connie indicates the hammered-gold armlets they are wearing.
I tell them to hand over the coiled serpents.

"Never!" they yell in unison, and explain that they are matched
symbols of the cow-headed Isis, wife of Osiris and the sacred goddess
of motherhood and fertility. Their serpentine shape adds an ironic
quality, of course, to the matched artifacts, which, presumably em-
blematic of the dormant phallus, function as engagement rings for
these two screaming refutations to bisexuality. "Never!" And finally,
they say the armlets, as far as anyone knows, are absolutely genuine
relics of the eighteenth dynasty (from the environs of Thebes) and
worth more than our four lives put together. "Never!" And they clasp
their opposite hands over the precious things.

Connie, though, is quite fixed in her determination to have them,
and so, this being no moment for disputation among thieves, I persist.
The nances are no less fixed until I threaten gruffly to shoot them
directly in their favorite parts. Whimpering pitifully, they fling the
armlets at us—and a volley of the shrillest vileness I have heard in
all my born days. Connie scoops them up coolly, puts them in the opal
dish, and covers me with steady trigger finger as I go and handcuff
their arms and legs together (Terry's arm to Jerry's leg and vice
versa—so they will not be altogether miserable). And we dash for
the door.

There are four landings to go. On the third she drops the Circe
clock. The crash is explosive. There is no pausing, though. We pant
on—and make it back to the apartment unseen and with no further
damage. She is laughing and crying and gasping for breath all at once,

and falls against me with relief and exhilaration over the shared tension of the experience. She pulls away in another moment and drops into a kitchen chair, drenched and parched and looking for the rest of the wine. She splashes some into a soiled glass and gulps it down, half choking, and when she recovers, all she can ask over and over is whether all men have ones that big and how on earth will she ever be able to accommodate them?

With so much in common, there is no longer any question that we will spend the night under the same roof. But, her whole manner makes it just as imperative, it is unthinkable that our bodies should mingle. We have shared our thrill for the night already, and the rest is mere civility. She drops her skirt and sheds her blouse and climbs into my bedroom bed in her underthings. It is now *her* bed. She closes her eyes and says good night and appears to be instantly asleep. I retreat to the living room, not a lascivious thought in my head, and fall asleep on the sofa in my underpants.

In the morning she comes to me, dressed and showered, and strokes my beard till I am conscious. She must go, she says, and I must be good, for she is fond of me. She looks down at my underpants, notes my rampant manhood, and says, "I hope *yours* isn't shaved." But she does not want to find out. She just goes. She is gone. Only when I am fully awake and reconstructing the night before do I notice that the golden serpentine armlets of the great goddess Isis are nowhere to be found. And so, as far as I know, is Connie Capehart Colton.

24

Routine Investigation

I AM A PARAGON OF INACTIVITY THE REST OF THE MORNING, AND an increasingly disconsolate one as the early afternoon comes slothfully on. No newspaper, magazine, book, or television show can hold my attention for more than a minute. All I can think of is the girl, the crazy engaged-to-be-married-sometime-if-he-really-loves-me-enough girl, with her French and her kites and purloined dodecahedrons. She turned it all on and then turned it all off, and I shall never be the same. Her presence is first disarming and second overwhelming and third beguiling, and her absence, once her presence has been known, is desolation. And yet I must not seek her. I must not—unless I want to possess her utterly, for there is no other way to have her. But there is no saying she is to be had even if I want her more than anything else on earth. Why do I think our episode was something more to her than a spontaneous interlude, the sort of chance encounter she evidently thrives on? And why do I think I could bear twenty-four hours a day of her nonstop quirkiness? Only because no hours of it seem a Sahara of tedium. Where are you, Connie Capehart Colton, with your hundred pairs of shoes and succulent stews and your dear little rat look? And what are you up to? And don't you think you should have asked for dibs on the golden armlets of the sacred Isis instead of just stealing them like that? I mean you're entitled to a share of the swag but you shouldn't've just up and left with it like that, dammit. Where are you, dammit to hell?

Suddenly I think I know. I throw on a coat and open the door— and practically flopping on his face into my foyer is a very rumpled fellow in a battered fedora and nondescript overcoat with the collar up. His dark eyebrows are undulating with suspicion.

"Pat Pratt," he says, collecting himself. "Twenty-second Detective Squad." He flashes his medallion.

The law! So soon? A chill splashes through me.

"I—was just going out. Is there anything I can do for you— Detective?"

He flicks a couple of sideways glances. "You've got a nice place here."

"Why—thanks. Yes, we like it fine."

"I hope I didn't disturb your family, Mr. Kwait."

My name. He has my name. Clearly he is not browsing.

"No—no one's home just now."

He looks quizzical. "Oh?"

"They're on vacation."

"I see," he says, taking off his hat and fiddling with the brim. Is there a warrant inside that dreadful hat? What *is* he up to?

"I—I'm joining them in a few days."

His look suggests approval.

"I'm sorry to trouble you, Mr. Kwait, but I have a few questions to ask you."

I have a sudden impulse to murder Detective Pratt. I will excuse myself, fetch a carving knife, and do him in. One quick thrust to the heart. And do what with the body? And say what to the other cops who will follow? That he never came to my apartment? But there is the elevator man to testify. Must I murder him, too? And who else? Shall I run down the street stabbing witness after witness until there are no more witnesses—or the blade snaps off?

"Questions?"

"Strictly routine, Mr. Kwait. You know about the robberies, I guess."

"The Lifeline apartment—yes, I read about it in the paper. Quite a haul."

"Biggest one the precinct's had in years."

"Yes, I'd imagine."

He is scratching the back of his neck now. "Say, would you mind if I took off my coat?"

"Oh, not at all," I say and take my own off, too. I have no choice but to invite him into the living room.

He sinks pleasurably into the sofa. I remain standing.

"Last night's job was routine by comparison."

"Last night's?"

"You don't know about it?" he asks, eyes on the floor.

"No—no, I haven't been out yet. What happened?"

"A couple o' fairies on the seventeenth floor were robbed."

I register shock and dismay. "Gee—and this is supposed to be one of the safest buildings in town."

"Yeh, that's what's got us a little shook."

"Is it just a coincidence?"

"We don't know, but the guessing now is no. The description of one of the robbers is the same."

"The same as what?"

"As the guy who robbed the Lifelines. It's the same M.O."

"The pirate mask, you mean?"

"That, and the way he talked."

My eyes widen. "Strange."

"What's even stranger is the getaway—clean as a whistle both times. Not a trace. There's no way to get down to the basement at night without going through the lobby. And none of the elevator men or doormen saw anybody even slightly suspicious either time."

"Odd—very odd."

"That's what we think."

"Of course the building staff is not the most alert crew I've ever seen."

Pratt looks up with interest. "What do you mean?"

"I mean—they sort of doze at night—in any nook they can find."

His eyes narrow.

"I—I'm not blaming them, you understand. I mean they're all pretty old and shaky— You know?"

"Yeah," he says, crossing his arms over his chest. "Well, I admit they aren't the sharpest bunch I've run into. But we gotta go with what there is. And these guys say they saw a whole lot of nothin'."

I shake my head. "Very strange."

"And so that's why I'm here, Mr. Kwait."

Is he playing cat-and-mouse with me? Under that tatterdemalion exterior is there a wily mastermind at work? Christ, he looks dumb enough.

"What is?"

"We think maybe they were inside jobs."

My impulse now is to run. Out the back door. Down thousands of stairs. From the building. Away. Forever. Someday, somehow, I will send for the family. Unless I like it without them.

"Inside? I don't understand. You mean one of the elevator men?"

"Maybe. One of the elevator men—or handymen."

"Gee, I hope that's not so."

"To tell you the truth, we don't think it is. The guy—the robber in the pirate mask—didn't sound very much like an elevator man or a handyman. He sounded pretty educated."

I gasp. "You mean—you think it was one of the—the *tenants?*"

His eyes are roving all over me for any telltale traces of insincerity.

"It's just possible," he says.

"But that's ridiculous! All the tenants in the buliding are—rather comfortable."

"We know."

"Why on earth would any of them—?"

"People do strange things sometimes, Mr. Kwait."

I am shaking my head with disbelief. "Maybe so," I say, "but that's a bit much."

"Just doing our job, Mr. Kwait."

"Oh, right, right. I didn't mean to suggest—"

"We're questioning every man in this wing of the building."

"Oh. Well, I imagine that adds up to quite a few."

"Seventy-seven, as a matter of fact. But we've already eliminated thirty-two of them, because they live above the fourteenth floor."

I frown. "I'm sorry—I don't quite follow. I thought the robbery was on the seventeenth floor."

"It was. But they dropped one of the things they stole last night on the fourteenth-floor landing."

"Oh." I sit in a chair across from him. "Well, thirty-two from seventy-seven—that's forty-five suspects."

"We've whittled it down to twenty-three."

"Oh. Now, how did you do that?"

"General size and voice description."

"Oh."

"Mr. Kwait," he says, taking out a little note pad, "would you mind telling me where you were last night between ten and eleven o'clock?"

He knows nothing. Nothing. I know it. I feel it. He is a dumb groping flatfoot in mufti. Pat Pratt. Pratt as in pratfall. Pratfall as in Keystone Kops. Pat Pratt in a huge-patterned sport jacket and brown tieless shirt. Pratt of the Twenty-second Detective Squad, plodding upholder of law and order, you are no match for the Pirate Robber.

"Not at all."

He wets his pencil on the tip of his tongue. When I volunteer nothing, he looks up and says, "I mean could you tell me, please?"

"Oh, sorry. Yes, sure—I was here. I'm not sure what I was doing exactly just then—reading a book, I guess, or a magazine." I sneak a look at him—his face is buried in the note pad—and decide to make a veiled bid for comradeship: "Or maybe I was in the crapper." I follow with a feeble little laugh.

He glances up. "For the whole hour?"

"What?"

"In the crapper?"

My God! One of nature's truly pitiable simpletons.

"No—not the whole hour. I'm not even sure I was in it at all."

He double-checks his notes. "You just said, 'Or maybe I was in the crapper.' "

"Right. I was—kidding." I turn on a big smile.

He looks up. "Why would you be kidding, Mr. Kwait?"

"I—I'm sorry. I've never been investigated before."

"And you're a little nervous?"

"I—I wasn't aware of being nervous. I—I'm sorry, detective. Look, I don't remember exactly what I was doing then, okay? Is that clear enough?"

He scribbles away noncommittally. "And were you alone, Mr. Kwait?"

It catches me off guard. I waver for a second. To delay any longer is to risk arousing real suspicion, even in a brain as sluggish as his.

"My family's on vacation," I say. "Remember?"

He looks up at me slowly. I look back, an agreeable smile pasted in place. "Right," he says, "but you're not answering the question."

Barely perceptible, but there it is—a tiny stiffening in him, a hint of rising wariness. And now I make a hundred flash calculations and decide in my final instant of grace that I have only one real choice: to lie. The truth, given the circumstances and the girl, is infinitely more perilous.

"Yes, of course," I say, "I was alone."

He nods a few times. "And you didn't see or hear anything unusual about that time?"

"Not that I remember."

He nods some more and then flips the pad shut decisively. "Okay," he says, expelling a large sigh. "Thanks a lot."

"Don't mention it."

"We really hate to bother people like this."

"Look, it's your job—"

"I'm glad you understand."

"Of course."

"Some people don't—you'd be surprised."

"Gee, that's too bad. It must make the job tough."

"Some of the time," he says, and before I know it he has shucked his stern pose entirely and is becoming depressingly chummy. In another minute he says, "Could I bother you for a favor?"

Oh, God, what now? Go. I want you to go. You are trespassing. You have done your duty; now get your big ass the hell off the premises.

"Sure."

"I'm dyin' for a cup of coffee."

"Coffee?"

"If it wouldn't be too much bother. Instant would be fine."

Mirabile dictu! Here I am, not fully detumesced from my début as a criminal, and Pat Pratt of the Twenty-second Detective Squad, hat in hand, badge in wallet, revolver in holster, has taken an unbearable shine to me.

"Sure, sure," I say, and head into the kitchen to boil the water.

Two steps into the pantry, I spot my crumpled pirate mask on the floor beside the back door, precisely where I had carelessly discarded it after returning victorious from the last heist and snatching it off my steaming face. Half a second later I am aware that Pratt is following me into the kitchen! Without breaking stride, I kick the mask sideways into the dark corner of the pantry next to the washing machine. If Pratt has seen the fancy footwork, he gives no sign of it. Suddenly I realize how thoroughly thrilled I am by his lingering presence, for it heightens the utter improbability of the entire undertaking. I begin to warm to the situation. I ask Pratt how long he has been on the force (twelve years), where he lives (Bensonhurst), how big a family he has (a fat wife, three girls, and a boy who wants to be a priest but he's only seven), and how he likes being a cop ("so-so—but it's a lot better than pushin' a truck all over the East Coast, which I did for five years and that was no picnic"). All that established, I am convinced that he cannot make ends meet on a police dick's salary. I am on the verge of asking how he manages when he volunteers that the pay scale discourages guys of high caliber from staying on the force— a pension after twenty years is the main financial inducement—and that almost all the guys moonlight.

"I run a rug-cleaning business myself," he says. "It goes great with the job." And, to my astonishment, he launches into a short but well-rehearsed commercial, describing the quality, speed, and attractively low price of his service. Before I know it, I am holding a small calling card that tells me to call Rug-Nu anytime of day or night for a pickup within twenty-four hours in any part of the city except Staten Island. He adds that the rug-cleaning business is doing so well that he is almost ready to quit being a cop. "Only there's something kind of nice about it," he says. "The way the kids look up to me, maybe— the way they wouldn't if I was just a regular rug cleaner."

So what he is is an entrepreneur whose tours of police duty are devoted, in large measure, to soliciting new customers, precisely as he is doing now in my kitchen. He is therefore, I assume, likely to be less than ardent about his pursuit of wrongdoers, and so I relax and join him in a cup of coffee. Before we are done, I promise him all our rugs. He can come tomorrow for them. And no rush about getting them back.

"Oh, there's something else I wanted to tell you," he says at the end.

I freeze.

"We're also going into furniture cleaning now, too. It'll be like a separate division. I'm calling it Chair-Nu—you know, to go with Rug-Nu?"

Take. Take them. Take all my chairs. All my sofas. And the drapes. And my clothes. And this whole jar of Yuban. "Tomorrow," I say.

"Could it be next week, maybe? We're a little jammed right now."

Next week. Next month. Next year. Whatever you want, Pat Pratt, you are one of nature's noblemen. Now get your rump out of here before I murder you on general principles. And do not think I am not capable. I am, at the moment, capable of anything—and feeling excellent about it.

25

The Kite

I STEER THROUGH THE GRAY RAW AFTERNOON ALONG THE PARK drive, the collar of my great woolly Scottish coat shielding half my head from the fitful early-winter wind. I move at a purposeful pace, rimming the boat lake that is just begining to grow its first glazed crust of the season. A few people are out walking the dog, but most of the park is white and still and the fresh light snowfall is so far unsullied. The footpath swings uphill at the Seventy-second Street exit. I trudge onward, southward, mindlessly absorbing the sporadic gusts. As the edge of the Ramble gives way to the great meadow, my eyes instinctively search above the bony traceries of treetop. Nothing there but dappled grays. Nothing and more nothing. Until finally there is something, something moving up there against the dour overcast. Is it a bird? No, the birds are far away. A plane? No, it is too slow and bobbing too much. An unidentified flying object it remains until my squint can determine at last that it is red and boxy and, yes, distinctly kite-like. A kite like the kite I have come hoping to find. It is way up and being buffeted angrily.

I come past the last clump of trees and the vast white blanket of meadow opens up before me. Toward the middle, a doll-like figure gambols freestyle in the snow. I want to romp to it, but I am not sure yet, not entirely sure. The snow creeps up and over my loafers as I plow the shortest straightest course to the circling dancer, who is looking up—that is clear now—up toward the kite. A dozen more steps bring me within eye range of the string itself, straining to yank its small owner into the slate sky like a tail on the bobbing, jerking red kite. The mangy coat is identifiable now, as are the general size and contours of its wearer. The black beret and black sunglasses and high black boots are new to me, but beyond any question I have found her.

She never takes her eyes from the sky. She lets the string in and out with the dexterity of a virtuoso. Her skill is particularly remarkable in light of the adverse kiting conditions. She is so rapt that I fear I am intruding on a transcendental experience. But there is no place else to go, and so I stand there right next to her, watching silently. Twice she must dodge around me, and that is the only way I know she knows that I have materialized. Then, a step at a time, she begins to recede from me. At first I think I am imagining it, but when she has moved off twenty or thirty yards, I cannot pretend it is just the kite and the wind that are bearing her away. Reluctantly I follow. I catch up with her just as the wind ebbs for a time and she is less harried by the physical contest. Still her eyes never stray from the kite, which is nearly motionless for the moment.

Without looking at me, she says, "Go away, whoever you are."

"I am not whoever-you-are."

"I never talk to strangers, so go away. Scat."

"Scat rat—I am not your regular park-prowling stranger."

"I don't know you."

"You're not looking at me."

"Well, I'm busy—isn't that obvious?"

"I don't mind that you walked off with the serpents."

"I don't know what you're talking about."

"The gold serpents of Isis—the armlets—I don't mind, if that's what you think."

"I haven't the slightest idea what you're babbling about, and if you don't stop bothering me, I'm going to scream."

There is no detectable vestige of whimsy in her voice. It is as cold as the day, with an edge as cutting. It is plain mean. I do not know this voice. "Connie?"

"I am not Connie, it so happens—my name is Olivia, and you've obviously mistaken me for someone else, so I would greatly appreciate it if you would go away this minute."

I snare the kite string out of the air. "You know something?" I say. "You're being a fresh, nasty child."

"Give me my kite back!"

"Not till you're ready to talk like a grown-up."

"I don't want to talk to you—Mr. Whoever-You-Are."

"My name is Christopher Kwait."

"I told you—I didn't want to know your name!"

"I'm called Kit—like some other Christophers."

"I don't care what you're called—just give me my kite back!"

"Connie, what's the matter? What did I do to you? You came voluntarily last night—I didn't drag you. What's happened since 8 A.M.? What did I do that was so terrible?"

She turns around and walks away, slowly and not very far. She circles about for a time, brooding. I wait awhile and then move after her. She is staring at the snow. Suddenly the wind picks up and tugs the kite string right out of my hand. I make a feeble jump to recover the very endpiece, but it whips away too fast and up the kite soars, spinning and pitching to its doom. At the sight of it, Connie flops in the snow and bursts into great heavy sobs.

I sit beside her, the wet cold telegraphing my bladder of its inroads, and wait till she stops. "I'll get you another one," I say finally, as I would to any five-year-old.

She promptly socks me on the arm. "It's not the damn kite, stupid," she whimpers and snuffles.

"What is it then? Are you pregnant or something?"

"No!" she blurts. "I am a ratty-looking virgin and not the slightest bit pregnant!"

"Then what is it? What's going on?"

"You are, stupid! I'm all shook up—can't you tell that? What's the good of your being a damn grown-up if you can't tell what's going on inside people?"

"Inside who? What? Say it in English, for crissakes!"

She lifts her sunglasses and looks straight at me with her teary almond eyes. "You are complicating my life," she says, giving each word of the charge an independent and immensely dramatic emphasis.

"How come?"

"You intruded on it—I asked you not to but you insisted."

"Oh."

"I shouldn't have let you—the way you were being so hideously unfunny with that terrible shoeshine kit."

"It teaches humility."

"Whatever it's supposed to do, it wasn't doing it to you."

"Oh. And so you hate me—"

"No, stupid man, I don't hate you."

"Call me Kit."

"No, stupid Kit, sitting there in the stupid snow—I don't hate you. And I don't love you. But I want to be with you. Something happened to me when I was with you. You are kind and funny and interested and grown-up—yes, you are grown-up and don't deny it—and when I'm with you, I think I am a real person and not so terrible or fat or ugly."

The joy is leaping out of me—the joy and the portent of travail—for, having sudden testimony of her caring, I see exactly what she means about my complicating her life, since she is doing no less to mine. All I can think of for the next ten protracted seconds is Anne, who dearly loves me and whom I dearly love, and our little children, what's-their-names, who worship me and whom I adore. How can I do anything, anything at all, to hurt these little vulnerable people who

depend on me utterly for their well-being? I am the center of their
solar system. I am the provider. The protector. The sower and the
reaper. Am I really on the verge of abandoning all that? For what?
For whom—this very strange girl crying next to me in the snow?
About whom I know nothing? Has she told me one word that is true?
What is admirable about her? It is impossible, all of it. It defies every
rule of logic, every principle of human kindness, every concept of
adult responsibility. Yes, and that is precisely what impels me toward
her. I have broken out of all those magnetic fields, am free from all
those gravitational pulls. I am not even orbiting. No, I am free-float-
ing. I am Eagle. I am the archetypal spaceman. With no way back to
earth, even if I wanted to get there. And for the moment, anyway, I
am relishing my weightlessness. I will take it as it comes. So tell me
I am marvelous, Connie Colton. Tell me you cannot live without me,
Olivia Ottway. Tell me you are mine, Cricket Kiteperson.

I touch her chin. I have not touched her anywhere before. I touch
her chin and say, "You are not fat and ugly."

"I'm fat—fat fat fat."

"A trifle plump."

She is laughing and crying together now. "Fat is fat, and don't try
to be nice to me or I'll hit you hard."

"Okay, you're fat and ugly."

"Fine. Now, what do you want from me? Why are you here? How
did you know where I was? What am I going to do?"

"What do you want to do?"

"I want to marry Paul."

"So marry him."

"He insists on knowing where I was last night."

"How does he know you weren't home?"

"Because he was there all night."

"Where?"

"At my apartment—he has the key."

"And Paul therefore thinks he owns you?"

"Yes, of course. He owns me and a Mercedes."

"Which does he love more?"

"He loves us both."

"Then why doesn't he marry you?"

"He's going to."

"Then why did you spend the night in the apartment of a strange man?"

"I never did that before."

"Really?"

"Really."

"Are you sorry you did?"

"No."

I scoop up some snow. "I see your problem."

"It's a terrible problem."

"Terrible."

"I wasn't sure it was until you showed up here. I mean I thought we'd both just let it go. But here you are. And here I am. And I don't know what to think."

"Do you want to just let it go? I will if you say so."

Her head slumps. She picks up a gloveful of snow and starts nibbling at it. "I have to think. I mean I don't see the point in going on with it unless—unless we—go on with it. And you're married. And have children. Oh, God, how I hate children!" She flips the snow away. "I mean it can only get terribly complicated—isn't that so?"

"Why don't we just play it by ear?"

"What does that mean?"

"Take things as they come."

"What does that *mean?*"

"I mean don't let's make a big thing of it. Let's see if any of it makes sense."

"Oh, goddammit to hell, what *are* you talking about?"

"What are *you* talking about? I mean we don't have to live together starting in fifteen minutes. We can—see each other once in a while. We're civilized people. We like each other. Let's—just—see each other once in a while."

"I'm not a once-in-a-while person. I don't see one person and then another person. I—just don't work that way." She lifts her head up high. "Okay, I'll think and you'll think and we'll both see what we—think. Okay?"

"Huh?"

"I mean you go away now and I'll go away and let's decide separately."

"Decide what?"

"Whether to—what you said—see each other."

"Oh. Well, I've decided."

"Well, I haven't. So go away."

"When will you decide?"

"I don't know."

"Oh. Well, when you do, let me know."

"Yes, I promise."

"You can leave word for me at the bar."

"What bar?"

"The bar where we met yesterday—The Bottom of the Barrel. Just give Shag the message."

"Who's Shag?"

"The owner. The co-owner. I own the other half. I'll be there some of the time."

"All right."

"Either way you decide, you can keep the snakes."

"What snakes?"

"The armlets—the gold armlets."

"What do you mean?"

"You know what you are? You're a robber-robber. That's a robber who robs from robbers."

"I don't know what on earth you're talking about."

26

Ecstasy Loves Company

JIMBO JEHEAVENSOCKER, HEAD BARKEEP AND CHIEF CASH-REGISTER looter of The Bottom of the Barrel, is overseeing the process of re-christening the place Xanadu City, as Shag and I have agreed. Madly twirling his handlebar mustache, Jimbo directs a squad of half a dozen volunteers who are painting a psychedelic mural the entire length of the wall opposite the bar. Each volunteer has his own section of wall to fill and, to ensure maximum spontaneity, is forbidden by the rules of the happening—or paint-in, as it has been inevitably designated by all concerned—to see what his neighbors are up to until everyone has just about finished, at which point a frantic effort will be mounted to execute transitional passages to make it all seem to hang together, at least vaguely. They are using a raucous palette of Day-Glo colors: a screechy green and voluptuous sort of lavender are the drabbest on hand. In his booth at the back, meanwhile, Shag Shaughnessy is dickering with a faggot sign painter, who is insisting on a Beardsleyesque style for the big sign that will hang out front. Shag has been opting for a sort of Oriental-modern arrangement, with each letter a different color. I am asked to mediate.

"What you want," I tell Shag, "is something in the neo-fandango school—that's not going to date as fast as this kind of crap." Having imparted that oracular wisdom, I wander off before I am asked for details and pick up the station abandoned by one of the mural volunteers who has gone off to the bathroom or for a fix or to the moon. He has been working with a kind of austere paisley pattern that I am not fond of, so I start making Hans Hofmann-like slashes of red and white and green and yellow, and then I draw some stick figures till someone hisses at me for being too representational and I go in for fingertip-type whorls that soon take me beyond my authorized territory. My intruded-upon neighbor becomes testy and I respond by seizing a roller sodden with orange paint and running it down the length of his navy sweat shirt. He inspects the design I have created with minute interest and then, gently almost, dumps half a can of red directly on my pants. As would any two civilized men, we agree the score is even at this point and retire to the bar for a mug of beer.

Old Orangestain turns out to have been a marvelously talented actor who, by steadfastly refusing to make TV commercials and to play in traveling autoramas while waiting for the Real Thing, has managed to run up an impressive skein of consecutive months without a job. Fortunately, he confides, he is being kept by a fortyish widow sporting a well-dispersed collection of warts and an insatiable case of lust. "She," he says, "is my full-time job."

I am on the verge of telling him I do not believe a word he has said when the abominable Action appears precisely on schedule. I tell Orangestain the beers are on me, in gratitude for which he gives me a telltale squeeze high on the thigh, and I excuse myself to conduct my business with my one legitimate link to the underworld.

To my astonishment, Action is anything but his abrasive, professionally hard-boiled self. No, he is all peaches and cream this afternoon and eager to know how soon he can get his mitts on the goods. It seems I have committed an already infamous robbery and the network linking denizens of the outlaw community has been pulsing for two days with inquiries over the ultimate disposition of the haul. The jewelry is of such renowned magnificence that it is generally agreed the newspaper stories undervalued its retail worth by half, for reasons nobody quite understands (though the hand of the insurance company is suspect). Spirited behind-the-scenes bidding ensued, Action boasts, when word got out that he had a pipeline to the stuff. Yes, adds Action expansively, we will be able to work out something quite satisfactory all around. And now, he says, where is it? Emboldened by his news, I demand to know his price first. He says he has to see the stuff first, but I remind him that, by his own testimony, its exquisite quality has been universally acknowledged. No, he must state a satisfactory price here and now or I will take my business elsewhere. The size of the prices in the offing has obviously loosened his illicit middleman's tongue beyond the limits of prudence, he recognizes belatedly, but how often do his sordid circumstances allow him something to boast about? He does not contest my point and is ready to knuckle down to hard numbers. He has fifty thousand in mind; I have two hundred thousand. For twenty minutes he tells me how preposterous my expectations are, and than we settle on the even and quite splendid figure of one hundred thousand. Dollars. To be paid in small bills. Many packets of. As soon as he has the stuff and checks its authenticity. I hand him the key to the locker in the Port Authority Bus Terminal (checking first to make sure it is not the key for the locker with the Caravaggio in it) and we agree to reconvene this evening at ten. End of transaction. No handshake.

I wonder, as he evaporates in seemingly dismembered sectors (to thwart easy identification), whether I shall ever see him again. I ponder the recourses available to me in that not totally implausible event. None, I decide, and to my mingled pleasure and horror I find I am unexercised over the possibility. Should my daring be rewarded if it is dependent for its harvest on such reptiles? But what choice have I? And Action, I tell myself, has compelling professional reasons not to slink off into the night with my gems in tow—his survival chief among them. The likelihood of my having to pursue him to, say, Tasmania and gun him down in the midst of their broadest boulevard seems remote at the moment, so my head fills instead with visions of impending wealth and the steadily-broadening freedom it will afford me and the new extramarital adventure I am embarked on with unabashed zest (if problematic prospects). It is all in the offing, but the imminence of it is not quite enough to sustain me. I cannot contain the yeastlike rise of my elation. I must share it. And since Shag is preoccupied with completing the redecorations before the main contingent of the after-work crowd storms the place (and he is not, anyway, precisely the sort of confidant I most crave at the moment), I telephone the one man in town who will serve me, and I him.

Gibby Good, not quite midway through his sabbatical, responds at once and affirmatively to my call. He has not seen or heard from me since blessing my undertaking and dimly promising to participate after I had broken ground. He will be here in twenty minutes, he says. He makes it in forty-three, blaming subways and buses and the polluted air that has so saturated his lungs that he cannot go faster than a shuffle for two blocks without becoming winded. He comes bearing the first three finished chapters of his book, called, as he has threatened all along, *The New Dionysian Ego*. Now, though, it has grown a new subtitle: *Studies in Twentieth-Century Perversity*. He wants me to read it and tell him that I admire it without reservation. "If you hate it," he says, "I don't want to know."

"Suppose I hate it but tell you I like it?"

"You wouldn't do that."

"I wouldn't want to make you feel bad."

Already he is fretting. "Now if you say you like it, I won't know whether you mean it."

"That's right."

"Only if you say you hate it will I know you're telling the truth."

"Exactly."

"And I don't want to know if you hate it."

I hand him the book back. He takes it, nodding thanks. We then establish that our healths are good and our families thriving. The next minute I am pouring out my perverse story to him in its every unthinkable detail. I am a walking case study, of course, for his book, and part of his dumfoundedness at my disclosures is attributed to the exemplary way I have demonstrated the validity of his premise. Besides being a case study, though, I am also still a friend, and, having originally encouraged my daredeviltry and now accepted my narrative without even token disbelief, he professes shock and alarm that belie the moral radicalism presumably rampant in his book. I point out the discrepancy.

"No," he says, "you don't understand. I'm not championing the trend—I'm describing it. I'm trying to synthesize it in some manageable way—to diagnose the causes—to pave the way for a more understanding response when all these varieties of perversity begin to be recognized for what they are: the culminating stage in the normative behavioral cycle of the century."

"Which is jargon for saying it's a fucked-up world."

"That's probably not the most felicitous way to put it," he says, cleaning his glasses with his tie, "but I suppose that's what it comes to."

"You sound disapproving."

"No, no—I'm trying to stay morally neutral. If I become a spokesman for or against, I lose all claim to dispassion. And without dispassion, I'm nothing."

He has retrogressed badly in the past few weeks. It has had something to do, I take it, with the process of converting outrageous thoughts into palatable scholarship. "If you are really dispassionate, you wouldn't be scolding me," I tell him. "After all, what am I but a walking case study of twentieth-century man entering the culminating stage of his normative behavioral cycle."

"Very funny," he says.

"Yes, I think it is."

"Well, I don't think it is—it or you. You've been doing some very stupid things."

"You didn't think they were so stupid when I told you I was considering them."

"I was just testing you. I didn't think you'd ever go through with it—not this far, anyway."

"Neither did I. I just started and kept going. And I don't know where it's going to stop."

"Kit, are you crazy? You've got to stop—right now."

"Why?"

"Why? You tell me the police are beginning to sniff around you, you're on the brink of an affair that could jeopardize your family, you've neglected your job completely, and you're consorting with a host of despicable and/or irresponsible types who will lead you to ruin. And you ask why. What's all this getting you, I'd like to know."

"It makes me feel good. Wonderful, in fact."

"No."

"Yes. Absolutely yes. Expansively wonderful. Full of limitless possibilities. And rich—I'm going to be rich. And powerful. And I will become even more rich and more powerful. And notorious—secretly, of course, but still notorious. And I will carry on a second love life—and maybe more. Men need it—all biological and historical evidence supports me. Monogamy is clearly unnatural; you know it as well as I do. It's got nothing to do with Anne. Of course I love her, and will keep right on loving her. But that can't keep being my whole life. No, I want it all. And I'm beginning to get it. And every bit of it—the thrill, the money, the fame, the power, the love, the freedom—it's wonderful. I'm really doing it—and loving it. I'm a new man—a total man. You ought to try it instead of whining at me as if all of a sudden you're manning the last goddam bastion of gentility with a ping-pong racket."

"Well—"

"But you know all this."

"I know it."

"In your head, though, not your glands. Your glands are up-tight, baby. And your book's not going to be anything until you really let go—until you really find out what it's all about and not settle for a cop-out fling at buggery."

He looks dejected. I know I have pinked him where it stings. He broods for a moment while I order us beer. Then he faces up to it. "Shall I tell you the truth? The truth is you're right and I know it. But I've been afraid to let go—to really let go. And you know why? Because if I let go, I'm panicked that I'll never be able to grab on again—that I'll get addicted—that I won't be able to bear the whole fucking routine I manage to stomach now because I can't see any viable alternative. I'm too old to reorient my whole way of thinking— and being—and that's what it takes. You—well, you're making history, doing what you're doing. That doesn't mean it's good, particularly. I mean if the cops catch you and you rot in jail for ten or fifteen years, I'd say you weren't very bright about it all. If you get away with it, though—and you don't ruin half a dozen lives in the process—then maybe you'll deserve a medal. The first Pulitzer Prize for Polymorphous Perversity by a Living Heterosexual American."

The beer comes and he downs it greedily. And another. And another. He keeps asking details about my adventures, and the more he hears, the more ogle-eyed he becomes. Minute by minute he is letting go, moving past the misty frontiers of Waltermittyland, with its antiseptic projections of a dwarfed and thwarted self, toward the dank rain forest of unleashed depravity. Once my mentor, he now becomes my protégé. My escapades, however modest to date, have transfigured all those sublimated yearnings and incorporeal theories he has been diddling with for so long now. But it will not happen in one hugely daring leap. He is moving to the brink sideways.

"Look," he says through foam-flecked lips, "I know what you're doing to me and why you're doing it. You want company—it validates what you're up to—and spreads the risk. Ecstasy loves company, right? Right. So okay. So I want in—a little. And don't tell me it's got to be all or nothing; I don't buy that. I mean nobody's going to con me into anything."

Spewing pugnacity all the way, he applies for associate membership in whatever ranks I am assembling. He wants to help plan and execute the next episode. I tell him I don't believe much in planning, that it violates the spirit of the thing, and he agrees. "But the money," he says, "what are you going to do with it—just stash it in a safe-deposit box and forget about it?"

"I don't know yet. I'll figure it out when I get it."

"Of course it's not really all that much."

"No, not really—not yet."

"You ought to try to parlay it—invest it in things with huge risk and huge profits. What's the point of a little money? It's worse than none. You ought to go all the way—millions or nothing."

I admire his sudden new zest for enterprise, even if it is my money he is ready to wager so recklessly. I designate him my official financial adviser.

"But I don't know anything about money. My checkbook never even adds up right."

"Then you're obviously the perfect one."

That settled, we both proceed to get stupefyingly drunk. Every other word out of Gibby's mouth is pornographic. In between, he starts proposing heroic projects we will undertake when my fortune reaches five million dollars. He has just suggested blowing up the Pan Am Building on a lazy Sunday morning when in come Daryl Divot and his standard entourage. Every booth is taken, so Shag, secretly craving the patronage of the Daryl Divots of the world and all their comely satellites, pays his daily homage to them by summarily ejecting the occupants of the booth preferred by the Divot party. When the ejectees protest, Shag explains the booth is reserved nightly for this time and these people. That fails to satisfy them, though, and they refuse to get up. Shag begins to bully them and I begin to move. The offended party has risen now but is refusing to pay its check. Shag has just threatened to summon the police when I lay a heavy hand on his shoulder and urge him to forget it.

"Fuck off," he says.

"You can't talk to your partner that way."

"You're not my partner—you haven't paid me yet."

"I am so the hell your partner—we shook hands on it."

"That doesn't mean dick legally, so butt out, buster, before I get sore."

"I'm a half owner, Charlie, and I'll sue your ass off to prove it. I say these people stay—and this big shit here can wait his turn like everyone else."

Divot overhears our exchange. "Well," he says to me, "if it isn't old fatlip sticking his two cents in again."

"I don't want this no-talent phony in my place," I tell Shag.

"Your place?"

"You heard me."

"What's eating this guy?" Divot asks Shag. "Sounds like he needs a quick trip to Lobotomyville to get rid of his hostility."

His lackeys all laugh.

"Of course if I had a face like that," Divot goes on, "I'd be hostile, too."

More lackey laughs.

"I must have heard wrong, Shag," Divot winds up. "You couldn't possibly have taken this certified schmuck in as a partner—could you?"

Shag's neck stiffens. The glare he has been inflicting on me turns now into narrowed slits aimed at Divot. "Why couldn't I?" he asks.

"Because he's a dumb, ugly, obnoxious schmuck."

Shag looks at me. "You gonna take that from him?"

"Certainly not."

"What are you gonna do about it?"

"Punch him in the nose."

"No, the eye—it hurts more."

"Okay." And I start my swing in a graceful arc. Divot's fist interrupts me in the belly and I sink to the floor vomiting beer. Seconds later Divot joins me in the swill. He is wearing a glazed and peaceful look. A small melee ensues, at the end of which I see Divot, still glazed and peaceful-looking, being borne toward the door on the shoulders of his faithful retinue.

They finish swabbing the floor before anyone bothers to pick me up. It is Shag who hoists me to my feet, gives me a little shaking out, and says, not unaffectionately, "A bouncer you'll never be."

"Check."

"But I like your spirit, champ."

"Yeah, next time I'll get him."

"Sorry, champ—I banned him for life. Nobody calls my schmucky partner names like that and gets away with it."

I try to embrace him but he fends off my reeking garments and we settle for a handshake renewing the covenant so sorely tested only a moment earlier. He helps me to the washroom and looks on solicitously as I fill the basin and dunk my face in it. I am given somebody's leftover sweat shirt and ushered back to the saloon proper and the seat of honor atop the lifeguard stand where Shag himself generally presides when he is in a presiding mood. It affords an excellent view of the scenery. Part of the scenery is Gibby Good, proud if cautious possessor of a New Dionysian Ego, slumped asleep drunk in his chair, mouth open in the classic fly-catching manner.

27

Unearned Increment

THE QUICKEST WAY TO THE MADHOUSE IN AMERICA IS TO BECOME agitated over the discrepancy between people who have money and people who deserve to have it. Not that people in America who deserve it never get it. Or that people who get it never deserve it. More often than not, though, both those things are true.

This matter of just deserts going unbestowed is particularly acute
in America because (1) there is so much money being bestowed, and
(2) so many nimble, predatory, and otherwise crummy people are
making off with so much of it that there is not enough left to properly
nourish (a) those who deserve it but don't ask for very much, and
(b) those who are systematically denied the chance to claim their
share. There is, of course, nothing particularly new about any of this.
It was named Social Darwinism some time back, and while a number
of steps have been taken to mitigate the more oppressive implications
of the doctrine that the fittest shall thrive, the doctrine by and large
still prevails. And probably will for quite a while.

Being neither Communist nor Socialist nor anarchist nor vegetarian
nor agitator of any stripe or intensity, I have long since learned to
live with this state of affairs, even while recognizing its inequities. To
fret about them unduly without the power or inclination to rectify
them—that way lies madness. One could say, I suppose, that the
course I have chosen to this point in the narrative—jettisoning the
conventions by which I have lived in order to gain some vague sense
of what life's larger possibilities hold for me—is scarcely less than
madness. I am prepared for that. It is, for example, what Anne would
say—has to say—for she is Anne, and Anne is the whole way of life
I have found both agreeable and intolerable. But in fact I am not
mad, and if in fashioning my liberation I have practiced a bit of
civil disobedience, I have harmed no one who could not stand a bit
of harming. The truth is I have not had the wherewithal to do much
more than vent my private fantasies in relatively harmless ways. Now,
though, as the story moves to its dénouement, the money starts to
arrive—money that is of course unmerited by any of the usual standards of achievement. I, in other words, am about to become a beneficiary of the American way of life. I am about to join the ranks of
the unwarranted rich. I do not mind the prospect, naturally, since I
have never objected very strenuously to their prevalence (because
there was always the possibility that I might someday be among

them). Mine is to be a textbook case of unearned increment. And the only way I will not lose my sanity altogether, I sense from the beginning, is to wield this ill-gotten wealth as a weapon against the injustice of the system that spawns it. It is to be the culminating act of perversity in the total redeployment of my—of my what? My psyche? My will? My being? Whatever it is called, it is performing, by all prevailing standards, in a perverse and depraved manner. I, for my part, am arguing that perversity has its reasons that reason knows not. Or, if you will (and since I am full of tedious aphorisms): perversity, like beauty, lies nowhere if not in the eyes of its beholder. Do you see? Shall we vote on it?

Yes, the money. I have not forgotten.

It begins the next day. Action, as he had pledged he would on returning from the bus-terminal locker the night before, has auctioned off the ice with almost unseemly speed. His being a strictly cash-and-carry trade, he appears at the saloon in the middle of the afternoon carrying a small suitcase. "It's all here," he says, "minus twenty-three-fifty for the suitcase."

I do not doubt for an instant that it is, in fact, all there. What would be the point in its not being? I am, apparently, a valuable new source of supply to the stolen-gems market, and, like any pearl, worth cultivating. Action and I seal the deal over beer, exchanging small talk about the weather, the psychedelic mural, and his fond memories of the year he spent in jail for a heist that yielded nothing but the realization he was in the wrong end of the business. His advice to me is to lie low for a while and, when I am ready to go back to work, to hit another town. He urges me to think creatively about the suburbs, where the potential take is enormous and few really skilled operators ever work.

I head for the toilet when he leaves, grabbing an oversized salad bowl from the kitchen en route. In the privacy of the booth I open the suitcase and scoop out great fistfuls of bills; I put them in the bowl and mix them all up in a crackling tangle. Draping my jacket over the bowl, I place the money salad in Shag's private booth in the back and then climb the lifeguard's tower to stand watch—sit watch, I suppose would be more accurate—until it is discovered.

While I am up there, numbly exulting, a telephone call comes from Bobby Butterfield, our faggot college classmate now ensconced as an associate curator at the Metropolitan. His news is dizzying: both Lifeline and the museum have agreed to the Caravaggio proposal, and I will be paid the fifty thousand dollars next week. Joyful beyond words, I nevertheless have the presence of mind to point out that a check would prove an awkward means of payment, and Bobby agrees that it should be done with small bills. He promises to exchange the marked bills he will almost certainly be given to transmit for nice regular ones, so that the chances of my being apprehended may be reduced to a minimum. In jail, he understands, I will be unavailable for fondling.

Just as I am concluding my business with Butterfield (I am to mail him the key to the bus-terminal locker where the painting is stored, and he will come to the saloon the following day with a bursting attaché case), a piercing yelp fills the air. Shag has happened on his salad. "You're beautiful, baby," he says and gives me a deal-consummating clop on the back. To celebrate, he pumps four quarters into the juke and orders us a small mountain of chili. While it is forthcoming, he reports fully on his plans to expand the kitchen and triple the food volume as well as inaugurate a series of cultural events of a thus far undetermined nature. "They've got to be boffo, though. I was thinking maybe of a series of debates. Like we could lead off with Bill Buckley going three rounds against Bertrand Russell on disarmament, see? And then maybe Jimmy Baldwin going against George Wallace on 'But Would You Want Your Daughter to Marry One?' And then Allen Ginsberg against Walter Lippmann on—on—what could they do?"

"How about 'Is Mao Tse-tung AC/DC?' "

"Good, that's very good. And maybe we could put Gibby in charge of cultural affairs. It would be all very respectable. And then maybe we could . . ."

I try unsuccessfully to restrain a gaping yawn as Shag rampages on and on with idiot schemes to turn the place into a mecca for rich swingers. He wants to buy out the thrift shop next door and turn it into a discothèque and then rent up the rest of the tenement that the saloon is in, using the second floor to show underground movies running at least eight hours each, the third floor as the studio for an artist-in-residence whom we will finance (provided the customers can watch him while he works), the fourth floor for a marijuana den (Shag is convinced narcotics will be legalized momentarily and he wants to be ready), and the fifth floor as a whorehouse. I agree it is not a totally unattractive plan, and on the strength of that muted vote of support, he vows to talk to the landlord the following week about dispossessing the other tenants in our favor. There remains a totalitarian streak in Shag Shaughnessy not terribly far below the surface. I am thinking of ways to put it to use.

My plunder now totals $129,976.50 (counting what I have subtracted to pay Shag) and I should be euphoric. But it is more than twenty-four hours since I last saw Connie Colton and I am despairing of her ever showing up. I keep one eye riveted on the door, but each passing hour lengthens the odds against her appearing. Gibby checks in around six and distracts my drooping spirits with a report on his conversation during the day with a hot-shot stockbroker who has briefed him on all the known methods for turning a little bundle like mine into a king's ransom. "Most of them," Gibby says dutifully, "are frankly speculative. I think you have to admire his candor for telling us." I say that's true, and so Gibby goes on at length, referring to several pages of notes he has taken outlining the various options and their accompanying degree of risk. The most promising, he concludes, all things considered, is investing in puts and calls. "It's a little complicated," he says, "so he's sending me a booklet explaining it all." I thank him for this faithful and immediate discharge of his new duties as my principal financial adviser and suggest that he go home now before his supper gets cold. "Screw that," he says with Dionysian disdain and runs on another unbearable half hour describing the virtues of investing in the stock market as compared with real estate or soybean futures. He is not yet done when I get up, ostensibly to pee, so I duck out the back door and walk around the block five times. He is enough miffed when I come back to announce that he is leaving. I thank him again, and we agree that we should pursue the matter next week. Meanwhile both of us will begin reading the *Wall Street Journal* in earnest.

Torpor inundates me for the next hour. Every minute of it I verge on calling Anne and telling her I am on my way to join them all in the winter wonderland. But I keep on drinking as a preventive to such rashness. I am practically senseless when bursting through the door in her mangy coat, irrespressibility rampant on her tapered face, comes Connie Colton herself—and a small round man about forty-five or fifty, with grayish hair. I am too numb to wave. The most I can manage is a few stiff blinks to make sure it is she. It is. She sees me. She is coming. Him with her. Now who in hell is that? No, not Paul. He is too old for that.

"My God," she says, "what have you been doing? You look absolutely terrible."

I nod.

"I mean scandalously bad. Corrupt, even."

I keep nodding.

"Well, aren't you going to say something?"

"Uh—who the hell is that?"

"This is Octavio—Octavio Ortiz."

"Tha's wonderful."

"He's my favorite person in the world."

"Hello, favorite person. Wha'd you do to qualify?"

"He's my guitar teacher. Also my mentor."

"Nice."

"Well, aren't you going to shake his hand?"

I shake his hand.

"Thank you for inviting us to sit down," she says.

" 'Scuse me. Everybody sit down."

They sit down.

"I have some truly excellent news," Connie says. "But I don't know if I ought to tell you when you're like this."

I dimly inspect Octavio, who is wearing a tieless shirt of sort of green burlap and a thin rumpled pea jacket, which means he should be freezing his dangles off out there in the cold. He has a shaggy mustache and shaggy hair, giving rise to my suspicion that great swirling clumps of hair sprout on him from chest to ankle—a feature that would explain his apparent insulation from winter. "Pop," I say, friendly as can be, "you get much off old Connie here?"

Octavio looks puzzled.

"Ass—do you get much ass off her?"

"Kit!" Connie screams. "Don't be vile!"

"I thought that's what mentors were for," I say thickly.

"Octavio and his wife have been absolutely marvelous to me for four years now—they're my surrogate parents." She is calm now, as if acknowledging my stewed condition. "So you keep a civil tongue in your head or we're walking right out of here—and taking your twenty-five thousand dollars with us."

"Oh."

"I mean we don't exactly have it yet—but we will next week, when the man from Chicago comes."

"Oh."

"That's where I've been all day."

"Chicago?"

"No—with Professor Moriarty. He thinks they're authentic."

"Oh."

"I was there when he called the man in Chicago. He's actually going to fly in Monday to look at them."

"Oh." I give my head a shake to try to clear it. "To look at what?" "The serpents. The gold armlets I stole from you. Well, not 'stole' exactly—I was just afraid you wouldn't know what to do with them. So I took them to Professor Moriarty—he's the biggest Assyriologist in the city. He wears white socks. I took a course with him once. I made up a very involved story about this friend of mine's having picked up the armlets at an antique shop in Piraeus. Oh, you should have seen him get excited."

"Why does he wear white socks?"

"I don't know. Maybe all Assyriologists wear white socks. He also has a big beer belly. He was naked from the waist up when I came. He's really very gross. But he has this great big magnifying glass and little lens things you plug into your eye socket, and he got them all out and looked at the armlets for about an hour. Then he called this man Petrie in Chicago—he's some sort of assistant director at the Oriental Art Institute. It's part of the university. Petrie practically jumped through the telephone wire. Moriarty says they'll pay at least twenty-five thousand for them if Petrie's convinced they're authentic. Isn't that lovely?"

"I missed you," I say. "Why didn't you call or something?"

"I wanted to surprise you."

"I was waiting to hear—"

"You don't seem very happy. I thought you'd be happy—at least twenty-five thousand dollars' worth."

"Keep it for your dowry."

"Don't be silly. It's yours."

"You're entitled to your share of the haul."

"But I wasn't a real partner. I just came along."

"The hell you did. You're a veteran robber—you told me. You even made a list. Besides, you're the one who insisted on taking the snakes. I say they're yours, pal."

"I won't hear of it."

"Then it's fifty-fifty, you and me."

"But that would make me a professional robber. I'm just an amateur thief. I don't rob really. I just sort of—pilfer."

"You're trying to buy me off. You're going to give me the money and then tell me we're through before we even begin."

"I am not!"

"You're not?"

"No. In fact that's why I brought Octavio along. I've been talking to him about you ever since you lost my kite." She looks stern. "That was damn mean, by the way."

"It was an accident."

"No, it wasn't. You were jealous of the kite."

"Paul—not the kite."

"Same thing."

"All right, I'm jealous of Paul—madly jealous—"

"Well, he *is* much younger than you. And thinner."

"So marry him already."

"I don't think I'm going to."

"Why not?"

"Because he sleeps with other women."

"How do you know?"

"He tells Octavio."

"And Octavio has a big mouth."

"Octavio is very protective toward me."

"Do you let Paul sleep with you?"

"I told you—I'm unviolated."

"So what's wrong with Paul's sleeping around?"

"Because he likes it so much he keeps putting off the marriage."

"Oh."

"Besides, Octavio says Paul doesn't have a beautiful soul."

"Oh."

"And that's why I asked him to meet you."

"To see if I have a beautiful soul?"

"Well, sort of. I mean it takes a while to figure out."

"Oh."

"But Octavio can tell about a man after a while."

"I can save him the trouble. I have a very ugly soul. It's all gnarled and green and slimy—"

"Now, stop—"

"And excretes poisons with a sulfurous stench."

"You're being a self-pitying idiot!"

I throw back my head and shoulders. "Okay, maybe we can speed up the screening process." I turn to Octavio. "Tell me, my hairy friend, could you by any chance stand to pick up a little bread by doing a regular gig here—maybe an hour or two a night?"

Octavio looks to Connie for the translation.

"He doesn't play in *bars,*" she says indignantly. "He plays in concert halls."

"When was his last concert?"

She stares at the table.

"Well?"

"Some time ago."

"All right, then you ask him."

"I won't."

"Why?"

"Because he still has his pride. If he didn't, I would've given him all the money from the serpents and never told you a thing about it. But he wouldn't dream of taking a cent from me. Do you know he even gives me lessons for free? I started paying for them and then I had this big thing with my family and stopped taking any money from them and I told Octavio that I'd have to stop the lessons but he wouldn't let me. He absolutely insisted that I take three lessons a week for nothing."

"That's wonderful. But why do you do it?"

"Because he likes me. He'd take it as an insult if I stopped."

"How do you make it up to him?"

She shrugs. "I play the guitar as well as I can."

There is something affecting about the way she says it, and I know I am defiling something hallowed. "Okay," I say, "I withdraw the offer. But if he's so big on character, why'd you bring him to see me? If he doesn't approve of Paul's philandering, why should he want you seeing a married man with two kids?"

"Because he's got two wives and ten kids himself."

"Who—Octavio here?" I look at him, brow bent with disbelief.

But Octavio is all smiles. He holds up two fingers to show he understands and to confirm the bigamy.

"Both wives know all about it, of course," Connie explains. "Octavio is entirely honorable. It's just that he couldn't bear the life in Santurce after a while; he had all this talent and no way to use it. But Carmela didn't want to go trooping around the world with Octavio and their seven kids while he studied and gave concerts and tried to scrounge out a living."

"Quite a sensible sort, it sounds like."

"Ah, Carmela!" Octavio says with an exquisitely wistful sigh.

"He sends her money," says Connie, "when he has any."

"Does he ever have any?"

"Oh, sure. He gets five hundred dollars for a concert—" She remembers again that it has been some time since the last five-hundred-dollar performance. "Oh, and he made a couple of records once and he gets some royalties from them every now and then. And then he gives lessons." She shakes her head. "Most of them for nothing. The truth is if it wasn't for Marguerita, they'd probably all starve. He met her when he was studying in Siena. She's marvelous. I mean she never went to school or anything—all she knows is that Octavio makes beautiful music. And she'll do anything to let him keep playing. She works as a cook in the East Village."

"What's that do to Pop's pride?"

"It doesn't help it very much."

"Then how do you know he wouldn't want to play here a couple of hours a night?"

"That would be even worse. Whatever he is, he's not a sellout."

I look at Octavio again, trying hard to convince myself a noble heart beats inside that hairy breast. All I see in those large wet soulful eyes, though, is defeat.

"All right," I say, aiming a finger at Connie, "then *you're* going to play here—and pay Pop for all those lessons you've been grubbing."

Her face lights up and then swiftly dims. "But I play classical guitar. I mean I don't do Pete Seeger things."

"Do whatever you do—you'll be a smash."

She is on the brink of elation. "But—your partner, I bet he'd hate it."

"No, he's very hot for culture. It's just what he wants."

She explains it all to Octavio in broken Spanish garnished with a phrase or two of Italian. He nods his great mane, slowly at first and then faster. Then he breaks into an approving smile and gives my arm a pair of kindly raps to signal that the booking is set.

"How much?" Connie asks, a grin lurking behind the suddenly feigned sternness.

"How much what?"

"Money."

"Oh, I don't know—whatever's fair. How about twenty bucks a night?"

"Wow!"

"Plus all the chili you can eat."

"Spectacular!"

"Plus booze. We'll turn you into an alcoholic for nothing."

"Oh, stunning. And what happens if you hate the way I play?"

"We'll pour the chili into your guitar."

Great rejoicing ensues, during which Pop bombs out on Jack Daniels, Connie agrees to play every night for a month, and I am invited to spend the weekend at her apartment. "But," she cautions, "nothing carnal. If it has to be carnal, stay home. We're just going to be friends. We're just going to see if we like each other." She sees my joyless look. "You'll just have to sublimate. It's very good for you."

28

Trouble in Malaguena

WHETHER IT IS GOOD FOR ME OR NOT REMAINS TO BE SEEN, BUT I spend a substantial part of my lips-off, hands-off, degenitalized weekend with her stealing the circular Y-centered radiator ornament off the hood of every parked Mercedes-Benz we can find. Despite historic German fanaticism for constructing machines of all types so they cannot be dismantled without a squad of drilled mechanics functioning in perfect unison, the widget comes off quite handily when a little Venezuelan ingenuity is applied—Paul taught her how, she says —by giving the thing a twist at a certain angle, thereby releasing the spring on the underside of the hood that holds it in place. We bag at least a dozen of them—why, I am not sure, though I do not doubt that the theft produces a gush of irritation in the victim well out of proportion to the gravity of the crime. Connie keeps popping them into a shopping bag that gets to clanging noticeably as the weekend wears on. Between thefts I hear about all fifty-three complexes and phobias that plague her at least intermittently (she has written them down somewhere), including the conviction that she will die of suffocation before she is thirty. "I have unbelievably teeny lungs," she explains. "The doctor told me." She also still sleeps with a Teddy bear.

As a respite from our plundering, I take her to King Wu, a feebly lighted basement on Doyers Street in remotest Chinatown where they serve the most succulent Chinese food in the entire Occident. Midway through our tureen of ecstasy-provoking hot-and-sour soup, Connie in her joy confesses that she cannot bear to have anything to do with most of the people on earth. "Ninety-seven per cent of them are stupid and ugly," she says. "Just look around—anytime, anyplace—and you'll see. I mean I know I sound like an absolutely hideous snob, but it just happens to be true."

"What shall we do about it?"

"I don't know. But it makes me sick."

"But ugly people's ugliness isn't their fault. Or stupid people's stupidity—most of the time, anyway. Let's face it, nobody wants to be stupid or ugly. How can you hate them when it works out that way?"

"I didn't say I hated them. I said they get me sick."

"Is there a difference?"

"I don't know—I don't care."

"Oh, but it's all a guise on your part. Actually, you feel terribly sorry for them—right?"

"Wrong."

"A teeny bit sorry for them?"

"Double wrong. People get what they deserve out of life."

"You don't really believe that."

"Absolutely."

"Poor people deserve to be poor and rich people deserve to be rich?"

"Of course."

"What about Octavio?"

"I never said he was flawless."

"You are saying cruel and crazy things."

"And you are extremely conventional and sentimental beneath this pose of your as a big tough emancipated robber type."

"Naturally."

"Then you're doomed. You have to be an absolutist about it all."

"You know what you are? You are an intellectual Fascist."

"Also a virgin."

She is right, of course. She is a twenty-two-year-old fanatic who's never been laid, and the two qualities—fanaticism and chastity—are, in her case anyway, indisputably linked. She has fierce views and preferences about everything on earth there is to view or prefer. What is that fierceness if not the sublimation of all the painfully compacted and long-thwarted desire throbbing in her? I suddenly want to put the child out of her misery by casting the table to the ground and violating her yearning delta here and now amid all these pungent aromas and clucking Chinamen.

But I desist as I have pledged, and desist the weekend long. I sleep on the living-room sofa Friday night and advance to her bed, with her in it, Saturday and Sunday nights, but nary an ear lobe is fondled. Enormous will power is required to maintain such abstinence, and I muster it, largely because we are on the go nearly every moment, museum-hopping and kite-flying and window-shopping when we are not stealing radiator ornaments off Mercedes-Benzes or cookie boxes from Gristede's or watching the snub-nosed scows fight their way through the murky East River because she loves the murky East River with a passion bordering on mania. "There," she says, gesturing toward a particularly grubby-looking boat, "is the sixty-two-year-old *Ezra Sensibar.*"

"Where?"

"There—right there." She means the grubby scow.

"How do you know?"

"His name is there—see, in teeny letters?" She is waving at the boat frantically.

I see the teeny letters. "Yes—well, what about it?"

"It's my favorite East River boat."

"Why?"

"Because I see him all the time. In fact every time I get a chance,

I come over here and look for him. And if I wait long enough—along he comes."

"Boats are 'she's,' not 'he's.' "

"Not ones called Ezra." She keeps waving. "Isn't Ezra wonderful-looking?" No one is waving back.

"It looks like a floating garbage can."

"Yes, that's exactly what it is."

"How do you know it's sixty-two years old?"

"There was an article once in the *Times* about the city river boats."

"I thought you didn't read the papers."

"Only things like that—and very rarely."

She waves on with unrequited devotion until the foul thing is out of sight.

Sunday she makes me go to mass at St. Patrick's Cathedral just to see what the inside looks like ("unspeakably pagan," she says). From there we proceed north to St. John the Divine ("I prefer it unfinished," she says) and finally to the Cloisters for the better part of the afternoon, where she adores the madrigals and instructs me in them with what seems authentic mastery of the subject. I propose we end the day with a movie but she says she cannot bear movies, and so we go to her place where she prepares an eight-course dinner of staggering delectability, attended, quite on the spur of the moment, by Octavio and Marguerita and their three remarkably subdued children. Afterward Marguerita and the children do the dishes while Octavio and Connie play guitar nonstop until the rest of us have all fallen asleep. Rather than wake the children, the Ortizes simply stay the night in the living room, and Connie and I repair to our immaculate bed.

Monday morning the strain of abstinence is beginning to take its toll on both of us. Connie breakfasts on her usual macaroons and tea-with-milk while I fiddle listlessly with a buttered roll and a cup of the most expensive brand of espresso sold in North America. The tacit question of where we go from here is on both our minds. Given her ground rules discouraging the kind of ebb and flow of intensity permissible during most weekend-long relationships between consenting adults, we have had a surfeit of consuming but inconclusive togetherness. She does not invite me to move in to stay, nor do I have a constitution that can indefinitely tolerate such uncertain prospects of fulfillment. Our disembodied liaison, that is, has run its course. Connie, I see now, had quite shrewdly anticipated that course when I came upon her kite-flying in the park. She is not the kind of girl whose essence is revealed slowly, like an artichoke's. She is all there from the very first, holding none of herself back—except that sanctified pudendum whose inviolability she equates with the rareness, the specialness, the talent, and the brilliance that set her being apart from every other nubile female on earth. She will bestow it ultimately, I have no doubt, but I wonder what price she will demand in return. Her self-control (if that is the word for it) qualifies, I am now convinced, as a full-fledged psychosis. We agree only that we will see each other this evening at Xanadu City—and that I am to lead the applause for her performance with clamorous enthusiasm. "I'll just die," she says, "if they ignore me."

The rest of my morning is devoted to renting safe-deposit boxes at half a dozen of the city's more impregnable-looking banks. It will not do for me to be indefinitely toting thousands of dollars around town in a suitcase. That burden lifted, I check in at home, where there is a telegram waiting for me: "I'M A WHITE-HOT FURY. DID A TRUCK HIT YOU? WHERE ARE YOU? WHAT'S HAPPENING? CALL AT ONCE OR WE'RE COMING HOME MONDAY AYEM BUS. UNREQUITED LOVE. ANNE." It is dated Saturday.

Did I really forget all about them? Have I soared that far off into my new world? What on earth shall I tell her? The truth, I decide in a surge of retroactive fidelity. And she will of course call on me to cease and desist forthwith and to begin a protracted period of rehabilitation through psychotherapy. She will not grasp for a moment that the therapy resides precisely in my not ceasing and not desisting until I have spent my wayward impulses. I write her a note instead. It explains that I have been working tirelessly in an effort to finish my research assignment for Computron by Christmas and that I am sorry I couldn't join her and the children in snow heaven and that I will be out of town the coming week but will call tonight without fail, and will she try to understand? It is a tactic that gives me maximum maneuverability for the time being. And the time being is very much the element in which I am thriving.

I pack a few things in my suitcase and check in at the saloon, where Shag is in one of his more expansive and painfully playful humors. "How'd you like to sell me back your half of the business?" he says.

"I thought you wanted a partner."

"Oh, I did, I did."

"Haven't I been silent enough?"

"Hell, yes—you've been perfect."

"Then what's the matter?"

"I've just reconsidered."

"Too late."

"I'll pay you twenty-five thousand dollars. That's a pretty good profit for three days of sitting on your ass."

"My price is a million dollars."

He looks at me suspiciously. "I think you're wise."

"To what?"

"To what's been going on here today."

"Of course. I command a vast network of agents and couriers whose loyalty to me is sworn every sunrise in a ritual bath of nearly coagulated blood."

He half believes me. Only when I confess finally that I have no notion of what he is talking about does he reveal the news. As threatened, he checked with the landlord to see if the rest of the tenants in the building could be evicted so we might expand our cultural and social operations. Their eviction, it develops, has been contemplated for several months—a disclosure that had Shag rhapsodic until he learned that their eviction was to be followed closely by *our* eviction: unbeknownst to Shag, the landlord has sold out, and the new owner's plans call for immediate demolition of the building.

"Oh," I say. "That's too bad."

"No, it's not," says Shag.

"How do you figure?"

"The landlord can evict all these peons upstairs who hang out the windows in their undershirts—that's a snap. They're just month-to-month tenants. But we—we have a lease. A good lease. A five-year lease, as a matter of fact. And the only way they're going to get us out of here is with money—lots and lots of money. And whoever the new owner is has it because *my* informed sources report that he—or they or it—has bought up every single property on the block within the past six weeks."

"Any word on who it is?"

"It's a deep dark secret, the theory behind it being that the seller's price is likely to skyrocket if he thinks he's dealing with a fabulously wealthy buyer. A perfectly justified theory, by the way, since our price is going up every hour on the hour."

"What is it at the moment?"

"Oh, about ten million dollars."

"Out of which you were just trying to bilk me of five million."

"Right. There's nothing petty about me, you've got to admit that."

I admit it. I even commend him for his duplicity and assure him I would have done the same in his place, perhaps with even more guile, to which he says his heart wasn't really in it and I say that was apparent and he is a true chum of a partner. We agree that ten million is a sensible starting price for our lease purchase and that we will budge from it only when we are told who the real buyer is. I then break the news about my invitation to Connie to perform on the guitar starting tonight. Shag is noncommittal till I suggest how beautifully she will dovetail with his over-all cultural expansion program.

He yields and asks bluntly what my intentions toward her are. I explain that it is a very complicated situation. He says he reserves the right to make it even more complicated, since I am a married man and, according to all the laws of church and state, have no business prowling in her pants. I remark that his notion of a partnership is obviously more elastic than mine and that, at any rate, she is not his type but he is welcome to find out for himself since her and my relationship at the moment is volatile.

Connie shows at about seven-thirty, with Octavio in tow. She is panicked and he wants bourbon. I try to get a drink in her but she will not dream of it. Shag proposes that she perform up on the lifeguard tower, a suggestion she rejects as outlandish. He then proposes she play while strolling around the place, a suggestion she abhors. We settle on a corner table, though Shag notes that four less customers can therefore be accommodated. We then discuss her program. She proposes Tárraga's "Recuerdos de la Alhambra"; "Leyenda" and "Sevilla," by Albéniz; "Fandanguillo" and "Suite Castellana," by Moreno-Torroba; and a number of things by Villa-Lobos—some *chôros,* Etudes 1 and 7 and maybe 11, and perhaps Preludes 1, 2, 4, and 5, depending how it all goes.

"What happened," says Shag, "to 'Malagueña'?"

"Oh, God," says Connie, and looks at me.

I clear my throat significantly.

"What'sa matter with 'Malagueña'?" Shag asks.

Connie says "Oh, God" again and gets ready to make for the door. Octavio is already well into his bourbon and not following the discussion. I tell Shag that "Malagueña" is perfectly fine but that I promised Connie total freedom to play what she likes. He grunts his misgivings and goes off to sample the evening batch of chili.

Now, I am no connoisseur of flamenco but I know at once that Connie Colton, a smallish plumpish frightened girl alone there in a dark corner of a crowded East Side pub, is the genuine article. She is terribly taut at first and obviously hesitant to come on strong enough to quench the undertow in the big high-ceilinged room. But her confidence grows with each number, and by the time she hits "Suite Castellana" she is sweating and vaulting and very much in charge. Octavio has his back to her but he hears every chord and does not drink except between numbers when his impassive face says, by its very lack of perturbation, that it goes well. I look over at Shag, and he is gripped. For the first thirty or forty minutes, in fact, she has the whole place entranced. Then, though, doing a Villa-Lobos *chôro,* she screws up—I can tell by the wince Octavio cannot quite restrain —and becomes all untracked. She finishes the piece uncertainly but, not wanting to quit on a sour note, decides to plunge into the études. Only she has lost command, both of herself and the crowd, which detects the change in her, suspects it has been tolerating a gifted but untried amateur, and begins by coughs and murmurs and scraping chair legs to demonstrate its growing restlessness. Flustered, Connie compounds the setback. Some brute, probably drunk, yells, "Do 'On Top of Old Smoky'!" There is thin edgy laughter. Connie plucks on, head down now, trying desperately to rekindle the magic. She begins muffing chords, and out of the dark someone tosses coins toward her that chink in loud disparagement against the tabletop. She still does not quit, though. She finishes the piece and, in retribution, goes on— until someone shoves a coin in the jukebox and the sudden caterwauling of falsetto rock drowns her. I bolt from my seat, grab the lapel of the guy who fed the juke, and jerk him toward the door. His suit rips and he swings. In my rage I register no pain but whack him back uncontrollably until Shag's restraining clutch disables me. The guy threatens to sue, at the top of his lungs, all the way to the door through which Shag ushers him with cordial firmness.

She is still sobbing against Octavio's chest when I get back to her. It is unclear whether she is angry with herself for her own ineptness, with the audience for its unkindness, or with me for getting her into the thing in the first place. All three, probably. She herself will not say. And I can think of no words to ease her mortification. Then the little heaves of misery suddenly stop, and she collects her purse and coat and Octavio grabs the guitar case, and off they go into the night without another word.

Remorseful, I trade shrugs with Shag and sit drinking beer for the next hour. My sense of distress for her grows, though, and soon I am hailing a cab and giving her address. The building has no doorman, just one of those intercoms that you push and the tenant buzzes the lobby door open for you. I consider ringing her, then decide she will not let me in. I hang around a minute or two until I see a couple coming out of the elevator. I pretend I am about to use the intercom but then, suddenly seeing them, I stop. They hold the door open for me and I thank them, thinking how pitifully easy it would be for the Pirate Robber to knock off the place. I take the elevator to her floor and wonder what balm I can possibly spread over the still-fresh wound. But I am sure that if I had not come now, I would be disqualified from further contention for that strange but alluring heart— and the body it defiantly beats in.

I touch the buzzer but withdraw my finger before it produces the rasp of a clumsy intruder. Instead I rap softly on the door. Nothing. I rap again. Still nothing. I try the door. It opens. The living-room lights are all on. The guitar case is leaning against the wall. Connie's dress is sprawled across the sofa. A pair of rumpled pants and a pea jacket are lying on a chair. And the bedroom door is closed. Tight. Numb with disbelief, I write a note: "I came to say I was sorry. Now I'm even sorrier. Compared to lying, stealing is a virtue. I think you need help. KK." And tiptoe out.

On the street I walk for blocks. There are no thoughts in my head, just fumes of billowing resentment. I ask myself why I harbored hopes that something would come of our encounter. She certainly promised nothing. It was her whole—*persona,* I guess we say nowadays, the wonderfully ingenuous way she opened up and was all there at once, serving her mercurial essence to me in a bubbly potion and compelling swift and complete adoration. How could I ever have thought her real?

I am aware of a telephone booth on the upcoming corner. Simultaneously I am aware that I must call Anne; Anne Kwait; Anne, my wife; Anne, the mother of my children; Anne, my loving companion of nearly a decade of connubial heaven on earth—Anne, to whom I can say nothing coherent at this moment. It will be very bad. I dial her and say I am in Pittsburgh.

"Why are you there?" She sounds little and far-off.

"Where do you want me to be?"

"I want you here—right now."

"I'll be there Saturday—if not before."

"That's what you said last week." The urgency in her voice is pitiable.

"Anne, now, stop!" God, I am cruel beyond belief. She does not deserve it; I have known that from the start, but I have not confronted it really till this moment. "The thing is taking a helluva lot out of me."

"What thing?"

"What do you mean 'What thing'? This thing I'm doing. Do you think I like it any better than you?"

"Yes."

Do not crack, my heart. Hold together, O epicenter of my addled will. "Anne, honey, get a grip on yourself."

There is a gush of tears on the other end. "Kit," she says through them, "what is it? What's going on? Something's happening and I don't understand it."

My throat constricts painfully. "Annie—"

"Kit, have you done something terrible?"

I fight the valve open. "Annie, you're panicking—"

"Kit, tell me what it is!"

"Anne, everything is all right!"

There is a pause. Then the beckoning little voice says, "Are you ever going to come back to us?"

I am speechless with guilt. My trajectory wavers in midcourse. But my hands never leave the badly vibrating controls, and I dismiss the sharp urge to turn back to base and be done with it all. Besides, my instruments tell me I have passed the point of no return some time ago. "Yes," I say, "of course. Stop being an idiot."

She seems slightly reassured. I ask after the children. They miss me. One has an infected splinter in his big toe. The other wants a dog or will die. Kiss them for me. Yes, I love you. Yes, yes. I will come back, yes. Yes, I promise, yes.

I spend the night at my college club.

29

Shaughnessy's Army

BOBBY BUTTERFIELD COMES THROUGH ON SCHEDULE. FIFTY THOU-sand dollars in a battered attaché case. Bobby, full of glad tidings and priapic entreaties, takes my arm warmly. Now that they have the painting, though, I remind him, they may put him under unbearable pressure to disclose the thief's identity. No, he assures me, he will never yield a speck of information. Good, I say, because I have every intention of implicating him if he does. He asks how, and I explain that I will claim he was an accomplice. He cannot believe his ears. They *know* I'd never do anything like that, he says. I snort and then suggest that we not be seen together again. Ever. For a moment he is sad. At the end of it he sees he has been used. And now he is being discarded, like an old dildo. He is angry. And angry nances have been known to do vile things out of spite. And so it is decidedly not

in my interest to deprive Bobby Butterfield of some small token of
my esteem. The token he has in mind, however, is not one I am
anxious to deliver to him. Unlike Gibby Good, I have no professional
stake in documenting the manifold delights of anal gratification. Yet
Bobby must be serviced. I am pondering this sticky wicket when
who should saunter in but my affectionate friend, Old Orangestain,
the idle actor who at our first encounter claimed to be a hard-working
stud but soon thereafter latched on to my thigh and would have
grabbed for pay dirt in another moment had I not broken away to
do my business with Action. Today Orangestain has on his navy
sweat shirt, still orange-stained from our previous playful exchange,
and a pair of skin-tight jeans that reveal his erogenous clump in alluring detail. Bobby Butterfield is at once riveted by the spectacle. In no
time at all, I have promoted a match blessed in sphincter heaven. I
leave them to each other, giving Bobby a knowing wink that asserts
I have now discharged my debt to him, and turn to less perverse
matters.

My cash position has now reached so substantial a total that I
begin seriously mulling Gibby Good's advice. Surely I will not just
squirrel the money away in steel cubbyholes in ten or twenty banks.
I must put it to work. In spectacular ways. I have momentum on my
side now and cannot stint. When Gibby comes by in midafternoon,
he is delighted to find me ready to listen to his fiscal scheming.

He has brought a twenty-page pamphlet with him entitled *The
ABCs of Puts and Calls* that his hustling banker friend has sent him.
It looks forbidding. "Actually," says Gibby, "it's not all that complicated. Not after you read it ten times." I indicate I am too rich to
have to read anything ten times. "Oh, you don't have to," he says.
"That's why I'm your financial adviser. I will read you certain
selected passages that make the whole thing clear." I do not want to
hear selected passages. I only want his broker to take my money and
double it in a week. And double it again the next week.

"Don't you even want to know the principle involved?" he asks.

Not totally bereft of the financial acumen I have gathered after ten years in the business world, I tell him the principle is that the investor purchases an option to buy or sell a certain amount of a certain stock at a certain price within a certain time span, right? Disappointed that he cannot parade his newly acquired expertise, he nods solemnly, and I say fine, I will open an account for fifty thousand dollars and let the broker have absolute discretion over how the money is to be invested.

"Absolute?"

I nod.

"Suppose he's a jerk?" But my financial adviser is not supposed to place my affairs in the hands of a jerk. "I know," he says, "but how can I tell if he's a jerk ahead of time?" That, I agree, is a problem. We decide the chances can be calculated only by instinct. "Well," he says, "my instincts tell me he's honest and well-informed." Qualities, I am compelled to point out, that do not preclude jerkiness. Gibby shrugs, and I place a reassuring hand on his shoulder. Let the fellow do his damnedest—maximum gain in minimum time, that is the sole philosophy I am prescribing—and I pledge no recriminations if he loses it all. Better that, I say, than winding up where we started.

"He will have to dabble in a great many speculative issues, you understand," Gibby says. I brush the caveat aside and refuse to hear any more about the particulars. All I want henceforth is a daily report on the net worth of my holdings. Gibby reflects briefly over the simplicity of my instructions, then heads for the telephone to put me in business.

"Oh," I say after him, "better tell your man I deal strictly in cash—if he doesn't mind. If he does, we'll take our business elsewhere." Gibby understands. "And let's make up a name so there's no way I can be traced."

Even as I am being plunged into the vortex of venture capitalism from which there is no return (the instant Gibby picks up the phone to summon Wall Street, I discount the entire fifty thousand dollars and

my frame of mind improves immeasurably), Shag lumbers in with the
daily mail—and confirmation that our seamy saloon will be
worth far more dead than alive. He has a letter from a lawyer in a
firm with many WASP names sculpted in sumptuous intaglio across
the top, inviting Mr. Shaughnessy to his office to discuss the possibility of negotiating a purchase of Mr. Shaughnessy's lease on the
aforementioned premises, hereinafter referred to as "the Bar," sometime at Mr. Shaughnessy's convenience in the near, if not to say the
immediate, future. Yours truly, very very truly, Chauncy C. Cudlipp.
Truly.

The "C.," we decide, is for "Christian." About the rest of him, we
have divided opinions. Does he have a deposed Italian nobleman
come by each morning to shave his ruddy face to a silken smooth-
ness? Shag says yes. I submit no one by that name would permit anything so unsightly as facial hair to grow upon him. Does he have his
shoes shined every hour? I say yes. Shag says he throws them away the
moment they are scuffed. Does he limousine into town from Purchase
or is he borne hence in a sedan chair by four and twenty blacka-
moors? Do he and Mrs Cudlipp share bed chambers? And does he
say "excuse me" after drilling it into her each Sunday following "The
Ed Sullivan Show"? And who, who on earth, could have enough
money to hire his services? Only, we figure, a titan of American industry, only an enterprise whose volume dwarfs the gross national
product of Turkey and Afghanistan put together. And so, we resolve,
Chauncy C. Cudlipp must pay the ultimate price for being Chauncy
C. Cudlipp if he hopes to do business with the partnership of Shaughnessy & Kwait: he must come to us—sometime at his convenience in
the near, if not to say immediate, future—and have a beer on the
house. Two beers, even. We draft a reply. Gibby promises to have it
typed tomorrow on the electric typewriter in his departmental office.

In the immediate afterglow of the executive session, Shag is giddy
with plans for the money he is sure Chauncy C. Cudlipp will shower
on us. For the first time, he broaches the project dearest to his heart,

the undertaking that will finally bring his flabby manhood to full flower. I assume, of course, that he is joking about it, since nothing could be more imbecilic in this day and age than enlisting, equipping, drilling, and deploying a private army. An army all one's own. Amphibious, too, he says. And bristling with weaponry of the latest make and most proficient deadliness. Not too big an army, of course; it would be too costly and unmanageable if it got above, say, two hundred men. But two hundred fiercely trained, powerfully equipped, and brilliantly commanded troops, says Shag, can conquer the world.

"And what will you do with the world once you have conquered it?"

"I will bring liberty and justice to all men," he says.

"And how will you do that?"

"By deposing tyrants everywhere."

"And then?"

"Well," he says, "there are a lot of tyrants to depose."

I am hardly the one these days to be throwing stones, but if some-one were to ask me in the next sixty seconds whether I had run across any certifiable maniacs lately, I would point to the beer-bellied ex-Marine with the coldly gleaming eyes who is sitting directly across the table from me. I know he means every word he says. He will field an army—Shaughnessy's army—and it will march unswervingly wherever he tells it to, up to the moment of its ultimate destruction, leaving more charred flesh and scorched real estate in its wake than any witless, heartless, two-hundred-man militia that ever tramped through history. Mankind's only hope is for C. C. Cudlipp to play it cool with whosoever money he is empowered to lavish on the vest-pocket Caesar I am in business with.

Before Shag begins shooting beer cans off the bar with the pearl-handled revolver he keeps in the cash register for killing robbers—he once blew one's head open—I go home to sleep. Too much of him at one time and you want to start disemboweling old ladies.

It is Gibby who awakens me. He telephones through the murk to say our stockbroker is off and flying. I am not sure if that means the fellow has absconded or is doing well by me. Gibby is reassuring. "He made you forty-five hundred dollars the first day out—on paper, of course. And you're nowhere near fully invested yet." I ask why he's dawdling. "He doesn't want to grab just anything for you. Some situations smell right to him, some don't." Tell him, I say, that if my paper profits aren't up one hundred per cent by this time next week, I am closing out the account and giving it to someone with flair. Gibby groans but promises to relay the ungrateful message.

Gibby is still at the saloon when I come by for dinner, and to my astonishment he has been totally proselytized by the resident warrior chieftain. "I think it's terrific," Gibby says to me. "It's the most exciting thing I've ever heard of."

"What?"

"Shag's army."

"Oh, God."

"And I'll be in the high command. He promised. And I can conduct in-depth interviews with all two hundred men who join up. I will replace Oscar Lewis as the nation's Number One fictional sociologist."

"Why are you encouraging him? You know he's a Fascistic war nut—"

"He's not Fascistic—we just had a very long talk about that."

"Then what is he if he's not a Fascist?"

"He's a radical positivist."

"What in hell is that?"

"Someone who uses extreme means to gain concrete ends."

"That's a Fascist."

"You're assuming evil goals. He has very lofty ones."

"He is feeding you a line. He's a latent mass-killer."

"Then why are you his partner?"

"Because Fascists are excellent businessmen—particularly at running beer halls. Besides, everyone's a latent mass-killer. And who knew he'd have an opportunity to convert his festering secret mania into practical everyday terror?"

"What terror? This is an army of liberation!"

"Who is it liberating?"

"We haven't figured that out yet. We will, though. That's one of the jobs of the high command."

"I see. And which other genuises are on the high command—Chiang Kai-shek?"

"Very funny."

"Then who?"

"Shag, me—"

"Yes."

"You—"

"Oh, no."

"And Connie."

"Connie?"

"Yeah, Connie. She's all excited about it."

My hair is rising. *"How does she know anything about it?"*

"Shag told her last night."

"Last night? You mean she was *here* last night?"

"Sure. She plays the guitar every night."

"She came *back*—after what *happened* the first night?"

"Yeah. Shag thought it was very gutsy of her."

"And he let her *play?*"

"He said you'd made a deal and he'd stick by it."

"So she *played?*"

"Sure—and she was terrific."

I don't believe it. "I don't believe it."

Gibby shrugs. "I never heard anyone play 'Malagueña' that way."

I believe it. "And the old guy—was he with her?"

"Octavio? Yes, he came. Hey, what exactly is their relationship?"

"Very basic—he fucks her."

"That's ridiculous."

"You tell her that."

"Tell her yourself—here she comes."

Bundled in her mangy coat and lugging her guitar case through the door as if in pain. I am in a state of heavy-breathing shock. She marches straight to Shag's booth in the back and gives him a little peck on the head. He waves her into a seat and, smoking fiendishly, continues poring over the papers spread in front of him. Gibby tells me they are organizational plans for the army. "He's trying to figure out what the whole thing will cost. He's very hot to have some tanks if we can afford it, but that might seriously restrict our theaters of operation."

I sit there stunned while Gibby goes over to say hello to Connie, who is her fully animated self and in no apparent way inhibited by my being in the place. I stay where I am and she stays where she is, our glances never crossing (which is to say she is not giving me a tumble). I do not know what to make of this strange and alluring girl who never stops surprising me. Is her coming back just sheer defiance? Or does she want to explain? But explain what? What is there to explain? Anyway, she is not an explainer. She is what she is—a creature of fiercely contesting impulses—and if the ones in her that vent themselves are unattractive to her companion of the hour, then he is free to steer clear. And so I sit, steering clear. And trying hard not to grab her and shake her and make her submit. She goads me now even worse by effervescing quite audibly over whatever it is Shag in his mania is murmuring into the woodwork. A lateral glance discloses her patting his wrist to reinforce some point or other. Oh, it is so transparent, this spiteful little display of hers.

Gibby returns to report that Shag is firm about wanting a parachute detachment. "He's thinking of two C-47 Dakotas—two."

I sit there glumly.

"They'd be a little rickety, of course," Gibby says, "but they work. And they're very reasonable, money-wise."

I sit there.

"He says you can pick them up for five or six thousand apiece—unarmed, of course. And you can probably get them even cheaper if you settle for a big rubber band instead of engines."

I sit.

"I was joking about the rubber band."

I am unmoved.

"What's the problem?" Gibby says.

"I'm just thinking about the whole thing."

"No, you're not. You're thinking about Connie and the old-timer."

"All right."

"I just asked her about it."

"Oh, Christ."

"She didn't mind at all. In fact she laughed when I told her you think he gives it to her."

"No—"

"She said you must have got the wrong idea."

"Cut it, will you? You weren't even talking to her."

He looks sheepish. I tell him my evidence. He says it is only circumstantial. "Why don't I go put it to her for you?" he volunteers.

Naturally, no red-blooded American would consent to such a thing. Not since John Alden went to bat for Miles Standish—procuring, I think we call it now—has one man sanctioned another to do his bidding for him and been honored for it. "Okay," I say, "just tell her I told you about it and you wondered if maybe she could fit you in sometime when the old man's not scheduled."

He waits till Shag leaves the table, then slides into the booth opposite her. I turn my back to them and await the shrill outburst. None comes. The five minutes they talk are eternal. Then he is back, long-faced and subdued.

"Well?"

"She says you are a pompous, hopelessly conventional, phony son of a bitch."

"She is a fat, lying whore."

"Shut up till I'm done!" He looks uncharacteristically stern.

"All right."

"She also says you are a dirty sneak, and the next time you break into her apartment uninvited, she is going to call the police."

Ah, the righteous indignation of a dissembler caught in the act. "The fact remains," I point out, "that she was in the hay with him."

"No," he says, "she says she wasn't."

"I see."

"She says he was taking a bath."

I slap my cheek in astonishment. "Oh, my God, of course!"

"She says he doesn't have a real bathtub in his apartment—"

"Right, right, I forgot."

"So he bathes at her place once a week."

"Right, of course. He is extremely antiseptic. And she was in there scrubbing his back when I wandered in."

"Yes."

"What do you mean 'Yes'?"

"I mean yes, she was in there scrubbing his back when you— wandered in."

"She didn't tell you that!"

"She did—just now."

I jump up and scream at her across half the room, "That's a goddam lie and you know it!"

Her tapered head pivots swiftly around. The face is placid-seeming till it barks back, "Oh, shut up, stupid!"

I march over and confront her. "Why was the frigging door closed if you were just scrubbing his back?"

"You are repulsive," she says quietly, and takes her sunglasses out of her purse and puts them on and starts reading some of Shag's papers, as if her remark had triggered a trap door and whisked me out of sight.

"And you," I say, "have a terribly guilty conscience."

She reads on without acknowledging my bristling presence.

"Even if this preposterous fable you've invented were true, didn't you think I was entitled to an explanation?"

"Don't get sanctimonious with me, you weasel, you. I mean first you come around prying like a miserable Peeping Tom. And then you go off blabbing dirty stories about me all over town."

"I only told Gibby."

She dissolves into tears before my eyes. I sit beside her and consider trying to comfort her but she is having none of it. She is purging herself, douching away the guilt that her large, free-flowing, but remarkably silent tears so clearly confess to me now.

"He wasn't taking a bath," I say.

She shakes her head.

"And you weren't scrubbing his back."

She shakes it again.

"You were in bed with him."

She nods.

"And performing— God, it's almost incest!"

"No! Believe me, no!" And she pushes her face against my sleeve and goes on a new crying binge.

I take her glasses off and wipe the longer rivulets from her face. "All right," I say, "I'll listen."

"We just—I just—it was like you and me. We were just lying down, that's all. I mean I wouldn't ever— Not with Octavio. He's— someone very special. He was just—trying to comfort me."

"With his pants off."

"Yes, yes—with his pants off! I didn't think anything of it and I'm sure he didn't, either. He just didn't want to get them wrinkled, I guess."

I want so much to believe it that I will not admit the enormity of her story. It is so absurd, I tell myself, that she would not try to purvey it unless it was true.

"I guess I shouldn't have done it," she says, calming down. "It just happened so naturally—" She looks at me for the first time. "I know—you don't think I should go to bed with someone unless we have relations."

"I never said that."

"I mean what's so terrible about sleeping next to someone you like a lot without—doing it?"

"Nothing. In fact it's very endearing—in a compromising sort of way."

She smiles a little. "Do you hate me?"

"Does it matter?"

"Yes, *stupid*—it matters." She snatches her glasses from me and adds poutingly, "Are you glad you got me to say it?"

"Yes, I'm glad. No, I don't hate you."

"Do you believe me?"

"I don't know."

"Please believe me—"

"Or what?"

"Or I'll keep stealing all day again tomorrow—the way I did today."

"Why, does stealing improve your disposition?"

"Oh, immensely!"

"And what did you steal today?"

She thinks for a moment. "At the supermarket this morning I found a little black purse lying among the potato chips and Fritos and Chee-Wees and stuff. It had five dollars and fifteen cents in it, and two house keys. So I took the five dollars and put the purse with the keys and the fifteen cents in it back on top of a very prominent box of Cheerios."

"Yes, well, that certainly mitigated the crime."

She smiles a bigger smile now. "Shall I tell you what else I took?"

I shake my head disapprovingly.

"Well, I took a bag of jellybeans from a drugstore, and I took two booklets—one on Iranian art and the other on the ancient Near East —from the Met, and, oh, also four coin reproductions from the Met, and I took a pen-sized flashlight from—I can't remember where, but it didn't have any batteries—and I took an architectural rule that you use to reduce drawings—that's worth about two-fifty—and I took a French magazine—and—and—that's all I can think of."

When it is over, I sigh and ask her, "And are you proud of yourself?"

"It doesn't have anything to do with being proud," she says. "Besides, everyone's a robber. I just happen to admit to it."

30

Neediest Cases

"THE SERPENTS!" SHE SHRIEKS AT ME ON THE PHONE THE NEXT morning as I am waking in my cell-like room at the club overlooking sunless West Forty-third Street. "The serpents—they're real!"

"Well, congratulations."

"No, don't congratulate me. The money's all yours."

I am still groggy and cannot remember what we had agreed on but I do not think it was that. "I thought we said fifty-fifty."

"No, no—that'd make me a professional, remember?"

"All right, then," I say, "I'll give your share away."

She gasps. "You can't do that!"

"Why not?"

"It's—wasteful."

"Not if we find a worthy recipient."

"Like who?"

"I don't know. Come bring me coffee and a doughnut and let's talk about it."

"Come where?"

"Here."

"I—just like that?"

"Sure. Oh, now don't tell me you're shy? You, the great unconventionalist?"

There is a pause. "It's just that I've decided I'm not going to get into the same bed with a man any more until—I'm ready."

"Who said bed?"

"Oh."

"Just come."

"All right."

"Black with sugar."

"All right."

"How much did we get?"

"For the serpents?"

"Yes."

"I was afraid you'd ask sooner or later."

"It wasn't twenty-five thousand dollars?"

"Not exactly."

"How about twenty-five dollars?"

"Closer to that than the other."

"Oh."

"Just five thousand."

"Well, it's something."

"That's what I figured."

"Of course if I weren't a wonderful and marvelous person, I might suspect that they actually paid twenty-five thousand and you're keeping the difference."

"Oh," she says, "I never thought of that."

"Of course not."

"It's a good idea, though."

"I'm full of good ideas."

I shave, hating it and torturing myself with visions of Connie's inaccessible breasts, which by now I am certain, despite the exemplary

way she declines to exhibit them, are more lavish than any two caressing hands can contain. I conjure them as vast, beautifully conical,
geometrically identical peaks against the sides of which I dream of
hurling myself and in the cleft between which I dream of languishing
for days on end. Oh, she could produce such rapture if she would
unfurl them! But no, she keeps them locked away like twin princesses
the king is saving for some lisping heir to the throne of Araby. I
could scream.

And then she is at the door, actually bearing them hence mounted
like great warm embellishments on her lovely front. She smiles, then
steps demurely in. My fingers contract reflexively at the sight of her.
She presents me the coffee with one hand and a money order for
five thousand dollars with the other. Choked with gratitude, to say
nothing of desire, I grab her impulsively and kiss her on the cheek.
And then the mouth. And the eyes and nose and neck and behind the
ears, which are warm and fragrant. Producing in her a trance-like immobility. So I do it again. All over. And again. Wondering every instant how I can bear to stop. Aware every instant of those wonderful
warm frontispieces pressed tight against my naked chest. Oh, my
merciful Father, Who art in heaven! We cling that way—motionless,
sightless, speechless, breathless. It is a moment of exquisite duration.
Ended only when I let the coffee drop to the floor with a terrible
splat.

The spell broken, the ultimate temptation receding again for the
time being, we ponder how to give away twenty-five hundred dollars
while I finish dressing and she cleans up the floor. We consider and
dismiss all the usual philanthropies, like the Salvation Army (which
we agree does some good work but is Fundamentalist in its teachings
and thus retrogressive) and the American Cancer Society (whose
work, I argue, should be financed instead by the national government
if it ever stops killing Commies in the name of the white Christ and
the white God it thinks enfranchised it to save the world). Then
there are SNCC and CORE and the Urban League and the NAACP,

whose very mention triggers Connie's confession of a recurring nightmare in which her maidenhead is punctured by a glistening ebony buck, whose outsized member tears through not merely the cervical canal but the northern wall of her uterus as well and lodges finally deep inside her entrails. A matter for therapy, I suggest, but she thinks it is a consummation being devoutly, if subconsciously, wished. I tell her it can be arranged but she scoffs, and it is clear we are getting nowhere.

"I think we ought to go out on the street," I say, "and just give it away to the saddest-looking people we can find—like our very own Hundred Neediest Cases."

She is horrified. "That will just encourage malingering," she says. "All those stupid, ugly, self-pitying parasites—I *hate* them." Her eyes are narrow with scorn.

"You," I say, "are a heartless bitch. You have been spoiled silly by indulgent parents whose only reward has been your unflagging contempt. You have not known a moment of deprivation or suffering in your entire life. It is time you saw a little of how the other half is mired in misery and despair."

"I don't want to see."

"That's too goddam bad—you're going to."

"No."

"Why not—what are you afraid of?"

Her haughty look falters.

"Well?" I demand.

"The truth?"

"Yes, for a change."

"Oh, shut up! I always tell you the truth—sooner or later."

"Let's have it the first time around."

"The truth is I can't bear to face it."

"Why?"

"Because secretly I know how terrible it is—and I want to cry every time I think about it—because I keep imagining I am one of them—one of those sick, stupid, ugly people who just take up space and air and food and contribute absolutely nothing to anybody's well-being including their own. I just *hate* them! I hate them because they're so useless. And I hate them because I'm afraid to pity them. I'm afraid because my bleeding heart would ooze all over the place and I'd have to give my whole life to them somehow. And I don't want to. I want to live my own life. Why do I have to live for other people? All I have is one life. Why aren't I entitled to be selfish with it?"

"Oh, you're entitled—"

"Yes, I *am,* thank you."

"Only why does it have to be a bleeding heart or a stone heart? Can't it be something in between?"

"But that's not the way I am. I'm all or nothing."

"So you're a stone heart—Miss Rich Bitch, who kicks mendicant lowlifes in the crotch while stepping daintily into her crystal coach."

"I don't *actively* hate them. I just—show them no mercy, because once I do I'm cooked."

"Well," I say, "you're about to bleed a little."

We go to her bank, where she deposits the money order (since I cannot risk having my own bank account show a sudden large increase). She will withdraw it a little at a time starting in a week or two and feed it to me. Meanwhile we go to my nearest safe-deposit box and I draw out twenty-five hundred dollars in small bills. We are ready for our début as spontaneous philanthropists.

I have, till now, never played the Good Samaritan, for I have a recurring nightmare to match Connie's. The featured players in mine are always me and some dwarf or hunchback or blind man or panhandler I happen on and, moved by his plight and the knowledge that fate could easily have reversed our roles in life, I offer kindness and money. Sometimes my beneficiary is lying in a gutter with a shattered bottle beside him; sometimes he is slumped in an alleyway afflicted by some terrible wound or illness. But whoever he is, however dire his need, he always responds to my outstretched hand the same way; he slashes out with some lethal weapon of his own devising and comes within an ace of killing me. The dream ends as I scurry off to safety, vowing never again to volunteer succor to the needy. But Connie's candid appraisal of her turning aside in the face of such encounters makes me suddenly see my own imagined response for what it is: a subconsciously generated excuse to avoid just exactly the kind of outgoingness I accuse her of denying the unblessed of the earth. What in fact have I ever done beyond an occasional quarter dropped furtively into a blind beggar's cup or a five-dollar check to a neighborhood youth center? Have I ever worked in a settlement house? Collected for a charity? Donated to a blood bank? Tithed? I will do it all when I am rich, I have always told myself, and then it will be something truly magnificent. But how heartfelt is the charity of the rich? Is it any more than ransom to allay those infrequent twinges of guilt? To mean something, mercy must come from the heart of one who himself is sorely tried; otherwise what is it but a mechanical dole like that of the millionaire who secretly fears they will come one day and take it all from him if he does not volunteer some token from his hoard? Oh, who am I to don the mask of an avenging pirate when I have sinned no less than those I victimize?

We begin on the Bowery. It is warmer today and the winos are out in force, knowing, I suppose, that the *nouveau* almsgivers are putting in their seasonal appearance. There is no elation—or lethal weapon flashed—as we make our way downtown dispensing five- and ten-dollar bills to any bum who will take them. They seem to understand they are doing us a favor and not the other way around. We have passed out about fifteen or twenty bills when Connie (who does it gingerly so as not to have to touch or smell or, almost, even look at the pathetic creatures) says, "You know, this is absolutely stupid. It doesn't have anything to do with anything. We're not doing these— these zombies one bit of good. They're going to take the money and go buy up a week's worth of muscatel. What's the point? Let's find one who looks salvageable and give him a whole lot of money and maybe he can start his life over with it."

It is a noble idea. But no promising candidate presents himself by the time we reach Canal Street. So we taxi back to midtown, tip the driver lavishly, and set out across lush Fifty-seventh Street in search of a reclamation project. It is hard to keep from being bowled over by the rejoicing shoppers who swirl relentlessly out of every store, their faith in mankind renewed by their latest purchase. The bell-ringing Santa Clauses are raking it in on the street corners, and so we steer clear of them. Between Madison and Park Avenues, though, we come upon an enterprising young beggar who surely must be working harder than any other in town. He is a young violinist with long hair, though it is not of an unseemly length, and he is playing gypsy music at an enormous speed. His violin case is open and a cardboard sign is tilted up against the green plush lining. It says, "I AM A MUSIC STUDENT—PLEASE HELP ME CONTINUE MY STUDIES." Connie and I stand over by the curb and watch him for a few moments. He drops down to *andante* and his collections immediately begin to pick up, and when he offers a positively soulful *larghetto,* the chink of falling coins turns into a steady clang. The virtuoso of Fifty-seventh Street, hair flying with Bernsteinesque showmanship, face full of passion, dedication beyond dispute. I think it is just terrible.

"Why?" says Connie. "At least he's doing something for the money."

"He's pathetic."

"He's courageous," she says, "but not very talented."

"Doesn't he have any pride?"

"Why don't you go ask him?"

"All right."

I wait till his tempo has dwindled to a particularly mournful *largo* (drowned out, nearly, by the cascading coins) and I put my question. His eyes remain sealed. I repeat the question, but still there is no acknowledgment. Finally I take hold of his upper arm, and the music—and the coins—stop. "Have you no pride, son?"

The eyes are deceptively calm. "Bug off, dad," he says.

"How can you do a thing like this?"

"You're freezing the action, man."

"I'll give you a thousand dollars if you'll promise never to play on the street again."

"What are you, a pervert, mister?"

"I mean it—I think it's terrible what you're doing."

"Who cares what you think?"

"It's you I'm thinking of."

"Hit the road, Mac."

"A thousand dollars—"

The blow lands on the side of my head, above the temple. I stagger backward and black out briefly. Then Connie is leading me into a drugstore. I slump on a stool and she inspects the wound. No skin is broken but it is throbbing nicely. "It didn't do his violin much good, either," she says.

My recovery is swift enough, but I lean now to some less hazardous form of philanthropy—like mailing ten dollars to the first hundred names I pick out of the phone book. Connie, though, has warmed to our direct method and will not hear of abandoning it despite my concussion. "You *were* bugging him," she says, and steals some rubber bands and a package of Switzer's licorice from the drugstore. The rubber bands she wraps around the remaining money to produce a tight cylindrical bundle easy to bestow; the licorice she unpeels the celophane from and nibbles at as we promenade. I complain about her not offering me any. She apologizes and then offers me half, which I of course decline as gut-clogging garbage. Thus, playfully, we resume our mission of mercy. We have gone about a block when we see him—a classic blind beggar, wearing a sign ("GOD BLESS THE CHEERFUL GIVER—THIS IS MY ONLY SOURCE OF INCOME"), rattling a tin cup to give voice to his plight, and being led down the avenue by a faithful dog with remarkable intelligence and a continuously panting tongue. I have never quite overcome the suspicion that every blind beggar I see is masquerading. This one, though, besides the real or feigned affliction of sightlessness, is black, and black blind beggars seem to me at least twice as forlorn a spectacle as white ones. I think, watching this one shuffle slowly along the sidewalk, that his chances of extricating himself from his bottomless despair—by getting a job, say, and renewing his fruitful participation in the human race —hover around zero. Connie and I eye him for a while. Does he have no one to take care of him? Does the city have no means of providing for him? Is there nothing else he can do with his waking hours but shuffle through the streets displaying his misery? Why are we so brutal a people?

Connie wants to give him the rest of the money—or a major portion of it. I resist at first. "But why?" she says. "Isn't he terrible enough for you?"

I am at a loss to explain my hesitancy. It just seems such a prosaic way to bestow the money. I try to say something to that effect.

"What did you have in mind," Connie asks, "a Seminole leper who was once a concert pianist? You're being ridiculous. Also prejudiced."

"I am not prejudiced against Negroes."

"No, just blind Negroes."

"You don't understand."

"No, I don't. He's a perfectly good case of utter hopelessness and you're holding back because you want some kind of exotic creature."

"Who said exotic? I just mean someone who—can do something constructive with the money."

"Constructive? What do you mean—a blind carpenter?"

"Don't be wise."

"Well, I'm giving him the money. It's my money, anyway, and I say he's as good as any other beggar you're going to find." And she promptly marches up to him, sticks the wadded bills into his cup, and retreats in embarrassed haste. I ask her if she told him how much money it is. "No—should I have?" I think so. I think she should go back and tell him, so he doesn't leave it in the cup where anyone can see it. "I *can't* go back," she says. "I just can't. Besides, who'd steal from a blind man?"

The words are no sooner off her lips than we see a little man in glasses with disheveled gray hair and a soiled coat and baggy pants flash his hand into the cup and make off with the wad of bills. The dog whirls around and shows his fangs and barks furiously after the thief, who slips swiftly away through the crowd.

We pause a nearly critical second too long; then I grab Connie's wrist and we are off in awkward pursuit. I catch a glimpse of the thief's coat and hair bobbing westward on Fifty-seventh. He is not running but moving with all deliberate speed through the maze of shoppers who, themselves scurrying, take no notice of his abnormal pace. We hurry after him, running now to close the gap to a respectable thirty or forty yards. He never looks over his shoulder or slackens his gait. It is a battle to keep up without giving our intentions away. At Fifth Avenue he turns the corner and heads north out of sight. We burst into a sprint, brake ourselves as we hit the corner, and hustle uptown after him. For a moment we do not spot him, there are so many people. But Connie sees him cross to the west side of the avenue on a red light, and we dodge through the idling traffic after him. We close the gap to about twenty yards now as he approaches Delman's shoe store and, to our astonishment, stops to study the window. We could in fact charge now and grab him. But we both understand, without either of us speaking, that it is impossible for us to seize him here in the crowd, since all he needs to do is scream that he is being robbed. We hang back and wait till he moves on. His first destination is the Fifty-ninth Street crosstown bus. We are no more than a dozen feet in back of him now. Even so, we have to hurry to make the same bus as he, for the driver is of that legendary stripe who, in the holiday season more than any other, manipulates the doors like a pair of pincers to exclude any dawdlers.

Our runty thief is midway back in the bus. We go past and take seats that allow us safe and careful inspection of him. He looks scarcely more affluent than his victim. He stares straight ahead and gives no sign that he is under stress, and certainly none that suggests he knows he is under scrutiny. Who is he? What sort of vermin would steal from the cup of a blind man? What events in his tawdry life could have led him to this abominable depth? Is such a life worth living? Shouldn't it, I even find myself asking, be taken from him if it is this far past redemption? I reach the tentative conclusion that whatever the specific circumstances driving him to such an unspeakable act, he is not the first man to want to alleviate his misery at the expense of the most vulnerable (if not the first) lamb to wander by.

No window is open even an inch and the bus, like all New York buses in winter, is overheated to begin with. In another moment I grow flushed and then furious as my effort to budge the nearest window proves utterly ineffective. Our thief, though, obliges by getting up and off at Columbus Circle. We pursue. He is headed for the subway. I am still fumbling for change while he pops his token in the turnstile and shoves through. For a panicky instant, we hesitate just as we did in the first moments after the crime itself—and then our course is clear; we vault the turnstile and never look back. The thief is a hundred feet ahead of us. We hurry to catch up. Soon we are only an arm's length away from him on the Seventh Avenue I.R.T. uptown platform. His back is toward us, but I brace myself in case he wheels around the moment the train roars into the station and tries to drive us onto the tracks. It is a silly notion, for he is a little man and almost certainly malnourished, but there is no telling what anyone so desperate may try. The wait turns out to be an uneventful five minutes, during which we examine the local graffiti exhibition, including such high points as "LOVE FOR SALE" (in lipstick), "ADAM CLAYTON POWELL IS WHITE—ONLY HIS HAIRDRESSER KNOWS" (in black Magic Marker), "GOD BLESS MY UNDERWEAR" (in crayoned cursive), and "SPEAK SOFTLY AND CARRY A BIG SCHTICK" (in tiny letters enclosed in a rhombus). On the "I GOT MY JOB THROUGH THE NEW YORK TIMES" poster, the occupation "TRAFFIC MANAGER" has been crossed out and "BIG PIMP" substituted. The station, we decide, can use a new writer-in-residence.

The train is uncrowded, and Connie and I sit on the same side of the car as the thief. The woman sitting on the other side of me is reading a cookbook. The page she is on gives a recipe for potato salad yielding thirty-three pounds. I try to imagine a thirty-three-pound mound of potato salad. And then how many carloads you would need to make a potato salad the size of the Empire State Building. My subway neighbor moves on to coleslaw and I abandon the project.

Our anger is abating with each passing station and we are beginning to feel as sorry for the little thief as we did for the blind black beggar. Still, the pursuit cannot be abandoned. There must be a confrontation. The subway rushes onward. Our thief looks as if he is settling in for a ride to the end of the line. Above the 181st Street stop, though, he begins to stir a bit, and as the train bursts out of the tunnel and into the daylight at the Dyckman Street stop, he is definitely fidgeting. At 215th Street he stands up. At the 225th Street stop he, and we, leave. He bundles up his scrawny body and makes his way down the steep stairway from the elevated tracks to the street. Half a block to the rear, we follow him up Broadway to 228th Street. The store windows here shabbily mirror the gloss and tinsel of the downtown emporiums, but still there is a wreath or string of colored lights or midget tree or glowing Santa face in each and they all serve to relieve the grimness of the vast shadow cast by the great black trelliswork of the elevated subway. And then our trip is over. We see our prey turn in at one of the shops in the middle of the next block. We slow our pace and talk over strategy. No alternative to abrupt accusation occurs to us.

It is a shoe-repair store. There is a small red paper wreath in the door with a candle in the middle, a tiny bulb glowing at the top to simulate a flame. It is hard to be very Christmassy about repairing shoes. The slope-shouldered, sunken-chested, gray-faced little man we have chased across the city for nine miles is talking to his assistant as we enter. His first quick glance at us through those steel-framed glasses says at once that he knows why we have come. He tells his assistant to quit hammering and go to lunch; then he picks up the hammer himself and resumes re-heeling an old black shoe. He is smoking as he works and refuses to look up at us. We wait a minute or two. He hammers on till the shoe is done, then picks up its mate and fits it on the foot-shaped little anvil.

"We want the money."

"Hah?"

"The money you took—you have to give it back."

"Whaddaya talk?" There is a faint Slavic or Greek or Mediterranean tone.

"From the blind man."

As his face straightens up, his glasses catch the overhead light in a way that makes him look like a fierce insect. "You wrong," he says. "Must be some other fella you want."

"We were there. We saw you take it. We followed you all the way."

He looks at us for a long moment, then he lowers his head and begins hammering again. He is thinking. We let him. He finally stops hammering and says, "You cops?"

"No, but it's our money."

"Whaddaya mean 'syour money?"

"We gave it to the blind man—and thirty seconds later you took it from him. That's not nice, mister."

He gives a little nod and then starts hammering again. He hammers till he finishes the shoe. He is thinking very hard now. While he is thinking, he shoves the re-heeled shoes in a crackly bag, wraps the bag with thin cord a few times, sticks a ticket beneath the cord at one end, and tosses the package onto a long shelf where all the shop's humble handiwork sits wrapped and waiting to be claimed. He turns to us, eyes swimming behind those blurry, glittering glasses, and breaks into a heart-wrenching monologue. He is a very poor man, he says. The shoe-repair business, he says, is a very hard business. He has a very large family, he says—a wife and three daughters and a son with a rheumatic heart and a penniless old mother on the other side and a sick brother who has a big family and can't manage and and and—and I am a very honest man, he says. I swear on my sacred mother I never stole a penny in my life before this. Never. I swear it. But I was walking by and there is this big wad of money in the blind nigger's cup and and and—and I know I got no money for presents for my kids on Christmas morning and and and—and I know I ain't sent nothing to my poor old mother for months now and and and— and I need new clothes awful bad and—and my brother's family and —and there was all that money just sitting there in the blind nigger's cup and and and—and I took it. "Whaddaya want from my life?"

"What about the blind man?"

His face drops again. "I know," he says softly. "Everybody got problems."

And so this is the way the world is. It is as Connie says (oh, she is wise beyond her years). Everybody robs what he can—including a blind black beggar with, for all I know, perfectly good eyes. Can a downtrodden little shoemaker be blamed more than anyone else if the basic nature of the human animal is predatory? I am about to give up. Connie, though, is less permissive about the trait than I.

"But he was a blind beggar," she says. "How could you steal from him?"

The shoemaker shrugs.

"Is it because he was black?"

Another shrug.

Connie looks at me. The look says: okay, we're all culpable and okay, you have to take into account the circumstances that drive a man to robbery, but this poor disheveled cruelly burdened little shoe-maker, beneath his heart of purest gold, is a dirty rat.

"I'm sorry about your troubles," I tell him, "but you'll have to give us the money back."

Across the counter the sallow face remains expressionless. I detect my reservoir of sympathy for this downtrodden creature rapidly draining dry. He picks up his hammer. He wets his lips. He is the picture of a drowning man pretending to be wily at the instant of direst distress. "I ain't got no money," he says, and starts to turn away.

"But we *saw* you take it!" Connie says, the sparks beginning to come.

"Your word against mine," says the shoemaker. "G'wan now or maybe I call the cops!"

"You're a filthy lousy rotten bastard!" Connie shouts.

The shoemaker shows us his back and bends to get another pair of broken shoes.

"Give us the money," Connie screams and charges the counter, "or I'll tear your hair out!"

In one fluid motion the shoemaker rises, pivots, and hurls the hammer at her. It sails wildly over her head—and shatters the main window into a thousand parts. Faces congregate instantly. Somebody shouts. In another moment a cop materializes with positively uncivil promptness. What's the trouble here? What's the trouble?

Just the human race, officer, just the race.

The shoemaker and we eye each other hatefully, and swiftly calculate what we have to lose by baring the dispute. He—he has a thousand dollars to lose, more money than he has accumulated in his entire life. We—well, where did the money come from in the first place? And what exactly is Connie's relationship to me? And how long will it take even the blockheaded Pat Pratt of the Twenty-second Detective Squad to add two and two and two and get Kit Kwait? We —we have everything to lose.

"Well?" the cop demands.

"We—just had a little disagreement, officer."

He wants to know the nature of it. It is about the quality of the shoemaker's craftsmanship, officer—and the outrageous price he asks for it.

" 'Sthat right?" the cop asks the shoemaker.

The shoemaker sizes up the situation with unerring instinct. "Man comes in and says I'm gyp him. How you like someone call you cheat?"

"So you threw the hammer at him?"

The shoemaker turns up his palms.

"I'm afraid I was a little sharp with him, officer."

The cop is puzzled over the speed of our *détente*. But there is nothing for him to do but urge the shoemaker not to go hurling his hammer around so casually—and me to keep a decent tongue in my head. The shoemaker nods. I nod. "Better clean the glass off the sidewalk before someone gets hurt," he tells the shoemaker. The shoemaker nods. "It's gonna be awful cold in here with the window like that." The shoemaker nods. "It'll cost you a lot of money to fix." Nod. "I got a brother-in-law in the glass business—maybe he'd give you a break." Two nods. "You want his name?" Three nods.

On the subway downtown, Connie wonders if our blind beggar will be walking the same beat tomorrow. We agree he is entitled to another wad, even if he sees better than the two of us put together.

31

The Mammoth Gap

GIBBY REPORTS THAT MY PAPER PROFITS ON WALL STREET ROSE by approximately nine thousand dollars on the day. My lightning calculations disclose a two-day profit of about 30 per cent. "Not enough," I say. "Tell him to stop pussyfooting with widows'-and-orphans' garbage. I want *movement*. Tell him to look into soybeans."

Gibby snaps his little black tote book closed with a shake of his head and accuses me of being unreasonable.

"Of course I'm unreasonable. If I were reasonable, I'd stick my money in a savings account and forget about it. Did Howard Hughes get to be a billionaire by being reasonable? Was Genghis Khan reasonable when he crossed the Rubicon? I am an adventurer—your broker friend has to understand that. Remind him of the ennobling words of Harry Truman, who once said, in a moment of rare insight, 'If you can't stand the heat in the kitchen, you shouldn't be a cook.' Or something like that."

"It was Abraham Lincoln," says my Fascist partner, intervening at this point to advise that he has heard from Charlie Cudlipp.

"Who's Charlie Cudlipp?"

"The lawyer—from the fancy firm—what wants to buy up our little old exorbitantly priced lease."

"It's not Charlie—it's Chauncy. What is Chauncy Cudlipp offering us?"

"He is offering to come have a beer"

"When?"

"Tomorrow."

"Ahhh. You know what that means?"

"Since he is a very high-powered and fancy lawyer—do they wear spats any more?—and must have an impossibly crowded schedule, I am inferring from the swiftness of his response that he is very hot to buy us out. Maybe we should ask twenty million for openers."

On the strength of this encouraging development, Shag has steamed ahead on his do-it-yourself army. It has advanced from the figment stage to the projection booth. He leads me to the high-command tent, where he dons a khaki officer's hat heavily embellished with stars and eagles and griffins and unicorns and hands me a stapled five-page hand-printed document, each new page of which I read with heightening anxiety:

COMBAT SCHEME

I. FORCE—Approximately 200 men, light weapons, one parachute detachment (aircraft available, two C-47 Dakotas), usual radio equipment, if possible a radio link with aircraft (this is important).

II. BATTLE GROUPS (A and B the same)
   Battle Group Commander (with radio operator)

   1st Platoon—30 men, including platoon commander
      Blue Squad—15 men, including squad commander
      Red Squad—15 men, including squad commander
   2nd Platoon—30 men, including platoon commander
      White Squad—15 men, including squad commander
      Green Squad—15 men, including squad commander
   Heavy-Weapons Platoon—10 men, including platoon commander
   and radio operator

                                        Total—70 men each group

III. PERSONNEL

   1. Each infantry squad has following strength:
      (a) Commander—automatic pistol and submachine gun, probably a .45 Colt Automatic and a Thompson .45-caliber submachine gun with 4 spare magazines.
      (b) Two men to handle 1 light machine gun (probably a British Bren gun, .303 caliber). One man is gunner, and carries gun

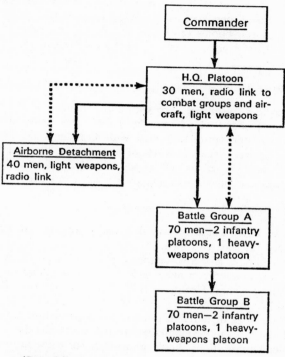

(Dotted line = radio link)

and 4 magazines. Second man is loader, carries 8 magazines
and spare barrel for MG.

   (c) Twelve infantrymen, armed with .303 Lee-Enfield rifles, 60
      rounds of ammunition, two grenades.

2. Heavy-weapons platoon has following strength:

   (a) Commander—auto pistol and submachine gun.

   (b) Radio operator—auto pistol.

   (c) Four men to handle heavy machine gun (.50 Browning)—
      one man carries barrel, one man (gunner) carries breech,
      one man carries tripod, one man carries belts of .50-caliber
      ammunition in metal boxes. Each carries a pistol as personal
      weapon.

(d) Four men to handle one 81-mm. mortar—one man carries barrel, one man carries baseplate, two men carry sights and mortar bombs (each bomb, 9 lb. 6½ oz., range 4,500 yds.). Total weight of mortar barrel and mounting, 51 lb.; baseplate, 25 lb. Each man carries a pistol.

IV. AIRBORNE DETACHMENT

20 men to an airplane, each with a commander. Each airplane has a separate squad—1 commander (pistol and submachine gun), 1 radio operator (pistol), 2 men with Bren gun, and 16 riflemen. Total airborne detachment (both aircraft) is 40 men. Every precaution must be taken that troops from both aircraft join up, and that each commander can take over if other is killed.

V. MISCELLANEOUS

1. A bazooka would be useful if tanks are likely to be met with. Needs at least two men.
2. Should have a doctor for force.
3. Tracer ammunition must be issued to all machine gunners.
4. Someone should carry a roll of plastic explosive to deal with bridges, obstacles, etc.
5. Spare fuses of different times to be supplied for grenades.
6. Radio links to be maintained between all units and headquarters —communications should go to HQ, *not* between units.
7. All men must wear steel helmets, colored stripes to indicate unit, and armbands for identification.
8. Each commander to carry flares and flare gun for marking position and signaling in case of radio failure.
9. All airborne troops to wear special helmets, kneepads, and jump boots.
10. *All* troops to carry: full pack with groundsheet, blanket; clean socks (2 pairs), spare shirt; washing kit; canteen, mess kit; first-aid kit; bayonet; rifle-cleaning kit (pull-through 4" x 2" cloths and oil); entrenching tool; 48-hour rations (six K rations); penknife; watch; all *necessary* maps; compass; flashlight with spare bulb.
11. No written orders to be carried. All objectives to be given code names. All orders to be confirmed. Password to be changed at

fixed intervals. All maps to be supplied with map reference overlay grid.

VI. CHAIN OF COMMAND

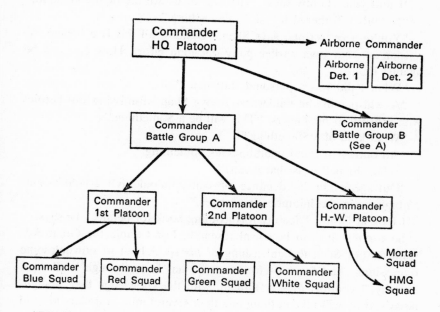

"I," Shag says, in case I have somehow missed the central point, "am the commander."

"I," Gibby says, with an antic dedication that makes unmistakably clear he is going along with the gag till it runs its course, "am in charge of passwords. Today its 'Rumpelstiltskin.'"

"I," says Connie, with the newly minted valor of one who has never known carnage, "will mend the tatters and tend the wounded and lift my voice in song before, during, and after each battle."

"And what," I ask, beginning now to grasp the scenario to the elaborate masque the three of them are concocting, "will be the first objective of this crack legion?"

"That," says Shag, "will be determined in concert as soon as the means to finance it are forthcoming."

"And who," I ask, "will be in the concert?"

"I told you," Gibby says. "The four of us are the high command."

"Nobody's bothered to ask if I'm willing."

"You're a conscript," says Shag. "Besides, all this is a logical extension of your own earlier puny one-man effort. How can you be against it?"

"What I did was a personal statement."

"A whisper in the wilderness," says Shag, dismissing my heroics with a brush of his fingers. "This will be a Something."

"What kind of a Something?"

"An outrageous and unambiguous Something."

"What the hell does that mean?"

"Outrageous in its defiance of conventional civil conduct—unambiguous in the iniquities it avenges."

I look at Gibby. "See my forthcoming book for details," he says.

So for him it is to be social research. For Connie the Great Adventure. For Shag the unleashing of *his* special set of unwholesome repressions. And for me—for me, who has been through it all now, insanity. I comfort myself, though, with the knowledge that Shaughnessy's army will take nothing less than several million dollars to send into battle, and such sums are not readily come by.

But that comfort, it turns out, is not long-lived. In fact it all but vanishes the next afternoon. Shag debates all the next morning whether to wear a shredding denim shirt and soiled jeans to the big meeting with Cudlipp, to suggest that he is beat and therefore hopelessly irrational and therefore all but impossible to budge from his absurd demands, or to throw on a tweed jacket and buy a pipe, thereby suggesting he is a squire who speaks Cudlipp's language and will not be easily gulled. The arguments are strong on both sides, so he compromises: tweed jacket over denim shirt and soiled jeans. He actually buys a pipe and spends an hour trying to break the thing in, then hurls it into the spittoon and settles, ten minutes before Cudlipp's coach-and-four is due, on a big black stogy. To strengthen the impression that he is dealing with big-time operators, Shag wants to advise Cudlipp that I am not only a partner in the saloon but a genuine attorney-at-law as well. "That could get a little embarrassing," I say. "Suppose he says something legal?"

"So say something legal back—like *Marbury v. Madison.*"

"He might want to go into it a little deeper than that."

"Tell him you'll have to reserve judgment because you wouldn't want to do anything arbitrary and capricious. And throws in a few 'whereas's.' "

I agree, on the proviso that Gibby is fobbed off as our accountant and required to sit in on the discussion. Shag agrees. Gibby balks. Shag threatens to leave him off the Shaughnessy expeditionary force. Gibby yields, pointing out, however, his ineptness in these matters. I counter-testify by citing Gibby's skill at administering my burgeoning stock portfolio. He says it is burgeoning only on paper so far but acknowledges a certain unexpected flair on his part for such claptrap.

At the appointed hour we are there in council, but there is no Cudlipp. Shag begins puffing more heavily on his terrible black cigar. He is well along on his second one when a burly young fellow with an attaché case appears and asks for the proprietor. He is ushered to the council table looking to us nothing the way a Cudlipp should—which turns out to be all right, since he is in fact not a Cudlipp but a Frogg. "Francis Frogg," he says. "Mr. Cudlipp got terribly tied up and sends his apologies."

"And a flunkey in his place," Shag says to me, with ill-concealed contempt, out of the side of his mouth. He is piqued over the twin implications of Cudlipp's no-show and Frogg's tardiness.

Frogg, though, apologizes quickly for being so late. "Actually," he says, "I've been walking up and down the avenue for half an hour looking for The Bottom of the Barrel—no one bothered to tell us you changed the name of the place."

"Surely, Mr. Fogg, you had our address," says Shag.

"Frogg," he says, "but I thought perhaps the office had made a mistake."

Shag dons his dark glasses and decides to be difficult. "Mr. *Frogg,*" he says, "how do we know you are in fact Mr. Cudlipp's authorized surrogate in this matter?"

Frogg laughs.

"I don't see that it's a laughing matter."

"Surely you're kidding," says Frogg.

"The hell I am."

Right then it begins to dawn on Frogg, precisely as Shag intends it to, that he is dealing with a very prickly customer, not to say a madman. "Well," he says, "I suppose you could call the office and ask him."

Shag waves it off as if to suggest he has made a concession—his last one of the day. Then he introduces Gibby and me as his professional henchmen. Frogg asks what firm I am with.

"I, uh—have my own office."

"He's the best goddammed ambulance chaser in town," says Shag, poking his ember at my chest as if to brand me with the title. "And since he's used to working on a contingency basis you may find him more pliable than me." He then announces he will not discuss the topic at hand unless Frogg tells us whom he is representing in the matter.

"I'm afraid that would violate a confidential lawyer-client relationship."

"In that case," says Shag, turning away and picking up the afternoon paper, "our negotiations are at a standstill."

Frogg turns to me in a near panic, since he has obviously been instructed to finalize the matter with dispatch and at a price the client can live with. "But what difference does it make who the client is?"

"Use your imagination," I say.

He thinks for a minute. "You mean," he says, "you're asking all the traffic can bear?"

"I don't know as I'd put it all that briskly."

Frogg crosses his arms over his chest. "Don't you agree, then, that we have all the more reason to protect our client by not disclosing his identity?"

"Of course," I say. "Only Mr. Shaughnessy declines to negotiate in the dark."

"But that's the way we always go about it."

"Mr. Shaughnessy feels you must be inventive in dealing with his situation."

"But he's asking something we can't grant."

"Mr. Shaughnessy believes—if I'm quoting him correctly—that he has your client by the balls."

"Oh," says Frogg. He reflects for another moment. "Well, suppose I tell you—strictly off the record, you understand—that we're representing a sizable organization."

"That's a start," I say. "Is it perhaps the Boy Scouts of America?"

"I don't think I ought to be any more specific."

"Well, is it a profit-making organization—surely that's not classified."

Frogg closes his eyes for further soul-searching. "You know," he says finally, "I could get in a whole lot of trouble for this—"

"But you'll get in even more trouble if you don't wrap this thing up in a nice neat package."

His face tells me I would have made a splendid lawyer. His mouth tells me, after a heavy sigh, that his client is indeed a profit-making organization.

"Ask him," says Shag from his redoubt behind the newspaper, "if its sales last year were over a hundred million."

I nod in Shag's direction.

"Now, really!" says Frogg.

"That means yes," I tell Shag.

"Then tell him our price."

"Our price," I say, "is ten million dollars."

"No, goddammit!" Shag shouts, glaring over the top of the paper, "I thought we said twenty."

There are tears now in Francis Frogg's eyes.

"Oh, yes, sorry," I say. "Twenty is our price. Million."

Clearly we are asking more than Frogg has been authorized to pay. In the interests of moving the negotiations off dead center, I ask him precisely what offer he had in mind.

"Twenty-five thousand dollars."

We order drinks. A double bourbon for Frogg, who turns out to have graduated from college the same year as the three of us, though he is a Yalie and therefore a rival. Before long, he and Shag are reminiscing about famous football games of our era, specifically Royce Rippem's legendary performances in a soggy Yale Bowl. Time passes and nobody mentions business. Until Shag decides that Frogg is midway in his cups, at which point he says to him, "I'll tell you a sceret if you tell me one."

Frogg glowingly consents.

"Ole Kwait over there is no more a lawyer than Grandma Moses."

Everyone, Frogg most of all, agrees that is rich.

"Okay," says Shag, "now you tell me one."

Frogg looks up at the ceiling for a while, then leans closer to us. "You know ole Cudlipp?" he says. We nod. "Well, confidentially," he says, "Cudlipp is a shitty-ass-rat-fuck."

From there, it is but two more bourbons and forty-five minutes till we have pried loose the revelation that the client after our lease is no less an enterprise than Mammoth Motors (sales for the preceding twelve-month period: five billion dollars and a whole lot of change). Ole Frogg is rewarded with a final bourbon before we send him home cockeyed in a cab. Gibby is assigned to write a new letter on his departmental electric typewriter, telling solicitor Cudlipp that our price is ten million dollars, firm, and if his client doesn't like it, it ought to seek a new location for its mammoth Eastern headquarters.

32

The Jackpot

AFTER TWO DAYS OF HARD-NOSED SILENCE, SPATS CUDLIPP HIM-self comes calling—a juiceless type, as expected, with chilling blue eyes and a cruelly flat gut—and advises that Mr. Frogg has walked the plank for his unfortunate improprieties in dealing with us earlier in the week, as a result of which his party recognizes that it is at some-what of a tactical disadvantage in negotiating with us and is therefore prepared to make a most generous lease-purchase offer, "provided," he adds, "that you understand it is absolutely our final bid."

Shag, uncowed by those mineral eyes, says if he wants to make us a new bid, to make it without the song and dance but that under no circumstances, and regardless of the bid itself, would we accept unless Mr. Frogg is restored to the firm's roster as a member in good stand-ing.

"That," says Cudlipp icily, "is an internal matter." Then, says Shag smugly, the discussions are closed. So Cudlipp agrees to raise the matter with his colleagues, and Shag says he will agree to entertain the new bid only conditionally, pending clarification of Frogg's status, and by the way what is the bid? "Three hundred thousand," says Cud-lipp offhandedly, and asks the way to the men's room.

I am ready to accede at once to this new and wonderfully generous bid. But the Gaelic stubbornness running deep in Shag's bloodline asserts itself at this juncture and he says that the new bid, which is twelve times larger than their opener, confirms his hunch that we have them by their collective proverbials. And so with a straight face (mine, as I turn away, wears a look of pained disbelief) Shag tells Cudlipp on his return that we reject his bid but, to show good faith, are lowering our asking price to $8,300,000—and alludes vaguely to tax problems to explain the somewhat arbitrary figure. Cudlipp gives a sputter of astonishment and then suggests we are being utterly unreasonable. Shag, throwing back his head and scratching his neck languidly, suggests that this is not your classic bargaining situation and that Mammoth Motors can no more jettison its investment in the property surrounding us than it can admit that its new Tornado sports car is a lemon. "That," says Cudlipp, "remains to be seen," and, declining all offers of bourbon, goes his way with the promise to keep his bid in effect for the next twenty-four hours only.

The supreme gambit, Shag is convinced. The real McCoy, I insist and urge us not to blow the whole bit by being greedy. And so, borne aloft by visions of imminent wealth, we cruise through the entire night and the next day endlessly weighing our options. My own inclination to take the offer is strengthened when Gibby breaks in at midafternoon to advise that the stock market has closed and my intrepid Wall Street put-and-caller has, as ordered, doubled my fifty-thousand-dollar investment in the week allotted to him—though, as a result, he is on the edge of a nervous breakdown. I instruct Gibby to send the wretch two thousand for a week's vacation in Acapulco, at the end of which I will submit my portfolio to an agonizing reappraisal. Thus the value of my robbery-derived holdings has now passed the two-hundred-thousand mark, which prompts Shag to accuse me of turning hypercautious just at the moment in our Mammoth negotiations when a stout heart is required. That, he says, is the problem with having too much money; it clips your wings. On the contrary, I argue; it better enables you to fly. We trade limp metaphors for hours till finally he gets me to agree I can afford to share his mad gamble.

Cudlipp calls at precisely the moment the twenty-fourth hour of grace expires. I have prevailed on Shag at least to the extent of getting him to couple the rejection of their last offer with a drop in our asking price to six million. The most excruciating—and surely the most expensive—pause I have ever endured follows. Shag's face is a mountain of inscrutability surrounding a fiercely burning cigar. Suddenly the face erupts in a huge smile and he covers the mouthpiece to shout, "A million, baby—a million!" I leap. Connie and Gibby do a little jig. It is beyond all belief. Our Shag has outgambited one of the great horned titans of American enterprise. I will follow him to the ends of the earth.

But wait! What is he saying? No, it cannot be! The dumb stupid stubborn Irish bastard! He is telling Cudlipp that it is not enough! He is shooting crap with *my* half a million dollars! And I cannot stop him! I try beating him on the head. He lashes out with a vicious roundhouse that I barely elude, and without looking at me or varying his tone of voice he tells Cudlipp that our price is a (I could die) firm four and a half. Another unbearable pause—and then Shag is beating *himself* on the head: Cudlipp has gone to a million and a half! I am moaning with blind ecstasy. Gibby is pounding the walls with both fists. Connie is guzzling bourbon straight from the bottle. But Shag—oh, I am swooning now with frustrated fury—Shag *still* will not yield! Three and a half, he demands. A million seven, says Cudlipp. Three, says Shag. A million eight, says Cudlipp. I am making fifty thousand dollars a second. Connie is pouring bourbon on Shag's scalp. Gibby is burbling French epithets. Shag grabs the bottle from Connie and chugs half a pint. Two and a half, he yells at Cudlipp, the bourbon cascading down his chin. A million nine, says Cudlipp. Shag's knuckles are white as he grips the phone and shouts, "Two million, you bastard, and you've got a goddam deal!" The final pause. No one breathes. And then—then Shag heaves the bottle at the wall-length mirror and gives a terrible bellow of triumph! Connie falls on me. Gibby falls on her. We roll across the floor in delirium, upending every table and chair we touch.

"But what about Frogg?" we hear Shag shouting hoarsely into the phone. We untangle ourselves and sit up suddenly in stunned silence. Oh, God! Can it be? Shag's lip is curled in anger as he listens. Then he looks over at us. "He says it's no deal if we make 'em rehire Frogg."

Principle grapples with expediency for a single heart-wrenching moment. And then, as it is wont, principle turns tail. "Fuck Frogg!" I yell.

"Yes, fuck him!" Gibby yells.

"Oh, God, yes!" Connie yells.

Shag, his valor spent, relents, takes the two million as a consolation prize, and tells Cudlipp he will be hearing from our lawyers shortly. Then he calls up Frogg, hires him for a one-per-cent fee (which we later agree he has more than earned), and invites him over for the last uproarious spree the old saloon will ever witness.

All I can think of as the roistering swirls on and on into the evening is that I am now—I, Christopher Kwait, known as Kit, estranged from all I have been conditioned to hold sacred and to the continuing peril of my mortal soul—I am now, by dint of furious defiance and uncalculating courage and monumental luck—I, by hook and by crook and the careful husbanding of my seminal fluids—I, at thirty-two, with my muscle tone not altogether dissipated, my passion to learn and to grow and to feel not altogether quenched—I am worth one million dollars. It is the magic number in the United States of America. It is, in fact, the only really meaningful American number. Below it, you are discussing petty cash. Beyond it, superfluities. But the number itself—and the moment of reaching it—ah, they are cause for celebration. How few places are there left on earth where such an accumulation is both possible and not entirely unconscionable. For me, it is not the chattels or commodities or comestibles the money can buy that is so thrilling; it is the freedom it purchases. A million dollars sitting lumpishly in a bank, or twenty banks (as prudence would dictate), throws off a pre-tax dividend, at prevailing rates, of fifty, for crissakes, thousand dollars a year—vastly more, in all probability, than I would be earning after twenty-five more tit-lapping years as a militant dissembler for Computron. I have, in short, made it. I can live, henceforth, off the fat of the land. I can dwell amid a grove of banyan trees and, if I desire, levitate all day. And night. My season of toil is done. God Bless the Cheerful Taker—This Is My Only Source of Income.

I must tell Anne at once.

It is after midnight as I complete that last homeward lap. Odysseus returning by stealth to Ithaca could have felt no keener anticipation. His Penelope, though, fared better at fending off would-be usurpers of the bed linen, it appears, than my own sweet pining bride. For whom do I run squarely into on leaving the elevator but a slouching cumbersome bundle—Muffie's Marvin. Making his post-midnight getaway from—from—*my* invulnerable nest! For a glaring imbecilic moment, we lock horns speechlessly. What, frankly, is there to say? And then he is by me taking the same elevator down that has just brought me home. As the door closes, I fill with sudden remorse that I have not detained him long enough to pound his fat head against the mail chute several dozen times. But the true object of my awakened wrath is, of course, the unimpeachably devoted lady of the house, mother of my children, light of my life, to whom I have returned with such joyous tidings and whose neck I am now perforce about to wring.

It is a classic confrontation. One of the great set pieces in the human behavioral cycle. I crash through the door. Anne in her nightgown flies down the hall toward the sound, sees me, sees I know all, recoils, then falls on her knees weeping instantly and copiously— less, I choose to assume, from joy than guilt. I break away while she is still blubbering out her delight at my return and I drag her into the living room. She reassembles herself in a corner of the sofa while I parade fiercely before the fireplace for a demonstrative few moments. Finally I face her and, with all the overworked eloquence of

a fledgling matinée idol in a third-string road company, demand:
"Well?"

"Well," she says, subduing the last few sniffs, "welcome home."

"Yes—some welcome."

"Marvin you mean?"

"I'm glad at least I didn't break up the party."

"There wasn't any *party.*"

"I'd think you could do a lot better than him if you were so determined—"

"It wasn't anything like you think."

"What was he doing here, playing checkers? And where are the children, for crissakes?"

"They're at my mother's till the weekend. And Marvin was here for sympathy—he and Muffie have split. He wanted my advice."

"And you were giving it in your nightgown?"

"I—"

"Just cut it."

"But I'd—"

"Let's be grown-ups about it."

"—changed before he called and asked if he could come over. I mean he's an old friend. I didn't feel as if I had to—"

"Anne, did you or did you not just commit adultery with that fatassed idiot?"

"I did nothing of the kind!"

"Oh, please!"

"But I'll tell you the truth," she says, standing up now and injecting a dose of stridency in her voice. "I was thinking about it—I really was. With Marvin or the delivery man from the grocery or anybody else who came by."

"What are you talking about?"

"I'm talking about you. I'm talking about the woman you brought up here for the night while I was away with the children. Don't think I don't know what you were up to. I could tell on the phone."

"You're crazy."

"Am I? That's not what Detective Pratt says."

My stomach gives a spastic revolution.

"He's been looking for you," she says. "He says the elevator man has a distinct recollection of your bringing a woman up here with you the night of one of the robberies."

"You don't think—?"

"I don't think what? What am I supposed to think?"

"Anne—nothing happened."

"Oh, right—nothing at all."

"I'm telling you the truth."

"Oh, sure."

"She's just a girl I know."

"Sure, sure—you just brought her up here for companionship. And then after a cozy little candlelight dinner, you went out together and pulled the robbery."

"As a matter of fact, yes—if you want the whole truth."

"Kit! I'm not an idiot! Whatever else you think of me—whatever's driven you to—to—do this to me, I'm not an idiot. Don't start treating me like one now."

"Goddammit, I'm not treating you like an idiot. I'm telling you the truth. The truth is I'm a robber—and I'm worth a million dollars— and nothing happened here that night."

"What about all the other nights? Where have you been? Shacked up, I suppose."

"A robber—"

"Sure, I heard."

"A million dollars—"

"Right, right." She rakes her hands through her hair. "I guess it's just the male animal—it's got to go roving sooner or later." She looks away. "Somehow I'd convinced myself we'd built something better than that."

"God, you certainly are consumed with self-pity."

"It's not self-pity! It's just—disappointment that you're so common."

"Just a goddam second! Don't start getting sanctimonious with me, Anne! I practically catch you in the hay with a guy and you want me to believe he was here just crying on your shoulder. But when I tell you nothing happened with the girl I had up here, you're utterly convinced it was adultery. Why should I believe you if you don't believe me?"

"Because of the whole pattern. You're up to something, I can tell. You've always been perfectly honest with me before this, but now—"

"I *am* being honest with you, but you won't listen. I'm telling you I've become a robber—and I'm worth a million dollars."

Anne shakes her head and fights back tears. "Stop it, Kit!" she says. "I can't stand your playing with me like this. Just admit you had the girl. I mean it's not the end of the world—it happens every day."

"I'll admit it if you'll admit it."

"Admit what? That Marvin Miller laid me?"

"Yes."

"He didn't—he can't. That's what broke up his marriage. In fact he thinks he's turning homosexual."

"Why should I believe that?"

"Because I'm telling you."

"And *I'm* telling *you!*"

"What are you telling me? Are you also telling me you didn't lay Muffie Miller?"

"Muffie . . . who told you that?"

"What difference does it make?"

"Was it Muffie?"

"Marvin told me—just tonight—if you must know."

"How does he know?"

"Muffie told him. Muffie tells him about everyone who lays her."

"She *is* a bitch."

"Then you admit it?"

"No—I deny it. I mean I almost did but I didn't. I didn't do it—not with her and not with Con— Not with anybody. I— Oh, Christ!"

"Yes, Christ. There is a large body of evidence against you."

"I'm leaving. You don't believe me, so what's the point?"

"Leave—I don't care. And don't come back till you admit it like a man."

Beautiful. It is perfect, absolutely consistent madness. I head for the door. "What does Pratt want?"

"He wants to talk to you about your girl friend. Evidently you lied to him, too. He says his list is down to six names and yours is still on it—whatever that means."

"Where did you tell him I was?"

"In Pittsburgh—wasn't that what you told me?"

"What'd he say?"

"He asked me where in Pittsburgh—and of course I couldn't tell him since I didn't know. He thought that was very strange. He said to tell you to call him when you get back."

My hand is on the doorknob. "Thanks."

"Kit—" So soft and plaintive and wounded, the way she says it. "Yes?"

"Kit, don't—please don't—destroy everything."

She is so very sweet.

"I don't know what's driving you to it, or what I've done or where I've failed you—"

And so very dedicated.

"But I'm sorry, really and truly sorry."

And so forlorn.

"Maybe," she ends in her most tentative tiny voice, "we can get you some medical help."

My God, she is a pitiful bore.

33

Man to Man

HELLO, PAT PRATT, IN YOUR TERRIBLE HAT, NOT TO MENTION YOUR unspeakable brown shirt, which you have taken to wearing as the uniform of your sadistic calling—hello. Yes, I just blew in from Pittsburgh, where my wife faithfully reported me to be and so I just got your message, and rather than calling I thought I'd come right over to headquarters and try to clear up the whole thing once and for all, because I don't like being on anyone's list, least of all Pat Pratt's. I forget—is it all right to call you Pat, Pat? Thanks, Pat. Well, Pat, let me begin by—yes, thanks, I wouldn't mind—yes, black, with sugar, is fine. Pat, let me begin by leveling with you all the way— which of course is what I should have done all along, but the truth is I *had* something to hide. No, not from you, Pat. The truth is, Pat, that I haven't been in Pittsburgh at all. The truth is, Pat, that I've been on the lam from the missus—just the way I was that night when you came by and asked if I'd been alone all the evening of the robbery and I said yes when in fact I was running up the flag on a chippie with a very big ass and a very mean box. Oh, I see the disapproving look in your church-affiliated eyes; you think I am a bounder and a rotter, and that is why I did not call you as instructed but knew I had to come over here to lay it on the line to you man to man. Pat, do you know what I—mmm, the coffee's not half bad, thanks, only a little more sugar'd help; yes, enough, thanks—Pat, do you know what I found when I came home tonight like a repentant husband and devoted father of two wonderful kids I'd give my right arm for, do you know what? No, you don't, so I'll tell you. I found the missus

tucked between the sheets beside a large hairy ass I'd never seen
before. Well, I mean I knew the guy but I'd never seen his— No, I'm
not shitting you, Pat. That is the truth. I know you have reason to be
suspicious because you found me out once in a lie, but, Pat, you do
not know, you cannot know, what it is like to be married to a cheating wife. Pat, she had driven me to it by that night of the robbery.
Oh, I've had plenty of evidence of what she's been up to before tonight, believe you me, but tonight was the first time I'd caught her
at it barehanded—or bare-assed, I guess is more like it. So that's what
I was up to that night you questioned me about—cheating on my
cheating wife. And I didn't know you and didn't see how I could tell
you what was going on without making you think the worst of me
unless I went into the story of my life the way I am doing now. Oh,
sure, you can check it out with the missus; I don't give a crap—the
fat's all in the fire now. We each know what the other's up to. She'll
probably deny it to you, getting caught that way tonight—anything
to make it tough on me. The girl? Which girl? Oh, that one. Hell, no,
I don't mind if you check it out with her, but if you find her, I wish
you'd tell me her name and where I can find her again—she was
good, Pat, real good. Oh, sure, I knew her first name, but that was
as far as we went; you can understand that, my being a married man
and the possibilities of blackmail and all that. And so that's why I
haven't called you yet about shampooing our rugs, which I have
pledged without fail to you. I'm not on the premises much and I'd
hate to have your guys come in and get the evil eye from my missus
when they start rolling up the place. But I'll get to it soon, I surely
will, Pat. No, I'm not sure how or when we'll work it out—maybe
I'll just murder her, how's that? No, you'd be on me like a rocket,
now that you know my motive. I'll just let her cool off for a while, I
guess, and stay where I've been staying. No, not the Y, Pat—it's a
club. You can reach me there if you need me. What's that sheet of
paper you've got there? Oh, the suspect list. I forgot about that.
Whose name is that you're crossing out, Pat old boy old pal old sock

old buckeroo? Oh, well done, Patrick O'Pratt. Say, why don't you come by the little bar I hang out in when you knock off tonight and we can hoist a few? It's going out of business next week and they're using up the stock fast.

34

Conditional Surrender

IT IS FOREORDAINED THAT PAT PRATT AND SHAG SHAUGHNESSY should meet and promptly coalesce. The twelve- or fifteen-year difference in their ages means nothing once their mutual interests and neuroses begin meshing. Pratt's entrepreneurial activities are quickly revealed as Poujadist—and a gossamer façade behind which a latent lust for violence has been churning away since it was implanted at places like Tarawa and Saipan and by no means fully exorcised there. Oh, he likes blood, does Pat Pratt of the Twenty-second Detective Squad, to which he had been transferred, he confesses to Shag and me over his seventh or eighth beer, for getting a bit too frisky with his night stick while bringing in one or two black bandits. ("Got this one big ape right here," he says, indicating his skull just behind the ear, "and another one square in his raping nuts.") Shag and he go at it for hours, a couple of ex-Marines extolling the best years of their lives, and before the night is done, Pratt not only has been fully briefed on Shaughnessy's army but has accepted the assignment to head up Battle Group A and become Shag's principal field officer. He had been getting ready to quit the cops anyway, he confides, and the rug-cleaning business practically runs on its own as it is.

Shag claps him on the back at the end of their hard-swilling, loud-belching session during which they have exchanged every known barbaric intimacy short of seeing who could pee farther across the room—and they would have done that, too, if Connie had not been hovering on the scene plucking at her guitar. It is decided that they will begin at once to enlist recruits in this most ennobling of causes, whatever it is, and Gibby is instructed to draw up a help-wanted ad for the *Times* and the *News*. Interviews are to be held with prospective recruits from noon to four every afternoon so that Pat can be on hand before he reports for duty to the precinct. When they have their full complement, Pat will resign and direct a six-week training program.

Next day, Francis Frogg, known among us quite naturally as Bull, is added to the suddenly burgeoning high command. Frogg, a former jet pilot and third-string fullback at Yale, has decided to practice law on his own and so readily accepts designation as Shag's adjutant general for a small annual retainer. Gibby asks him if becoming a pirate does not conflict more or less directly with the Canon of Judicial Ethics. Frogg denies the conflict and advises that every American citizen is entitled to counsel, pirates included. That settled, Shag assigns him the task of arranging for a conveniently located training site and then turns to Gibby and me for an intensive examination of his financial resources.

Shag has, of course, assumed my ardent interest in the project despite my having registered more than one loud disclaimer. What he wants now is not so much my ardor as my money. He argues, not altogether implausibly, that since his letting me buy into the saloon cheap in the first place and his high artistry at negotiating with the redoubtable Chauncy Cudlipp in the second place are what have produced the lion's share of my newly acquired fortune, he has a substantial claim to putting the money to whatever use he wants so long as I am allowed to retain my proportional share of the equity. I nevertheless reject his argument, on the ground that it is confiscation. He tells me I cannot. I tell him he is mad. He tells me he will turn me in to Pat Pratt as a tinhorn robber if I do not go along. I tell him I

will murder him before they cart me off to jail if he rats on me.
"You'd never be able to pin it on me," he says. "Besides, how do you
know Pratt isn't joining up for the sole purpose of continuing his in-
vestigation of crimes to which you are already suspected of being a
party?" I don't, I say. Shag nods and reassures me of his fidelity, but
his implied power to do me in swings the tide of debate. He has me.
It is simple blackmail. Yet, strangely, I am not badly riled, for I am,
moreover and to tell the truth, absolutely fascinated with the idea of
unleashing a two-hundred-man legion against the unrepentant villains
who abound in the land. And now that I am no longer being asked
to judge the wisdom of the project and thereby sever the last of my
badly frayed links to the mainland, now that I am being *told* that I
may disapprove this mindless enterprise only at peril to my liberty,
now that I have no will of my own to invest in or withhold from this
rapacious daredeviltry, I am free—I am obligated—to give in utterly
to the incredible venture and enjoy the hell out of it. So I submit,
with two provisos. First, that I retain absolute veto over the objective
of every mission. Shag readily agrees. Second, that the force be totally integrated. Shag even more readily agrees, proclaiming that the
black man is well known for his natural grace and ferocity as a
fighter—and dier.

These principles on record, the rest is as quickly disposed of. It
is agreed we will sign on the first two hundred cutthroats we can find
and pay them five thousand dollars each for six months of active
duty. With the other million dollars we will train, equip, and sustain
them. In return, the hirelings are to hand over all plunder to the high
command, which will retain the first two million dollars to pay itself
back the original investment. All additional plunder will be divided
between the high command and the soldiers, every soldier sharing
equally, with those who excel being eligible for bonuses dispensed
at the whim of the high command. At the end of six months, sur-
vivors may be invited to re-up—if there is anything left to re-up in.
There is a Randolph Scott/John Wayne/Brian Donleavy sort of re-

hearsed go-for-broke quality about Shag's tone as he outlines the plan and somberly says he expects casualties, maybe a lot of them. "We will take no prisoners," he adds, confirming my long-harbored suspicion that the Japs and Chinks and other varieties of Oriental gooks are not the only ones who shoot their captives in the back. "And there will be no dropouts," he concludes, with a few wiggles of his trigger finger. Taken all together, it does not sound exactly like Operation Madball. Indeed the methodical nature of the undertaking begins to frighten me for the first time. Two hundred armed brutes will be straining at the leash that I, nominally at least, am to hold.

I confide—mistakenly, it turns out—in Connie, whose ardor for the project knows no bounds. She has already volunteered to do all the cooking at the training camp.

"You're not going near the camp."

"Why not?"

"You'd be the only woman on the premises."

"Yes, isn't that exciting?"

"They'll rape you black and blue."

"Why would they do a thing like that? I'm on their side."

"You would also be available."

"You're being silly."

"Look, get the idea out of your head, will you? You're not going."

"You don't own me," she says, tightening the strings on her guitar for her last performance ever at Xanadu City.

"You're being a child."

"You're being a father figure."

"You seem to need one."

"I've had too many."

"Why are you all excited about this thing?"

"Because it's exciting, that's why."

"But you haven't the slightest idea what it's up to or what it stands for."

"It stands for knocking the stuffings out of stuffed fatheads and phony phonies."

"You sound like a dropout from *The Catcher in the Rye*—and just as adolescent."

"All right, then I'm adolescent. That doesn't make it any less exciting than being a robber with you was. Was that adolescent, too?"

"That was different."

"Why was it different?"

"Because—"

"Because what? Because that was your show and this one is Shag's? Because it's a bigger deal? Because you're running out of guts?"

"I—"

"Because what? Because what?"

Because I— Because they— Because it— Because because. "Are you sleeping with Shag?"

"Oh, Christ," she says, "will you please go away?"

35

The Putti Problem

THREE WEEKS PASS BEFORE THE DEMOLITION CREWS APPEAR TO begin wrecking the saloon. In the interim, there are Christmas and New Year's, during which I am so drunk that few pangs of regret over the disoriented circumstances of my life can penetrate. There are moments, though, when I dimly sense the sentiments of the season seeping through, when I hear the bells and chimes summoning me back to my nearest and dearest, when I wander thronged streets con-

sumed by my aloneness and no longer celebrating the absoluteness
of my freedom. I am neither here nor there. I am neither as bold as
I have been nor ready yet to renounce this deviant course I have will-
fully taken. Mostly I talk with Connie Colton about everything under
the sun and wonder when there will be a sign that she is ready to
surrender her body to me. But no sign is forthcoming. She is infuriat-
ingly even-handed about bestowing her attentions among the members of the high command, and all the while I am riven by the suspicion that she is copulating, on some sort of rotation basis, with all
of them but me.

While Shag Shaughnessy and Pat Pratt and Gibby Good sit around
a table in the now shuttered saloon and interview a steady stream of
jailbirds, prison guards, truck drivers, stevedores, village smithies,
grape pickers, hod carriers, gandy dancers, lumberjacks, ex-Bundists,
cowboys, stockyard workers, failed internists, college dropouts, ex-
roller derby stars, merchant seamen tattooed from head to toe, assorted rednecks, roughnecks, no-necks, and a great many black men
with no visible or invisible means of support, Connie Colton sits in
one corner serenading us all wistfully and I sit in the opposite corner
with a scratch pad and compose haiku in praise of Xerxes, Kemal
Ataturk, and Ivan the Terrible. It is hard to concentrate amid the
reveling that goes on between interviews as the high command sifts
through the qualifications of the would-be recruits, each of whom to
warrant selection is required to be (1) physically intimidating but
docile till provoked, (2) on intimate terms with one or another form
of lethal weaponry, and (3) devoid of compromising ties to family,
nation, or God.

Bull Frogg has meanwhile selected a summer boys' camp in the
Berkshire Hills as the training site. The place lies fallow until May
each year when it is put into shape for the summer flock, and so the
owner is only too glad to rent it out for three months at five thousand
dollars per month to a group of health nuts who plan to run an intensive physical-training course for adults trying to regain the muscle

tone of their youth. For our money we get seventeen bunks, an outdoor swimming pool, a lake, a mess hall, and the unmonitored run of four hundred well-treed acres. It is, of course, cold in the Berkshires in the middle of winter, but our forces, after all, are not being sent there for a suntan. We drive up for a weekend. Shag pronounces it ideal and sets to work at once with Gibby, Pat and Bull acquiring equipment, well before the recruitment process is completed.

There are trips to internationally renowned traffickers in arms in Alexandria, Virginia, to secluded warehouses in New Jersey, to Teterboro Airport, to the Portsmouth, New Hampshire, shipyards. There are phone calls all day and all night, and various foreign accents are heard on the premises as the murmured haggling goes on and deals are clinched with measured, if not swashbuckling, professionalism. By the time we are required to vacate the saloon, Shaughnessy's army has on order:

200 rifles @ $20 + ammo	$10,000
200 uniforms and personal equipment	10,000
10 20-mm. cannons @ $100 + ammo	1,500
10 mortars @ $75 + ammo	1,500
5 bazookas @ $100 + ammo	1,000
5 light tanks (stripped) @ $10,000 + arming	60,000
2 C-47s, very old, @ $6,000 + gas and refurbishing	15,000
2 LSTs @ $25,000	50,000
5 small trucks @ $1,000	5,000
Radio equipment	3,000
Medical supplies	500

Which totals $157,500. Plus three dollars a day to feed each man, times 180 days, adds $108,000 to the operating budget. Throw in some chicken feed for miscellany, and it's getting up near $300,000. Plus, of course, the million dollars previously allotted for the soldiers' pay.

"I think," says Shag, surveying the lists and numbers with satisfaction, "we are in business."

"What about hand grenades?" Gibby asks.

Shag looks at him, then at Pat, then at the ceiling. "Check," he says. "Get a thou worth," he tells Pat. Pat nods.

Everyone looks to me as the resident skeptic for some word of commendation for their industriousness. So I commend them. Only I don't quite understand how they propose to train a miniature army in the bucolic Berkshires without being swarmed all over by local, state, and federal authorities. "I take it," I say, "that twenty-millimeter shells produce a considerably bigger bang than a moose hunter's pop-gun."

"We are not about to defoliate the countryside," says Shag, explaining that there will be no target practice up there, only physical and mental conditioning and reacquainting the recruits, all of whom are to be ex-servicemen, with the equipment.

"Suppose they're all lousy shots?"

"Our stress," says Shag, "will be on swift physical movement and hand-to-hand combat. We're not planning on any extended campaigns."

"Then what's the artillery for?"

"It makes me feel good," he says. "And it's cheap."

"And where will you keep all the equipment?"

"I, it so happens," says Bull, "own a small deserted island in lower Penobscot Bay. I know the Coast Guard patrol schedule inside out, so there shouldn't be any problem running the LSTs up there from Portsmouth and keeping them hidden in any of several deep coves. It's pretty rocky terrain, but there's one passably level strip about a third of a mile long that you can bring a C-47 down on—if you're good. We've got five guys signed up who say they can fly a Tin Goose. We'll let 'em practice and pick out the best pair."

"How will you know who's best?"

"Whoever doesn't crack up."

"And the tanks?" I ask.

"They'll go in the LSTs."

"How are you going to get them there—the Merritt Parkway?"

Shag, Pat, and Bull exchange heavy looks.

"We'll have to dismantle 'em," says Shag. "Do we have any good dismantlers signed up?"

Pat checks down his list. "Well, there's about a dozen of 'em who say they have mechanical skills—"

"Like tying their shoelaces," says Shag. "Look, I don't want to depend on a couple of glorified grease monkeys. Let's get ourselves half a dozen first-rate mechanics."

"Where?" Pat asks.

"I don't care—go kidnap some freshmen from M.I.T."

"Maybe try an ad in the *East Village Other*," says Gibby. "Some of those artsy-craftsy types secretly know a lot about retreading tanks."

And so on into the night, refining and reshaping and redeploying— it is decided, for instance, that three of the twelve infantrymen in three of the eight squads making up Battle Groups A and B will be converted into tank crews and that two other infantrymen in five of the squads will function as bazooka teams—until what at first seemed to me an utterly preposterous business begins to emerge as yet another perverse miracle of modern technology.

Connie, meanwhile, is surrounded by a hundred discarded sketches of possible insignia for the army as she hunches on the floor wielding Magic Markers of every color made and peering over the tops of her sunglasses, in mock desolation, at her whimsical renderings. She has done a lion rampant on a field of buttercups ("A visitation of wrath, tempered by mercy," she explains, and crumples it), a turtle in a helmet with guns poking out the ass part of its shell pillbox-fashion ("Slow and steady wins the war," she explains, and crumples), an alligator clutching a bow in its teeth and firing an arrow with its tail (she crumples without explaining), variously shaped bolts of lightning slashing across variously colored backgrounds, and flaming swords held aloft by every manner of man and beast. They are all abominations, she announces, but keeps scribbling away, consuming hundreds of Magic Markers in the process and tattooing her arms, legs, and face with assorted grotesque patterns till she has all but disappeared from sight. After three days of creative agony, she gives a little yelp of ecstasy and announces, "Success!" Everyone comes flocking around. With great zest, she unveils the winner: a clenched upright fist, encircled by five fluttering cherubs.

A long silence. It is Shag who finally responds. "What," he asks, "in Christ's name is that?"

"That's our new official insignia," Connie says, all beamish and not at all quenched by the sour looks confronting her. "It is totally wonderful."

"I understand the fist," Shag says, "but what are those little flying fuckers doing there?"

"They," she says coolly and not deigning to repeat his grossness, "are nothing of the kind. They are *putti.*"

"What the hell's a *putti?*"

"*Putti,*" she says haughtily, "are more than one *putto.* A *putto* is a heavenly emanation. It has wings—for locomotion—"

"I see them, I see them."

"The insignia," she says, "stands for militant rectitude—represented, naturally, by the erect fist—tempered with loving-kindness and understanding and compassion and—all that—and represented, as you can very well see with your hostile and insensate eyes, by a flock of—"

"Fucking *putti,*" says Shag.

"Yes."

"Terrible," says Shag.

"Faggy," says Bull.

"Esoteric," says Gibby.

"Too complicated," says Pat.

"It's absolutely perfect," I say, yearning to install my head between her militant breasts.

"Majority rules," says Shag. "Back to the drawing board."

"I am not going back to any damned drawing board," she says. "I absolutely and unalterably insist this be the official insignia. It must be worn on every uniform and painted on every tank and every plane and every boat, and I am going to make a big enormous huge flag with a giant fist and thousands of *putti* and raise it over the training camp myself every morning, and everybody's going to salute it or or or or —or you can get someone else to cook your damned meals and play your damned guitar and lick your damned wounds—that's what you can do, goddammit to hell!" And she runs out the door, not to be seen again for five hours. On her return, she brings stencil-making material with her and sets to work at once cutting out her fist-and-*putti* pattern. Nobody objects. By midnight she has transferred the involved pattern to two hundred little canvas arm patches that she will sew on every uniform the moment the shipment arrives in camp.

36

Operation Scattergood

FEBRUARY. A BERKSHIRE HILLSIDE, SLOPING IN THREE TERRACES to a spotless frozen lake. Patches of snow on the ground. The sky is clear and without portents. Mount Greylock is plainly visible ten or twelve miles to the north across a vista of lake and hillocks.

Arrayed in a horseshoe around the flagpole (with Connie's flag giving an occasional cherubic flutter above them), Shag Shaughnessy's fighting force assembles for the first time. In the center, wearing fatigues and combat boots like everyone else but sporting a brimmed, heavily eagled-and-starred hat and slapping his thigh at regular intervals with a mean-looking riding crop, stands the Commander-in-Chief. His legs are spread in accepted authoritarian manner. He surveys them all darkly from behind his oversized sunglasses until they begin to shuffle with anxiety. Finally, he speaks: "All right, gentlemen, are there any questions?"

There are none, naturally, since nobody has been told anything yet.

"Fine," he says, "then let's get it straight from the start. You're all here voluntarily—nobody made you come. But now that you're here, you're here to stay. If you don't like the way things are run, if you think too much is being asked of you, if you want another portion of mashed potatoes and nobody will give you one, if you wet your bed or get a hernia or break a leg, if it's so cold out you're afraid you'll freeze your nuts off, if you don't like the way your bunkmates talk or smell or comb their hair—that's tough titty. You're in for six months, like it or lump it. And if you lump it loud enough, you're gonna have me to reckon with." He smacks his riding crop into his palm half a dozen times. "Now this camp, gentlemen, has three main objectives. First, to get the lead out of your asses and the fat off your gut. Second, to teach you how to use your weapons—and everybody gets to learn how to use every weapon. Third, to mold the mangy lot of you into a fast, smart, coordinated bunch of killers." He grinds his jaw a little. "Our hope is that we'll never have to kill a soul. But if we're forced to, we'll be ready. There's not gonna be a lot of parades around here in front of a lot of fat-assed generals. But there's gonna be one helluva lot of running, jumping, climbing, and push-ups. Oh, I'm a big push-up man, I am. Why, every last one of you'll be able to do a hundred push-ups by the time we break camp or know the reason why." He wigwags the riding crop. "Now, the whole while you're here, we're gonna be watching you—looking for the strongest guys, the guys with most guts, the guys with most endurance, the guys with most brains—and they're gonna be the squad commanders by the time we head out to the field. It's gonna be a tough, brutal process and there's no one here to hold your hand when the going gets roughest. But when we're done, gentlemen, you're going to be the finest, toughest, smartest, fastest, best-equipped, best-trained, deadliest fight-

ing force on the face of the earth." He circles the flagpole for a minute to let his rhetoric sink in. Then he gestures over to the high command, clustered behind the flagpole under a towering blue spruce.
"Actual operations here will be under the immediate direction of Vice-
Commander Pratt. Mr. Pratt is the possessor of the Silver Star with
three oak-leaf clusters, the Purple Heart with five oak-leaf clusters,
the Distinguished Service Cross, the Croix de Guerre, the Victoria
Cross, the South Korean Medal of Honor, fifteen battle ribbons, and
a Colt .45. He has two general directives from me. First, shape you
guys up. Second, shoot anyone who disobeys." He raps his wrist hard
with the riding crop. "Pat, you wanna add anything?"

"I think you said it all, Commander."

"All right, then, Pat," Shag says, with a half salute and a smart
about-face, "they're all yours."

A great roar goes up from the men.

And so begins the first week of the ordeal. In the beginning the
program is the same for all the men: running, jumping, and climbing
before breakfast, followed by breakfast, followed by cleanup, followed by rifle and pistol instruction, followed by more running, jumping, and climbing, followed by lunch, followed by a five-mile hike with
full pack, followed by mortar and hand-grenade instruction, followed
by milk and cookies, followed by a mandatory five-minute freezing
swim, followed by half an hour of free time, followed by supper, followed by map reading, followed by still more running, jumping, and
climbing, followed by a Red Skelton movie, followed by lights-out-
and-keep-your-mouth-shut-or-you-get-a-rifle-butt-in-the-nose. As the
week wears on, the five-mile hike turns into ten, the climbing turns
into scaling telephone poles with a packful of rocks, and the five-
minute freezing swims become an endurance contest, with the man
who stays in longest serving as drillmaster during calisthenics the
next day. The men assigned to the airborne detachment, all of whom
allege they have served in the paratroops at one time or another, are
broken off from the main contingent for special jumping and landing

training in the empty swimming pool. As the second week begins, the primary after-supper activity becomes a mass wrestling contest in the rec hall in which the recruits strip to their shorts and divide themselves into four equal groups. One group at a time positions itself inside a chalked circle and, at a whistle blast from Pat, everyone tries to throw everyone else out of the circle, no holds, kicks, or bites barred; last man left is the winner, the four group winners pair off in semifinals and then finals, and the Big Winner, who is invariably naked and bleeding by this time, is rewarded with a pound of raw hamburger and a quart of beer. There are no repeat Big Winners but plenty of bruised necks and kneed groins after the first week of it, at which point the gala event is curtailed to a twice-a-week schedule in the interest of not decimating the ranks.

Through all this, the high command is hard at work on the sidelines. Shag is everywhere at once running things. He has dubbed the entire operation "the Scattergood Scout and Health Camp" and opened bank and charge accounts in that name in the nearby town. He makes sure the place is properly patrolled at all times, day and night, and that the actual field exercises are shielded from the eyes of the temporary kitchen and maintenance help. He shows up unannounced a dozen times a day, his dress hat poking its insistent brim out from under the hood of his oversized parka, to check on progress in the field and brandish his riding crop with menacing flourishes. Every night at ten, he and Pat huddle to evaluate the daily performance and to plan the next day's regimen. In time, temporary platoon and squad commanders are named and brought into a second daily skull session during the morning cleanup hour. It is all frighteningly well organized.

Bull Frogg, in mufti, checks in and out of camp overseeing fulfillment of the equipment orders and ferrying back and forth in a Piper Cub to his Penobscot Bay island to work with the C-47 pilots and the LST commanders. Connie, cutting her hair even shorter than usual and wearing fatigues just like the men, directs the kitchen crew and resists all temptations to concoct gargantuan ragouts, curries, mousses, and other belly-bursting exotica. When she is not in the kitchen, she is playing toe-tapping records on the camp p.-a. system, including "On the Sunny Side of the Street," "Marche Militaire," "Pack Up Your Troubles in Your Old Kit Bag," "Semper Fidelis," and "When the Saints Go Marching In." The music, everyone agrees, has a singularly salutary effect on the otherwise unrelievedly somber proceedings. And when she is not playing records or tasting the food, she is in the field, cheering the men on, joking with them freely, applying medicines to minor wounds with tenderness, and fast becoming everybody's favorite person in camp. So much a part of the scene is she that in time she is invited to watch even the mass wrestling matches and bats not a lash at the dozens of dangling genitalia exposed in the course of the brutal spectacle.

Gibby, in tennis sneakers (despite the intermittent snow), green corduroy pants, thin zippered jacket and navy-blue wool ski cap, interviews the men at every conceivable moment, including ones of peak stress, as when they are double-timing on the ten-mile, full-pack daily hike. At first nobody wants to answer his questions. But then Pat makes it clear that cooperation is compulsory, and so everyone assumes Gibby is the resident shrink and they tell him what they think he wants to hear. They decide, at any rate, that he is harmless, though of course Gibby's findings are duly reported to Shag and Pat and figure importantly in their decisions as to who will command the platoons and squads.

I come upon Gibby going over his notes in the rec hall late one night toward the end of the second week of camp. "What tentative conclusions have you reached with reference to the dominant personality types?" I ask him.

"It's too early to tell," he says. "We'll know more when they are put to the crucible of ultimate stress in the next few weeks."

He is ever the cautious scholar. But I am a friend of long standing and will not hold him to his preliminary judgment. "Don't shit me, buster."

"They're very interesting, actually."

"And how would you describe them?"

"Most of them, I would say," he says, plucking at his lower lip, "are frustrated maniacs."

"And their potential?"

"Trained, armed, and acting in concert, in my professional judgment, their capacity for destructive action is"—he checks his notes for a moment—"incalculable. But it is probably quite substantial. Statistically significant, even. Ultimately, I would guess, they will turn so vicious that they will have to be institutionalized."

Four of the five tanks on order have been disassembled and routed to Portsmouth for shipment by LST to Bull's off-Maine island hideaway. The fifth tank arrives in camp right on schedule in eighty-nine cartons of assorted sizes and shapes. Bull has escorted them on their rail-and-truck trip up from Virginia, counting them tirelessly at every transfer point and triumphantly at their destination: the camp arts-and-crafts shop. All six of our ace mechanics tinker through the night with the hideous thing under the direction of one of the star recruits, a veteran of the Afrika Korps who clicks his boots every time Shag comes within fifty yards of him. By daybreak it is ready, and two hours are set aside each afternoon thereafter to teach everybody in the place how the contraption works. Its symbolic value is so high and keeping its presence from the outside world so vital to him that Shag will not settle for padlocking the crafts shop each night. He decides to throw a mattress on the front hood and sleep there with a loaded rifle under his pillow.

Through all this, I am the grimly detached observer, charged solely with planning the army's ultimate objectives and meanwhile slipping deeper into the doldrums by the day. For one thing, I have long since defaulted on my obligation to produce a stunning field report to Mooring, my single-minded superior at Computron headquarters. The punch card bearing witness to my company performance has surely been punctured beyond recognition by now. I have been AWOL for a month and filed not a jot with Mooring or anyone else. Yet some badly shriveled impulse in me dictates a telegram that I ask one of the kitchen help to dispatch in town:

HAVE BEEN HAVING NERVOUS BREAKDOWN DIRECT RESULT TEN THOU-SAND FIELD INTERVIEWS. RELUCTANTLY REPORT LITTLE WONDER #301 UNLIKELY TO ACHIEVE PROJECTED VOLUME UNLESS SHORTWAVE STEREO AND PAPERCUP DISPENSER ADDED TO DICTATING/PHOTOCOPY-ING/PENCILSHARPENING FEATURES. RECOVERING IN SHANGRILA. HOPE TO RETURN BETTER THAN EVER. YOURS FOR ENHANCED EARNINGS. KWAIT.

Do I hope against hope to restore a shattered career with that one absurd gesture? Hardly. It is just something I know I must do—a wire from the underground to tell them all that I live. Its effect is of no interest to me. Of far more immediate concern are reports that begin to reach me during the early part of the fourth week at camp. They have to do with the alleged promiscuity of everybody's camp favorite, Connie Colton, who has reverted to her pseudonym for the duration—Olivia Ottway—but who is now familiarly known, I hear, as just plain Everybody's.

I have been aware from the start of training, of course, that she is going out of her way to avoid me. But I am not prepared to believe the rumor that her services are for hire each night after lights-out in a small shack just off the main campus. The rumor is embellished by a later report from no less a source than Gibby Good that she has taken to bestowing her favors gratis upon any black recruit who manages to win the semiweekly mass wrestling contest—and quite a few blacks do—but she will submit to whites for money only. I am utterly incredulous. I try nevertheless to confront her with the steeliest look of reproach I can manage, but every time I catch her in the kitchen, she is wielding a butcher knife or cleaver or the like with such practiced dexterity that I retreat to regroup my forces and still my heightening rage. But when I hear, the following evening, that Pat Pratt himself has countenanced her accessibility to the troops and, the ever-alert moonlighter, has in fact been functioning as her whoremaster, I can no longer forbear. I grab an axe from the toolshed behind the crafts shop, shove it inside my greatcoat, and burst into the moonlight.

"Password," says the sentry on duty on the main campus.

"Oh, for crissakes," I say, "it's just me."

"Sorry, sir, I need the password."

"I can't remember the goddam password."

"Sorry, sir."

"Can I guess it?"

"You only get one guess, sir."

"Oh, I remember—it's 'shoo-fly pie and apple pandowdy.' "

"No, sir, that was last night."

"Let me by, fella."

"Sorry, sir. I have my orders."

"How would you like your head split in half with an axe?"

"I wouldn't try it, sir. I'm a trained killer—sir."

In my passion, I have quite forgotten. So, my rage redoubled, I go back to the rec-hall office and ask Shag for the password. He can't remember, either. He telephones down to Pat's command post on the main campus. The sentry on duty reports Pat is "making the rounds." To hell with it, I say, and decide to resort to an elementary tactic of deception. I reapproach the campus but steer clear of the main path this time, slouching through the underbrush instead. When I am just beyond the sentry's range, I pick up a conveniently discarded canteen from the ground and hurl it far down the path, where it bounds along with a terrible clatter that immediately draws the sentry from his post. I slip behind him and through the checkpoint like a flash—or as much of a flash as a man can manage with an axe inside his coat. On the balls of my feet, I make my way behind the trees and dart past the showerhouse to a position just to the rear of the shack where I was told the loathsome concubinage occurs. A second sentry is on duty in the general vicinity. From what I can make out of him through the high grass in which I crouch, he is asleep on his feet. I duck-walk a yard or two along the frosted earth. Still he is motionless. I take another yard, then another—suddenly the sentry stirs. I freeze. He stretches his arms once, twice, gives a little groan of fatigue, and heads off down the path. My chance is now. I pull out the axe. Its gleaming edge picks up cold glints of moonlight. I give it a heft and, adrenals flooding my system with instant stamina, make a dash for the shack. I grab the doorknob. Locked. I wrench it. Locked. I hoist my axe high, in classic posture for delivering a blow of maximum retribution—and then feel it wrenched cruelly out of my grip and an arm whiplash around my neck bearing me to the ground. Over and over we roll in silence and then the other has braked the roll and is on top of me, clapping my arms back with a strength that nearly extracts them from their sockets. I look up—into the unrelenting face of Pat Pratt.

"Then it's true!" I gasp.

"What?"

"She's in there."

"Who?"

"You know goddam well who!"

"What are you talking about?"

"Don't deny it. She's humping half the camp."

"You're crazy!"

"You're lying!"

"*I'm* lying? *I'm* lying? You been lying so long, Kwait, you wouldn't know the truth if you stepped in it."

"What are you talking about?"

"The robberies, you crummy son of a bitch!"

"What robberies?"

"*Your* robberies!"

"Oh," I say, "those."

"Yeah, those. And don't bother denying it. She's confirmed everything I'd already guessed."

"Then she *is* in there."

"Yeah, she's in there, but she isn't humping half the camp. She only humps who I tell her to."

"You dirty pimp!" I cry, and lunge for his throat in a burst of supreme rage. But my strength cannot overcome his. He repins me and takes an even tighter hold. "Know something, Kwait? She's good. She's *really* good—and getting better all the time."

I suddenly see the whole picture. "You're still a cop, aren't you, Pratt—I knew it," I pant. "Admit it—you're a fucking undercover agent, and the second anyone turns his back here, you're going to beat it and spill the beans on the whole setup and get your fat ass promoted to fifty-third deputy commissioner."

He tosses his head back and gives a contorted laugh. Then his face tightens with hatred as it bears steaming down on mine. "You know what I'm going to do to you, Kwait? I'm gonna reach back and grab that axe and then I'm going to chop your head off—and no one around here's gonna stop me, because they are fanatically devoted to their vice-commander."

I believe him—oh, I do indeed. And with the last grain of energy that the body can summon in its moment of ultimate duress, I pitch him off me and lurch after the axe. He recoils almost instantly but his gesture is so violent that he slips on the icy ground, flops down, strikes his head on a sharp rock, and is instantly at peace. Leaving the axe behind, I slink off into the trees, come up to the main guard post from the rear, jump the sentry, and sprint the whole way back up to the rec hall to alert Shag and Gibby.

To my dismay, the pair of them scoff at my allegation that Pat is a spy and suggest that his threat to do me in was mere bluster in the tradition of army camps the world over. I protest at this whitewash, and Gibby accuses me of incipient, perhaps even advanced, paranoia.

As to Connie, Shag says he has taken her for a strumpet all along and sees no harm in her providing a few of the boys with a little diversion so long as they have the energy to keep up with the training routine. I bellow savagely but the two of them deride me for naïveté.

Our talk has gone on for half an hour when a call comes from the main campus. Shag looks thunderstruck as he listens. He says we will be right there and hangs up limply. "They found Pat in a stall in the showerhouse," he says.

"What about him?"

"They found his head in the sink and an axe in the toilet bowl."

I veer off from the rest of them and make a beeline for Connie's shack. I shout in to her what has happened, and she unlatches the door at once and flies naked into my arms, sobbing, "He made me do it, he made me do it! He said he'd turn us both in if I didn't do it!" I clutch her tight and shield her from the cold. I run my hands through her short hair as the moon beams down on us and her sobbing turns into a sporadic whimper and finally ceases altogether. Then she gives a little laugh and says, "It's all right, though—we've had our revenge."

"I'm not sure I approve of such a ghastly method."

"Oh, that," she says. "That's not what I mean."

"Then what is?"

"A little secret I've been keeping from you."

"What's that?"

"I've been nursing a nasty dose of gonorrhea for a couple of months and that's why—"

"You *what?*"

"I—have—the clap."

"Oh, God."

"And I hope I gave it to every one of those slimy brutes."

"But I thought you—"

"I must have sat on an infected toilet seat somewhere."

"Oh, God."

"Or maybe it was from too much masturbating. I masturbate a lot."

"Ooohhhh."

"Of course it might have been that Egyptian sailor who tied me to the bed and made me submit to him for ten straight days."

"Ooohhh."

"He was pretty dirty. But he did bring me a bedpan when I asked for it."

"Oh oh ooohhhh."

"He said he only wanted to listen to my sitar records. It was a very sobering experience."

"And—and—and that's why you—never let me—"

"Of course."

"And you never told me?"

"I didn't think you'd believe that an Egyptian sailor tied me to the bed and made me do it. I thought you'd think the worst."

"Ohhhhhhh," I say, my head reeling, and drop her on her ass in the snow.

37

Battle Stations

IF MY SUSPICIONS ABOUT THE LATE PAT PRATT ARE WARRANTED, THE New York fuzz will be on our necks in short order. In which case, we are faced with two choices: to flee at once or to sit tight and maintain the fiction that we are no more or less than what we announce ourselves to be—the Scattergood Scout and Health Camp. The former course will brand us all murderers and lead to a nation-wide dragnet—and a conspiracy charge as well, in all likelihood, if we are caught. The latter course will require the immediate removal-without-a-trace of every piece of military equipment in camp and the perpetuation forever by two hundred brigands of a big, if not altogether implausible, lie. Neither choice, on reflection, appears particularly attractive to the high-command-less-one.

If my suspicions are proved groundless, there nevertheless remain the noisome problems of how to dispose of the two-part corpse and what to do about replacing the fallen vice-commander. And there is, of course, the further matter of the implications of his death. All that is clear at the beginning is that it was almost certainly not a suicide. Somebody has done him in—body or bodies. Why, is the question. Gibby reports that in his field interviews of late he has detected a certain undercurrent of resentment against the vice-commander. But anyone in his position would have been the object of such hostility, and if this is the way our hand-picked army responds to a stern taskmaster, it will be hard indeed to keep it supplied with taskmasters.

As the high command sits around the campus headquarters of the late vice-commander and ruminates on these large policy questions, something becomes clear beyond the conviction that Pat Pratt did not chop his own head off; namely, that he engendered more than a normal portion of resentment among the recruits. One by one, his victims come forward to testify; he was nothing less, they say, than a sadistic monster. They produce burned fingernails, lashed backs, and bruised genitals as evidence. Without anyone confessing to anything, the high command soon holds the opinion that the vice-commander was disposed of in a manner that met with popular acclamation in the ranks. Its unseemliness is the source of some alarm among us—until Gibby reflects that it would be utterly contrary to the nature of this kind of men and of the ordeal they have been enduring for them to have tiptoed behind Pratt's back and informed the rest of us of his excesses. And so, coming upon their tormentor in the prone and defenseless state in which I left him, they acted much the way any other group of two hundred frustrated and badly abused maniacs might.

So we have two hundred murderers on our hands, and the fact that it was not exactly premeditated and was, if we are to believe our eyes, prompted by the victim's own villainy does not entirely mitigate this laying on of hands—or steel, as it were. Murder has been done. But since we have no choice other than tacitly to countenance it (for we are outnumbered, unless the high command takes to the tank—a strategy briefly considered and swiftly rejected, on the ground that it is ultimately self-defeating), we decide not to press an inquiry. Implicit in the decision are two other decisions: first, to bury the body without resort to the local undertaker, who, being practiced in such matters, is certain to notice the ununified state of the deceased and therefore unlikely, for any price, to overlook the missing death certificate. Second, having determined to bury the remains by ourselves (unofficially, so to speak, but nevertheless very deep), we then adopt a tactic to counter the possible arrival of a contingent of New York cops greatly agitated over the sudden short-circuiting of their secret agent. Accordingly, the whole camp gathers about Shag, who, addressing them by moonlight, reports that, to his great chagrin, the distinguished vice-commander has disappeared this night and that if any outside authorities should appear in search of him, it would be best to put the matter as simply as that: Pat Pratt just disappeared. Phffft. Meanwhile all military gear will be removed from camp for a week, during which physical conditioning will continue apace; after a week, the military phase of training will be resumed.

"Who's gonna take over for Pratt?" someone shouts out.

"I am," Shag says. "And the first son of a bitch who comes within ten feet of me gets a bullet between his eyes." And he turns his back on them and shouts over his shoulder, "Dis-*missed!*"

It turns out, of course, as the week unfolds, that they love him beyond imagining. He is tough but not sadistic, fair but not averse to singling out stalwarts for praise or malingerers for scorn, and stern but not so forbidding that his charges are busier hating him than absorbing what he has to teach. He is, in short, in his element, and the morale of the whole camp responds immediately. By the end of the week, anxiety over the possible imminent arrival of Pratt-hunting cops has lifted, the weapons have been returned to the men (along with a certain swagger stemming directly from the totemic value of the arms), and the first intimations of spring are in the air. Sensing it, the maximum leader sheds his parka, and to demonstrate his self-confidence in the troops' estimate of him as a commander, he discards his sidearms and moves easily and intimately among them, squeezing an arm here in reprimand, patting an ass there in commendation. He relishes the *esprit de corps* he has excited and spurs the ranks to efforts and achievements they thought beyond their power, including the hundred push-ups that every man in the place is now capable of. He drills and hikes along with them, never trying to match the men in stamina but always giving the impression he can take on any one of them in a man-for-man face-off. Shag Shaughnessy's army, that is to say, has about shaped up.

The important question now—the only question, really, and the one that I had put at the start—is how to unleash this splendidly orchestrated collection of muscle and machinery: how and when and where and toward what objective. Answering it has been my special assignment all along. But until now I have not been moved to grapple with it. For one thing, I had been pretty much shanghaied into the undertaking at the start. For another, I had genuine doubts about Shag's aptitude for generalship, not to mention his sanity and politics. For another thing, it has been cold and dreary and damp up here in these wintering hills and I have wanted nothing more than to linger before the giant fireplace in the rec hall and ponder the eternal void. And, finally, Connie and I have been estranged, irreparably I had supposed, until the cause was revealed and violently remedied. All together, the timelessness and placelessness and purposelessness of my being have left me a listless husk.

Now, though, the sap is rising in me anew. Shag in the field has ignited real hope that it will not all end in a bloody disaster. Bull

Frogg has the logistical situation well in hand. Gibby, nearly a daily commuter between the camp and the city, holds out high hopes for our grand gesture of organized defiance, whatever it is to be. And Connie, dear quirky sad-eyed clap-stricken Connie, is at my side now all day, wolfing cupcakes—she eats the paper wrappers, too, insisting they are made of seaweed and gelatin and are entirely digestible—and promising to quench my overheated celibacy the moment the medicines I put her on conquer her contagion. For the moment, though, that protracted celibacy serves to focus my energy on the problem at hand, and it is no small one.

Connie suggests that we conquer Switzerland.

"We need a grievance," I say, twiddling my pencil over the pad on which I am listing all possible targets for our stouthearted band of terrorists.

"Well—they *are* hoarding all that money there."

"People give it to them to hold."

"Yes, but what kind of people? Terrible people. Dictators. Embezzlers. Robber barons. Crooked commissars. Let's steal it."

It is not the worst idea proposed. The Swiss army, we agree, would prove a less than formidable barrier. But there are only two hundred of us, and the logistics of the operation, considering that our air force amounts to two C-47s that begin to rattle badly above five thousand feet, look hopeless.

Gibby, for his part, is pressing us to invade and lay waste the state of Mississippi.

"It's already been laid," says Bull. Besides, we agree, there are many upright and only moderately depraved Mississippians who would surely fall victim to our whirlwind, as would large, slow-moving portions of the black population whose feudal and degraded state we would all too effectively end. No, we need a more manageable, more clearly delineated target, the destruction of which must be a symbolically endowed blow in the name of the—the—the New Jerusalem that shall flourish upon the earth and beckon unto the—the—

the wronged and the grieved and the unblessed whose pain and deprivation shall be alleviated forever and who shall be free to have and
to hold the fruits of their labors and to multiply in a place where
there is sunlight and bird song and life is good for however long it
may be granted to mortal men, amen. And so I surround myself with
every manner of book and journal and map and astrological chart
and logarithmic table, seeking Good Causes that will hasten the coming of that heaven on earth. Slowly I accumulate a list. And talk endlessly with Shag about our realistic capabilities violence-wise, with Bull
about our range of operations maneuverability-wise, with Gibby about
the cultural and social priorities in American life abomination-wise,
and with Connie about her progress clap-wise. The men in the field,
meanwhile, are being honed to a fine fighting edge, and Shag advises
that they cannot be held in check very much longer.

Grimly I convene our high command and present my battle plan.
It is met with enthusiasm on all sides. The final round of preparations
begins at once, among them a series of phone calls I place to the other
side of the continent. Bull Frogg is dispatched to Penobscot Bay with
a dozen men to convoy our LSTs to the mainland, loaded to the
gunwales with every stick of armaments at our disposal. He sells the
LSTs the moment their cargoes have been covertly transferred to a
dozen of the biggest trailer trucks he can buy in a hurry. The trucks
lumber across New England to our camp by cover of night and within
a week are converted by our tireless corps of mechanics into the most
exotic columns of armor ever sent into battle. Slits, portholes, peri-
scopes, sliding panels, and pneumatic ramps are installed at strategic
points. Bunks, latrines, showers, and a field kitchen are added and the
trucks all linked by radio. Money, with the great moment at hand,
is no object. One truck, of my own devising, is given over entirely to
great drums of paint in many colors, all rigged to a high-powered
pumping system.

Thus outfitted, the motorized armada takes on ten days' worth of
supplies, all our assembled armaments except the C-47s (which are

hangared, for the moment, in Rockport, Maine, roughly adjacent to Bull's island), and our full complement of combat-hungry troops except the airborne detachment (which is dispatched by delivery truck to Rockport). The high command climbs into a microbus piled high with maps, flares, radio equipment, five cartons of Fig Newtons, and ten cases of beer in dry ice. At ten o'clock on the moonless night of April 15th, without benefit of bugle blare or whistle blast, unadorned by banners or insignia or any visible designation (Connie's fist-and-*putti* flag having been hauled down at sunset and packed away as a bad, if serviceable, joke), unheralded by any press releases, lavish layouts in slick magazines, or other public disclosure, Shag Shaughnessy's army begins its assault, one truck at a time at two-minute intervals, upon the desecrated land. There has been no dry run. It would have violated the spirit of the thing.

38

Over the Top

AND THE SPIRIT IS HIGH, INDEED ROLLICKING. OUR CAUSE IS JUST, our strength formidable, our intended victims deserving beyond debate of the wrath about to be visited upon them. Connie launches a medley of marches on the guitar that our radio hookup carries to the trucks, careening ahead of us through the night. We are moving south along Route 7 as it wends its peaceful way past the picture-book village greens of westernmost Massachusetts, where everything is painted white. Every half hour the trucks count off and report their location. Eight are carrying troops, three are carrying heavy equipment (including the tanks, which are ready to crank down the reinforced hydraulic ramps at a moment's notice), and one is carrying paint. In the morning the C-47s will begin hopscotching across the continent to our final rendezvous—the only one of the steadily escalating encounters on our schedule in which an air arm will be of any practical value.

At the first check, all trucks are present and accounted for and proceeding in the order in which they began. The night is calm, the ride pleasant, and Shag soon breaks out the beer. Before long he is proposing a toast to the memory of Pat Pratt, whose earthly remains we have left in the hospitable Berkshire Hills.

"Not only that," he says, taking his eye off the road and flashing it sideways at me, "but I have decided we should make an appropriate financial gesture to his family in the form of a living, interest-bearing memorial."

"But he abandoned his family to come with us."

"All the more reason for us to do right by them."

"But he left them a thriving rug-cleaning business."

"Rug-cleaning businesses are notoriously precarious without the chief rug cleaner on the premises. Besides, he had a sizable family, as I understand it."

"How big a living memorial did you have in mind?"

"A hundred thousand dollars."

"Of which *I* am to put up half?"

"More, if you'd like."

"After what he did to Connie?"

"Stop being a Grade A schmuck, will you? He didn't do anything to Connie she didn't want done to her."

"You dirty pederast!" Connie screams.

"Kiss my rosy red!" Shag shouts back at her.

"Don't talk like that to her," I say.

"I'll talk any goddam way I want to the bitch, you love-struck asshole!"

"Who's a pederast?" Gibby asks in the interest of the behavioral sciences.

"He is!" Connie shouts, poking Shag in the back with her guitar.

"Don't lie, whore!"

"I saw it with my own eyes!" She turns to me and Gibby. "That's why he hates me and says such rotten filthy ugly things—because he's a pederast and I caught him at it and I know now this whole crazy thing is a sublimation of his thwarted, shriveled, pitiful little sex."

"Who'd you catch him doing it with?" I ask.

"Pratt—who else?"

"Lying bitch pig whore nymphomaniac cunt!" Shag shrieks.

"How do you know he has a pitiful little shriveled sex?" Gibby shouts in the further interest of science.

"She was sleeping with Pratt and every goddammed one else in the place with a dong!" Shag yells. "And loving it!"

"Because he tried to slip it to me," she outyells him, "and couldn't."

"Who?"

"Him," she says, and raps Shag with the guitar again.

"You do that again," Shag yells as we swerve out of our lane, "and I'll ram that thing up your diseased crevice!"

"You couldn't ram anything anywhere, you impotent Hitler, you!" She turns to me again. "That's why he wants to give Pratt's family money—to relieve his dirty little conscience!"

"You open your mouth one more time," Shag says, "I'm stopping this thing and throwing you the hell out on your ass!"

"You throw her out, I go, too."

"You—you're not going anywhere. You're going the route, Charlie. And you're putting up fifty thou in memory of poor Pat Pratt's severed head—or I'll bash *yours* in."

"Look, I didn't kill the dumb bastard."

"No? I'm not so sure of that."

"What are you talking about?"

"How do you know he wasn't dead when you left him?"

"I—I *don't* know. But I certainly didn't cut his head off."

"Maybe that was just a little post-mortem the troops performed. You wanted him dead, didn't you?"

"I—look, he'd just threatened to kill me."

"That's my point."

"You're—" Out of your blooming mind is what I want to say. But I have always known that was true, and there seems no point, at this critical threshold in our adventure, to announce what is manifest anyway. If he were not such a madman, how could he have carried the thing this far along? "You're—right. I'm in for fifty—all right? How'll you get it to the family?"

"Anonymously, of course. A bank check—"

"You're just gutless!" Connie screams at me. "I always knew it." And she turns toward the window in a furious pout.

A minute passes in simmering silence. Then Gibby says, "Say, Shag."

"What is it?"

"Did you really play ugly with Pratt?"

Shag looks back murderously over his shoulder, then bursts out laughing. "Yes, and I also rut with kangaroos."

"No, seriously."

"Seriously you can't be serious."

"I am—for my book. I want to know what satisfaction you got out of it."

"Didn't you hear me deny the foul bitch?"

"Yes, but she denied your—um—charge, too."

"Then you'll just have to take your choice."

"But both of you could be telling the truth. There's nothing mutually exclusive about the two alleged perversions."

"Or we could both be lying."

"Yes."

"That leaves you with four possibilities."

"Yes."

"What more could any social scientist ask?"

"The truth, of course."

"When you get right down to it," Shag says, looking straight ahead now and waving out the window as we pass the first of our trucks, "and under all the gloss of jargon, a remarkably pedestrian brain is at work in your fat head."

And so, tempers fraying ever so slightly as the point of no return passes and the moment of overt action nears, we hurtle through the unsuspecting night. The tiny towns of western Connecticut—Canaan and Kent and Cornwall Bridge and Gaylordsville and New Milford —are behind us and then we are swerving through Danbury onto super Interstate Highway 84, following it across the state line into Putnam County, New York, till we veer south onto NY 22 and close in on what is left of the bucolic northern reaches of Westchester. Katonah, Bedford Center, Bedford Village, Pound Ridge, and then, about five miles from anywhere, floodlit in all its stark-modern flatness and angularity, our first target comes glittering through the blackness: the Electronic Data-Processing Division headquarters of the Continental Computron Corporation.

Inside it, a billion electronic impulses surge through ceaselessly whirring Computrons in the division's Information Retrieval Center, where a thousand giant corporations have stored duplicate magnetic tapes on which every bit of business they have ever transacted has been recorded. Some of the transactions go back two hundred years. All the data can be summoned instantaneously, should any of Computron's distinguished clients have the need. Every company buying or leasing an EDP system from Computron is entitled to the retrieval service, a stellar feature that has given Computron an important advantage over its competitors—and indeed such domination of the field that a flock of federal antitrust lawyers hovers perpetually over Computron's hulking shoulders in order to build a case against the company as an unconscionable and monopolistic leviathan. Which it most assuredly is. It also puts people out of work. In fact, the more the better. That is one of the EDP Division's prouder boasts: every working day we make one hundred more jobs obsolescent somewhere in America. And since, for the most part, they are clerical jobs held by no-account drones begrudging an honest day's work for an honest day's pay, society can be said only to benefit from this job-displacement process. The displaced, presumably, are to be retrained for more exacting and creative tasks, the better to utilize their God-given wits and fulfill their destiny. Except for those drones who have no wits or destiny, about whom it is too bad, but that, the company implies in a variety of elusive ways, is what Human Evolution is all about.

Two of the trucks join our microbus for the assault. The other trucks circle back to Mount Kisco for a coffee break calculated to last no longer than it takes us to complete our mission and catch up with the main force. No unsightly gate mars the vista that the building presents. From several articles that I have read in *Concepts,* the Computron house organ, I know that the sprawling place is guarded by three watchmen and that the Information Retrieval Center maintains an around-the-clock staff behind locked doors (though the night shift is no more than token—or just enough for the company to boast legitimately that its operations in this area never end). The Red Squad from the first platoon of Battle Group A supported by the Green Squad from the second platoon have been assigned the task.

They slip noiselessly out of their trucks and scurry over the edges of the lush lawn. The watchmen are overpowered at precisely the same moment the power and telephone lines are cut. The locked door to the Information Retrieval Center is battered down with an axe and the half-dozen clerks monitoring the Computrons are lined against the wall and held at gunpoint. Wearing sunglasses and gloves, I stride into the secured building and demand the magnetic tapes on which the vital data are stored. The clerks eagerly assist in dislodging them from the memory-unit Computron and packing them in airtight containers. The support squad, working in relays, moves them rapidly to one of the trucks, where space has been reserved for them. The watch-

men and the clerks are then ushered outdoors and instructed to lie
flat on the ground at the edge of the lawn farthest from the building
while our demolition crew goes nervelessly about its handiwork. In
no time, they are ready. The firing mechanism has been thrust into
my hand. The entire operation has consumed but twelve minutes.

At 1:33 A.M., with a slight depression of my vengeful right index
finger, our defiance is dealt to all the Malefactors of Corporate Wealth,
to all the Manipulators of Massive Dehumanization, to all the Pro-
prietors of Modernity-at-Any-Price; that flat sleek glazed fluorescent
transistorized tabernacle to programmed man bursts apart at the seams.
Snap crackle pop BAROOOOM! Holocaust! Doom and damnation to all
button-down cutthroats everywhere! *Sic semper tyrannis!* I bequeath
you, Continental Computron Corporation, a nonrecurring plant cost
of seventeen million dollars on the next annual statement.

Our troops march off in well-ordered retreat. The trucks have been
moved half a mile away, out of sight of the horizontal company people. The big truck doors clank shut, their bolts are bolted, and their
husky motors, kept running throughout the hostilities, bear us away before the dust has settled at the site of our first glorious violent gesture.

But the night's devastation is by no means over. Our two trucks
rejoin the main convoy just below Armonk and, at one-minute intervals, peel off southward along the White Plains Post Road, through
haughty Scarsdale and Tuckahoe and Bronxville and Mount Vernon
till the procession pounds across the city line and begins traversing
the whole depressing length of that archetypal melting pot, the Bronx.

Along the way, my secret weapon gets unlimbered. A small metal
panel slides open on the side of the paint truck and the nozzle at the
business end of the pumping system is shoved into the aperture. On
instruction from me in the microbus, now traveling directly in front
of the paint-laden monster, a many-colored ejaculation snakes through
the air—a spurt of colored liquid moving faster than the eye can
follow—and douses whatever passing landmark curries my displeas-
ure. We start by purpling a few homes of the overprivileged along

the Scarsdale roadside. By Bronxville we are bluing the slightly more secluded homes of the tastefully anti-Semitic. And by the time we hit the Bronx, we have raised our sights and increased our pressure and are joyfully splattering brightness upon the unrelieved gloom of the high-rise apartment houses and the low-slung tenements of the ethnically unassimilated. Oh, it is a thing of beauty—very nearly Jackson Pollockian in the explosive patterns and enveloping skeins with which we adorn every surface in range.

Assured of the effectiveness of the weapon—of its suppleness, its adhesive quality, its capacity for harassing without inflicting permanent damage—we are eager to direct it at more prominent targets. The paint truck (or "PT," as it is officially designated) detaches itself from the main caravan, which has followed the Post Road to Fordham Road, thence west to Broadway, thence south to the Washington Bridge, thence west to New Jersey, where it dawdles while the microbus and PT follow Broadway all the way down to Columbus Circle. We circle the Circle twice to make certain no police car is in the vicinity. Then the little panel slides open, the nozzle pokes forward, and an enormous spritz of orange paint douses the whole northern façade of that marbled Swiss cheese, Huntington Hartford's Gallery of Modern Art. We continue around the Circle, watching our handiwork spellbound as the paint oozes unevenly down the great slab; it is in process of becoming the world's largest action painting. On the second go-round we give it a blast of royal blue, and oh the vigor of the configurations! The exquisiteness of the pigmented harmonies! The something of the something else! It is all so marvelous we cannot resist a third sally—red, this time, though Connie wanted green—and of course it ends up a mess. Still, it is better than it was before we redecorated.

Down Broadway we go and then east, looping a great yellow splat onto the Pan Am Building, America's most superfluous skyscraper. Though we do not slow down to assess it like connoisseurs, I estimate that the fried-egg stain, when dry, will run from the tenth to the thirty-first floor, and easily half the width of the wretched pyre. We turn down Lexington and go as far as Twenty-third, then swing over to Third Avenue and proceed to Fourteenth, where we run the one short block west to Irving Place. There, on the corner, looms yet another beacon glittering in the American night, yet another monument to American ingenuity and enterprise, yet another bastion against the world-wide forces of collectivism that miss no opportunity to besmirch the American achievement even while ogling and trying vainly to ape it—the headquarters of Consolidated Edison.

Connie, for one, wants us to blow up the place simply because they had once billed her $11.27 for a six-week period when a pair of hundred-watt bulbs were the only electric installations on the premises. "Mine," she wrote the company, "is the last household in America without a toaster. I couldn't use up $11.27 worth of your stuff if they installed an electric chair in my bathtub and did away with an axe-killer every night of the week. There is no other electric company listed in the yellow pages of my phone book (the phone people at least *list* their charges and we get along fine with each other), and so I suppose you have me at a disadvantage. But that is all the more reason why you ought to be nice to dear little fat-legged people like me whose power you can shut off anytime you like if you want to be brutes about it. Can't you see there's been an awful mistake made?" They wrote back and said they had sent someone to double-check the meter and the meter said that the tenant had consumed $11.27 of Consolidated Edison's power during the period indicated and could she please remit the proper payment promptly. She wrote back: "Does anybody at your place actually *read* letters like mine or am I writing to a machine? Look, I never doubted that your meter readers can read meters. I was just telling you that somehow—I don't know how; I don't even know what electricity is—I have been cruelly overcharged. And I think you ought to be gentlemen about it. Because if you're not and I have to pay, I'm going to take a blunt object—a hammer is what occurs to me first—and bash in about a dozen of your damn meters and then you'll be sorry." The company, though, would not relent. Nor would Connie. They shut off her power and she took to using candlelight—and bashed in a dozen meters at selected locations around the city. That, though, was not enough for her, and now here she is imploring us to call in the tanks and reduce the home office to rubble—bomb it, even, from the C-47s.

Instead, with an artful display of paintsmanship, we trace a lightning pattern in jagged orange down the whole front of the building. Unassuaged, Connie pokes her pistol out one of the curtained windows of the microbus and, before anyone can stop her, aims a single shot at the ornamental fixture burning on the crown of the building. It misses. We tug her back to cover and sit on her until we are out of the neighborhood.

On the ride uptown, we unleash our final painterly assault on the least lovely metropolis in all creation—a fat green swath at the seventh-floor level for block after block along the city's most luxurious architectural disaster area, the new Third Avenue. Surely no civilization has lavished such wealth on dwellings more tedious to look at, on vistas more dispiriting than these of stacked brick and sterile glass. Our single swift stroke does more to relieve the monotony of that cityscape than a thousand sissy decorators sent to hang paisley banners from every sooty terrace on the avenue.

39

J'Accuse

WE CROSS THE HUDSON, DIZZY OVER OUR POWER TO DEFY, TO DE-nounce, to deface, to besmirch. But the moment we begin plying the flotsamized arteries of north Jersey, we are stunned by the inade-

quacy of our new weapon to affect local conditions, which are clearly
terminal. The devastation is so far-flung—the gas stations so frequent, the billboards so clamorous, the hot-dog stands so bacterial,
the flashing lights so glaring, the sulfur and gas fumes so pervasive,
the bargain stores so cluttered with shiny artifacts of instant perish-
ability, the used-car lots and junkyards so redolent of the manufac-
tured rot that is the chief nutrient of that sprawling compost heap—
that no detergent can attack the stain, no purgative can repair the
pollution, no antidote can combat the toxic rampage. Surgery is the
only hope. And so our two trucks with tanks in them are pressed into
service. Turrets pivot into position, other metal panels slide open, and
terrible flame-spewing spouts are aimed at the appalling spectacle.
Every quarter mile, the microbus signals for a new burst of napalm—
and another small patch of the infection is cauterized. Soon the bazookas open up, splintering billboards and empty frozen-custard
stands. Then the shell-lobbing tanks take over from the flame-throwers,
demolishing gas stations and, farther along, in a still more pointed rebuke to the hegemony of the internal combustion engine, igniting the
pastel storage tanks of the Linden oil refineries. Fire spreads in chain
reaction. The whole night is aglow. The air fills with klaxons and the
roadways behind us clog with rescue vehicles, discouraging all pursuit
of the bringers of this righteous mayhem. We have charred the face
of foulmost Jersey (as we will other scabrous stretches along our
lengthening path) and markedly improved its aspect.

We swing onto the Jersey Turnpike at the first opportunity, speed
down the diagonal corridor past Philadelphia and the truck farms at
the bottom of the state, cross the Delaware below Wilmington, and
follow Route 40 as far as Aberdeen, Maryland, where we pitch camp
for the night. The trucks pull over to the side of the road or into
diners or shopping-center parking lots, roughly half a mile apart so
as not to attract attention. The high command checks into a motel—
Shag and Gibby in one room, Connie and I in a second. The various
group and platoon commanders are summoned for a conference in

Shag's room, where commendations are lavishly dispensed with the beer and plans are confirmed for the next leg of the campaign. The trucks meanwhile are refueled and checked and the troops allowed, in unobtrusive groups, to stretch their legs in the immediate vicinity.

Connie and I withdraw from the fringe of the revelry to catch a few hours of sleep. It is the first time I have slept with her—or beside her, to be perfectly accurate about it—since our weekend together months and months before. My passion to possess her has never died entirely throughout the intervening rise and ebb of our fortunes, but it has been so effectively distracted and rechanneled that lately when I think about it at all, I have very nearly come to conceive of lust as a vice. How marvelous not to be tyrannized by it, I would think. Energy that would have gone to replace squandered body fluids has gone instead to sustain my gallantry in combat. And yet the instant Connie and I fall in together hand in hand at the motel, so naturally, so innocently, all those pockets of disenfranchised hormones are stirred up and there seems only one wholesome and truly expressive way to crown the triumph of the long night. "How's your disease?" I ask as I turn the key.

"Oh, better."

"How much better?"

"Oh, much better."

"Much, *much* better?"

"Much *much*."

My whole pelvic zone swells with anticipation of the long-deferred event. I hesitate a moment, then add, *"All better?"*

"Yes, I think so."

"You think it's safe?"

She tosses off the pea jacket she has taken to wearing and falls backward on the bed, exhausted. "If you really wanted me, you wouldn't ask."

"Really wanted you? I've wanted you from the moment I saw you."

"Then what's a little clap to worry about? Oh, I know, you think it'll turn your brain soft. So what—so you'll take a couple of doses of penicillin like me."

"It's not that."

"Oh, I know. You're too polite to say it. I just don't turn you on when I'm infected, right? Your little old subconscious back there is saying, 'Easy, buster, she's got a putrid pussy and you don't want to mess with *that*.'"

"I never thought *that*. Not *that* way, anyway."

"Maybe not. But you don't really want me, even now—I can tell."

"You're crazy."

"No, I'm not. I mean me personally—not me generally, me generically, me woman. I'm just a symbol to you."

"You really *are* crazy."

"No, no, I'm absolutely right. You'd see it the moment after we did it. You don't want me. You want what I stand for away in the back of your head where you've hidden all your frumpy old conventional ways of thinking about things. Oh, don't misunderstand—I think you've made a *wonderful* effort to transform yourself, the way you've broken heartlessly with your family and tossed away your career and become a real outlaw and a murderer and all."

"I am *not* a murderer!"

"Don't be embarrassed—he deserved to be murdered."

"I did not murder Pat Pratt!"

"Okay, okay. But you're implicated—we all are."

"He was trying to murder me!"

"All right, so it wasn't murder—it was self-defense—but how did he get involved in the thing in the first place? Through you—right?"

"But that's ridiculous! He decided to come all by himself."

"He wouldn't have come if you hadn't bought him off."

"Bought who off?"

"Pratt."

"That's a goddam lie!"

"He told me you'd paid him twenty-five thousand dollars to take your name off the suspect list."

"Never!"

"You corrupted him, Kit."

"Oh, my God!"

"Why deny it this late in the game? I mean he's dead now, and I'm not going to testify against you."

"This is utterly insane."

"Look, I don't blame you."

"He was lying. He was just trying to get you to squeal."

"Sure, okay—whatever you say."

I slap her face.

"Ohhhh," she moans. "Kit Kit Kit Kit Kit."

I fall on her. "I want you, buddy."

"I want *you,* buddy." Her hands are all over me. "Only we can't."

"Why not?"

"It's my period."

"I don't care."

"*I* do."

40

Rupert!

BALTIMORE AND WASHINGTON WE STORM IN BROAD DAYLIGHT, SO bold have we become. The former, actually, has so few worthy targets that we spare our paint and shells and napalm, except to knock over a couple of the fat brick factory chimneys that tower above the seamy downtown—the loftiest and loveliest structures anyone in the area has seen fit to erect. It is a pinched, tight-assed town that we kick dust on as we barrel ahead to the nation's capital.

Washington! O shrine of each patriot's devotion! O temple of gleaming alabaster! O marbled halls of freedom! O stately seat of justice—take that black splat on your sanctimonious White House portico! And that green one on your idolatrous Lincoln Memorial! And that red one on your Sam Rayburn Office Building sarcophagus! And that orange one on your cankerous Foggy Bottom! And on, without looking back, into the ripening hills of the Old Dominion, where the dogwood is beginning to bloom and the foxhounds run, while Gibby Good pipes over and over at the top of his lungs:

"Carry me back to old Virginny,
There's where the cotton and the corn and 'tatoes grow,
There's where the birds warble sweet in the springtime,
There's where the old darkey's heart am longed to go.
There's where I labored so hard for old Massa,
Day after day in the field of yellow corn,
No place on earth do I love more sincerely
Than old Virginny, the state where I was born.

"Carry me back to old Virginny,
There's where the cotton and the corn and 'tatoes grow,
There's where the birds warble sweet in the springtime,
There's where this old darkey's heart am longed to go.

"Carry me back to old Virginny,
There let me live till I wither and decay,
Long by the old Dismal Swamp have I wandered,
There's where this old darkey's life will pass away.
Massa and Missis have long gone before me,
Soon will we meet on that bright and golden shore.
There we'll be happy and free from all sorrow,
There's where we'll meet and we'll never part no more."

"Shut the fuck up," Shag says after the fifteenth rendition, "or you'll never make it past the Dismal Swamp."

"I didn't know heaven was integrated," says Connie.

"Bet yaw honky ass," says Gibby, who insists on chattering in his
Uncle Remus dialect all the way down the Piedmont, past Culpeper
and Orange Counties, past Spotsylvania and Louisa Counties, past
Cuckoo, Virginia (which is ten miles due west of Bumpass, Virginia),
past Goochland and Powhatan and Cumberland and across the Ap-
pomattox River into the voluptuous lotus land of Prince Edward
County, riotous even this early in the year with redbud and laurel,
azalea and rhododendron. And here, here in God's untrammeled
garden, resides our old classmate Ronald Renfrew Redfield III, lawyer, farmer, latter-day Cavalier, keeper of the flickering flame of white
supremacy, scion of a landed aristocracy whose moment in the sun
has been protracted so far beyond justification that its beneficiaries
no longer doubt that God Himself smiles on their mansions and nour-
ishes their field and blesses every thought that penetrates their be-
nighted heads. It is in the blood. And God purifies their blood and
sanctifies their women's breasts, and will vent his wrath now or in the
hereafter on all who would defile either. But now the time has come
to demonstrate to Ronald Renfrew Redfield III that his way derives
not from divine providence so much as from accidents of geography
and history—and the relentless defense of assumed privilege.

We swing off the road from Kingville to Hollyhock and follow it
to the Redfield place, arriving at twilight. We park the microbus at
the head of the long, cypress-lined driveway that turns into an oval
before the gabled mansion, and Connie goes to the front door on the
pretext of seeking directions to Petersburg but really to learn if the
master is home. A liveried butler, a black liveried butler, gives the
directions. There is no sign, she says, whether anyone is home. We
make her go back to the door and tell the butler with feigned em-
barrassment that she is an old flame of the master's and wants very
much to say hello after all these years. "But suppose he's there?" she
says. "Kiss him passionately," says Shag, "and ask what's for supper."

She goes. The master, it turns out, is over at his mother's plantation, where a costume gala is in progress to benefit the local private

school, of which Ronald serves as chief trustee—an academy established, Gibby recalls from the tenth-reunion book, to avoid court-
ordered integration of the county's public schools. "Go ask how to get
to the plantation," Shag commands. Connie balks, but goes for a
third time. "He is a very suspicious darky," she reports, along with
the directions.

"With good reason," says Shag. "He is about to be emancipated,
like it or not."

Our trucks are strung out behind us about a mile apart. We radio
them to stand by till darkness takes hold. Through the gloaming, the
muted lilt of spirituals reaches us as our units materialize and form
a vast cordon about the plantation. The Blue Squad from Battle
Group B moves in through the southwest quadrant and startles the
resident colony of black field hands gathered on the platform of a
big wooden tobacco-aging shed to watch the merrymaking on the
distant flagstone terrace behind the glowing Georgian manse. The
White Squad moves in through the northeast quadrant and encounters
a transient colony of Latin fruit pickers who have stopped over to
help bring in the spring crops before heading north for the summer
to the Jersey truck farms. The blacks, murmuring fretfully and im-
ploring Jehovah to spare them, are ushered into the shed and con-
tained by half a dozen rifle-toting troops. The Latinos, lounging indifferently along the rutted road that runs through their tar-paper
village, know at once whom our men are after and drift along in their
wake to watch the fireworks with relish.

In close now, the troops flop on their bellies. Shag hands me the
binoculars. The terrace is festooned with colored lanterns, and the
guests, in their ante-bellum costumes, waltz and fox-trot decorously
as a procession of chefs bearing chafing dishes and candelabra emerges
from the mansion. The night air carries the savory aromas to us:
tender deviled crabs from Virginia's shores, plump Virginia oysters
from the tidelands roasted and dripping with melted butter, turkeys
cooked with an art that began when all Virginia turkeys were wild,

hickory-smoked Virginia ham cured and aged the way the colonists learned from the Indians—all accompanied by red-eye gravy and flaky biscuits and hot Sally Lunn rolls and delicate spoon bread.

Shag bellies forward a few more yards, checks his watch, then fires a brilliant red flare into the night. In thirty seconds, Tara is ringed by very visible Union troops and the gaily whirling gentry freeze in mid-cotillion. Ronald Renfrew Redfield III, sword bobbing at the side of his pearl-gray trousers, marches to the edge of the terrace and confronts our less grand commander, whose identity is hidden from him by a peaked officer's hat and sunglasses. "I demand to know the meaning of this outrage, sir," bellows Ronald Renfrew Redfield III, squire of Hollyhock.

"You're surrounded, schmuck," Shag says calmly.

"You are trespassing on my property," says Redfield, undeterred.

"We'll get off soon enough," says Shag.

"Then state your business."

"Our business?" He pauses to hold a cigarette lighter to his cigar. A thousand eyes converge on the tiny flame. "Our business," he says, billowing smoke in Redfield's face, "is retribution."

Redfield coughs away the smoke. Some snickers come from the Latinos, bunched behind our ring of troops. "Who let those wetbacks up here?" Redfield asks, teary-eyed.

"They thought they were invited," says Shag. "And the food smelled good."

"Very funny," says Redfield.

" 'Wetbacks' is a pejorative term, Mr. Redfield, sir. A man of your eminence ought to have better manners—at least in public."

"I'm not in public, mister. This is my family's land and I'll say what I damn well please on it. Now, what exactly's on your mind?"

"It's that school of yours, specifically."

"I knew it," Redfield says, turning to the heavy-breathing patricians clustered behind him. "I knew it the minute I saw them."

"And in general the greed, rape, robbery, and inhumanity to man you have been genteelly practicing in these parts for roughly three hundred years."

"They're just a bunch of nigger-lovin', Commie-kike, rabble-rousing Yankee bastards." He points to someone in his group. "Jeb, you want to run inside and call the sheriff and ask him to get on over here?"

"Your telephone lines have been cut," Shag says, flicking off an ash.

"Take your car, then, Jeb."

"If Jeb takes one dainty little step, he will get the 'Stars and Bars' tattooed on his ass by fifty rapid-fire rifles."

Jeb stays where he is.

"Now, then, Mr. Redfield, sir," says Shag, clearing his throat, "we have traveled many moons and come in good faith to make you a humanitarian proposition."

"I don't want to hear propositions from any bolshevik sons of bitches."

"Fine," says Shag. "Then we'll burn the place to the ground right now." And he starts to turn.

"Don't bluff us, mister."

"Ronald," says the chastening voice of his dowager mother, stepping forward from the group, "they appear to have a considerable number of armed roughnecks at their disposal. Why don't we let the gentleman state his proposition?"

Shag gives a semi-bow to the woman in her fifty crinolines.

"All right," snarls Redfield, his *machismo* diminished, "let's hear it."

"The school you and your friends are operating here is a blatant circumvention of the law of the land and an effront to human dignity. We ask you to close it down at once and send your children back to the public schools. We ask you, furthermore, to convert this superb ancestral property of yours into a fully integrated community college, financed entirely by local charitable funds, which you yourself will take the lead in raising. The school will be a model for the South—and North, too, for that matter—in the fruitful mingling of the races so that black and white, hand in hand, can march hopefully into the future." He puffs his cigar. "You have thirty seconds to think it over."

Someone on the terrace behind Mother Redfield laughs out loud. Then someone else. Then everyone else. Now they are roaring with laughter, nudging each other with elbows, falling down with fat tears rolling across their bloated cheeks.

Ronald Renfrew Redfield III, though, is not laughing. He is standing bolt upright and glaring at his antagonist in the khaki uniform. He seems to understand that Robert E. Lee is not about to lead a relief column from over the nearest hill within the allotted time. "Why—" he says, and falters. "But why are you doing this to us? We want only to be left to our own divinely ordained way of life."

"Who says it's divinely ordained?"

"Why—" he looks startled, "all our bounty comes from the Almighty."

"And the bounty, I take it, is evidence of your sanctified state?"

"Why, yes. The Lord rewards those who deserve rewarding."

"And you deserve it because of your lofty moral qualities?"

"Why, yes, I believe that's so."

"And the Lord punishes those who deserve His wrath."

"Yes, of course."

"Like the blacks?"

"I wouldn't say that."

"Would you say He's rewarded them?"

"Some of them yes, some of them no."

"How do you tell which are which?"

"Why—the ones that are getting on in the world have been rewarded. Those who aren't haven't."

"And is God white?"

"Why—I don't know."

"Well, is He black?"

"No."

"Is he Technicolored perhaps?"

"You are a blasphemer!"

"Just answer me."

"I don't presume to know what color God is. He's no color. He is an immanence."

"And He made the races different colors because He wanted them kept apart?"

"Different colors, different smells, different brain capacities—yes."

"It's all very clear?"

"Yes, very."

"Suppose I told you I was an angel?"

"A what?"

"An angel, an angel."

"I wouldn't believe you."

"Do you believe that Jesus Christ is the Son of God and was sent to earth to spread His word?"

"Yes, of course."

"Then why won't you believe God has sent me here to tell you that you are getting His message all screwed up?"

"Because you are smoking a cigar."

"Who says an angel can't smoke a cigar?"

"You're trying to make a fool out of me."

"Somebody beat me to it," Shag says. He drops his cigar on the terrace and steps on it. "Do you agree to our proposition?"

"Of course not."

"Then we're going to burn the house down."

"Go ahead."

"And the tobacco shed."

"Go ahead."

"And set fire to the fields."

"Go ahead."

"And by your own faith, do you believe it will be the hand of God visiting this retribution upon you?"

"It will be the hand of nigger-lovin', Commie-kike, rabble-rousing

Yankee bastards—and you will not escape Prince Edward County alive."

Shag orders four of the soldiers to clear everyone out of the house. Then he turns and signals across the fields. From the tobacco shed, the oldest black man on the plantation, his mouth toothless, his hair frizzy white, his overalls patched in a dozen places, is brought to the terrace. At the sight of the white folks in all their finery, he falls to the ground, understanding not at all that their distress, for once, is equal to his. Shag lifts him upright. He sags badly. "What is your name, old man?" Shag asks him.

"Rupert, suh,"

"How old are you, Rupert?"

"Don't know for sure, suh."

"*About* how old"

" 'Bout sebenty, suh."

Shag shows him his cigarette lighter. "You know what this thing is, Rupert?"

"No, suh."

Shag lights it for him. "You just press down the button." He tosses it at him. "Try it."

Rupert lights it. "Very nice, suh." He tries to hand it back.

"No, you keep it, Rupert. I'll tell you why."

"Yes, suh."

"In one minute, I want you to walk over to those big open double windows there on the ground floor of the house—you see the ones where those nice gold drapes are blowing?"

Rupert squints. "Yes, suh, I see 'em."

"I want you to walk over to that window and set those drapes on fire with the cigarette lighter."

"Oh, Lawd, no, suh! I couldn't do that, suh!"

"Why not, Rupert?"

"Why, I'd burn de place down if'n I did that, suh."

"That's right, Rupert, that's just what you'd do."

Rupert is trembling now. "Dat would be a terrible thing, suh."

"Why, Rupert?"

"Why de folks would kill me for doin' it, suh."

Shag looks him in his rheumy old eyes. "Rupert," he says, "the folks have been killing you for seventy years."

The rheumy eyes narrow.

"When you finish setting the drapes on fire, you can come away with us—unless you've got a family here."

"No, suh. Mah family left a long while back."

"Then come with us, Rupert, and we'll take everyone else among your people who wants to come with us, and we'll make sure you all have enough money to make a new start somewhere else."

The four soldiers come out of the mansion and give Shag an all-clear signal. Everyone is assembled on the terrace.

"All right, Rupert," says Shag, "this is your shining moment."

Rupert does not budge.

"You owe it to yourself, Rupert."

Rupert is transfixed by the flagstone.

"Rupert," comes Mother Redfield's voice softly.

Rupert looks up. "Yes, ma'am."

"We've provided for you, Rupert."

"Yes, ma'am." His feet begin to stir.

"Mr. Redfield's old hunting jacket—remember it, Rupert?"

"Yes, ma'am—it fit me real nice." There is a measurable shuffle now. Toward the house.

"And the time we drove your daughter to the white folks' doctor, Rupert?"

"Oh, yes, ma'am." He is striding fully now.

"And, Rupert—are you listening, Rupert?"

"Yes, ma'am, I hear you good." He is running now.

"Chicken every Sunday, Rupert—"

"Yes, ma'am, mah favorite."
Running hard, bearing a torch.
"RUPERT!"

41

Armageddon

"ACTUALLY," SAYS CONNIE, SOMEWHERE BETWEEN OLNEY AND
Flora, Illinois, "I didn't get along so wonderfully with the telephone
company, either. They cut me off three times on the same call once
and I got so angry I broke the receiver in half against my dresser.
They accused me of doing it deliberately, so I told them to take the
phone out completely and I borrowed my neighbor's whenever I
really had to make a call, which wasn't very often. I also borrowed
her refrigerator after Con Edison turned off the electricity. All I ever
kept in it were milk and pickles and tuna fish. Mostly I ate up whatever I opened. Except cookies. I kept cookies in the medicine chest.
My grandmother owned a refrigerator for eighteen years without ever
plugging it in. She also used to take her dog to the beach in a doggy
bathing suit and four little thong sandals."

Day and night, stopping only for gas and an occasional stretching
of well-muscled limbs, the convoy rolls across the great American
heartland. The blacks Rupert has brought with him from the Redfield
plantation have been accepted without incident by the troops amid
whom they spread a festive air until they are dropped off by twos
and fours along the route in likely-sounding towns. Under St. Louis's
six-hundred-foot-high wicket known grandly as "the Gateway to the
West" we speed and head out US 50 as far as the Missouri, which

we cross at Jefferson City, then strike off onto US 54 and follow its enormous arc southwestward. The towns are called Eldon and Osage Beach and Camdenton and Macks Creek and Hermitage and Collins and Eldorado Springs and Nevada and then we are past the undulating Missouri upland of wheat and cattle farms and hurrying over the mineral-rich, corn-covered pancake of Kansas. US 54 in Kansas: Fort Scott, Redfield(!), Uniontown, Bronson, Moran, La Harpe, Gas (Hitler is alive and well in Gas), Iola, Piqua, Yates Center, Toronto, Neal, Eureka (where Rupert himself debarks and is roundly blessed), Reece, Rosalia (the air is clear and hearts are pure in Rosalia, anyone passing through in a microbus can tell), El Dorado, Augusta, Wichita—Wichita! Straight down Kellogg Street through the heart of downtown Wichita we roll, wafting a phlegmy blob of turquoise paint onto the city hall as we pass, and proceed to Wichita Municipal Airport, where our rickety C-47s are waiting for us with fresh ammunition, for we have used up most of what we had brought with us to demolish billboards and pelt junkyards and otherwise register pique over the disfigured vista. Oh, the eagle has befouled his own transcontinental nest and it is a sight to see, these endless guano-caked miles of it.

We coordinate final plans with our airborne units and roll on again out US 54 across the shimmering prairie, across the spongy breadbasket, bisecting little nowhere towns named Goddard and Garden Plain and Waterloo and Kingman and Calista and Cunningham and Cairo and Pratt and Cullison and Wellsford and Haviland and Brenham and Greensburg and Mullinville—it runs to the end of the earth, US 54 does in Kansas—and Bucklin and Kingsdown and Bloom and Minneola and Fowler and Meade and Plains and Kismet and Hayne and Liberal, and that is not even the westernmost extent of Kansas but we have come 365 miles from Fort Scott on the Missouri-Kansas border and now we are at the Kansas-Oklahoma border and suffering unendurably from the vastness of the great republic.

Somewhere between Kismet, Kansas, and Hayne, Kansas, there is a field lying fallow and we stop by it, and in a big hole marked only by the top half of a beer can protruding from the fragrant earth we bury the airtight cartons of magnetic tapes rescued from the Information Retrieval Center of the Electronic Data-Processing Division of the Continental Computron Corporation, late of Westchester County, New York. The exact whereabouts of that hole in that field in that stretch of unplowed soil is of interest to no mortal soul this moment residing in or passing through that boundless acreage known as Seward County, Kansas—no one except me. I mark the spot on a map.

The highway unravels obliquely across the thin Oklahoma panhandle and the wheat fields and oat fields and sorghum fields and alfalfa fields and then it is Texas, a piece of it, anyway—the hilly, bleak northwest corner of the great panhandle—for not even a hundred miles, but it is all so stupefyingly monotonous that we are in Logan, twenty-five miles beyond the Texas border, before any one of us knows we have reached New Mexico, home of the Apachaho Indians, whom we have come all this way to champion in their death struggle with the deputies of the Great White Father.

While our army was still in training camp, newspaper articles about the tribe's latest tribulation sent me scurrying to the well-stocked library in the nearby village where I found what I was looking for—a dog-eared copy of Edmund E. Edmund's classic study in para-anthropology, *Apologies to the Apachahos*. It is an appalling chronicle of red men uprooted from their happy hunting ground by the relentlessly westering, pestilence- and firewater-bearing paleface, who spent the next fifty years trying to ghettoize the savages in the arid badlands. Neither as fierce nor as predatory as their cousins the Apaches, neither as numerous nor as enterprising as their other cousins, the Navajos, the hard-riding Apachahos nevertheless shared with both of them a certain reluctance to stay on the reservation; about once a year they would come whooping across the desert and do in the nearest Army stockade in a most barbaric manner—an act that would sooner or later send a punitive expedition of government cavalry thundering

across the desert in the opposite direction for a few parching weeks
during which they would find no trace of the renegades. Whereupon
the territorial commander would visit the reservation, caution the
council of chiefs (who regularly denied all knowledge of the atroci-
ties), and remind them of the treaty confining them to their trackless wasteland. In time, the Apache clans quarreled among themselves, the doves drifting off to join other, more pliant tribes while the
hawks continued rampaging, though on a reduced schedule, until their
numbers dwindled so severely that they were readily rounded up and
deported to a hermetically sealed reservation in Oklahoma. The Navajos made out better. Populous enough to pose a continuing threat to
the white man, they kept brewing trouble until they were ceded a
desert empire of more than fifteen million acres, at least some of
which were fertile enough to feed large numbers of sheep, who produced large amounts of wool, which the Navajos converted into large
quantities of blankets, which they sold to large white tourists.

The Apachahos were a different story. They stayed a cohesive,
untamable tribe, living more by their wits than their daring. To avoid
the white soldiers, they perforce became nomads; to sustain themselves (and not caring a feather for sheepherding), they became pirates, raiding the villages of their red brethren, preferably while the
braves were out massacring the local Army stockade. Such tactics,
Edmund E. Edmund points out, "endeared the Apachaho neither to
the career military men charged with pacifying the area nor to the
other, more valorous and forthrightly unregenerate tribes on whom he
preyed." Other chroniclers have been more charitable toward the
Apachaho sensibility, arguing in effect that valorous is as valorous
does. Nor is there any gainsaying, by Edmund or any other of the
conventionally minded observers of that dreary desert saga, the extraordinary survival quotient of the Apachahos; they were, quite simply, uncontainable throughout the nineteenth century. Shortly before
New Mexico and Arizona attained statehood, though, an expedition
of local militiamen, seeking to convince the nation that all surviving

red men in the area were thoroughly domesticated, set out to contain
the elusive gypsy tribe. The main body of Apachahos was surrounded
one night just as they were in the midst of rustling five thousand head
of Navajo sheep. The terms of the treaty called for the Apachahos
to lay down their tomahawks in perpetuity and be confined to ten
thousand acres of particularly hard-scrabble desert where the Gila
monster was the only form of fauna thought capable of surviving.
Now just as the Treaty of Versailles has been said to have provided
tinder for a still worse holocaust than the one it ended, so the treaty
with the Apachahos assured their long-smoldering rancor. And so
every once in a while they would waylay a passing freight train with
their rifles. The authorities claimed this was a blatant violation of their
treaty, but the Apachahos noted the treaty had ordered them to lay
down only their tomahawks and made no mention of other weapons.
The treaty was duly revised to cover all weapons, but the Apachahos
continued their occasional forays, robbing cars and trucks on Route
285 while apparently armed with nothing more than an extra coat of
war paint. Whereupon the Department of the Interior advised that if
the Apachahos ever again wandered off their reservation for any reason whatever unless duly approved by written request to the Secretary, they would have their worthless land taken away from them
"forthwith" and be declared outlaws. Well, Apachahos being Apachahos and none of them knowing how to write (to the Secretary or
anyone else), some of them sooner or later wandered off limits, for
no reason more menacing, according to their venerable chieftain,
Shining Toe, than to see the sights of Albuquerque. A couple of them
got drunk, the matter came to the attention of the Secretary of the
Interior, and quick as a flash the treaty with the tribe was declared
null and void and all surviving Apachahos were designated wanted
criminals. Nobody wanted them very badly, though, because Chief
Shining Toe continued unmolested to operate the one legal enterprise
ever attributed to the tribe—a hamburger stand on Route 44 near the
Blanco Trading Post. It was there that I reached him on the tele-

phone—he was listed under the "T"s in the San Juan County directory—after I had read in the paper that the tribe had reasserted its claim to their reservation, where geologists from the University of New Mexico had just discovered vast deposits of petroleum.

Our deal with the Apachahos was straightforward enough. Bull Frogg would immediately petition the federal courts to rule that the Secretary of the Interior had denied them due process of law in unilaterally voiding their treaty with the government. Those ten thousand acres, and everything beneath them, belonged in perpetuity to the sovereign Apachaho peoples, Frogg's landmark petition would assert. To pursue *Shining Toe v. Udall* to its ultimate adjudication, though, might take years, by which time all the oil in Christendom and Islam together could be sucked from the earth, and so the other prong of our two-pronged befriendment of the much-abused Apachahos: our army would move at once to the scene and, possession being nine-tenths of the law, spearhead Shining Toe's reclamation of his rightful homeland.

What complicated matters was the federal government's decision, in the light of the newly discovered petroleum deposits and at the behest of two dozen registered and unregistered representatives of the lustful oil lobby, to garrison the vacated reservation pending a high-level decision as to how the pie would be sliced among the corporate monoliths contending for it. Thus two Quonset huts were hastily erected and a federal platoon from Fort Sill dispatched to post the suddenly coveted acreage. They are patrolling the spread day and night, according to Shining Toe's scouts, and have orders to shoot all interlopers on sight.

Yes, here beyond question is a cause worth our undertaking, a flagrant example of man's inhumanity to man, an opportunity to intervene in this playing out in microcosm of the most pathological tenets of Social Darwinism; and so here, now, fully trained and equipped and mentally disciplined, our might is poised to right the wrongs done these hounded savages. We are to link up with Shining

Toe's braves five miles southwest of the reservation, proceed together
to disperse the government troops, proclaim the Apachahos' lawful
repossession of the territory, arrest the nation's attention and capture
its imagination with our daring in so just a cause, and force the courts
to an early decision affirming the Indians' claim. In return for which
we have asked for nothing more than a voice in directing the oil ex-
plorations that will follow. And 50 per cent of all revenues accruing
therefrom.

D-Day. The operation is due to begin at dawn, before the heat can
take hold. The troops are up at two o'clock, working mostly by flashlight. Tanks roll down truck ramps and are hovered over continuously
by mechanics. Guns are cleansed, mortars and bazookas inspected,
canteens filled, bayonets sharpened. The battle plan is rehearsed over
and over, and Bull Frogg's airborne unit, squatting on a tiny field in
Alamosa, Colorado, about a hundred and fifty miles north of us, is
radioed periodically to make certain everything is in order on that
end. Shag is all over the place, spot-checking, scolding, heartening,
bringing his men back to the fighting edge that has necessarily dulled
during the long haul Westward. Gibby slaps closed his twelfth loose-
leaf book of notes and tries to make himself useful by passing around
coffee. Connie, in fatigues, polishes her pistol and loads it unflinch-
ingly. And I—I on the brink—I believe. I believe in the unquencha-
bility of the liberated soul, in the irresistibility of defiant passion, in
the invincibility of slowly acquired and suddenly unleashed rectitude.
I am as close to being ready to die, to immolate myself in the name
of this larger-than-I, as I shall ever be. Yet I am equally convinced
at just this critical juncture that I shall live forever.

It is zero-minus-60. I am at the wheel of the microbus. Shag is
beside me, manning the radio. Connie and Gibby are where they have
been throughout—in the back seat—but now they are helmeted and
bearing arms and swallowed up by the surge of it all. Every unit
checks in with Shag. All present and accounted for. I turn the key.
The motor gags, and dies. I turn it again. This time it catches. The

snubnosed microbus eases forward past the tanks, slowly, slowly, over the sand and into the starry night. And now we are rolling, the microbus slightly in the lead, the headquarters platoon and support tank right behind, the two battle groups on either flank a few hundred yards distant. All our headlights are on and the desert unfolds in a gray spool before us. We are unstoppable.

At zero-minus-40 our map readers in the headquarters platoon buzz Shag and tell him we are at the rendezvous point. The stars have faded now. The first smear of light is detectable on the eastern horizon. We halt. Gradually the outline of a dune becomes visible to the west of us. Shag has his binoculars trained on it. A minute passes. Then another. And then—no hoofbeats or dust clouds to announce them—they are there! Perched on the crest of the dune, resplendent in full battle regalia, the remnants of the Apachaho tribe have come to reclaim their birthright, their nationhood, their rightful parcel of the American continent. Shining Toe, on an enormous pinto, raises his hand, holds it there for a long moment, and then brings it sharply down. Now the desert swirls with the fury of them. So swiftly do they come that for a fleeting instant I think they mean to waylay us and not our mutual foe. It is their grand moment, and they play it well. At the last second they rein up and fall in behind the headquarters platoon. Murmured greetings are exchanged behind the microbus while their horses whinny apprehensively at the sight of the tanks. Their war paint shows lustrous in our headlights and their long-outlawed tomahawks, reactivated for the occasion, dangle unsheathed from their belts. The gray smear on the horizon has fanned out to fill the eastern sky. It is zero-minus-30. The combined force advances now together. It is five miles to forbidden ground—and open insurrection against the United States of America.

Our scouts range ahead. They tell us to keep coming. We move up the long tapering back of a low-lying ridge—it is not steep enough to make a butte—that runs nearly to the gates of the reservation and shields our coming from any ground observation post there. At zero-

minus-5 we halt for the last time and snap off our lights. And we
wait. We wait for the planes. We wait for them because they could
not wait for us if, for any reason, we had been delayed. While we
wait, there is nothing more to say. Or think. We are hanging like
sprinters on their starting blocks, asses in the air, every muscle straining for release. Shag is standing beside the microbus now, holding the
radio mike in one hand, his binoculars in the other, scanning the
slate sky. Gibby's Adam's apple is yo-yoing up and down. Connie is
asking me how to fire her pistol straight. And I—I am in a state of
total disembodiment.

Coral stains in the east. The pall of night has lifted. A new day is
dawning. And there it is, precisely on schedule—a distant hum stirring through the breathless desert air. At the same moment we hear
it, Bull Frogg's voice comes chattering through Shag's earphones
saying he can see us, though Shag cannot yet pick them out of the
sky with his glasses. "Move it out!" he says with jutting jaw, and we
move, we move fast and we move straight. No Army patrol has been
spotted by our scouts on this stretch of the reservation's border, and
we roll unimpeded through the barbed-wire fence. The planes are
droning in now a mile or so to the east of us. In another minute their
stubby silhouettes pass us. It is zero-minus-90 seconds. Our mighty
blows will land simultaneously. The Indians are whooping wildly.
The sand is flying. Hearts are pounding. A new day is—

And then it explodes all at once. The doors of the C-47 are thrust
open—outward instead of into the planes, which were never built to
accommodate paratroopers—and are snapped off in the wind. Half a
dozen men without chutes on are sucked out into the void. Those with
them on, horrified at the sight, must follow almost at once, and
whether because they are panicked or were betrayed by our suppliers,
most of them meet the same fate; only two chutes are seen to open.
Our pilots are sobbing openly into their microphones. And there is
no more Bull Frogg; he was the first one sucked out when the doors
were opened.

Shag is wild-eyed with disbelief. But there is no turning aside. We shall overcome even with our air arm missing. The Quonset huts are in view now. Our guns are primed. At zero-minus-15 seconds Shag shrilly orders them to get ready, at zero-minus-5 to aim, at zero to open up. A great roaring red volley springs across the desert—and is answered by a deafening cannonade that stops us in our tracks. The Quonset huts have been abandoned and off to the left and right, behind what we took to be innocent clumps of sagebrush, crack troops from what must be every law enforcement agency between here and the Berkshire Hills are crouched and gunning at us. They have trailed us three thousand miles to lie in wait here, and now they are gunning at us and shredding our armor and butchering our men. Our army lunges backward and, like a great wave, sweeps over and past the microbus, scrambling in utter disorder as the air fills with fire and whizzing steel and rearing horses. The Apachahos, recoiling by instinct, begin falling on our men with their tomahawks, the better to later claim they had been duped. Shag is behind me screaming into the volcano's mouth but his voice is engulfed by the flaming chaos. I glance up, see a tank bearing down on us (ours or theirs, I do not know), and reach for an abandoned bazooka on the ground in front of me. I can barely lift it. I can barely aim it. Desperately I fire at the clanking metal monster. The bazooka goes off backward, to my great astonishment, and destroys Shag Shaughnessy most horribly. Humiliated, I barely notice the Apachaho on my back. I catch the glint of his weapon and struggle against it. I cannot resist him. My scalp will be ripped from my head in another bloody instant. I hear a gun shot louder and sharper than all the others. The Indian falls to the ground. I look up. Connie is waving at me, her pistol still smoking. Gibby wheels the microbus over the Indian, orders me and Connie in, and jams the gas pedal to the floor.

42

. . . And the Home of the Brave

"DO YOU HAVE ANY MONEY LEFT?" SHE ASKED.

"About seventeen dollars," he said. "Why?"

"Gas—and food."

"You don't need food. You're fat, remember."

"And hungry," she said.

"Gibby, how much have you got on you?"

Gibby was asleep in the back seat.

"He must have something. We'll get there."

"Or walk."

"Yes, or walk. You'll be a mere sliver on arrival."

"Right," she said, and looked out the window at Kansas going by the other way. "Goodbye, Kansas," she said. "I shall never your way come again."

"You can never tell."

"*I* can tell."

He looked in the rear-view mirror by habit, but he had seen nothing that could pass for a pursuit vehicle for three hundred miles now. "Why don't you play something?" he said to her, indicating her battered guitar. "A dirge maybe."

"I don't feel like playing. I feel all washed out."

"I know."

"I think I'll become a nun."

"Yes, you'd make a marvelous nun."

"Nuns are creepy, though."

"I understand they never bathe."

"Oh, that's not true. I've stayed at some abbeys in France—lady travelers can do that there—and they have quite excellent bathing facilities."

"Oh."

"Of course I only know about France."

"Then become a French nun—they're the chic-est."

"Yes, and the perfume's cheap." And she faded out the window again, contemplating the changeless vista.

"Do you have any money left back in the city?" she asked after a while.

"Some."

"Enough to go live in Marrakesh?"

"For a while, I suppose."

"Wouldn't you like to go live in Marrakesh?"

"I hadn't thought about it."

"It's warm and lovely there, and everything is cheap."

"So I've heard."

"I've never been to Marrakesh."

Kansas. Endless Kansas. Warm and lovely Kansas, where everything was turning green. "Is that what you want to do with your life —go to Marrakesh?"

"For a start. Have you someplace better in mind?"

"Not offhand."

She looked at him. "Tell me what I'm going to do, Kit."

"You're not going to jump out of a window."

"No, I promise."

"You are warm and lovely and bright and funny—"

"And wonderful and marvelous."

"Yes—and you will have a long and happy life."

"Doing what?"

"Not robbing."

"I promise—no more robbing."

"You will go back and marry your long-time fiancé, what's-his-name."

"What's-his-name doesn't deserve me, though I love him dearly. He has missed the boat."

"Then you will change your name to Maria Segovia and become the world's first great female classical guitarist and tour the world and live like a queen and have a thousand lovers from many lands."

"My fingers are too short and stubby."

"Take pills for them."

She laughed. "Besides," she said, "I don't want a thousand lovers."

"How many do you want?"

"One good one."

"But not me."

"You are warm and lovely and bright and funny—"

"And wonderful and marvelous—"

"And wonderful and marvelous, but no, not you. You have a lover. And you are going back to her."

"How do you know?"

"I can tell. You don't want me any more now that you can have me, so what else could it mean?"

"It could just mean I'm emotionally drained by everything I've been through."

"That's really the same thing."

Missouri now. She drove for a while.

"She may not have me, of course," he said.

"Why not?"

"She thinks I'm an adulterer."

"I'll testify."

"She doesn't even know about you. It's someone else—a friend of ours—who turns out to be a nymphomaniac because her husband's thing doesn't work."

"That's too bad."

"The truth is, I never touched her—technically."

"Technically is important."

"She asked for money at the crucial moment, so I backed off."

"And she told on you."

"Yes, to be a bitch. I told her I'd kill her if she told."

"And now what are you going to do?"

"I'm going to make her admit she was lying."

"And if she won't?"

"I'll kill her."

Gibby drove through Illinois and announced that his next major work would be a reappraisal of the redoubtable Apachahos. "Someone absolutely must take Edmund Edmund apart," he said, "and show him up for the blowhard he is."

Everyone agreed that someone absolutely must.

"And you," she said to Kit in Indiana, "and your life—what will you do?"

"I will become Lance Trevalyan, the Don Juan of the tennis courts, and tour the world and live like a king and have a thousand concubines from many lands."

"No," she said.

"No," he said.

"You will go back to work for that horrid company, I know it."

"Perhaps."

"But they probably fired you."

"But I have all the tapes from their wonderful and marvelous Information Retrieval Center, which blew up most mysteriously about a week ago, according to the *Wall Street Journal*."

"They would arrest you the moment you set a foot in the door with them."

"I'd work out a scheme."

"What kind of scheme?"

"I don't know yet. I may just leave the tapes in the ground forever and take my money and buy a yacht and put my family on it and sail around the world till I get tired of it."

"No, you won't."

"Probably not."

"What will you do with the money?"

"Send my kids to college. And buy an extra pair of shoes with what's left over. I'm usually very stingy when it comes to shoes."

They ran out of gas and money at the Carlisle exit of the Pennsylvania Turnpike. They abandoned the microbus there and hitchhiked back to New York. When they got there, Kit Kwait had a beard, Gibby Good had a dozen loose-leaf notebooks full of their adventures, and Connie Colton had a busted guitar and a million dollars willed to her by her bachelor-uncle, who had died of a heart attack while she was away.

ABOUT THE AUTHOR

RICHARD KLUGER was born in Paterson, New Jersey, in 1934. Educated at the Horace Mann School and Princeton University, he has published his own weekly newspaper in Rockland County, New York, reported for the New York *Post,* reviewed for *The New Republic* and *Harper's,* and served as the book editor of the New York *Herald Tribune.* He is presently the executive editor of Simon and Schuster, book publishers, and lives in New York City with his wife and two sons.

Format by Katharine Sitterly
Set in Linotype Times Roman
Composed and printed by York Composition Co., Inc.
Bound by The Haddon Craftsmen, Inc.
HARPER & ROW, PUBLISHERS, INCORPORATED

697071727387654321